John Brown, Richard Davis Webb

The life and letters of Captain John Brown

1859

John Brown, Richard Davis Webb

The life and letters of Captain John Brown
1859

ISBN/EAN: 9783337175948

Printed in Europe, USA, Canada, Australia, Japan

Cover: Foto ©Raphael Reischuk / pixelio.de

More available books at **www.hansebooks.com**

THE LIFE AND LETTERS

OF

Captain John Brown,

WHO WAS

.

EXECUTED AT CHARLESTOWN, VIRGINIA, DEC. 2, 1859, FOR AN ARMED
ATTACK UPON AMERICAN SLAVERY ;

WITH NOTICES OF

SOME OF HIS CONFEDERATES.

EDITED BY
RICHARD D. WEBB.

LONDON :
SMITH, ELDER. AND CO. 65, CORNHILL.
———
MDCCCLXI.

" I have no regret for the transaction or which I am condemned. I went against the laws of men, it is true; but 'whether it be right to obey God or men, judge ye' Christ told me to remember them that are in bonds as bound with them, to do towards them as I would wish them to do towards me in similar circumstances. My conscience bade me do that. I tried to do it, but failed. Therefore I have no regret on that score."—*Brown's letter from prison to a clergyman in Ohio.*

" You would not call John Brown's movement treason, you would not call it murder, you would not call it a wicked act, if white persons, your own relations, had been chained and claimed as property, tortured, and condemned as a race of chattels; you would call it justice, heroism, piety."—*Cheever.*

PRINTED BY ALFRED WEBB, GREAT BRUNSWICK-STREET, DUBLIN.

PREFACE.

THE following pages are an attempt to give a faithful portraiture of the life and character of Captain John Brown, whose name has attained celebrity in connexion with the seizure of the arsenal at Harper's Ferry, Virginia, on the night of the 16th October, 1859. The interest excited by this event was widely felt on this side of the Atlantic, but still more intensely in the American Union. In the Slave States, fear and danger produced their natural results in numberless deeds of cruelty and outrage against Northern citizens; in the Free States, the heroism, self-devotion, and firmness of Brown and his handful of young and devoted confederates, called forth admiration and respect, and awakened a fuller recognition of the enormity of slavery, and its gross inconsistency with the national boast of freedom. Thus the inherent difference between North and South was widened; and it is not too much to say that but for Brown's enterprise the

B

North would not have been prepared so soon to defy the slaveholders by electing a republican President. The election of Lincoln was the pretence, if not the motive, for Southern secession; and the war which has followed secession—however much to be deprecated in itself—will, we trust, at no distant day work the overthrow of chattel slavery, which just before Brown's enterprise seemed as firmly established as the everlasting hills. Thus the object which he failed to accomplish—the commencement of the subversion of slavery —will probably through his means, as an instrument in the hands of Providence, be accelerated much more effectually than it could have been by his temporary success.

But John Brown's indirect agency in promoting this great political and moral revolution would not of itself entitle him to an elaborate biography. The interest excited by the affair at Harper's Ferry was intensified by the subsequent development of the remarkable character of the principal actor in that singular drama. It soon became clear that the attempt was not the deed of a capricious fanatic, but of a sagacious and practical man, who had given long years of deliberation to the project. Brown's whole demeanour while in prison and on his trial, and the calm dignity with which he faced

an ignominious death, made a profound impression on
the American people ; forbidding the imputation of
insane excitement or of a thirst for notoriety, and
showing forth his modesty, piety, and magnanimity,
his unhesitating devotion to the convictions of duty,
and his willingness to sacrifice life and all that was
near and dear, for the attainment of a beneficent
object. The life and character of such a man are a
subject of abiding interest, and worthy of a permanent record.

This biography has little pretension to the dignity
of authorship. It is simply an attempt to present
from all accessible sources such a memoir of Captain
Brown as will place him fairly before the British public.
The principal of these sources, of course, is Mr. James
Redpath's "Public Life of Captain John Brown,"
which was published in America about a month after
his death, and had a vast circulation in the Northern
States. That work contains a large amount of interesting matter, which was compiled and prepared for
the press with extraordinary industry and promptitude;
but it is overladen with comments and epithets, inap-
propriate scripture texts, and minute particulars of
events in Kansas. The arrangement is unsatisfactory,
and the nomenclature of the books and chapters is more

calculated to mystify than to assist the reader. For all these reasons it was thought that a new biography was a desideratum, and this the present work is intended to supply. Whilst pains have been taken to present a clear and unambitious narrative, a considerable number of interesting particulars have been introduced which never before appeared in a collected form, and some of which are now published for the first time. To the former category belong the conversations with Mrs. Brown respecting her husband and family, which were originally contributed to the *New York Tribune* by Mr. McKim of Philadelphia and Mr. Tilton of New York; also the interesting account of Captain Brown's funeral, written by Mr. McKim for the *National Anti-Slavery Standard*. Acknowledgments are due to Mrs. Lydia Maria Child for a letter respecting Brown's journey to Canada with the slaves he had rescued in Missouri, which was addressed to her by a gentleman, now resident in Kansas, who aided him in that extraordinary exploit; and especially to the editor's valued friend the Rev. Samuel May, of Leicester, Massachusetts, who selected for publication in this volume from a quantity of John Brown's letters, placed in his hands by Mr. Redpath (with liberty to make such a use of them), the letters and extracts given in the Appendix. The object in publishing these was mainly to show that the letters written under the ordinary circumstances of daily life were entirely consistent in spirit and tenor with those written from prison; and, making allowance for the difference of circumstances, equally indicative of the religious, upright, and self-possessed character of the man.

The chapter respecting Captain Brown's confederates, which has been gleaned from various scattered sources, contains many passages of romantic adventure and pathetic interest. None of these young men, all of whom were under thirty years of age, appear to have ever failed in veneration for their leader, or in confidence in the rightfulness of the cause to which they had pledged themselves.

In the preparation of this little work, it has been the object of the editor to allow John Brown to speak for himself in his conduct and conversation, his actions and familiar letters. Little space has been devoted to comment or eulogy; but the reader will find this omission amply supplied on turning to that portion of the Appendix which contains the views of several eminent Americans (who differed widely in their opinions upon other subjects) respecting the character of Brown, and the probable influence of his life and

actions upon the institution of slavery and the future
prospects of the United States.   The remarks of the
Rev. George B. Cheever are full of feeling, fervour,
and eloquence, and are especially commended to the
reader's notice.

Besides the sources of information already indicated,
the following have been consulted and quoted in the
preparation of this volume :—

"Report of the Special Committee appointed to investigate
the Troubles in Kansas."   Washington, 1856.

"The Narrative of Dr. John Doy, of Lawrence, Kansas."
New York, 1860.

"Six Months in Kansas," by Mrs. Robinson.   Boston, 1856.

" A Voice from Harper's Ferry : a Narrative of Events at
Harper's Ferry, with Incidents prior and subsequent to its capture by Captain Brown and his Men; by Osborne P. Anderson,
one of the number."   Boston, 1861.

The *Independent, Tribune*, and *National Anti-Slavery Standard*,
published in New York ; the *Liberator*, Boston ; and the *Anti-
Slavery Bugle*, Salem, Ohio.

CONTENTS.

CHAPTER XI.

November 2nd—December 1st, 1859.

CHAPTER XII.

December 2nd—December 8th, 1859.

CHAPTER XIII.

December, 1859—March, 1860.

APPENDICES.

LIFE

CAPTAIN JOHN BROWN.

CHAPTER I.

1800—1855.

JOHN BROWN'S ANCESTRY.—AUTOBIOGRAPHICAL SKETCH OF HIS EARLY LIFE.—HE MARRIES.—BECOMES A TANNER, A FARMER, AND A SHEPHERD.—DEATH OF HIS WIFE.—HIS SECOND MARRIAGE.—EMBARKS IN THE WOOL TRADE.— VISITS EUROPE.—REMOVES TO NORTH ELBA.—HIS CHARACTER.

JOHN BROWN, the subject of this memoir, was the only person executed for treason in the United States during the eighty-three eventful years which elapsed from the Declaration of Independence, in 1776, to the day that he perished upon a Virginian scaffold. But when we find that the "crime" for which he suffered was an effort to precipitate the abolition of American slavery, and that this "traitor" was eminently pious, upright, humane, modest, and fearless, it will hardly be thought remarkable that he was directly

descended from the famous stock of the Puritan founders of New England, and that his grandfather died
while serving under Washington, as an officer in the
army which achieved American independence.

In the burying ground near the Church in Canton
Centre, Connecticut, stands a marble monument, bearing this inscription :—

IN MEMORY OF
CAPTAIN JOHN BROWN,
WHO DIED IN THE REVOLUTIONARY ARMY,
AT NEW YORK, SEPT. 3RD, 1776.
HE WAS OF THE FOURTH GENERATION IN REGULAR DESCENT
FROM PETER BROWN, ONE OF THE PILGRIM FATHERS
WHO LANDED FROM THE MAYFLOWER
AT PLYMOUTH, MASS.
DECEMBER 22ND. 1620.

This Captain Brown fell a victim to an epidemic
then prevailing in the American camp. He left a large
family of young children, whom his widow reared with
singular tact and judgment in strict principles and
habits of industry, and who became distinguished citizens in the communities in which they resided. One of
the sons became a judge in Ohio, and a grandson was
president of a flourishing college in New England.
Owen Brown, another son, the father of the subject of
our narrative, married a daughter of Gideon Mills, an
officer in the revolutionary army, who was entrusted
with the command of the guard that had in charge a
large portion of the prisoners comprising Burgoyne's
army. Soon after Owen Brown's marriage, he removed
to Torrington, Connecticut, where our hero was born.
When the boy was about five years of age, his father

removed to Hudson, Ohio, and became one of the principal pioneer settlers of that town. He was chosen one of the board of trustees of Oberlin college, in the same state. He was endowed with energy and enterprise, and went down to his grave honoured and respected, about the year 1852 or 1853, aged eighty-seven.

Of John Brown's early life we have but few particulars ; but there fortunately exists a graphic sketch from his own hand, in a letter addressed to a son of Mr. Stearns, Medford, Massachusetts, for whom he had promised to write out some of the incidents of his boyish days. We give this letter entire. It was written during an enforced pause in his busy life, while detained on a journey by the delay of a promised remittance.

" Red Rock, Iowa, 15th July, 1857.

" Mr. Henry L. Stearns,

" My dear young friend,

" I have not forgotten my promise to write you, but my constant care and anxiety have obliged me to put off a long time. I do not flatter myself that I can write any thing that will very much interest you, but have concluded to send you a short story of a certain boy of my acquaintance, and for convenience and shortness of name I will call him John. His story will be mainly a narration of follies and errors, which it is to be hoped you may avoid ; but there is one thing connected with it which will be calculated to encourage

1*

any young person to persevering effort, and that is the degree of success in accomplishing his objects which to a great extent marked the course of this boy throughout my entire acquaintance with him, notwithstanding his moderate capacity, and still more moderate acquirements.

"John was born May 9th, 1800, at Torrington, Litchfield county, Connecticut, of poor but respectable parents—a descendant on the side of his father of one of the company of the Mayflower who landed at Plymouth, 1620. His mother was descended from a man who came at an early period to New England from Amsterdam, in Holland. Both his father's and his mother's fathers served in the war of the revolution. His father's father died in a barn at New York while in the service, in 1776.

"I cannot tell you of anything in the first four years of John's life worth mentioning, save that at that early age he was tempted by three large brass pins belonging to a girl who lived in the family, and stole them. In this he was detected by his mother, and after having a full day to think of the wrong, received from her a thorough whipping. When he was five years old his father moved to Ohio—then a wilderness filled with wild beasts and Indians. During the long journey, which was performed in part or mostly with an ox-team, he was called on by turns to assist a boy five years older (who had been adopted by his father and mother), and learned to think he could accomplish smart things in driving the cows and riding the horses. Sometimes he met with rattlesnakes, which were very large, and which some of the company generally managed to kill. After getting to Ohio, in 1805, he was for some time rather afraid of the Indians and of their rifles ; but this soon wore off, and he used to hang about them quite as much as was consistent with good manners, and learned a trifle of their talk. His father learned to dress deer skins, and at six years old John was in· stalled a young Buckskin. He was perhaps rather observing, as he ever after remembered the entire process of deer-skin dressing, so that he could at any time dress his own leather, such as squirrel, racoon, cat, wolf, or dog skins, and also learned to make whip lashes, which brought him some change at times, and was of considerable service in many ways. At six years old, John began to be quite a rambler in the wild new country, finding birds and squirrels, and sometimes a wild turkey's nest. But about this period he was placed in the school of adversity ; which, my young friend, was a most necessary part of his early training. You may laugh when you come to read about it, but these were sore trials to John, whose earthly treasures were very few and small. These were the beginning of a severe but much needed course of discipline which he after_ wards was to pass through, and which it is to be hoped has learned him before this time that the heavenly Father sees it best to take all the little things out of his hands which he has ever placed in them. When John was in his sixth year a poor Indian boy gave him a yellow marble, the first he had ever seen. This he thought a great deal of, and kept it a good while, but at last he lost it beyond recovery. It took years to heal the wound, and I think he cried at times about it. About five months after this he caught a young squirrel, tearing off his tail in doing it, and getting severely bitten at the same time himself. He however held on to the little bob-tail squirrel, and finally got him perfectly tamed, so that he almost idolized his pet. This too he lost, by its wandering away or by getting killed, and for a year or two John was in mourning, and looking at all the squirrels he could see, to try and discover Bobtail, if possible. I must not neglect to tell you of a very bad and foolish habit to which John was somewhat addicted. I mean, telling lies, generally to screen himself from blame or from punishment. He could not well endure to be reproached; and I now think had he been oftener encouraged to be entirely frank, by making frankness a kind of atonement for some of his faults, he would not have been so often guilty of this fault, nor have been obliged to struggle so long in after life with so mean a habit. John was never quarrelsome, but was excessively fond of the hardest and roughest kind of plays, and could never get enough of them.

"Indeed, when for a short time he was sometimes sent to school, the opportunity it afforded to wrestle, and snowball, and run, and jump, and knock off old seedy wool hats offered to him almost the only compensation for the confinement and restraints of school. I need not tell you that with such a feeling, and but little chance of going to school at all, he did not become much of a scholar. He would always choose to stay at home and work hard, rather than be sent to school ; and during the warm season might generally be seen barefooted and bareheaded, with buckskin breeches, suspended often with one leather strap over his shoulder, but sometimes with two. To be sent off through the wilderness alone to very considerable distances was particularly his delight, and in this he was often indulged, so that by the time he was twelve years old he was sent off more than a hundred miles with companies of cattle ; and he would have thought his character much injured had he been obliged to be helped in any such job. This was a boyish kind of feeling, but characteristic, however.

"At eight years old John was left a motherless boy, which loss was complete and permanent ; for, notwithstanding his father again married to a sensible, intelligent, and on many accounts a very estimable woman, yet he never adopted her in feeling, but continued to pine after his own mother for years. This operated very unfavourably upon him, as he was both naturally fond of females, and withal extremely diffident ; and deprived him of a suitable connecting link between the different sexes, the want of which might under some circumstances have proved his ruin.

"When the war broke out with England, [in 1812,] his father commenced furnishing the troops with beef cattle, the collecting and driving of which afforded him some opportunity for the chase, on foot, of wild steers and other cattle through the woods. During this war he had some chance to form his own boyish judgment of men and measures, and to become somewhat familiarly acquainted with some who have figured before the country since that time. The effect of what he saw during the war was to so far disgust him with military affairs, that he would neither train or drill, but paid fines and got along like a Quaker, until his age finally has cleared him of military duty.*

"During the war with England a circumstance occurred that in the end made him a most determined abolitionist, and led him to declare or swear eternal war with slavery. He was staying for a short time with a very gentlemanly landlord, once a United States marshal, who held a slave boy near his own age, very active, intelligent, and good feeling, and to whom John was under considerable obligation for numerous little acts of kindness. The master made a great pet of John, brought him to table with his first company and friends, called their attention to every little smart thing he said

---

* " He accompanied his father to the camp, and assisted him in his employment, seeing a great deal of military life—more, perhaps, than if he had been a soldier, for he was often present at the councils of the officers. He learned by experience how armies are supplied and maintained in the field. He saw enough of military life to disgust him with it, and to excite in him a great abhorrence of it. Though tempted by the offer of some petty office in the army when about eighteen, he not only declined to accept this, but refused to train, and was fined in consequence. He then resolved that he would have nothing to do with any war, unless it were a war for liberty."—*Henry D. Thoreau.*

or did, and to the fact of his being more than a hundred miles from home with a company of cattle alone; while the negro boy, who was fully if not more than his equal, was badly clothed, poorly fed and lodged in cold weather, and beaten before his eyes with iron shovels or any other thing that came first to hand. This brought John to reflect on the wretched, hopeless condition of fatherless and motherless slave children : for such children have neither fathers nor mothers to protect and provide for them. He sometimes would raise the question, ' Is God their Father ?'

" At the age of ten years, an old friend induced him to read a little history, and offered him the free use of a good library, by which he acquired some taste for reading, which formed the principal part of his early education, and diverted him in a great measure from bad company. He by this means grew to be very fond of the company and conversation of old and intelligent persons. He never attempted to dance in his life, nor did he ever learn to know one of a pack of cards from another. He learned nothing of grammar, nor did he get at school so much knowledge of common arithmetic as the four ground rules. This will give you some general idea of the first fifteen years of his life, during which he became very strong and large of his age, and ambitious to perform the full labour of a man at almost any kind of hard work. By reading the lives of great, wise, and good men, their sayings and writings, he grew to a dislike of vain and frivolous conversation and persons, and was often greatly obliged by the kind manner in which older and more intelligent persons treated him at their houses and in conversation—which was a great relief, on account of his extreme bashfulness.

"He very early in life became ambitious to excel in doing anything he undertook to perform. This kind of feeling I would recommend to all young persons, both male and female, as it will certainly tend to secure admission to the company of the more intelligent and better portion of every community. By all means, endeavour to excel in some laudable pursuit.

"I had like to have forgotten to tell you of one of John's misfortunes, which sat rather hard on him while a young boy. He had by some means, perhaps by gift of his father, become the owner of a little ewe lamb, which did finely till it was about two-thirds grown, and then sickened and died. This brought another protracted mourning season, not that he felt the pecuniary loss so much, for that was never his disposition; but so strong and earnest were his attachments.

"John had been taught from earliest childhood to 'fear God and keep his commandments,' and, though quite sceptical, he had always by turns felt much serious doubt as to his future well-being, and about this time became to some extent a convert to Christianity, and ever after was a firm believer in the divine authenticity of the Bible. With this book he became very familiar, and possessed a most unusual memory of its entire contents.

"Now some of the things I have been telling of were just such as I would recommend to you; and I would

like to know that you had selected these out, and
adopted them as part of your own plan of life, and I
wish you to have some definite plan. Many seem to
have none, and others never stick to any that they do
form. This was not the case with John. He followed
up with tenacity whatever he set about, so long as it
answered his general purpose, and hence he rarely
failed in some good degree to effect the things he
undertook. This was so much the case that he habitually expected to succeed in his undertakings. With
this feeling should be coupled the consciousness that
our plans are right in themselves.

"During the period I have named, John had acquired
a kind of ownership to certain animals of some little
value ; but as he had come to understand that the title
of minors might be a little imperfect, he had recourse
to various means in order to secure a more independent
and perfect right of property. One of those means was,
to exchange with his father for something of far less
value. Another was, by trading with other persons for
something his father had never owned. Older persons
have sometimes found difficulty with titles.

"From fifteen to twenty years old, he spent most of
his time working at the tanner and currier's trade,
keeping bachelor's hall, and officiating as cook, and
for most of the time as foreman of the establishment,
under his father. During this period he found much
trouble with some of the bad habits I have mentioned,
and with some that I have not told you of, his conscience urging him forward with great power in this

matter; but his close attention to business and success
in its management, together with the way he got along
with a company of men and boys, made him quite a
favourite with the serious and more intelligent portion
of older persons.   This was so much the case, and
secured for him so many little notices from those he
esteemed, that his vanity was very much fed by it; and
he came forward to manhood quite full of self-conceit,
and self-confident, notwithstanding his extreme bashfulness.   A younger brother used sometimes to remind
him of this, and to repeat to him this expression, which
you may somewhere find, 'A king against whom there
is no rising up.'   The habit so early formed of being
obeyed rendered him in after life too much disposed to
speak in an imperious and dictating way.   From fifteen
years and upward he felt a good deal of anxiety to
learn, but could only read and study a little, both for
want of time and on account of inflammation of the
eyes.*   He however managed by the help of books to
make himself tolerably well acquainted with common
arithmetic and surveying, which he practised more or
less after he was twenty years old.†

* When about eighteen years of age he undertook a course of
study, with a view to preparation for the ministry in the Congregational Church ; but he was compelled by this inflammation of
the eyes to relinquish it.   He is described at this time as being
" a tall, sedate, dignified young man."

† A friend, referring to a later period, thus writes :—" In his
early manhood he had been a surveyor, and as such had traversed
a large part of Ohio, Pennsylvania, and Western Virginia, and

"At a little past twenty years old, led by his own inclinations, and prompted also by his father, he married a remarkably plain, but neat, industrious, and economical girl, of excellent character, earnest piety, and good practical common sense, about one year younger than himself. This woman, by her mild, frank, and—more than all else—by her very consistent conduct, acquired, and ever while she lived maintained, a most powerful and good influence over him. Her plain but kind admonitions generally had the right effect, without arousing his haughty, obstinate temper. John began early in life to discover a great liking to fine cattle, horses, sheep, and swine; and, as soon as circumstances would enable him, he began to be a practical shepherd, it being a calling for which in early life he had a kind of enthusiastic longing, together with the idea that as a business it bid fair to afford him the means of carrying out his greatest or principal object. I have now given you a kind of general idea of the early life of this boy; and if I believed it would be worth the trouble, or afford much interest to any good-feeling person, I might be tempted to tell you something of his course in after life, or manhood. I do not say that I will do it.

" You will discover that, in using up my half-sheets to

was thus in some degree familiar with the locality where, it would seem, he intended to operate. This life in the woods, to which he was trained from a boy, gave him the habits and the keen senses of a hunter or an Indian. He was remarkably clearsighted and quick of ear, and knew all the devices of woodcraft."

save paper, I have written two pages, so that one does not follow the other as it should. I have no time to write it over; and but for unavoidable hindrances in travelling, I can hardly say when I should have written what I have. With an honest desire for your best good, I subscribe myself your friend,

"J. BROWN."

John Brown was married to his first wife, Dianthe Lusk, June 21st, 1820, at Hudson, Ohio, where he then carried on the trade of a tanner. His character as an upright man of business always stood high, and in accordance with this we find that he refused to sell his leather while it retained a particle of moisture, lest his customers should be cheated in value or weight. He afterwards combined with this trade the business of farming and keeping sheep. He had a great taste for rearing farm stock of all kinds, and cared tenderly for the beasts under his care. So keen was his observation, that he knew when a strange sheep had got into his flock of two or three thousand head.

In 1826, he removed to Richmond, Pennsylvania, still engaged in the tanning trade. About this time he joined the Presbyterian Church, with which he remained in communion till his death. Here his wife died in 1832, having brought him seven children, of whom five survived her. In the following year he married Mary A. Day, of Meadville, Pennsylvania, then only in her eighteenth year, and was again fortunate in his choice. By this marriage he had seven sons and six daughters.

In 1835, he removed to Franklin Mills, Portage County, Ohio, continuing his trade, and occasionally dealing in sheep and cattle. In 1840, he returned to Hudson, Ohio, and engaged in the wool business; he afterwards removed to Akron, in the same state; and settled in Springfield, Massachusetts, in 1846.

While at Akron, he entered into partnership with a Mr. Perkins; they opened a large woollen warehouse at Springfield, and sold wool on commission, chiefly for farmers living in Ohio and Western Pennsylvania. Here he was known as a peaceable citizen and a religious man, of unswerving integrity, attending diligently and successfully to his calling. But the New England manufacturers, who had been accustomed to purchasing the wool on their own terms from the wool-growers, were determined to keep the trade if possible in their own hands; they combined against the firm of Perkins and Brown, and refused to deal with it. Thus deprived of his market, Brown, in the year 1848, with his characteristic promptitude took about 200,000 lbs. weight of the stock of wool to England, in the hope of selling it to advantage. The speculation was unfortunate; it sold in London for about half its value, and was a heavy loss to the firm, reducing Brown almost to poverty. In reference to this journey, during which he also visited parts of France and Germany, a friend writes as follows :—

"I heard from him an account of his travels in

Europe, and his experience as a wool-grower. He had chiefly noticed in Europe the agricultural and military equipment of the several countries he visited. He watched reviews of the French, English, and German armies, and made his own comments on their military systems. He thought a standing army the greatest curse to a country, because it drained off the best of the young men, and left farming and the industrial arts to be managed by inferior men. The German armies he thought slow and unwieldy; the German farming was bad husbandry, because there the farmers did not live on their land, but in towns, and so wasted the natural manures which should go back to the soil. He visited several of the famous battle grounds of Napoleon, whose career he had followed with great interest. He thought no American could visit Europe without coming home more in love with our own country, for which he had a most ardent affection, while he so cordially hated its greatest curse—slavery.

"He was noted for his skill in testing and recognizing different qualities of wool. Give him two samples of wool, one grown in Ohio and the other in Vermont, and he would distinguish each of them in the dark. I heard the following story told of him while in England, where he went to consult wool merchants and wool growers. One evening, in company with several of these persons, each of whom had brought samples of wool in his pocket, Captain Brown was giving his opinion as to the best use to be made of certain varieties, when one of the party, wishing to play a trick on

new home among the mountains of the Adirondack
district. This was in the summer of 1849. He had at
this time ten children living; he had buried several;
three in the course of one month while residing in
the state of Ohio. His two eldest sons, John and Jason,
had by this time married. The farm at North Elba
was a wild, romantic, and dreary spot. The climate
was too severe for the growth of Indian corn, the great
staple of the American farmer; and it was with difficulty that they raised provisions enough for their own
use. Cattle must be housed during six months of the
year, while the snow lay on the ground. Their chief
stock was sheep; they spun the wool for clothing, and
had some over for sale; this was the only produce they
had to take to market. That Brown possessed some fine
cattle while on this farm is shown by an extract from
the report of a cattle-show held in Essex County, New
York, in 1850:—" The appearance upon the grounds of
a number of very choice and beautiful Devons, from the
herd of Mr. John Brown, residing in one of our most
remote and secluded towns, attracted great attention,
and added much to the interest of the fair. The interest and admiration they excited have attracted
public attention to the subject, and have already
resulted in the introduction of several choice animals
into this region. We have no doubt that their influence
upon the character and stock of our country will be
permanent and decisive."*

* A correspondent of the *New York Observer* wrote to Brown

2 *

The family remained at North Elba two years ; returning in 1851 to Akron, where Brown managed Mr. Perkins's farm and was again associated with him in the wool business.*   But when, in 1855, he started for Kansas, to aid his sons who had settled there, he again removed his family to the lonely farm at North Elba. There the widow and her surviving children still reside, and there he now lies buried.

In giving this rapid sketch of his movements, we have said but little of the man himself.   He will show himself most clearly in his own words, when that crisis comes which takes him out of the domain of private life and makes him an historic character.   We have a few testimonials during this long period from men who knew him well.   Mr. Baldwin, of Ohio, who had known him from 1814, "considered him a man of rigid integrity and of ardent temperament."   Mr. George Leech, who knew him from early boyhood, says that he

in reference to these cattle, and received a reply which he considered remarkable not only for the force and precision of the language, as a business letter, and for the distinctness of the statements, but also for its sound sense and honesty of representation.   He gave the following extract :—" None of my cattle are pure Devons, but are a mixture of that and a particular favourite stock from Connecticut, a cross of which I much prefer to any pure English cattle, after many years' experience of different breeds of imported cattle.   *   *   *   I was several months in England last season, and saw no one stock on any farm that would average better than my own."

* John Brown's name appeared as an exhibitor of samples of wool at the London Exhibition of 1851.

"always appeared strictly conscientious and honest, but of strong impulses and strong religious feelings." Mr. Otis writes :—" I became acquainted with John Brown about the year 1836. Soon after my removal to Akron, he became a client of mine; subsequently, a resident of the township in which the town of Akron is situated ; and, during a portion of the latter time, a member of a Bible class taught by me. In these relations which I sustained to Mr. Brown I had a good opportunity to become acquainted with his mental, moral, and religious character. I always regarded him as a man of more than ordinary mental capacity, of very ardent and excitable temperament, of unblemished moral character ; a kind neighbour, a good Christian, deeply imbued with religious feelings and sympathies. In a business point of view his ardent and excitable temperament led him into pecuniary difficulties ; but I never knew his integrity questioned by any person whatever."

Nothing could be more simple and unpretending than his daily life. He rose early and worked hard ; his clothing was of the plainest cut and material, but he was remarkable for cleanliness and neatness. He never used tobacco, wine, or spirits, cheese, or butter; nor did he take tea or coffee till a few years before his death, when he had occasion to be frequently from home, and found it gave less trouble to take what was set before him at a friend's table. He was a tender though somewhat strict father, a faithful and affectionate husband. He reared his children in habits of industry, independence, and filial obedience. The Bible was their earliest study ; morning and evening prayers, grace before and after meals, were the daily law of his house.

One of his daughters writes :—"My dear father's favourite books of an historical character were Rollin's Ancient History, Josephus's Works, the Lives of Napoleon and his Marshals, and the Life of Oliver Cromwell.   Of religious books, Baxter's Saints' Rest, the Pilgrim's Progress, Henry on Meekness ; but, above all others, the Bible was his favourite volume, and he had such a perfect knowledge of it, that, when any person was reading it, he would correct the least mistake. When he came home at night, tired out with labour, he would, before going to bed, ask some of the family to read chapters (as was his usual course night and morning), and would almost always say, 'Read one of David's Psalms.'

"He was a great admirer of Oliver Cromwell.   Of coloured heroes, Nat Turner and Cinques stood first in his esteem.   How often have I heard him speak in admiration of Cinques' character and management."*

---

* The Spanish schooner "Amistad" sailed from Havana on the 28th of June, 1839, bound to Guanaja, in the island of Cuba, under the command of her owner, Don Ramon Ferrer, laden with sundry merchandise, and with fifty-three negro slaves on board. About day-break on the 31st, the slaves rose upon the crew, and killed the captain, a slave of his, and two sailors—sparing only two persons, namely, Don Jose Ruiz and Don Pedro Montes ; of whom the former was owner of forty-nine of the slaves, and the latter of the other four.   These they retained, that they might navigate the vessel and take her to the coast of Africa.   Montes,

He imbued his children with the same hatred of oppression, and love for the oppressed coloured race, that animated his own mind. They were trained to heroism and self-sacrifice, and they were all ready and eager to second his views when the time came to carry them out.

His business habits were orderly and systematic; his account books and correspondence were kept with the greatest regularity. But, though diligent in business, frugal and careful in his style of living, and possessed of uncommon energy and shrewdness, he appears never to have accumulated money. Too honest and straightforward to avail himself of trickery in trade, unselfish almost to a fault, and reckless of consequences in carrying out his views of right, he was not a man likely to

availing himself of his knowledge of nautical affairs, succeeded in taking the vessel to the shores of the United States. He was spoken by various vessels, from the captains of which the negroes bought provisions, but to whom, it seems, he was unable to make known his distress, being closely watched. At length he reached Long Island sound, where the "Amistad" was detained by the American brig-of-war "Washington," Captain Gedney, who, on learning the circumstances of the case, secured the negroes, and took them, with the vessel, to New London, in the state of Connecticut. These negroes were native Africans who had been recently introduced into Cuba by the slave traders. Their leader was Cinques, whose skill and courage in conducting to a successful issue this conspiracy for the liberation of himself and his fellows excited great admiration in America, where the captives (who were eventually sent back to their native country) received important assistance from the abolitionists.

grow rich. He also speculated in land, and made
some unsuccessful investments, by which he was a
serious loser.

He was extremely fond of music. A friend writes :—
" I once saw him sit listening with the most rapt attention to Schubert's Serenade, played by a mutual friend;
and, when the music ceased, tears were in his eyes. He
was indeed most tender-hearted ; fond of children and
pet creatures, and always enlisted on the weaker side."

In his sketch of his early life, we have seen that
the cruel treatment which he saw inflicted on a slave
boy about his own age, at a tavern where he stopped
when driving his cattle through a slave state, sank deep
into his heart, and made him "a determined abolitionist." The indignant feeling of hatred to slavery, thus
early aroused within him, never slept, and about the
year 1839 he appears to have conceived the idea of
attempting the deliverance of the slaves. A gigantic
system of injustice was going forward ; the oppressed
slaves could not raise themselves; their cry had entered
into his heart, and aroused a fixed determination to lead
them to liberty. From the time he formed this resolution, he was on the watch for an opportunity to carry it
out, and he engaged in no commercial speculation which
he could not honourably and without serious loss to his
family wind up on short notice. Here was another
reason why he could not grow rich. Meantime he did
what was difficult for a man of his eager temperament
—he waited patiently.

CHAPTER II.

1854—1856.

BEFORE proceeding with our narrative, it will be well to give a short description of Kansas, and some account of the circumstances under which it was peopled and ultimately organized into one of the free states of the American Union.

Kansas lies directly west of the state of Missouri, and occupies nearly the centre of the North American continent. The country consists of undulating prairies, with a rich and fertile soil, and is well watered by streams flowing through picturesque valleys, generally bordered with woods to the distance of a quarter or half a mile of their high banks on either side.

The state, which is about as large as Scotland, has been divided into thirty-six counties, of which a large proportion are named after men eminent for their zeal

in support of slavery. Such is frequently the case in
the United States, where devotion to the interests of an
oligarchy of slaveowners has usually proved the surest
passport to the admiration of the multitude and the
favours of their rulers. Notwithstanding . the small
population of Kansas, we find on Colton's map no
fewer than twelve settlements dignified with the name
of cities.   There are Delaware City, Neosho City,
Mound City, Central City, Ohio City, Council City,
Riley City, Leavenworth City, Geary City, Diamond
City, Jefferson City, and Prairie City.   The last of
these has been described as consisting, so lately as
1856, of " two log cabins and a well."

According to the American census of 1850, the population of Kansas was 8,500, of whom less than 200 were
slaves ; but such is the rapid increase of numbers by
emigration in the new settled districts of the far west,
that, notwithstanding the struggle between freedom and
slavery which made the territory for years a prey to
the miseries of civil war, the population amounted by
the census of 1860 to 107,011 souls. During the time
in which John Brown was concerned in the events we
are about to relate, the number probably did not exceed
40,000. These were very thinly scattered over the
country, and were for the greater part settled in the
eastern districts bordering on Missouri. Nearly all the
places mentioned in our narrative are comprised within
a strip of territory one hundred and fifty miles in length
from north to south, by one hundred miles wide. It
will be observed that many of them have Indian names,

for there are several Indian reserves within the bounds
of Kansas, and the whole territory was until within a
very few years in the possession of native tribes.

Ever since the union of the free and slave states
in one republic, the demands of the slaveholders for
fresh privileges and concessions have been insatiable ;
and there were always pliant tools among northern
statesmen, who, for the chance of office and emoluments,
were ready to aid them in their designs. The slaveholders especially coveted new and fertile soil, after
having impoverished wide tracts of land by the wasteful
and exhaustive system of slave labour. By an act of
congress passed in the year 1820, commonly called the
Missouri Compromise, slavery was admitted into the
territory now forming the state of Missouri, on its
admission into the Union, in defiance of a previous
engagement by which that system was "for ever" prohibited in all the United States territory lying north of
36½ degrees, north latitude. Missouri was thus admitted as a slave state, by way of compromise, and to
avoid a dangerous collision between the free and the
slave states, but with the express understanding that
no more of the territory of the United States lying
north of the prescribed geographical limit should from
thenceforward be contaminated by the institution of
slavery. But about the year 1853, the slaveholders
threw longing eyes on Kansas, the most fertile portion
of the unappropriated territory ; coveting it not only
for its rich virgin soil, but in order to regain the
balance of power in the United States senate. The

free states were sixteen in number, the slave states only fifteen; and as each state, whatever its size and population, sent two members to the senate, it was important to recover this advantage for the south. As usual, when the southern interest had determined on gaining an object, it persevered with unflinching steadiness to its attainment. One of their most able and energetic northern allies, an aspiring politician, a member of the democratic party, and one of the senators for Illinois, Mr. Stephen A. Douglas, introduced a bill into congress for the purpose of organizing as territories the vast districts of Kansas and Nebraska, embracing an area more than four times as large as Great Britain. One of the provisions of this bill threw open the territories to slaveholders with their slaves, and thus virtually repealed the Missouri Compromise. Mr. Douglas maintained that he could see no reason why slaveholding should be restricted by arbitrary lines of demarcation; that as much right existed to establish slavery as to establish freedom in any territory of the United States. Unfortunately for the peace of Kansas, his efforts were successful; and on the 30th May, 1854, the territory was thrown open to slavery under the specious pretext of non-intervention on the part of the federal government with the right of settlers to order their own institutions—or, in the language of the day, with "squatter sovereignty." Settlers from the south were left at liberty to take their slaves into Kansas if they chose; and when the population was sufficiently large to procure its legal admission into the Union, the majority of the votes must decide whether it should enter as a free or as a slave state.

It cannot be doubted that but for this unhappy intervention of congress, the settlement of Kansas as a free territory, and eventually a free state, would have been rapid, peaceful, and prosperous. Its climate, its soil, and its easy access to many of the older settlements would have made it a favoured course for the tide of emigration constantly flowing to the west. But when the prohibition of slavery was removed, the aspect of affairs changed. The whole country was agitated by the reopening of a question which it was believed had been finally settled by the Missouri compromise. The excitement which always accompanies the subject of slavery was aggravated on the one hand by the hope of extending it into a region from which it had been excluded by law, and on the other by a sense of indignation at the dishonourable violation of a national compact. This excitement was naturally greatest in the border counties of Missouri and Kansas, according as settlers favouring free or slave institutions moved into the new territory. It was contended by the the proslavery party that the removal of the prohibition to hold slaves in the territory virtually established slavery there; and every movement hostile to slavery was regarded by them as an interference with their rights. As soon as the passing of the law was known on the western borders of Missouri, leading citizens of that state crossed over into the territory of Kansas held squatter meetings as citizens of Kansas, passed declaratory resolutions in that capacity, and then returned to their homes.   Among the resolutions thus passed were the following :—

" That we will afford protection to no abolitionist as a settler in this territory."

" That we recognise the institution of slavery as already existing in this territory, and advise slaveholders to introduce their property as early as possible."

This system of unlawful interference was acted upon in every important event in the early history of the territory.   Almost every election was controlled, not by the actual settlers, but by citizens of the state of Missouri who entered Kansas for the purpose, prepared to carry out their will by force of arms, if necessary. They were determined that Kansas should be a slave state.   A secret political society was formed in the state of Missouri, with a machinery of signs and passwords and secret oaths.   This society sent armed interlopers into Kansas to control the elections, and to prevent the return to office of any who were free-state men ; it also invited settlers from the slave states to emigrate into Kansas, aiding them liberally from its funds.   While the free-state settlers were relying upon the rights which they believed to be secured to them by law, and had as yet formed no combination among themselves for mutual protection, this hostile conspiracy was gathering strength.

Emigration flowed rapidly into Kansas, both from the north and south.   But, for a long time, all the advantages were on the side of slavery. Missouri was the jealous guardian of the interests of the southern states. Every obstacle was thrown in the way of the northern emigrants. They were driven back; they were tarred and feathered; their claims of land were seized; their cabins were burned down; they were often ordered, by committees of southern emigrants, or the Missourian rabble, to leave the territory at once, under penalty of death. A single paragraph from a speech delivered at St. Joseph, Missouri, in 1854, by General Stringfellow, a prominent citizen of that state, will illustrate the spirit of the Missourians :—

" I tell you to mark every scoundrel among you who is the least tainted with abolitionism, or free soilism, and exterminate him. Neither give nor take quarter from the damned rascals. To those who have qualms of conscience as to violating laws, state or national, I say the time has come when such impositions must be disregarded, as your rights and property are in danger. I advise you, one and all, to enter every election district in Kansas, in defiance of Reeder* and his myrmidons, and vote at the point of the bowie knife and revolver. Neither take nor give quarter, as the cause demands it. It is enough that the slave-holding interest wills it, from which there is no appeal."

On the 29th November, 1854, the first election was held in Kansas for a delegate to congress. On this

---

* The Governor of Kansas appointed by the United States government.

occasion about seventeen hundred Missourians crossed the border, and voted for the pro-slavery candidate, although actual settlers alone had the right to vote.* As these strangers were armed, it was dangerous to oppose them, and it was sometimes with great difficulty that the legal voters could get to the ballot boxes to deposit their votes. Many of the actual settlers took at this time but little interest in the elections; their settlements were scattered over a wide extent of country, and they were not aware that the question of free or slave institutions was distinctly at issue.

These outrages excited great indignation in the free states, and especially in New England; but instead of deterring they rather encouraged emigration; and

* In the district of Lawrence, where the late census report indicates but 359 voters, the election shows there were 1,000 votes polled, and yet a large number of our *actual* residents, and particularly those from a distance, did not exercise their right to the elective franchise, as they found they could not do so without endangering their lives. In the district of Tecumseh, Mr. Burgess, one of the judges appointed by the governor, was violently threatened; a pistol was three times snapped in his face, and a club flourished over his head, till finally he was compelled to proclaim the election adjourned. The mob then selected a new board, with two drunken secretaries, who took possession of the ballot-box, and allowed no person to approach it unless he was right on the "goose question,"—a slang phrase used among the Missourians, implying they are in favour of extending the institution of slavery over Kansas. No questions were asked the voter as to his citizenship or place of residence; no oath was administered, or other test required, save an assurance of support to the pro-slavery ticket.—*Kansas Herald of Freedom.*

amongst the settlers who then removed to Kansas from the state of Ohio were the four sons of John Brown by his first wife.

The two eldest of these, John and Jason, had families to take with them. John converted his landed property into cash. Jason dug up his vines and choice fruit trees, and conveyed them at considerable expense to Kansas. Owen and Frederick were to follow slowly with the waggons, cattle, and horses, wintering in south-western Illinois on the way. This plan proved very expensive, and was attended with great hardship to the two young men. A younger brother, Solomon or Salmon, was sent on to assist them, and all three arrived in Kansas with their teams and stock early in the spring of 1855.

" During this slow journey with their stock across the entire width of Missouri," writes their father, "they heard much from the people of the stores of wrath and vengeance which were then and there gathering for the free-state men and abolitionists gone or going to Kansas, and were themselves often admonished, in no very mild language, to stop ere it should be too late."

They settled in Lykins County, southern Kansas, near the small river Pottawattomie, and experienced their full share of the hardships of the settler's life, and the outrages to which emigrants from the free states were subjected. " The brothers," writes a friend of the family, " were all free-state men in opinion; but, removing thither with the intention of settling there, went without arms. They were harassed, plundered, threatened, and insulted by gangs of marauding border

ruffians, with whom the prime object was plunder; and
noisy pro-slavery partizanship was equivalent to a free
charter to plunder with impunity. The sons wrote to
their father, requesting him to procure such arms as
might enable them in some degree to protect themselves, and personally to bring them to Kansas."

We have seen that Brown was an eminently peaceable
man, and that he had even refused to train in his
youth, from his dislike to the soldier's calling. But he
had also declared eternal war with slavery, and here
was an opportunity of aiding to check the extension of
its innumerable horrors over a wide region of his
country. He was indignant at seeing justice trampled
under foot, and he keenly felt the wrongs to which his
sons were subjected. The federal government, under
the presidency of Mr. Franklin Pierce, had been repeatedly appealed to by the persecuted free-state settlers,
but it gave them no redress; and was indeed so far from
checking the pro-slavery party that it virtually encouraged them. Mr. Reeder, who had been appointed
governor of the territory, was found too ready to dis-
countenance the border ruffians; he was therefore
recalled,* and his place supplied by Governor Shannon,

---

* "Governor Reeder found the people whom he was sent out
to govern invaded by a lawless band of alien marauders. He
resisted them with such weapons as the constitution and the law
had placed in his hands, and no other. His resistance brought
upon him the hostility of those, and those only, whose piratical
schemes he foiled. They memorialized the President to remove
him; and he has removed him. By that act President Pierce has

a timid and irresolute compromiser. It was evident
that the settlers must defend themselves, or must retire
before the invaders, and relinquish their own property
and the cause of freedom in Kansas. Brown could not
hesitate between these alternatives. His spirit was
thoroughly aroused by the summons. Leaving Akron,
Ohio, he settled his wife and younger children on the
bleak mountain farm at North Elba, and took leave of
them for a time. In allusion to this parting, one of his
family says :—" On leaving us the first time he went
to Kansas, he said, 'If it is so painful for us to part,
with the hope of meeting again, how dreadful must
be the separation for life of hundreds of poor slaves.'"

He reached Kansas in the autumn of 1855, well
provided with arms for himself and his sons, funds
having been contributed for their purchase by generous
friends in New England, who were watching the unequal conflict from afar, and sympathized warmly with
the side of freedom. He did not purpose settling in
Kansas, but, to use his own words, " with the exposure,

given countenance and encouragement to those who have openly
defied the officers and laws of the federal government. By that
act he has taken sides with lawlessness and violence against the
people of Kansas and public peace. By that act he has made his
administration responsible for the composition of the so-called
Kansas legislature, and the outrages which prevented the citizens
of the territory from participating in its election. By that act he
has made himself a party to the schemes of Atchison and Stringfellow, and convicted himself and his administration of a determination from the beginning to make Kansas a slave state."—*New
York Evening Post, edited by the poet Bryant.*

3*

privations, hardships, and wants of pioneer life he was familiar ; and he thought he could benefit his children and the new beginners from the older parts of the country, and help them to shift in their new home."

We cannot here attempt to give minute details of the civil war in Kansas, but shall merely indicate the general course of the struggle in which Brown took so earnest a part during the two following years. With this view, we shall go back to a period shortly before his arrival in that country.

In March, 1855, the election took place for the legislative assembly of the territory of Kansas.   It was controlled and decided by an armed irruption of Missourians to the number of about five thousand. With this illegal assistance, the pro-slavery party prevailed.   Great irritation existed through the region ; the successful side, while assuming the title of the " law and order party," daily inflicted acts of reckless outrage on peaceable citizens, who were naturally aroused to make reprisals ; and the settlers of both parties now wore deadly weapons, even when engaged in their ordinary avocations.

The legislative assembly, thus illegally elected, met on the 2nd July, at Pawnee, the town appointed by Governor Shannon.   Here they passed a constitution and laws of a thoroughly pro-slavery nature, embodying some of the most barbarous clauses of the Missourian and other southern codes.   The punishment of death was awarded for aiding in the liberation of a slave ; no man known to be opposed to slavery was eligible to the bar, the bench, or the jury-box in cases affecting slave-property ; and all the enactments of this assembly breathed the same despotic and intolerant spirit. Laws passed by a legislature thus illegally imposed on the people, had, of course, no valid claim to their obedience, and were received with vehement opposition. The free-state settlers repudiated the code, and denied the authority of its framers, giving them the name of the *bogus*, or spurious, legislature. They resolved to convene a rival assembly, form a state government, and apply to congress for admission into the Union. A mass meeting was accordingly held in the town of Lawrence on 15th of August, 1855, "irrespective of party distinctions, and influenced by common necessity ; " at which they called upon all *bona fide* citizens of Kansas territory, of whatever political views or predilections, to elect delegates to a convention, to be held at the town of Topeka. A regular machinery was appointed for electing members, with the usual legal formalities, to a constitutional convention, to meet at Topeka on the 23rd of October. There was no illegality in this proceeding, for the right of the people to assemble and express their political opinions in any form, whether by election or convention, is secured to them by the constitution of the United States.

The convention met in October, as appointed, and adopted a constitution known as the Topeka constitution. It served as a rallying point for the free-state men, but technically had no legal validity, as the general government at Washington had meantime accepted and sanctioned the spurious constitution, with all its atrocious clauses, and was determined to enforce obedience to it with all its power and authority, regarding and treating all opposition as rebellion. Thus justice was struck down in the name of law ; and we find that the machinery of a free democratic government may be converted into a weapon of terrible wrong, when the people itself has become demoralized. In January, 1856, an election for territorial officers and legislators was held by the free-state party under the provisions of the Topeka constitution. Thus there were two codes of law in the territory; the one monstrous in itself, and passed by a body chosen illegally, but having received the sanction of the general government ; the other expressing the will of the majority of the actual inhabitants, but treated by the general government as a treasonable document. Such rival claims must of necessity be fruitful of deeds of violence in a community of men who habitually carried fire-arms and were rendered irritable by numberless outrages inflicted and endured.

No words can more vividly portray the reign of terror which prevailed at this time in Kansas, than the following description of an election, which we take from the correspondence of the Cleveland *Morning Leader*, under date of Leavenworth, October 2nd, 1855 :—

" Murder rules in Kansas. The armed assassins of Missouri have again invaded our soil, and, backed up by [Governor] Shannon and the usurping legislature which was imposed upon us by the same lawless marauders, are revelling in drunken but short-lived triumph over the honest, peaceful, and liberty-loving voters of Kansas.

" Yesterday was, you are aware, the day appointed by that fraudulently elected legislature for the election of a representative in congress from this territory ; you are also aware that the free-state convention resolved to resist and repudiate the action of the legislature; but the friends of freedom pledged themselves to commit no violence unless compelled to do so in self-defence. They resolved to maintain peace, good order, and obedience to all laws properly enacted, as far as lay in their power —yet never to yield. They accordingly stayed away from the polls.

" The Missourians came over in armed bands. They have carried the elections, of course ; and, encouraged by the apparent non-resistance of the friends of liberty, they rushed, in a drunken and riotous frenzy, to the last extreme of barbarity, and capped the climax of their atrocities by murder.

" The enactment passed by this infamous legislature, prescribing the qualifications of voters, declares that any one may vote who swears allegiance to the Fugitive Slave Law and the Kansas-Nebraska Bill, and pays the sum of one dollar. Such are the evidences of citizenship, such is the self-government which grows out of the Fugitive Law of 1850, the repeal of the Missouri compromise, and the institution of squatter sovereignty.

" On the day of election the motley crowd of voters,

composed of Missourians, recently arrived Virginians, and drunken Indians, were addressed by pro-slavery speakers from the steps of the hotel in this place. They were told that slavery was right for Kansas, and that Whitfield was the true representative of squatter sovereignty. They went and voted almost before the Missouri mud was dry upon their boots. With rifles in their hands, knives in their belts, bottles in their pockets, and whiskey in their bellies, they swaggered around the polls, drinking and shouting in exultation over their triumph.

"As night approached they became more turbulent and overbearing. They marched through the streets bespattered with mud, swearing, yelling, swinging their hats, and asking, 'Where are the abolitionists?'—'Let's cut the white-livered Yankees' throats!' At that time one of our citizens, Mr. James Fornam, was passing through the streets. As he passed the hotel, one of the Missourians, who wore a white slouched hat, a grey coat, and a pair of greasy corduroy pants tucked into the top of his mud-covered, cowhide boots, hailed him, and asked him to come in and vote. Mr. Fornam declined. One of the Missourians then asked him, 'Why do you not vote?' Mr. Fornam replied, 'Because I do not consider the election legal.' 'He is one of the free-state men,' said the crowd. Mr. Fornam, at this time seeing he had got into bad company, started to go; but he was too late. The crowd gathered round him, and began to cry out, 'Hang him! Lynch him! Tar and feather the Yankee!' One of the mob then seized hold of him, but being a quick, powerful man, he turned, knocked his assailant down, and fled. They gave chase, but could not overtake him. One of the desperadoes shot at him with a rifle. The ball pierced his hat, but though it did not hurt him, it penetrated the boards of a house, and killed a child who was playing on the floor. The mother ran out, shrieking, 'Murder! help!' The news spread, and the free-state men armed themselves. In the mean time another citizen had been insulted in the street, knocked down, and stabbed. This was young Thomas Newman. He died this morning. The marauders now began to be alarmed at their own acts. About one hundred free-state men, well armed, formed in a body, and marched to the hotel; but the Missourians had decamped. The free-state men pursued them to the river, and one of the villains has felt cold steel."

In the month of November, 1855, Mr. Dow, a peaceable emigrant from New England, was murdered by a pro-slavery settler named Coleman. The authorities, instead of arresting the assassin, leagued themselves with him, and seized an innocent free-state squatter, as a provocation to his party to rescue him in Lawrence; whereby they might have a plausible excuse to call on the Missourians to destroy the town, on the plea of enforcing the territorial laws. The prisoner was unexpectedly rescued several miles from Lawrence; but, despite this accident, the "territorial militia," as the pro-slavery interlopers were officially styled, were called to arms; and, in December, Lawrence was invested by a force of fifteen hundred armed men. Of this large body, it should be observed, not more than seventy-five were residents of Kansas. "Missouri," it was admitted by Governor Shannon, "sent not only her young men, but her grey-haired citizens were there. The man of seventy winters stood shoulder to shoulder with the youth of sixteen." They were well provided with arms and ammunition, having broken into a national arsenal in their own state, and taken cannon, muskets, rifles, gunpowder and all the munitions of war.

As the inhabitants of Lawrence were known to be in favour of making Kansas a free state, that town was peculiarly obnoxious to the pro-slavery party, and they had accordingly determined on its destruction. The free-state settlers flocked to its defence, and soon mustered about five hundred men, organized under Lane and Robinson. Though the invaders were three times as numerous, and far better provided with weapons, they hesitated to attack the place, but lay encamped around it nearly two weeks. During the continuance of this siege, Mr. Brown and his four sons arrived one day in Lawrence in their lumber waggon. They were armed with broad-swords and revolvers, and had long poles surmounted by bayonets standing upright around the waggon box. Brown's opinion was openly given for war. He longed to grapple with the invaders, not doubting that the right would conquer. But milder or more timid counsels prevailed. Governor Shannon hastened up from the Shawnee Mission, to effect a compromise. The northern men were willing to try the effect of negociation; nor can we wonder that they dreaded an open rupture with assailants so numerous and so barbarous. They had everything to lose if the day went against them; they were restrained by their leaders; and they apprehended treachery from some of their associates. On the other hand, their assailants were backed up by the authority of the United States government, and the military power of the nation. But Brown cared little for expediency and diplomacy. The idea of compromise with evil was foreign to his nature. When General Lane sent a message, requesting his presence at a council of war, his reply was characteristic :—" Tell the general, when he wants me to fight, to say so, but that is the only order I will obey." The result of the negociation was a treaty with the invaders. Although a peace was patched up for the time, Brown always maintained that this treaty and the policy which led to it served only to postpone the inevitable conflict then rapidly approaching, and to demoralize the spirit of the free-state party. It occasioned, he thought, the death of many northern men, whom the invaders, encouraged by this compromising policy, murdered in cold blood or in desultory warfare.

The Missourian border ruffians, on their way home after raising the siege of Lawrence, destroyed the free-state ballot-box at Leavenworth, and threw the press and types of the *Territorial Register* newspaper into the Missouri river. Strange to say, this paper was the political organ of Mr. Stephen A. Douglas, through whose influence the Missouri compromise had been repealed, and slavery admitted into Kansas. The leaders of the mob stated that the destruction of the press was provoked by an article of Mr. Redpath's which had appeared in the paper.

At the elections which were held throughout the territory in January, 1856, under the Topeka constitution, John Brown, jun., was chosen one of the representatives to the territorial legislature. At some places the elections were not allowed to be held; many fierce skirmishes occurred at the polls; and one atrocious murder was committed. At Atchison, a clergyman who admitted in private conversation that he was a free-state man, was tarred and feathered, and sent down the river on a raft, federal office-holders leading and encouraging the mob. Nevertheless, the assembly met, passed some enactments, prepared a memorial to Congress, and adjourned till the 4th of July.

In the month of February, 1856, President Pierce, in an official proclamation, denounced the Topeka, or free-state, legislature as an illegal assembly, confirmed the governmental sanction previously given to the pro-slavery code which was passed under the auspices of the Missouri border ruffians, and ordered the federal troops to aid the territorial officers in carrying out its enactments.

As spring advanced, troops of emigrants from the southern states of Georgia, Alabama, and the Carolinas arrived in Kansas, with the avowed intention of exterminating or driving out the free-state settlers. Numbers of these emigrants were enrolled as territorial militia by Governor Shannon, and armed with United States muskets, as if the more effectually to enable them to carry out their purpose. Another attack on Lawrence was determined upon, as that town was regarded as the stronghold of the free-state forces and the head-quarters of the Emigrant Aid Company.* The Missourians assembled in its vicinity, pillaging and destroying with impunity. Under pretence of serving writs on some of the inhabitants, the United States marshal entered the town on the 20th of May, at the head of eight hundred men. After making his arrests, which were peaceably submitted to, the marshal formally dismissed his attendants. They were immediately re-organized by the sheriff as his official staff, and under his orders a large hotel, erected by the Emigrant Aid Company, was battered with cannon and burned to the ground; the presses and offices of two free-state newspapers were completely demolished; and property of the inhabitants was destroyed to the estimated value of forty thousand pounds, sterling.

Further particulars are given in a letter from Mrs. Woods, wife of the editor of the *Kansas Tribune :—*

" After they had got all the arms they could, Atchison† and Jones proclaimed that Judge Lecompte had

---

* A company formed in Massachusetts to promote the permanent settlement of Kansas by a free and intelligent population.

† The *Missouri Democrat* gives the following report of a speech (from which we omit the blasphemy) made by Atchison to the posse assembled by Donaldson and Jones in Lawrence, just previous to the sacking of that town :—

pronounced the free-state hotel, the printing presses, and Blanton's bridge all nuisances, and had ordered them to remove the same. The presses were attacked first, and my descriptive powers fail me to paint to you the scene of desolation that the offices now present— the presses broken in every place that could break— the papers and books torn, and strewed all over the town—the ink smeared over all—the stoves battered and broken—the type thrown into the river, and strewed like hail through the streets. The hotel went next, as I have told you.

"The work of pillage and plunder still went on. When the party first entered, the women and children fled like frightened birds across the ravine to Jenkins's house, and about fifty houses were entered by the mob.

"Boys, this day I am a Kickapoo ranger. This day we have entered Lawrence, with southern rights inscribed on our banner, and not one —— abolitionist dared to fire a gun.

"Now, boys, this is the happiest day of my life. We have entered that —— town, and taught the —— abolitionists a southern lesson that they will remember till the day they die. And now, boys, we will go in again with our highly honourable Jones, and test the strength of that —— free-state hotel, and teach the Emigrant Aid Company that Kansas shall be ours. Boys, ladies should, and I hope will, be respected by every gentleman; but when a woman takes on herself the garb of a soldier, by carrying a Sharpe's rifle, then she is no longer worthy of respect. Trample her under your feet as you would a snake.

"Come on, boys. Now do your duty to yourselves and your southern friends.

"Your duty I know you will do. If one man or woman dare stand before you, blow them to hell with a chunk of cold lead."

They tore up beds, and ripped them open to find arms. They smashed looking-glasses, dishes, furniture, and even children's toys; ate everything they could, and destroyed the rest of the provisions; broke open trunks, and stole money and clothes from Johnson's house. · Mr. Stowell had about six thousand dollars stolen, in drafts and land warrants. They stole watches, chains, and all the ladies' jewellery and silk dresses they could find. The ruffians entered the stores, robbed the money-drawers, pulled off their old shabby duds, and dressed themselves in the best they could find. David Atchison, late Vice-President of our glorious republic, took two boxes of cigars from Brooks's store, and stole some shirts, one of which the owner recognized on Atchison's back the next day.

" Our people yielded for two reasons : first, because the demand of arms and removal of ' nuisances' were made and ordered by the court, Lecompte acting as judge, under the authority of the United States. The second, and I believe the greatest, reason was because Robinson, Deitzler, Brown, Jenkins, Judge Smith, and Branson were in their hands ; and it was well known that, should the first blow be struck by free-state men in defence of their rights, the helpless prisoners would have been assassinated by an infuriated mob."

A further description of the behaviour of this lawless horde is given in the able "Narrative of John Doy of Lawrence, Kansas,"* an emigrant from the State of New York, from which we make the following extract :—

* Published in New York in 1860.

" On the night of May 21st, 1856, when Lawrence was sacked, hotels burned, and printing presses thrown into the river, my beautiful brood mares and other animals were stolen by the invaders, my growing corn and wheat trampled down and ruined, and we were left without the means to cultivate our crops. On the next day twenty-eight men tied their horses to my fence, came to the house, and asked me :

" ' Are you from the East ?'

" ' Yes.'

" ' Then you're a damned abolitionist ?'

" ' Of course.'

" Without more words, they cleaned out my house of everything they wanted ; and this was a sample of their usual manner of proceeding towards the free-state settlers.

" One night we were awakened by a great light, and saw six houses burning, while the border ruffians, brought in by Colonels Titus and Buford to force slavery upon us, were laughing at and insulting the women and children as they ran from their burning homes in their night clothes. Men were murdered, women and girls were violated, and the invading mob treated the free-state people of Kansas as if they were conquered slaves and utterly devoid of human rights. Our appeals to the United States officials and to Washington were in vain. We were laughed at, and our oppressors aided. Armed with weapons from the government arsenal at Liberty, Missouri, they hoped soon to drive us away, and to deprive us of all claim to our common heritage ; to fix the blighting curse of slavery upon the soil of Kansas, and a padlock upon the lips of every man who wished to be free.

"The United States government, which should have protected us, looked on applaudingly. We were quiet, peaceful, industrious citizens, and wished to remain so, but we would not consent to bring up our children on land cursed by the toil of slaves. This was the only condition on which we could hope for peace.

" There was one other way, however, and that we determined to adopt. We could, and we would, conquer a peace. We could endure the present state of things no longer. We felt that they would go from bad to worse, and we swore to treat the invaders as noxious vermin ; we would drive them out or die. We formed ourselves into companies, we drilled, we made oath to stand by each other and by freedom for Kansas until death.

" During these troubles, the women and children made cartridges, and saw that we were properly fitted for every expedition. The war-spirit was as rife among them as among the men. Many a woman stood, rifle in hand, by the side of her father, husband, or brother, to resist the invaders ; and many a marauder fell by the ball from a rifle fired by a woman's hand. To the honour of the Kansas mothers, wives, and daughters be it said, that to them as much as to the men, the freedom of their country is due. The men, anxious for the safety of the dear ones dependent upon them, and sometimes dispirited by the gloomy aspect of the political horizon, might have given way, had they not been cheered and encouraged by the pious cheerfulness and perseverance of the women, whose lot was so much harder to bear than their own : it being much easier to meet the enemy in battle, amid all the excitement of a fight, than to sit at home waiting in anxious suspense for news, which might bring tidings of the death of those whom they loved, and upon whom their little ones depended for food."

CHAPTER III.

1856.—MAY TO SEPTEMBER.

BROWN IN THE ENEMY'S CAMP.—THE FREE-STATE MEN RESORT
TO LYNCH LAW.—ATTEMPT TO ARREST BROWN.—HIS CAMP.
—PATE'S BARBAROUS TREATMENT OF BROWN'S SONS.—
BROWN CAPTURES HIS PURSUER.—FREE-STATE LEGISLA-
TURE BROKEN UP BY FEDERAL TROOPS.—AFFAIR AT OSSA-
WATTOMIE.—MURDER OF FREDERICK BROWN.—DEFENCE
OF LAWRENCE.—OUTRAGES ON NORTHERN IMMIGRANTS
PASSING THROUGH MISSOURI.

WE have no desire to exaggerate the lawless deeds of
the invaders from Missouri, were such exaggeration
possible. We have compiled this history from contem-
poraneous documents, which no impartial mind can pe-
ruse without horror and astonishment that such a state
of society could have existed in our own day, in a nominally free, Christian, and civilized nation. Nor do we
mean to represent the settlers from the free states as
being always actuated by the highest motives. Doubtless many of them removed to Kansas more from the
hope of improving their worldly circumstances, than
from any special desire for the spread of free cultivation
or the discouragement of slavery. A large proportion
of these were imbued with the prevailing American
prejudice against the coloured race, and did not desire
their competition in the labour market. At a public
meeting which Brown attended while in Kansas, he
startled some who held these selfish views by the vehe-

4*

mence with which he opposed a resolution that Kansas should be a "free white state," implying the exclusion of free coloured settlers. He indignantly denounced the idea of excluding any man for the colour of his skin, and asserted the manhood and equal rights of the African race. This was the only political meeting he attended while in Kansas. He was not connected with any of the American political organizations; the Democratic party being in full sympathy with the slaveholders; while the Free-soil, or Republican party, although pledged against the extension of slavery into any of the northern territories, was yet fully committed to the execution of the Fugitive Slave Law, and the suppression of any attempt of the slaves to obtain their liberty by insurrection. He always regarded the maintenance of slavery as peculiarly criminal on the part of a people whose continual boast was that they had secured their own independence by a long and sanguinary struggle.

The pro-slavery party in all the district round Pottawattomie, near which Brown resided, now renewed their attacks on the free-state men, and he began to prepare for the defence of his neighbourhood. Accompanied by a few friends, he frequently entered the prairies where a number of the invaders were stationed, and, pretending to be engaged in making a survey of the country, he drove his imaginary lines through the middle of their camp, observing all that passed. He often adopted this way of learning the schemes of the enemy, and was apparently unsuspected by them, as they never made any inquiry respecting his political opinions. Believing him to be a surveyor employed by the United States government, they naturally concluded that he belonged to their own party, and accordingly they freely told him their plans. There was an old man named Brown, they said, who had settled in this vicinity, and was a great impediment to the designs of the slaveholders and their adherents. If this man and his sons could be forced to leave the country of their own accord—or more summarily disposed of, if no gentler means were found effectual—the other settlers would be afraid to offer any further resistance. They told him how Wilkinson, the Doyles, and a Dutchman named Sherman, all residing on Pottawattomie creek, had recently been in Missouri, and had succeeded in securing forces to expel or murder the Browns and several other prominent free-state men.

With this timely information Brown left their camp and warned the settlers who had been marked out for destruction, of the murderous designs of the Missourians. A meeting of the intended victims was held; and it was determined that on the first indication of an attack, the Doyles, Wilkinson, and Sherman should be seized, tried by Lynch law, and summarily put to death.

On the 24th of May, four days after the sacking of Lawrence, a brutal assault was committed during the forenoon on a free-state man at the store of Sherman, in which the Doyles were the principal and most ruffianly participators. These wretches, on the same day, called at the houses of the Browns; and, both in words and by acts, offered the grossest indignities to a daughter and daughter-in-law of Mr. Brown. As they went away, they said, "Tell your men that if they don't leave right off, we'll come back to-morrow and kill them." Thus forewarned, it was determined to forestall these ruffians, and on the following night they were taken out of their houses, tried by Lynch law, and shot.

In order to judge fairly of this act, we must endeavour to place ourselves in the position of these settlers. Harassed and threatened by men who would hesitate at no conceivable crime to gain their object, having numberless instances of outrage and murder already before their eyes, and aware of the indignities to which their women and children would be subjected if deprived of their protectors, can we wonder that they regarded it as an act of necessary justice to take the law into their own hands? No aid or redress need be hoped for from the authorities; indeed oneof these ruffians, Allen Wilkinson, was himself the magistrate for the Pottawattomic district. Brown was at Middle Creek that night, twenty-five miles away, and did not know what had occurred till next day; nor were any of his sons present. When accused of personal participation in the deed, he flatly denied the charge. "But remember," added he, "I don't say this to exculpate myself; for although I took no hand in it, I would have advised it had I known the circumstances; and I endorsed it as it was."

This was a deed which the authorities would be certain to notice, however ready to connive at all manner of atrocities on the other side. A body of troops set

out from Westport, Missouri, under the command of
Henry C. Pate, a Virginian, with the avowed intention
of arresting Brown, who had been charged with the
slaughter of the ruffians of Pottawattomie.*

Mr. Redpath was in Lawrence when Pate's troops
passed through that town, and their destination was discovered. Not a moment was to be lost in warning the
Browns of their coming and design. He immediately
rode after the troops, passed them, and though he was
followed and challenged by some of the party, and had
his horse stolen at the village of Palmyra, where he
passed the night, he arrived safely on foot next day at
Prairie City, and thence despatched a messenger to
inform the Browns, who lived only a few miles distant,
of the approach of the federal troops. Redpath himself remained some days in Prairie City, to ascertain the
condition of the country, which he thus describes :—

" I found that, in this region, when men went out to
plough, they always took their rifles with them, and
tilled in companies of from five to ten ; for, whenever
they attempted to perform their work separately, the
Georgia and Alabama bandits, who were constantly
hovering about, were sure to make a sudden descent on
them, and carry off their horses and oxen. Every man
went armed to the teeth. Guard was kept night and
day. Whenever two men approached each other, they
came up, pistol in hand, and the first salutation invariably was, ' Free-state or pro-slave ?' or its equivalent

* See Appendix A.

in intent, 'Whar ye from?' It not unfrequently happened that the next sound was the report of a pistol.
People who wished to travel without such collisions,
avoided the necessity of meeting any one, by making
a circuit or running away on the first indication of
pursuit."

As Redpath was walking in the neighbourhood of
Prairie City on the day of his arrival, he met a wild
looking young man of fine proportions, with half a
dozen pistols and a large Arkansas bowie-knife stuck
in his belt. He was bare-headed, unshaven, and wore
red-topped boots over his pantaloons, and a coarse blue
shirt, after the fashion of the settlers. He proved to be
Brown's son Frederick, who made himself known to
Redpath, and led him to his father's encampment in
the neighbouring woods, which is thus graphically described :—

"I shall not soon forget the scene that here opened
to my view. Near the edge of the creek a dozen horses
were tied, all ready saddled for a ride for life, or a hunt
after southern invaders. A dozen rifles and sabres
were stacked against the trees. In an open space, amid
the shady and lofty woods, there was a great blazing
fire with a pot on it ; a woman, bare-headed, with an
honest, sun-burnt face, was picking blackberries from
the bushes; three or four armed men were lying on red
and blue blankets on the grass ; and two fine-looking
youths were standing, leaning on their arms, on guard,
near by. One of them was the youngest son of Brown,
and the other was 'Charley,' a brave Hungarian, who

was subsequently murdered at Ossawattomie. Brown himself stood near the fire, with his shirt-sleeves rolled up, and a large piece of pork in his hand. He was cooking a pig. He was poorly clad, and his toes protruded from his boots. He received me with great cordiality, and the little band gathered about me. But it was for a moment only, for the captain ordered them to renew their work. He respectfully but firmly forbade conversation on the Pottawattomie affair; and said that, if I desired any information from the company in relation to their conduct or intentions, he, as their captain, would answer for them whatever was proper to communicate.

"In this camp no manner of profane language was permitted; no man of immoral character was allowed to stay, except as a prisoner of war. He made prayers, in which all the company united, every morning and evening; and no food was ever tasted by his men until the divine blessing had been asked on it. After every meal, thanks were returned to the bountiful Giver. Often, I was told, he returned to the densest solitudes to wrestle with his God in secret prayer. One of his company subsequently informed me that, after these retirings, he would say that the Lord had directed him in visions what to do; that, for himself, he did not love warfare, but peace,—only acting in obedience to the will of the Lord, and fighting God's battles for his children's sake.

" It was at this time that he said to me :—' I would rather have the small-pox, yellow fever, and cholera all

together in my camp, than a man without principles
It's a mistake, sir,' he continued, 'that our people make,
when they think that bullies are the best fighters, or
that they are the men fit to oppose these southerners·
Give me God-fearing men—men who respect themselves—and, with a dozen of them, I will oppose any
hundred such men as those Buford ruffians.'

" I remained in the camp about an hour. Never
before had I met such a band of earnest men. Six of
them were John Brown's sons. I left the spot with a
far higher respect for the great struggle than ever I had
felt before, and with a renewed and increased faith in
the noble and disinterested champions of the right."

In a published narrative, entitled the " Conquest of
Kansas," by Mr. Phillips, the cruel conduct of Captain
Pate to two sons of Brown at this time is thus re-
corded :—

" While near Ossawattomie on the 30th of May, he
contrived to seize Captain John Brown, jun. and Mr.
Jason Brown. These were taken while quietly engaged
in their avocations. Captain Brown, jun., had been up
with his company at Lawrence, immediately after the
sacking of the place, and at the time the men at Pottawattomie were killed. He had returned home when
he saw he could not aid Lawrence, and quietly went to
work. He and his brother Jason were taken by Pate,
charged with murder, kept in irons in their camp, and
treated with the greatest indignity and inhumanity.
While Pate was thus taking people prisoners without
any legal authority or writs, he was joined by Captain

Wood's company of dragoons,* who, so far from putting a stop to his violent career, aided him in it, and took from him, at his desire, the two prisoners, keeping them under guard in their camp, heavily ironed and harshly treated. While these companies were thus travelling close to each other, Captain Pate's company burned the store of a man named Winer, a German ; the home of John Brown, jun., in which, amongst a variety of household articles, a valuable library was consumed ; and also the house of another of the Browns ; and acted in a violent and lawless manner generally. Not being able to find Captain Brown, sen. at Ossawattomie, Pate's company and the troops started back for the Santa Fé road. In the long march that intervened, under a hot sun, the two Browns, now in charge of the dragoons, and held without even the pretence of law, were driven before the dragoons, chained like wild beasts. For twenty-five miles they thus suffered under this outrageous inhumanity. Nor was this all. John Brown, jun., who had been excited by the wild stories of murder told against his father, by their enemies, and who was of a sensitive mind, was unable to bear up against this and his treatment during the march, and afterwards, while confined in camp, startled his remorseless captors by the wild ravings of a maniac, while he lashed his chains in fury till the dull iron shone like polished steel."

Mrs. Robinson, whose husband, General Robinson,

* Belonging to the United States army.

was detained at Lecompton at this time on a charge of
high treason, thus describes the arrival of John Brown,
jun., in their camp:—"On the 23rd of June, the prisoners received an accession to their numbers in the persons
of Captain John Brown, jun., and H. H. Williams. The
former was still insane from the ill-treatment received
while in charge of the troops. He had a rope tied
around his arms so tightly, and drawn behind him, that
he will for years bear the marks of the ropes where they
wore into his flesh. He was then obliged to hold one
end of a rope, the other end being carried by one of the
dragoons; and for eight miles, in a burning sun, he was
driven before them, compelled to go fast enough to keep
from being trampled on by the horses. On being taken
to Tecumseh, they were chained two and two, with a
common trace chain, and padlock at each end. It was
so fixed as to clasp tightly around the ankle. One day
they were driven thirty miles, with no food from early
morn until night. The journey, in a hot June day, was
most torturing to them. Their chains wore upon their
ankles, until one of them, unable to go farther, was
placed upon a horse." This son was detained in camp
till the 10th of September, nearly four months, although
he was never indicted. Jason was kept prisoner for one
month.

To rescue his two sons from their captors became
the determination of Captain Brown. Like a wolf robbed of her young, he stealthily but resolutely watched
for his foes, while he skirted through the thickets of
Marais des Cygnes and Ottawa Creeks. Perhaps it was

a lurking dread of Captain Brown's rescuing the prisoners, that made Captain Pate deliver them to the United States dragoons. The dragoons, with their prisoners, encamped on Middle Ottawa Creek, while Pate went on with his men to the Santa Fé road, near Hickory Point. On the evening of Saturday, the 31st of May, he encamped on the head of a small branch or ravine, called Black Jack, from the kind of timber growing there.

On Monday morning, June the 2nd, two scouts brought tidings to Captain Brown that Pate and his men were encamped at Black Jack, four or five miles off. He immediately rode thither with a company of nine, accompanied by Captain Shore with nineteen men. When within a mile of the troops, they dismounted, leaving two of their number to guard their horses, and sending two others for additional assistance. The remaining twenty-six marched forwards against the enemy, sixty in number, who were entrenched in a strong position, with a ravine behind and a breastwork of waggons in front. Although his party was badly armed, Brown conducted the attack with such bravery and military skill, that, after firing had been kept up for nearly three hours, Pate's men began to give way. Many of them were badly wounded ; and others began to drop off one by one, by gliding down the ravine till they were out of range, running to where their horses were tied, and then galloping away. At last Captain Pate sent out his lieutenant and a prisoner with a flag of truce. Mr. Redpath thus describes the interview :—

" When they reached Captain Brown, he demanded of the lieutenant whether he was the captain of the company.

" ' No,' said the lieutenant.

" ' Then,' said Brown, ' you may stay here with me, and let your companion go and bring him out. I will talk with him.'

" Thus summoned, Captain Pate came out ; and, as he approached Captain Brown, began to say that he was an officer under the United States marshal, and that he wanted to explain this fact; as he supposed the free-state men would not continue to fight against him if they were aware of the circumstance. He was running on in this way when Brown cut him short :—

" ' Captain, I understand exactly what you are, and do not want to hear more about it. Have you any proposition to make to me ?'

" ' Well, no ; that is—'

" ' Very well, Captain,' interrupted Brown, ' I have one to make to you—your unconditional surrender.'

" There was no evading this demand, and just as little chance to deceive Captain Brown, who, pistol in hand, returned with Pate and his lieutenant to their camp in the ravine, where he repeated his demand for the unconditional surrender of the whole company."

In accordance with this summons, twenty-one men, exclusive of wounded, surrendered to Brown's party, of whom only nine men were at the time in sight. A quantity of arms were obtained, many of which had been taken from free-state men ; twenty-three horses

and mules, some of them also stolen from northern settlers; a portion of some goods plundered two days
before from the store of a free-state man; besides waggons, ammunition, camp equipage and provisions. The
prisoners, after having being disarmed, were taken by
Brown to his camp, together with a large portion of the
spoils. No one appears to have been killed during the
skirmish and but three of Brown's party were wounded,
one of whom was his son-in-law, Henry Thompson.
The wounded prisoners were carefully tended, and, on
their recovery, were admonished to behave better in
future, and were sent home to Missouri. Notwithstanding Pate's fiendish barbarity to Brown's two sons a few
days before this affair, he and his men were very well
treated while in his hands. They were allowed to use
their own blankets and camp equipage, which were
superior to anything Brown had; and were fed much
better than he could feed his men. These prisoners,
with the spoils taken at Black Jack, were given up by
Brown a few days afterwards, on the summons of
Colonel Sumner, who was in command of a body of
United States dragoons.

On the 7th of June, Reid, at the head of one hundred and seventy Missourians, sacked the town of Ossawattomie with circumstances of great atrocity. There
are many well-authenticated accounts of the cruelties
perpetrated by these ruffians, some of them too shocking and disgusting to relate. The mutilated bodies of
murdered men, hanging upon the trees, or left to rot or
be devoured by wild beasts on the prairies or in the

deep ravines, told frightful stories of brutal ferocity, from which the wildest savages might have shrunk with horror.

Every movement made by the free-state men to defeat and crush these organized marauders was thwarted by the federal troops ; and, on the 4th of July, 1856, when, elsewhere, Americans were celebrating the birthday of their liberty, the free-state legislature at Topeka was broken up by companies of artillery and dragoons of the United States army, by command of the government at Washington.

" This," says Mr. Redpath, " was the culmination of southern success.   The Missouri river was now closed against northern emigration, the roads were literally strewed with dead bodies ; the entire free-state population of Leavenworth had been driven from their homes ; almost every part of Kansas was in the power of the invaders ; the army and the government, federal and territorial, the bench and the jury-box, were in the hands of the oppressor ; and our state organization had been destroyed by the dragoons."

But the free-state men were not without resources. At Topeka, Aaron D. Stevens, who was afterwards intimately associated with Brown, was the chosen leader of eight hundred men, who were ever on the alert to defeat the designs of the invaders, and ready to march against them.   At the same time, General James Lane (who from this time began to play an important part in Kansas, and is at present one of her senators in the congress of the United States) was slowly approaching with his little army, and entered the territory early in August. The general confidence felt in the military ability of this leader made his arrival an event of some importance. Several revolting atrocities—for example, the mutilation of Major Hoyt, the scalping of Mr. Hopps, and a cruel and dastardly outrage on a northern lady—aroused once more the spirit of the free-state men to resume the struggle. The cowardice of the southerners, who were now vigorously assailed, displayed itself at every point; and the northern settlers, by a rapid series of surprises, drove the invaders from most of their strongholds.

After taking his wounded son-in-law Thompson to Tabor in Iowa, and leaving him there in the hands of friends, Brown returned and joined General Lane and his forces. After a skirmish at Franklin they proceeded to Rock Creek, with the intention of seizing the murderers of Major Hoyt; and Captain Brown took the command of a small company of cavalry there. On the 26th of August his company was at Middle Creek, eight miles from Ossawattomie, where there was a camp of one hundred and sixty southern invaders. The free-state forces, consisting of the united companies of Brown, Shore, and "Preacher" Steward,* and numbering sixty men, surprised and attacked these marauders, and utterly routed them in a few minutes, killing two, and taking thirteen prisoners, twenty-nine horses, three

* This gentleman is mentioned by Mr. Redpath as "having been in more fights and liberated more slaves than any man now in Kansas." He won for himself the title of the "fighting preacher."

waggon-loads of provisions, and one hundred stand of arms.

On the 17th of August, the Missourians, alarmed at the threatening aspect of affairs in the territory, issued at Lexington an inflammatory appeal for another expedition against the northern men in Kansas.

Thus appealed to, a force of two thousand Missourians assembled at the village of Santa Fe, on the border; and, entering the territory, divided into two forces—one division led by Senator Atchison, and the other wing under General Reid. The force under Atchison fled precipitately on the morning of August 31st, at the approach of Lane. That under Reid advanced to attack the town of Ossawattomie, about eight miles from the settlement of the Browns. The reception of this troop by Captain Brown is one of the most stirring episodes of Kansas history. They were between four and five hundred strong—armed with United States muskets, bayonets, and revolvers, had several pieces of cannon, and a large supply of ammunition.

This is Brown's own account of the affair :—

" Early in the morning of the 30th of August, the enemy's scouts approached to within a mile and a half of the western boundary of the town of Ossawattomie. At this place my son Frederick, who was not attached to my force, had lodged with some four other young men from Lawrence, and a young man named Garrison from Middle Creek.

" The scouts, led by a pro-slavery preacher named White, shot my son dead in the road, whilst he, as I have since ascertained, supposed them to be friendly. At the same time they butchered Mr. Garrison, and badly mangled one of the young men from Lawrence who came with my son, leaving him for dead.

"This was not far from sunrise. I had stopped during the night about two and a half miles from them, and nearly one mile from Ossawattomie. I had no organized force, but only some twelve or fifteen new recruits, who were ordered to leave their preparations for breakfast, and follow me into the town as soon as this news was brought to me.

"As I had no means of learning correctly the force of the enemy, I placed twelve of the recruits in a log-house, hoping we might be able to defend the town. I then gathered some fifteen more men together, whom we armed with guns, and we started in the direction of the enemy. After going a few rods, we could see them approaching the town in line of battle, about half a mile off, upon a hill west of the village. I then gave up all idea of doing more than to annoy, from the timber near the town, into which we were all retreated, and which was filled with a thick growth of underbrush, but had no time to recal the twelve men in the log-house, and so lost their assistance in the fight.

"At the point above named I met with Captain Cline, a very active young man, who had with him some twelve or fifteen mounted men, and persuaded him to go with us into the timber on the southern shore of the Osage, or Marais-des Cygnes, a little to the north-west from the village. Here the men, numbering not

5*

more than thirty in all, were directed to scatter and secrete themselves as well as they could, and await the approach of the enemy. This was done in full view of them, who must have seen the whole movement, and had to be done in the utmost haste. I believe Captain Cline and some of his men were not even dismounted in the fight, but cannot assert positively. When the left wing of the enemy had approached to within common rifle shot, we commenced firing, and very soon threw the northern branch of the enemy's line into disorder. This continued some fifteen or twenty minutes, which gave us an uncommon opportunity to annoy them. Captain Cline and his men soon got out of ammunition, and retired across the river.

"After the enemy rallied, we kept up our fire ; until, by the leaving of one and another, we had but six or seven left. We then retired across the river.

"We had one man killed—a Mr. Powers, from Captain Cline's company—in the fight. One of my men, a Mr. Partridge, was shot in crossing the river. Two or three of the party who took part in the fight are yet missing, and may be lost or taken prisoners. Two were wounded, viz. Dr. Updegraff and a Mr. Collis.

"I cannot speak in too high terms of them, and of many others I have not now time to mention.

"One of my best men, together with myself, was struck with a partially spent ball from the enemy in the commencement of the fight, but we were only bruised. The loss I refer to is one of my missing men. The loss of the enemy, as we learn by the different statements of

our own as well as their people, was some thirty-one or
two killed, and from forty to fifty wounded. After
burning the town to ashes, and killing a Mr. Williams
they had taken, whom neither party claimed, they took
a hasty leave, carrying their dead and wounded with
them. They did not attempt to cross the river, nor to
search for us, and have not since returned to look over
their work.

"I give this in great haste, in the midst of constant
interruptions. My second son was with me in the
fight, and escaped unharmed. This I mention for the
benefit of his friends.

"Old Preacher White, I hear, boasts of having killed
my son. Of course he is a lion.

JOHN BROWN.

"Lawrence, Kansas, September 7th, 1856."

The brilliancy of this exploit is only faintly traced
in Brown's modest and characteristic account. Nearly
five hundred men, as the Missourians afterwards admitted, all well armed, were arrested in their march of
desolation by a little band of sixteen, imperfectly
equipped ; for Cline's company, after firing a few shots,
retired from the conflict, being out of ammunition. A
tree is still pointed out near which Brown stood during
the whole engagement, quietly directing his men, and
using his own rifle with steady hand. The dispropor-
tionate loss of the invading force resulted from their
lawless character and want of discipline ; for, alarmed
at being fired at, they refused to obey orders, and hud-

dled round the dead and wounded instead of standing
to their ranks. Into these panic-stricken groups Brown
poured a deadly fire; and before the officers of the
enemy could restore order among their men, thirty-two
lay dead, and more than fifty were wounded.

The rest of the invaders, after proceeding to Ossawattomie, burning the town, and killing three men in
cold blood, returned to Missouri, boasting of their success; but the large number of corpses and wounded
men brought back, and a knowledge of the insignificant
force of free-state men that had opposed them, created
a feeling of terror in the state from which the Missourians never fully recovered. At the sacking of Ossawattomie, a man named Timmons, one of the most bitter
pro-slavery men in the vicinity, was killed. Some time
afterwards, Brown called at the log-hut where Timmons
had lived, and where his widow and children were living in great destitution. He inquired into and relieved
their wants, and supported them till the friends of Mrs.
Timmons, informed through him of her condition, had
time to come and convey her to her former home. Mrs.
Timmons fully appreciated the kindness shown her, but
never learned that Captain Brown was her benefactor.

We next find Brown at Lawrence, which town, always
obnoxious to the pro-slavery party, was again threatened by an armed band of Missourians. He had been
at Topeka, and, on his way home, stopped in Lawrence
during Sunday, the 14th of September. On the morning of that day news arrived that a large force of Missourians, under Atchison and Reid, was approaching,

and that Lawrence was the object of their attack. So many false alarms had constantly been set afloat, that little credence was given to this rumour. However, about four o'clock in the afternoon, the report was confirmed by the appearance of the smoke from the burning of the village of Franklin, a small place in the way of the invaders, about five miles south-east of Lawrence. There were so many points at which the free-state men had to exercise their vigilance, that Lawrence was almost unprotected, and the number of available men in the place who could muster for its defence was not more than about two hundred, while the number of the invaders was said to be upwards of two thousand.

As soon as it was known that he was in the town, Captain Brown was unanimously voted leader. Most of the people assembled opposite the post-office, and Brown, mounted on a packing-case, addressed them to the following effect :—

" Gentlemen—It is said there are twenty-five hundred Missourians down at Franklin, and that they will be here in two hours. You can see for yourselves the smoke they are making by setting fire to the houses in that town. This is probably the last opportunity you will have of seeing a fight, so that you had better do your best. If they should come up and attack us, don't yell and make a great noise, but remain perfectly silent and still. Wait till they get within twenty-five yards of you ; get a good object ; be sure you see the hind sight of your gun ; then fire. A great deal of powder and lead and very precious time is wasted by shooting too high. You had better aim at their legs than at their heads. In either case, be sure of the hind sight of your gun. It is from this reason that I myself have so many times escaped; for, if all the bullets which have ever been aimed at me had hit me, I would have been as full of holes as a riddle."

Brown now posted his forces in some breastworks, and in one or two unfinished churches on the south side of the town, from which direction the enemy were looked for. On the north of the town ran the Kansas river, and on the west was a ravine. Brown himself was constantly on the alert, visiting the various posts, directing the men, and exhorting them to keep cool and do their duty. Among other preparations for defence, some of the storekeepers produced a number of pitchforks, certainly no mean weapons if dexterously handled, and one of these was supplied to every man unprovided with a bayonet to his gun.

The invaders had meanwhile continued their march from Franklin, and at about five o'clock their advanced guard, consisting of four hundred horsemen, appeared in sight of the town, about two miles off, where they halted. Brown ordered out all the men who were armed with rifles, about one hundred in number, and marched them half a mile into the prairie, where he arranged them three paces apart, in a line facing the enemy, with orders to lie down on their faces, awaiting the command to fire. He soon, however, changed their position to a piece of rising ground, about a quarter of a mile to the left, where he stationed them as before, with their faces to the ground. A simultaneous movement of the Missourians brought the two bodies face to face, about half a mile apart, and with a field of Indian corn, containing eight or ten acres, between them.

Darkness was now coming on, but the firing commenced, and soon became general. The distance between the contending bodies was such as to give a deadly effect to the rifle bullets. Lest the small party of free-state riflemen should be surrounded and cut to pieces by the large body of horsemen, a twelve-pound brass cannon was sent, with a guard of twelve men, to their assistance; but, before it had arrived, a panic seized the Missourians, and four hundred men, well armed and mounted, fled before one-fourth of their number.

"That night," says one who was present, "T. and I took our blankets, and lay down immediately within the breastwork, with a stone for our pillow, and the clouds for a covering. We had been here for a few moments only, when Captain Brown came along, and said, ' With your permission, I will be the third one to aid in defending this fortification to-night.' He then lay down by our side, and told us of the trials and wars he had passed through; that he had settled in Kansas with a large family, having with him six full-grown sons; that he had taken a claim in Lykins County, and was attending peacefully to the duties of husbandry, when the hordes came over from Missouri, took possession of the ballot-boxes, destroyed his corn, stole his horses, shot down his cattle, sheep, and hogs, and repeatedly threatened to shoot, hang, or burn him, if he did not leave the territory ; that many times they endeavoured to put their threats in force, but were as often prevented by the eternal vigilance which he found to be the price of safety to himself and his family ; that they afterwards did kill and murder one of his sons, in cold blood, in his own hearing, and almost in his own sight ; and all because he hated slavery ! He told me that he held that promising son in his arms as he drew his last breath, and thought of the resemblance he bore to his mother."

The remainder of the night was passed undisturbed. The main body of the troops never came up; alarmed, doubtless, by the defeat of their advance guard, and believing the place to be numerously defended, they retreated to Missouri, and left Lawrence this time unscathed.

In order to give the reader some idea of the insults and outrages to which emigrants from the free states to Kansas were subjected in their passage through the semi-barbarous slave state of Missouri, we shall give an extract from a letter addressed to the Boston *Daily Bee* from Lawrence, on July 1st, 1856, by a Massachusetts barrister, then on a visit to Kansas. The editor of the *Bee* states that a few days before he left Boston, the writer of the letter called at his office and told him of his intention of visiting Kansas ; saying, " I wish to convince myself of the true condition of that territory. I believe that the stories we get about the out-

rages in Kansas are got up merely for political effect,
and for the purpose of increasing the northern feeling
now aroused throughout the free states. We are making fools of ourselves here at the north; as I shall
prove to you when I ascertain the facts relating to
matters in Kansas." The testimony of a witness who
expressed such opinions before leaving home is most
valuable.

On Saturday, June 22nd, he left St. Louis for Kansas, by steamer. On the 25th he heard that a number
of settlers from the eastern states had been stopped at
Lexington, Missouri, on their arrival by the 'Star of
the West,' and robbed of their rifles and other property.
These settlers were about seventy-five men, accompanied
by two women and two children. " A better looking
set of men could not be sent to Kansas. They would be
a credit to any country. At Waverley one of the rifles
taken from the passengers in the 'Star of the West'
was given to the captain of the 'New Lucy,' in which
I was embarked, and this was immediately hoisted to
the flag-staff head. We proceeded to Lexington, arriving there about noon. The plank was run out, and at
once some twenty or thirty ruffians boarded the boat,
with revolvers and bowie-knives suspended from their
waists; some had two revolvers and a bowie-knife.
The boat remained here about one hour. I left, in
order to gain information relating to the passengers by
the 'Star of the West.' All that I had previously
heard was fully confirmed. As my enquiries about
the rifles were numerous, a gentleman (by appearance)

inquired if I would like to see them.   On replying in
the affirmative, he led me into the rear part of Magraw's store, and, feigning to look for the rifles, declared
that he did not know where they were.   By this time
I was surrounded by about thirty ruffians, and then
and there was heaped on me a volley of oaths and
curses sufficient to sink the whole of the slave states.
Mr. William Allen, a brick-maker by trade, a stout,
athletic man, weighing over 200 lbs., one of five con-
stituting a vigilance committee appointed by the citizens of Lexington to prevent emigration to Kansas,
addressed me in the following gentlemanly and courteous language :—

" 'You want to see the rifles, do you ?'   I replied,
' Yes.'   ' You do, do you ?   Why didn't you bring men
with you to take them, you —— abolitionist ?   We 'll
hang you.*   Our boys would like to hang such a fellow
as you.   We have half a dozen ropes here now to hang
you with, and we 'll soon put a rope round your neck.
Boys, bring the ropes, and hang this —— abolitionist.'
I replied, ' If you intend hanging me, you had better
hurry up, for I would like to see you about it.'   At this,
he raised his hand, and, shaking it, said, ' Boys, stop a
moment !   I 'll tell you when.'   At this moment, another ruffian, a tall, slim man, who is in the employ of
Magraw, commenced with, ' Are you the —— rascal
who writes letters to Chicago ?   You —— abolitionist,
we 'll hang you, and every one we can catch.   Have

* The language in this and other speeches is so thickly inter-
larded with profanity that we are constrained to omit much of it.

you written any letters to Chicago?' I replied, 'That is none of your business.'

" Others joined in the same kind of threats and language, but, finding their threats of no avail, they gradually slunk away. Some of the armed ruffians took the control of the boat ; passengers were interrogated with impertinent questions, whether they were pro-slavery or abolitionists ; state-rooms were searched ; the ladies' saloon entered ; insulting language used to them, and every insult imaginable offered. A number of them remained on board as spies up the river ; during the afternoon, they left the boat. They delight in the name of ' border ruffian,' and boast that they are so called. I saw at this place an omnibus with the name of ' The Border Ruffian.'

" We had one border ruffian on board all the way up the river, brandishing his revolver in the faces of the passengers, and cursing and swearing about the '——— abolitionists' and Yankees, and declaring that he would kill every one he met with. Soon after we left Lexington we dined, and the armed ruffians took seats at the table. Such obscenity and profanity as came from their mouths are beyond belief. One of the ruffians, on leaving the boat, threw down his cap on the levee, stamped on it, yelled, cursed and swore, and behaved like a raving maniac. This man, if he can be so called, was one of those who insulted the ladies.

" On Saturday last, I visited the camp where are confined Governor Charles Robinson, Judge George W. Smith, George W. Brown, George W. Deitzler, and Captain Brown, jun. [son of Captain John Brown.] During the two hours I spent with them, the only regret they expressed was, that a great work was to be accomplished, and their assistance was needed. Until now I never could realise the forbearance, patience, and courage of the heroes of the American revolution. The free-state people of Kansas will equal those of that revolution, both men and women. I never saw such a set of people. Their motto is 'Liberty or death.' They are fearless beyond belief, and all for the cause of freedom. Every man, woman, and child is ready to lay down life for freedom in Kansas. In the New England states, people have no idea of the wrongs, insults, and cold-blooded murders that have been perpetrated in this territory by ' border ruffians,' ' Buford's men,' and others in the employ of pro-slavery people. No person or property is safe that passes through Missouri. The freedom of speech and the freedom of travel are prohibited. It matters not from what free state one hails, he is considered a ' —— abolitionist' and a ' —— Yankee,' and he must die, or go home to a free state, or take an oath to support slavery. Missourians will tell you there is no danger in travelling in Missouri, and that all the danger is over. Let me tell you that this is untrue."

CHAPTER IV.

October, 1856—November, 1857.

BROWN LEAVES KANSAS FOR THE EASTERN STATES.—DELIVERS
AN ADDRESS IN BOSTON BEFORE A COMMITTEE OF THE
LEGISLATURE.—VISITS HIS FAMILY AT NORTH ELBA.—
ORDERS THE MANUFACTURE OF A THOUSAND PIKES.—IS
DISAPPOINTED IN HIS HOPES OF AID FOR KANSAS.—RETURNS
TO KANSAS.

EARLY in October, 1856, Brown left Kansas with
four of his sons, by way of Nebraska territory.
While on his way, he found at Topeka a fugitive slave,
whom he carried along with him, covering him up in
his waggon. His own health was considerably broken
by hardship and fatigue, but his spirit was unsubdued.
He wished to obtain the aid of the friends of freedom
in the eastern states, in order to organize a more effective
opposition to the pro-slavery forces in Kansas. At this
period there was every prospect of renewed disturbances.
The need of skilled leaders had been greatly felt in the
recent conflict. Brown fully appreciated this necessity,
and hence he desired to have funds to equip a sufficient
force for the protection of the settlers, as well as to drill
a number of the young men of Kansas, who had proved
themselves faithful to the free-state cause. At Tabor,
in Iowa, a village of true friends of freedom, Brown
and his sons remained two or three weeks. About the
end of November he reached Chicago, and afterwards
visited Cleveland in Ohio, and Albany in the state of

New York. In all these places he pleaded in public and
in private the claims of the free-state settlers in Kansas,
but did not meet a very hearty response. Few could
comprehend the stern indignation which filled his
whole soul at the atrocious deeds he had witnessed. So
vehement were his words and gestures when expatiating
on this subject, that many thought he was mad. The
Cleveland Herald, in reference to his visit to that city,
says, "He was so demented as to suppose he could raise a
regiment of men in Ohio to march into Missouri to
make reprisals against the slave forces, and even asked
a friend if the power of the state could not be enlisted
in that matter. He was told by many that he was a
madman, and the poor man left sorrowing that there
was no sympathy here for the oppressed."

That such was also the opinion of Captain Brown's
half-brother Jeremiah, appears in the following passage
from his evidence, given under oath before the committee appointed by the senate of the United States, to
enquire into all the circumstances connected with the
outbreak at Harper's Ferry :—

" My brother John, from my earliest recollection, has
been an honest, conscientious man ; and this was his
reputation among all who knew him in that section of
the country. Since the trouble growing out of the settlement of Kansas territory, I have observed a marked
change in brother John. Previous to this, he devoted
himself entirely to business ; but since these troubles
he has abandoned all business, and has become wholly
absorbed by the subject of slavery. He had property

left him by his father, of which I had the agency. He has never taken a dollar of it for the benefit of his family, but has called for a portion of it to be expended in what he called *the service*. After his return from Kansas he called on me, and I urged him to go home to his family and attend to his private affairs ; that I feared his course would prove his destruction and that of his boys. This was about two years ago. He replied that he was sorry that I did not sympathize with him ; that he knew he was in the line of his duty, and he must pursue it, though it should destroy him and his family. He stated to me that he was satisfied that he was a chosen instrument in the hands of God to war against slavery. From his manner, and from his conversation at this time, I had no doubt he had become insane upon the subject of slavery, and I gave him to understand that this was my opinion of him."

Brown arrived in Boston in January, 1857. At that period an effort was made to induce the legislature of Massachusetts to vote an appropriation of ten thousand dollars, for the purpose of protecting the interests of the north and the rights of her citizens in Kansas. A joint committee was appointed to consider the petitions in favour of this measure. It held its sittings publicly. Eminent champions of freedom in Massachusetts, and men who had distinguished themselves during the conflict in Kansas, were invited to address the committee ; and Captain Brown, on the 18th of February, appeared before it to make a statement of his views. He said he intended to speak exclusively of matters of which he

82 LIFE OF CAPTAIN JOHN BROWN.

was personally cognizant, and therefore must be excused if he should refer more particularly to himself and
his family than he would otherwise do. He then read
the following statement 'in a clear, ringing tone' :—

"I saw, while in Missouri, in the fall of 1855, large
numbers of men going to Kansas to vote, and also
returning, after they had so done, as they said.

"Later in the year, I, with four of my sons, was
called out, and travelled, mostly on foot and during the
night, to help to defend Lawrence, a distance of thirty-
five miles, where we were detained, with some five
hundred others, or thereabouts, from five to ten days
—say an average of ten days—at a cost of not less than
a dollar-and-a-half per day as wages; to say nothing of
the actual loss and suffering occasioned to many of them
by leaving their families sick, their crops not secured,
their houses unprepared for winter, and many without
houses at all. This was the case with myself and sons,
who could not get houses built after returning. Wages
alone would amount to seven thousand five hundred
dollars; loss and suffering cannot be estimated.

"I saw, at that time, the body of the murdered Barber, and was present to witness his wife and other
friends brought in to see him with his clothes on, just
as he was when killed.*

"I, with six sons and a son-in-law, was called out,
and travelled most of the way on foot, to try and save

---

* By a United States office-holder, who was afterwards pro-
moted to a more lucrative post.

Lawrence, May 20th and 21st, and much of the way in the night. From that date, neither I, nor my sons, nor my son-in-law could do any work about our homes, but lost our whole time until we left, in October ; except one of my sons, who had a few weeks to devote to the care of his own and his brother's family, who were then without a home.

"From about the 20th of May, hundreds of men, like ourselves, lost their whole time, and entirely failed of securing any kind of crop whatever. I believe it safe to say that five hundred free-state men lost each one hundred and twenty days, which, at one dollar-and-a-half per day, would be—to say nothing of attendant losses—ninety thousand dollars.

"On or about the 30th of May, two of my sons, with several others, were imprisoned without other crime than opposition to bogus legislation, and most barbarously treated for a time, one being held about one month, and the other about four months. Both had their families on the ground. After this, both of them had their houses burned, and all their goods consumed by the Missourians. In this burning all the eight suffered. One had his oxen stolen, in addition."

Here Brown, laying aside his paper, said that he had now at his hotel, and would exhibit to the committee, if they so desired, the chains which one of his sons had worn, when he was driven, beneath a burning sun, by federal troops, to a distant prison, on a charge of treason. The cruelties he there endured, added to the

*6

anxieties and sufferings incident to his position, had rendered him, the old man said, as his eye flashed and his voice grew sterner, "a maniac—yes, a maniac."

He paused a few seconds, wiped a tear from his eye, and continued his narration :—

"At Black Jack the invading Missourians wounded three free-state men, one of whom was my son-in-law ; and, a few days afterwards, one of my sons was so wounded that he will be a cripple for life.

"In August I was present, and saw the mangled and disfigured body of the murdered Hoyt, of Deerfield, Massachusetts, brought into our camp. I knew him well.

"I saw the ruins of many free-state men's houses in different parts of the territory, together with grain in the stack, burning, and wasted in other ways, to the amount, at least of fifty thousand dollars.

"I saw several other free-state men, besides those I have named, during the summer, who were badly wounded by the invaders of the territory.

"I know that for much of the time during the summer, the travel over portions of the territory was entirely cut off, and that none but bodies of armed men dared to move at all.

"I know that for a considerable time the mails on different routes were entirely stopped ; and, notwithstanding there were abundant troops in the territory to escort the mails, I know that such escorts were not furnished as they ought to have been.

" I saw while it was standing, and afterwards saw the ruins of a most valuable house, the property of a highly civilized, intelligent, and exemplary Christian Indian, which was burned to the ground by the ruffians, because its owner was suspected of favouring the free-state men. He is known as Ottawa Jones, or John T. Jones.

" In September last I visited a little free-state town called Staunton, on the north side of the Osage (or Marais-des-Cygnes, as it is sometimes called), from which every inhabitant had fled for fear of their lives, even after having built a strong log-house, or wooden fort, at a heavy expense, for their protection. Many of them had left their effects liable to be destroyed or carried off, not being able to remove them. This was to me a most gloomy scene, and like a visit to a sepulchre.

" Deserted houses and corn-fields were to be found in almost every direction south of the Kansas river.

" I have not yet told all I saw in Kansas.

" I once saw three mangled bodies, two of which were dead, and one alive, but with twenty bullet and buck-shot holes in him, after the two murdered men had lain on the ground, to be worked at by flies, for some eighteen hours. One of these young men was my own son."

The stern old man faltered. He struggled long to suppress all exhibition of his feelings; and then, but in a subdued and faltering tone, continued :—

" I saw Mr. Parker, whom I well knew, all bruised

about the head, and with his throat partly cut, after he had been dragged, sick, from the house of Ottawa Jones, and thrown over the bank of the Ottawa Creek for dead.

"About the 1st of September, I and five sick and wounded sons, and a son-in-law, were obliged to lie on the ground, without shelter, for a considerable time, and at times almost in a state of starving, and dependent on the charity of the Christian Indian I have before named, and his wife.

"I saw Dr. Graham, of Prairie City, who was a prisoner with the ruffians on the 2nd of June, and was present when they wounded him in an attempt to kill him, as he was trying to save himself from being murdered by them during the fight at Black Jack.

"I know that numerous other persons, whose names I cannot now remember, suffered like hardships and exposures to those I have mentioned.

"I know well that on or about the 14th of September, 1856, a large force of Missourians and other ruffians, said by Governor Geary to be twenty-seven hundred in number, invaded the territory, burned Franklin, and, while the smoke of that place was going up behind them, they, on the same day, made their appearance in full view of, and within about a mile of, Lawrence; and I know of no reason why they did not attack that place, except that about one hundred free-state men volunteered to go out, and did go out on the open plain before that town, and give the offer of a fight; which, after getting scattering shots from our men, they declined, and retreated back towards Franklin. I saw that whole thing. The government troops at this time were at Lecompton, a distance of twelve miles only from Lawrence, with Governor Geary ; and yet, notwithstanding runners had been dispatched to advise him in good time of the approach and setting out of the enemy (who had to march some forty miles to reach Lawrence), he did not, on that memorable occasion, get a single soldier on the ground until after the enemy had retreated to Franklin, and been gone for more than five hours. This is the way he saved Lawrence. And it is just the kind of protection the free-state men have received from the administration from the first."

He concluded his remarks by denouncing the traitors to freedom.

The Chairman.—" Captain Brown, I wish to ask you regarding Buford's men.* Did you ever mingle with them ? And if so, what did you see or hear ?"

Captain Brown replied, that he saw a great deal of them at first ; that they spoke without hesitation before him, because he employed himself as a surveyor; and, as nearly all the surveyors were pro-slavery men, they probably thought he was "sound on the goose."† They told him all their plans; what they intended to do; how they were determined to drive off the free-state men, and possess themselves of the territory, and make

---

* Colonel Buford was the leader of several companies of Georgia and Alabama bandits, who came to Kansas in the spring of 1856, with the avowed intention of expelling or exterminating the emigrants from the North.

† Western phrase: equivalent to, a reliable friend of slavery.

it a slave state at all hazards—cost what it might. They said that the Yankees could not be whipped, coaxed, nor driven into a fight, and that one pro-slavery man could whip a dozen abolitionists. They said that Kansas must be a slave state to save Missouri from abolition; that both must stand or fall together. They did not hesitate to threaten that they would burn, kill, scalp, and drive out the entire free-state population of the territory, if it was necessary to do so to accomplish their object.

The Chairman then asked who commanded the free-state men at Lawrence.

His answer was characteristic. He explained how bravely the free-state men had acted, and gave everyone credit but himself. When again asked who commanded them, he said—No one; that he was asked to take the command, but refused, and only acted as their adviser!

In conclusion, he said, "We want good men, industrious men, men who respect themselves, who act only from the dictates of conscience—*men who fear God too much to fear anything human.*"

The Chairman.—"What is your opinion as to the probability of a renewal of hostilities in Kansas—of another invasion? And what do you think would be the effect on the free-state men of an appropriation by Massachusetts?"

Captain Brown.—"Whenever we heard, out in Kansas, that the north was doing anything for us, we were encouraged and strengthened to struggle on. As to the probability of another invasion, I do not know.

We ought to be prepared for the worst. Things do not look one iota more encouraging now than they did last year at this time."

To a gentleman who made his acquaintance during this visit to Boston, we are indebted for the following reminiscences :—

" He brought me a letter of introduction in January, 1857. His business was to raise money for the purpose of further protecting the free-state men of Kansas ; and for this purpose he desired to equip one hundred mounted men. His son Owen accompanied him. He immediately impressed me as a person of no common order, and every day that I saw him strengthened this impression. . . . His brown coat of the fashion of ten years before, his waistcoat buttoning nearly to the throat, and his wide trousers, gave him the look of a well-to-do farmer in his Sunday dress; while his patent leather stock, gray surtout, and fur cap, added a military air to his figure. At this time he wore no beard.

" I found him frank and decided in his conversation ; expressing his opinions of men and things with a modest firmness, but often in the most striking manner. I think it was in his second call on me that he used the language, 'I believe in the Golden Rule, sir, and the Declaration of Independence. I think they both mean the same thing; and it is better that a whole generation should pass off the face of the earth—men, women, and children—by a violent death, than that one jot of either should fail in this country. I mean exactly *so*, sir.' I have twice or thrice heard him repeat this sentiment, which I particularly noticed at the time. He staid but a short time in Boston ; but returned in February, and soon after appeared before a committee of the Massachusetts legislature. . . . . In March he visited Concord, and spoke at a public meeting in the Town Hall, where, I am told, he exhibited the chain worn by his son John in Kansas, and, with a gesture and voice never to be forgotten by those who heard him. denounced the administration and the south for their work in Kansas. He spent several days in Concord, and made the acquaintance of several of its citizens; among others, of Ralph Waldo Emerson and Henry D. Thoreau, who have testified so clearly to his nobility of character.

"Near the end of March, 1857, being on my way to Washington, I met Captain Brown in New York city, and spent a night with him at the Metropolitan Hotel. Captain Brown objected to the show and extravagance of such an establishment, and said he preferred a plain tavern, where drovers and farmers lodged in a plain way. We went on to Philadelphia, and while there I was taken unwell, and could scarcely sit up. Captain Brown nursed me as much as I had need of, and showed great skill and tenderness. In May he set out for Kansas, and I lost sight of him for nearly a year."

Mr. Emerson is reported to have said at this time that Brown was the truest hero-man he had ever met. Theodore Parker also said to one who spoke of Captain Montgomery as a man of more harmonious and cultivated intellect than Brown, "Do you know what you say, sir? John Brown is one of the most extraordinary men of this age and nation."

Mr. Stearns, an active and generous friend of Kansas, who made Brown's acquaintance at this time, said to him one day, half jestingly, "I suppose, Captain Brown, that if Judge Lecompte* had fallen into your hands, he would have fared rather hard." Brown turned round in his chair, and, in the most earnest tones, said, "If the Lord had delivered Judge Lecompte into my hands, I think it would have required the Lord to have taken him out again."

A meeting of prominent friends of freedom in Kansas was to be held on Sunday, as on no other day could a full attendance be obtained. Mr. Stearns, not knowing how the old puritan might regard this use of the day of rest, inquired if it would be consistent with his religious convictions to give his attendance. "Mr. Stearns," said he, "I have a poor little ewe that has fallen into the ditch, and I think the Sabbath is as good a day as any to help her out. I will come."

Brown spent the spring of 1857 in travelling; and also paid a visit to his family at North Elba. He spoke at different cities, and employed all his energies in collecting money. It is believed that a large sum was voted for his use by the National Kansas Committee, but that, through the dishonesty of an agent, he

---

* A notorious partizan of the border ruffians in Kansas, and as near a parallel to Judge Jeffreys as has yet appeared in the United States.

received only a very trifling portion of it. He published the following appeal, which was widely copied by the press, and very liberally responded to in some parts of the country :—

To THE FRIENDS OF FREEDOM :

The undersigned, whose individual means were exceedingly limited when he first engaged in the struggle for liberty in Kansas, being now still more destitute, and no less anxious than in times past to continue his efforts to sustain that cause, is induced to make this earnest appeal to the friends of freedom throughout the United States, in the firm belief that his call will not go unheeded.

I ask all honest lovers of *liberty and human rights, both male and female,* to hold up my hands by contributions of pecuniary aid, either as counties, cities, towns, villages, societies, churches, or individuals.

I will endeavour to make a judicious and faithful application of all such means as I may be supplied with. Contributions may be sent, in drafts, to W. H. D. Calender, Cashier, State Bank, Hartford, Connecticut. It is my intention to visit as many places as I can during my stay in the states, provided I am informed of the disposition of the inhabitants to aid me in my efforts, as well as to receive my visit. Information may be communicated to me (care of Massasoit House), at Springfield, Massachusetts. Will editors of newspapers, friendly to the cause, kindly second the measure, and also give this some half-dozen insertions? Will either gentlemen or ladies, or both, volunteer to take up the business? It is with *no little sacrifice of personal feeling* I appear in this manner before the public.

JOHN BROWN.

From his experience in Kansas, Captain Brown was of opinion that Sharpe's rifle was an inefficient weapon in the hands of unskilled and inexperienced men; and he expressed his belief that with pikes, or with bows and arrows, he could arm recruits more effectually for such warfare. When at Collinsville, Connecticut, he accordingly ordered a number of pikes from a manufacturer there, who gives the following particulars of the transaction :—

" In the latter part of February, or the early part of March, 1857, Old Brown, as he is familiarly called, came to Collinsville to visit his relatives, and, by invitation, addressed the inhabitants at a public meeting. At the close of it, or on the following day, he exhibited some weapons which he claimed to have taken from Captain H. C. Pate at the battle of Black Jack. Among others was a bowie-knife or dirk, having a blade about eight inches long. Brown remarked that such an instrument, fixed on the end of a pole about six feet long, would be a capital weapon to place in the hands of the settlers in Kansas, to keep in their cabins to defend themselves against ' border ruffians or wild beasts ;' and asked me what it would cost for one thousand. I replied that I would make them for one dollar each ; not thinking that it would lead to a contract, or that such an instrument would ever be wanted, or be put to use in any way if made. But, to my surprise, he drew up a contract for one thousand, to be completed within three months ; he agreeing to pay me

five hundred dollars in thirty days, and the balance
within thirty days thereafter."*

That Captain Brown was not satisfied with the results
of his trip to New England in 1857, may be gathered
from the following document, which was found in his
own handwriting among his papers at North Elba. It
forcibly and feelingly exhibits his sense of the ludi-
crous contrast between the boastful professions so habitual with popular orators in the free states, and the
backwardness of the people to make any sacrifices for
the maintenance of liberty in Kansas. It should be
observed that, in New England at least, orations in
celebration of the declaration of American independence, and the speeches of demagogues in laudation of
the people, are thickly sprinkled with allusions to
Plymouth Rock, near Boston, where the first puritan
settlers landed from the Mayflower in 1620; to the
monument erected to commemorate the battle of Bunker's Hill, &c. By coupling with these, "Uncle Tom's
Cabin," he intimates a suspicion that the extraordinary
popularity of that anti-slavery novel has resulted in no
great practical impression upon the American people,
whose prejudices against the African race, joined to

* Captain Brown having failed to raise the necessary money,
the pikes were left unfinished at this time; in June, 1859, he
was again at Collinsville, and completed the contract—but not
for the warfare in Kansas. They were forwarded, in the assumed
name of J. Smith and Sons, to Chambersburg in Pennsylvania,
whence they were conveyed across the country to Harper's Ferry,
Virginia.

their pro-slavery prepossessions, were far too deeply rooted to be removed by any work of fiction, however powerful and impressive. This document is entitled:—

OLD BROWN'S FAREWELL

TO THE "PLYMOUTH ROCKS," "BUNKER HILL MONUMENTS," "CHARTER OAKS," AND "UNCLE TOM'S CABINS."

He has left for Kansas. He has been trying, since he came out of the territory, to secure an outfit, or, in other words, the means of arming and thoroughly equipping his regular minuet-men, who are mixed up with the people of Kansas; and he leaves the states with a feeling of deepest sadness, that, after having exhausted his own small means, and with his family and his brave men suffered hunger, cold, nakedness, and some of them sickness, wounds, imprisonment in irons, with extreme cruel treatment, and others death : that, after lying on the ground for months, in the most sickly, unwholesome, and uncomfortable places, some of the time with sick and wounded destitute of any shelter; hunted like wolves; sustained in part by Indians—that, after all this, in order to sustain a cause which every citizen of this "glorious republic" is under equal moral obligations to aid, and for the neglect of which he will be held accountable by God—a cause in which every man, woman, and child of the entire human family has a deep and awful interest—that, when no wages are asked or expected, he cannot secure, amidst all the wealth, luxury, and extravagance of this "heaven exalted" people, even the necessary supplies of the common soldier. "How are the mighty fallen !"

Boston, April, A.D. 1857.

In April he made an agreement with Hugh Forbes, a drill-master, and an Englishman by birth, to instruct in drill and military tactics a number of Kansas young men, at Tabor, in Iowa. Brown was in hopes that, should the Kansas difficulties cease, the youths thus drilled would follow him to Harper's Ferry, which he had years before selected as his point of attack on slavery. In May he started for Kansas, but was delayed for some time in the central states. The following incident of this journey was given under affidavit, with the view of proving Brown's insanity, after the affair at Harper's Ferry, by Mr. Goodall, of Cleveland, Ohio :—

"During the summer of 1857, I met John Brown in the cars between Cleveland and Columbus. He was about to return to Kansas. I sought to gather some information respecting the probable advantage of wool-growing in that section ; but found his mind very restless on wool and sheep husbandry, and he soon began to talk with great earnestness of the evils of slavery, on which he soon became enthusiastic, and claimed that any course, whether stealing or coaxing niggers to run away from their masters, was honourable ; at which I attempted to point out a more conservative course, remarking very kindly to him that Kentucky, in my opinion, would have been a free state ere this, had it not been for the excitement and prejudices engendered by ultra abolitionists of Ohio. At this remark, he rose to his feet, with clenched fist, eyes rolling like an insane man (as he most assuredly was), and remarked that the

south would become free within one year were it not
that there were too many such scoundrels as myself to
rivet the chains of slavery. . . . I must, though,
in justice to Mr. Brown, state that when not under
excitement or mental derangement, he has ever manifested to me a kind, benevolent, and humane disposition, as a man of strict integrity, and moral and religious
worth."

Brown reached Tabor on the 7th of August, and
Forbes two days later. Being out of funds, they were
obliged to remain there inactive for nearly three months.

"During this interval of suspense," writes Forbes,
" Captain Brown advocated the adoption of his plan,
and I supported mine of stampedes*. The conclusion
arrived at was that he renounced his Harper's Ferry
project, and I consented to co-operate in stampedes in
Virginia and Maryland, instead of the part of the country I indicated as the most suitable. I perceived,
however, that his mind constantly wandered back to
Harper's Ferry ; and it was not till it had been defi-
nitely settled that neither of us should do anything,
unless under the direction or with the consent of a
committee, that I felt easy in my mind respecting his
curious notions of Harper's Ferry. He was very pious,
and had been deeply impressed for many years with the
Bible story of Gideon, believing that he, with a handful
of men, could strike down slavery."

In consequence of differences of opinion between

---

* The word stampede is here used to signify the running off of
a large number of slaves in company.

Brown and Forbes, the engagement between them was broken off. The latter was afterwards accused of having given information to the government of Brown's plans, entrusted to him in confidence at this time. On the 2nd of November, Forbes took steamer at Nebraska City for New England, and Brown started for Kansas in a waggon driven by one of his sons. He left two others at Tabor.

CHAPTER V.

November, 1857—October, 1859.

TRAINS HIS ADHERENTS TO ARMS.—CONVENTION IN CANADA.
— PRELIMINARY CONSTITUTION. — RETURNS TO KANSAS. —
PARTICULARS OF THE INTENDED ENTERPRISE.—FORTIFIED
POSITION AT BAIN'S CABIN.—RAID INTO MISSOURI TO LIBE-
RATE SLAVES.—TAKES THE FUGITIVES TO CANADA.—LET-
TER OF OLIVER BROWN.—THE KENNEDY FARM.—LETTERS
OF OLIVER AND WATSON BROWN. — FINAL PREPARATIONS
FOR HARPER'S FERRY.

THE published confession of John E. Cook, who was
executed two weeks after Captain Brown for his
complicity in the affair at Harper's Ferry, throws some
light on the events of this winter. He states that he
met Brown in November, at the house of a friend near
Lawrence. Brown told him he intended to organize a
company to put a stop to the aggressions of the pro-
slavery party. Cook consented to join him, and, being
asked if he knew any other young men who were perfectly reliable and likely to join, he afterwards introduced several to Brown; who finally arranged with a
party of young men to leave Kansas, and attend a military school during the winter. The party stopped some
days at Tabor, "where," says Cook, "we found that
Captain Brown's ultimate destination was the state of
Virginia" Some of the young men demurred to this,
their views being probably limited to the defence of the
free-state cause in Kansas; but at length they agreed

7*

to proceed with the rest.   At Tabor they procured
teams to transport their goods, consisting of blankets,
clothing, ammunition, and about two hundred revolvers,
also two hundred Sharpe's rifles, which had been stored
at Tabor during the previous year, and awaited Captain
Brown's orders.   These arms they conveyed to the
eastern part of the state of Iowa, whence they were forwarded to Ohio to be stored till required.   It was the
intention of Brown to sell his teams in Springdale,
Iowa, and with the proceeds to take his company of
young men to Ohio, and engage a good military in-
structor for them.   But as he was disappointed in the
sale, they remained at Pedee, Iowa, during the winter,
pursuing their military studies under Captain Aaron D.
Stevens, already mentioned as having been the leader
of the free-state men at Topeka in the summer of 1856.
" The people of the neighbourhood," says Cook, " did
not know our purpose.   We remained at Pedee till
about the middle of April, 1858, when we left for
Chatham, Canada, *via* Chicago and Detroit."

In Canada there are upwards of forty thousand fugitive slaves.   Many of these are intelligent and rich,
and all bear a deadly enmity to the system of slavery.
Some of them have, at great personal risk, made journeys to the south to help others to escape ; and they have
thus carried the " underground railroad " and the " underground telegraph " into nearly every southern state.
As Brown intended to make his projected attack on Virginia within a very few months, his object in visiting
Canada was to inspire the negroes with confidence in

his plan, and to induce them to participate in it. Accordingly, on the 5th of May, 1858, after his arrival in Chatham, Canada West, he called a secret convention of the friends of freedom in that place, for the purpose of agreeing upon an organized plan of attack. He issued a written circular, as follows, to various persons in the United States and Canada.

Chatham, May —, 1858.

Mr. ——. Dear Sir:—We have issued a call for a very *quiet* convention at this place, at which we shall be happy to see any *true* friends of freedom, and at which you are most earnestly invited to give your attendance.

Yours respectfully,   JOHN BROWN.

Cook, in his confession, tells us that "the names were left blank; but as they were directed by Captain Brown or J. H. Kagi, I do not know the parties to whom they were addressed. They were sent to none save those whom Captain Brown knew to be radical abolitionists. It was about ten days from the time the circulars were sent that the convention met. The place of meeting was in one of the negro churches in Chatham. The convention was called to order by J. H. Kagi. Its object was then stated, which was to complete a thorough organization and the formation of a constitution. Elder Monroe, a coloured minister, was elected president; and J. H. Kagi, secretary. Brown had already drawn up a constitution, which was read by the secretary. It was ordered that each article of the constitution be taken up, and separately amended and passed, which was done; it was then adopted. Most of the delegates to the convention were from Canada. After the constitution was adopted, the members took the oath to support it. It was then signed by all present. There were no white men at the convention save the members of our company. Men and money had both been promised from Chatham and other parts of Canada. When the convention broke up, news was received that Colonel H. Forbes, who had joined in the movement, had given information to the government. This, of course, delayed the time of attack. A day or two afterwards most of our party took the boat to Cleveland; J. H. Kagi, Richard Realf, William H. Leeman, Richard Robertson, and Captain Brown remaining. Captain Brown, however, started in a day or two for the east. Kagi, I think, went to some other town in Canada to get the constitution printed, which he completed before he returned to Cleveland. We remained in Cleveland for some weeks, at which place, for the time being, the company disbanded."

The constitution drawn up by Brown and passed on this occasion is a lengthy document, containing forty-eight articles. It gives minute details for the organization and maintenance of a provisional government, well adapted to preserve order in the community of liberated slaves which he hoped to form. When we bear in mind that his plan was not extradition into the north, but emancipation in the south—not to run off negroes to Canada, but to free them in Virginia, and to keep them there—the constitution is divested of the ridicule with

which it has been assailed. Brown and his confederates
sought no offensive warfare against the south, but only
to restore to the African race its inherent rights. Their
object was not revolution, but justice; not negro supre-
macy, but citizenship ; not war against society, but for
freedom.

The spirit and purpose of the constitution are shown
so clearly in the preamble, that we give it entire :—

"Whereas, slavery, throughout its entire existence in
the United States, is none other than the most barbarous,
unprovoked, and unjustifiable war of one portion of its
citizens against another portion, the only conditions of
which are perpetual imprisonment and hopeless servitude,
or absolute extermination ; in utter disregard and violation
of those eternal and self-evident truths set forth in our
Declaration of Independence; therefore, we, the citizens
of the United States, and the oppressed people who by a
recent decision of the Supreme Court are declared to have
no rights which the white man is bound to respect, together
with all the other people degraded by the laws thereof, do,
for the time being, ordain and establish for ourselves the
following provisional constitution and ordinances, the better to protect our people, property, lives, and liberties, and
to govern our actions."

The forty-sixth article plainly shows that no violent
revolution was contemplated. It runs as follows :—

"The foregoing articles shall not be construed so as in
any way to encourage the overthrow of any state government, or of the general government of the United States;

and look to no dissolution of the Union, but simply to amendment and repeal; and our flag shall be the same that our fathers fought under in the Revolution."

Only forty-four names are appended to this constitution, the convention having been summoned on very short notice. But we are given to understand by Mr. Redpath, that there were in Canada many hundreds of fugitive slaves, who were prepared to hasten southward and join the emancipators when the signal should be given at Harper's Ferry. Brown had acquired the reputation of a prudent man. Those who knew him best had as high an opinion of his caution and foresight as of his courage. Many of his preparations to ensure the success of his project can never transpire, but we have seen him gradually maturing his plans, and collecting and training a number of young men on whom he could depend as leaders. His own sons he could rely upon thoroughly, and he was wonderfully successful in infusing a portion of his eager, sanguine spirit into those around him. There was a contagion in his strong conviction that the work was the Lord's, and that He could save by many or by few.

Captain Brown's reason for not proceeding to Harper's Ferry immediately after the convention is thus stated by Cook :—"We stayed about two weeks in Chatham —some of the party stayed six or seven weeks. We left Chatham for Cleveland, and remained there until late in June. In the meantime, Captain Brown went east on business; but, previous to his departure, he had learned that Colonel Forbes had betrayed his plans to some extent. This, together with the scantiness of his funds, induced him to delay the commencement of his work, and was the means, for the time being, of disbanding the party. He had also received some information which called for his immediate attention in Kansas. I wished to go with him ; but he said that I was too well known there, and requested me and some others to go to Harper's Ferry, Virginia, to see how things were there, and to gain information.

" In this trip east, he did not realize the amount of money he expected. The money had been promised *bona fide;* but, owing to the tightness of the money market, they failed to comply with his demands. The funds were necessary to the accomplishment of his plans."

During Brown's absence from Kansas, the troubles of that unhappy territory had continued with little intermission. The free-state men stood their ground under their chosen leader Montgomery, but fearful atrocities were daily perpetrated by the pro-slavery party. Amongst these, a massacre committed at the farm of the Marais des Cygnes was conspicuous, and aroused almost the whole free-state population to take up arms. The news of this deed was the immediate cause of Brown's return to Kansas ; and the disclosures made by Forbes rendered it also desirable, in order to divert the attention of the government from his original plan.

Our hero's appearance on his return to Kansas at this time is thus incidentally described :—

"On the 25th of June, 1858," says Mr. Redpath, "we were at supper at an hotel in Lawrence, Kansas, when a stately old man, with a flowing white beard, entered the room, and took a seat at the public table. I immediately recognized, in the stranger, John Brown; though many persons who had previously known him did not penetrate his patriarchal disguise."

Another gentleman who had an interview with Brown and Kagi on that same day informs us :—

"On Sunday I held a very interesting conversation with Captain Brown, which lasted nearly the whole afternoon. The purport of it was, on his part, inquiries as to various public men in the territory, and the condition of political affairs. He was very particular in his inquiries as to the movements and character of Captain Montgomery. The massacre of the Marais des Cygnes was then fresh in the minds of the people. I remember an expression which he used. Warmly giving utterance to my detestation of slavery and its minions, and impatiently wishing for some effectual means of injuring it, Captain Brown said, most impressively :—'Young men must learn to wait. Patience is the hardest lesson to learn. I have waited for twenty years to accomplish my purpose.'

"In the course of the conversation he reminded me of a message that I had sent him in 1857,* and hoped I

---

* This message expressed regret that the writer could not then

meant what I then said, for he should ask the fulfilment of that promise, and that perhaps very soon ; and
further added that he wanted to caution me against
rash promises. Young men were too apt to make
them, and should be very careful. The promise given
was of great importance, and I must be prepared to
stand by, or disavow, it now. My answer need not be
stated. In this conversation he gave me no definite
idea of his plans, but seemed generally bent on ascer-
taining the opinions and characters of our men of anti-
slavery reputation.

"Kagi, at the same time, gave me to understand
that their visit to Kansas was caused by a betrayal of
their plans, by a Colonel Forbes, to the administration,
and that they wished to give a different impression
from what these disclosures had, by coming to the west.
Both stated they intended to stay some time, and that
night (Sunday) Captain Brown announced they would
go south in the morning, to see Captain Montgomery,
and visit his relatives."

He started next day, June 26th, with Mr. Kagi, for
southern Kansas, where they encamped about half a
mile from the border, and fortified themselves strongly
against all invaders. They were here joined by a few
of their companions ; and the presence of Brown in the
neighbourhood inspired confidence in the free-state
men, and checked the depredations of the Missourians

join him, in consequence of other engagements ; but promised at
any future time to be ready to obey his call.

in that quarter. He afterwards spent some time at the house of his half-sister, Mrs. Adair, near Ossawattomie ; and while there he was visited, in September, by the gentleman already referred to, who thus describes the interview :—

"Captain Brown had been quite unwell, and was then somewhat more impatient and nervous in his manner than I had before observed. Soon after my arrival, he again engaged in conversation as to various public men in the territory. Captain Montgomery's name was introduced, and Captain Brown was quite enthusiastic in praise of him, avowing a most perfect confidence in his integrity and purposes. 'Captain Montgomery,' he said, 'is the only soldier I have met among the prominent Kansas men. He understands my system of warfare exactly. He is a natural chieftain, and knows how to lead.' Of his own early treatment at the hands of ambitious leaders, to which I had alluded in bitter terms, he said :—'They acted up to their instincts. As politicians, they thought every man wanted to lead, and therefore supposed I might be in the way of their schemes. While they had this feeling, of course they opposed me. Many men did not like the manner in which I conducted warfare, and they too opposed me. Committees and councils could not control my movements, therefore they did not like me. But politicians and leaders soon found that I had different purposes, and forgot their jealousy. They have been kind to me since.'

"The conviction was expressed that trouble would

break out again in southern Kansas. At this time I
mentioned my intention of embarking in a newspaper
enterprise. Captain Brown, in an impressive manner,
reminded me of my promise to obey his call, and expressed a wish that I should not enter into any entang-
ling engagements, referring to my letter of 1857. He
said that he thought all engagements should be considered sacred, and liked my adhering to the one I had
at the time. That was the reason he had not sent to
me ; but now he hoped I would keep myself free. In
this connection he used words which I have often
thought of since.

"'For twenty years,' he said, 'I have never made
any business arrangement which would prevent me at
any time answering the call of the Lord. I have kept
my business in such condition, that in two weeks I
could always wind up my affairs, and be ready to obey
the call. I have permitted nothing to be in the way
of my duty, neither wife, children, nor worldly goods.
Whenever the occasion offered, I was ready. The hour
is very near at hand, and all who are willing to act
should be ready.'

"I was not at this time aware of his precise plans,
but had a general conception of his purpose. All
through that conversation I had the impression that
those blue eyes, mild yet inflexible, and beaming with
the steady light of a holy purpose, were searching my
soul, and that my whole being was as transparent to
him as the bosom of one of his own Adirondack lakes.
I shall never forget the look or the expression with

which he said :—' Young men should have a purpose
in life, and adhere to it through all trials. They would
be sure to succeed if their purpose is such as to deserve
the blessing of God.'

"After dinner, Kagi had some conversation with the
Captain apart. He then asked me if I would walk
down to the Marais des Cygnes, 'as he was going to
fish.' I acquiesced, and we started. About half way
to the river we stopped and sat on a fence. Kagi asked
me what I supposed was the plan of Captain Brown.
My answer was, that I thought it had reference to the
Indian territory and the south-western states. He
shook his head, and gradually unfolded the whole of
their plans, a portion of which only has been elucidated
in the Harper's Ferry outbreak. I shall not, for obvious
reasons, give the full details. A full account of the
convention in Canada was given, as well as of the
organization, its extent and objects, thereby effected.
The mountains of Virginia were named as the place of
refuge, and as a country admirably adapted in which
to carry on a guerilla warfare. In the course of the
conversation, Harper's Ferry was mentioned as a point
to be seized—but not held,—on account of the arsenal.
The white members of the company were to act as
officers of different guerilla bands, which, under the
general command of John Brown, were to be composed
of Canadian refugees, and the Virginia slaves who would
join them. A different time of the year was mentioned
for the commencement of the warfare from that which
has lately been chosen. It was not anticipated that

the first movement would have any other appearance
to the masters than a slave stampede, or local insurrection at most. The planters would pursue their chattels
and be defeated. The militia would then be called out,
and would also be defeated. It was not intended that
the movement should appear to be of large dimensions,
but that, gradually increasing in magnitude, it should,
as it opened, strike terror into the heart of the slave
states by the amount of organization it would exhibit,
and the strength it gathered. They anticipated, after
the first blow had been struck, that, by the aid of the
free and Canadian negroes who would join them, they
could inspire confidence in the slaves, and induce them
to rally. No intention was expressed of gathering a
large body of slaves, and removing them to Canada.
On the contrary, Kagi clearly stated, in answer to my
inquiries, that the design was to make the fight in the
mountains of Virginia, extending it to North Carolina
and Tennessee, and also to the swamps of South Carolina,
if possible. Their purpose was not the extradition of
one or a thousand slaves, but their liberation in the
states wherein they were born, and were now held in
bondage. 'The mountains and swamps of the south
were intended by the Almighty,' said John Brown to
me afterwards, 'for a refuge for the slave, and a defence
against the oppressor.' Kagi spoke of having marked
out a chain of counties extending continuously through
South Carolina, Georgia, Alabama, and Mississippi.
He had travelled over a large portion of the region
indicated, and from his own personal knowledge, and

with the assistance of Canadian negroes who had escaped from those states, they had arranged a general plan of attack. The counties he named were those which contained the largest proportion of slaves, and would, therefore, be the best in which to strike. The blow struck at Harper's Ferry was to be in the spring, when the planters were busy, and the slaves most needed. The arms in the arsenal were to be taken to the mountains, with such slaves as joined. The telegraph wires were to be cut, and the railroad tracks torn up in all directions. As fast as possible, other bands besides the original ones were to be formed, and a continuous chain of posts established in the mountains. They were to be supported by provisions taken from the farms of the oppressors. They expected to be speedily and constantly reinforced; first, by the arrival of those men, who, in Canada, were anxiously looking and praying for the time of deliverance, and then by the slaves themselves. The intention was to hold the egress to the free states as long as possible, in order to retreat when that was advisable. Kagi, however, expected to retreat southward, not in the contrary direction. The slaves were to be armed with pikes, scythes, muskets, shot-guns, and other simple instruments of defence; the officers, white or black, and such of the men as were skilled and trustworthy, to have the use of the Sharpe's rifles and revolvers. They anticipated procuring provisions enough for subsistence by forage, as also arms, horses, and ammunition. Kagi said one of the reasons that induced him to go into the enterprise

was a full conviction that at no very distant day forcible
efforts for freedom would break out among the slaves,
and that slavery might be more speedily abolished by
such efforts than by any other means. He knew by
observation in the south, that in no point was the
system so vulnerable as in its fear of a slave-rising.
Believing that such a blow would soon be struck, he
wanted to organize it so as to make it more effectual,
and also, by directing and controlling the negroes, to
prevent some of the atrocities that would necessarily
arise from the sudden upheaving of such a mass as the
southern slaves.   The constitution adopted at Chatham
was intended as the framework of organization among
the emancipationists, to enable the leaders to effect a
more complete control of their forces. Ignorant men,
in fact, all men were more easily managed by the forms
of law and organization than without them.   This was
one of the purposes to be subserved by the provisional
government.   Another was to alarm the [slaveholding]
oligarchy by discipline and the show of organization.
In their terror they would imagine the whole north
was upon them pell-mell, as well as all their slaves.
Kagi said John Brown anticipated that by a system of
forbearance to non-slaveholders many of them might
be induced to join them.

"In answer to an inquiry, Kagi stated that no politician, in the republican or any other party, knew of
their plans, and but few of the abolitionists. It was
no use talking, he said, of anti-slavery action to non-
resistant agitators. That there were men who knew of

8

John Brown's general idea is most true ; but, south of
the Canadian provinces and of North Elba, there were
but few who were cognizant of the mode by which he
intended to mould those ideas into deeds.

"After a long conversation, the substance of which
I have given, we returned to the house.   I had some further conversation with Brown, mostly upon his movements, and the use of arms.   In allusion to the terror
inspired by the fear of slaves rising, he said, that Nat
Turner, with fifty men, held Virginia five weeks.   The
same number, well organized and armed, can shake the
system out of the state.

"I remember also these sentences :—'Give a slave a
pike, and you make him a man.   Deprive him of the
means of resistance, and you keep him down.'—'The
land belongs to the bondman ; he has enriched it, and
been robbed of its fruits.'—'Any resistance, however
bloody, is better than the system which makes every
seventh woman a concubine.'—'I would not give
Sharpe's rifles to more than ten men in a hundred, and
then only when they have learned to use them.   It is
not every man who knows how to use a rifle.   I had
one man in my company who was the bravest man and
the worst marksman ever I knew.'—'A ravine is better
than a plain.   Woods and mountain sides can be held
by resolute men against ten times their force.'—'A few
men in the right, and knowing they are, can overturn a
king.   Twenty men in the Alleghanies could break
slavery to pieces in two years.'—'When the bondmen

stand like men, the nation will respect them. It is necessary to teach them this.'

"Much more was said which I cannot recall. The afternoon had more than half passed before I left for my destination. I rode over the prairies till sunset ; and in the glory of the grand scheme which had been opened to me, it seemed as if the whole earth had become broader, and the heavens more vast. Since that day, I have known what John Brown meant when he said :—'Young men should have a purpose in life, and adhere to it in all trials. They will be sure to succeed if their purpose is such as to deserve the blessing of God.'"

Brown, with some of his men, afterwards returned to southern Kansas, where they took up their residence near the Little Sugar Creek, at a house known as Bain's Cabin. They converted this dwelling into a regular stronghold, as they had reason to expect a renewal of hostilities. Brown had great skill in choosing his ground, and in erecting these rude fortifications, traces of which still remain in that neighbourhood. In November, during his absence at Ossawattomie, an attack was made upon Bain's Cabin by a force of more than a hundred men, led by the sheriff of the county ; their object being to arrest Brown and his men, and demolish their stronghold. Stevens and Kagi were the only persons there at the time, but they were joined by many of their neighbours when it was known that the sheriff's party were coming ; and a message was sent to Captain Montgomery, who hastened thither with some of his men. The assailants, finding the defence stronger than they had anticipated, retired without firing a shot.

In December, two hundred Missourians had assembled for a foray into the district in Brown's neighbourhood, but, hearing that he was recruiting his forces, they retired several miles within their own state. He now formed a plan to follow them into Missouri, and, by carrying off slaves, to teach the citizens of that state to attend to their own affairs. While his arrangements were in progress, a negro man named Jim came to him on Sunday, December 19th, and, saying that he, with his family and a friend, were about to be sold south, implored help for their deliverance. John Brown was not the man to turn a deaf ear to such an appeal. He decided on immediate action, and on the night of the following day two parties under Brown and Kagi, numbering twelve and eight men respectively, left Bain's Cabin, and crossed the border into Missouri.

Brown's party first visited the house of Hicklan, the master of Jim, and liberated that negro and four others. They then proceeded to the house of another slave-holder, Isaac Jarné, where they released five more. They also took Jarné prisoner, and carried him with them into the territory, to prevent his giving the alarm. John Brown acted on the principle that not only liberty, but compensation for unrequited labour, was due to the slaves. Therefore, after telling the slaves they were free, he asked them how much their

services had been worth, and proceeded to take property to the amount.

Kagi and his party went on the southern side of the
Little Osage river, and called at several houses for the
purpose of rescuing slaves. They found none till they
came to the house of David Cruse, who, on learning the
object of the party, raised his rifle to fire, but was shot
dead before he could pull the trigger. He had only
one slave, whom they added to their company. The
two parties now united and returned into Kansas,
taking Mr. Jarné with them. One of his late female
slaves sought to console him. Finding her endeavour
of no avail, the sympathetic negress remarked : " Gosh !
massa's in a bad fix ! Hog no killed ; corn no
gathered ; nigger run away. Laws-a-me ! What 'll
massa do ?" A little negro boy of the party grasped
his father by the leg, and asked : " How's ye feel,
fadder, when you's free ?" These liberated slaves constituted four families : one man, his wife, and two children ; a widow, with two daughters and a son ; a young
man, a boy, and a woman who had been separated
from her husband. They were taken several miles into
Kansas, where they remained for two or three weeks ;
Brown and Kagi returning to their fortified position at
Bain's Cabin.

This raid into Missouri created such a panic among
the slaveholders that in a few days the two border
counties of Bates and Vernon were cleared of their
slaves. Numbers were sold south ; many ran into the
territory, and escaped ; and the rest were removed

further from the border. The governor of Missouri
offered a reward of three thousand dollars for the arrest
of Brown, to which President Buchanan added a further
sum of two hundred and fifty dollars.

At this time Captain Brown addressed to several newspapers the following account of this expedition, contrast-
ing the course pursued by the federal government in reference to him and his followers, with their total neglect to
punish the perpetrators of a cruel slaughter of a number
of unoffending free-state men, which we have already
referred to as the massacre of the Marais des Cygnes :—

Trading Post, Kansas, Jan., 1859.

Gentlemen,—You will greatly oblige a humble friend
by allowing the use of your columns while I briefly state
two parallels in my poor way.

Not one year ago, eleven quiet citizens of this neighbourhood, viz. William Robertson, William Colpetzer,
Amos Hall, Austin Hall, John Campbell, Asa Snyder,
Thomas Stilwell, William Hairgrove, Asa Hairgrove,
Patrick Ross, and B. L. Reed were gathered up from their
work and their homes by an armed force under one Ham-
ilton, and, without trial or opportunity to speak in their
own defence, were formed into line, and, all but one, shot
—five killed and five wounded. One fell unharmed, pretending to be dead. All were left for dead. The only
crime charged against them was that of being free-state
men. Now, I enquire, what action has ever, since the
occurrence in May last, been taken by either the president
of the United States, the governor of Missouri, the governor of Kansas, or any of their tools, or by any pro-slavery

or administration man, to ferret out and punish the perpetrators of this crime?

Now for the other parallel. On Sunday, December 19,
a negro man called Jim came over to the Osage settlement
from Missouri, and stated that he, together with his wife,
two children, and another negro man, was to be sold
within a day or two, and begged for help to get away.
On Monday [the following] night, two small companies
were made up to go to Missouri and liberate the five
slaves, together with other slaves. One of these companies I assumed to direct. We proceeded to the place,
surrounded the buildings, liberated the slaves, and also
took certain property supposed to belong to the estate.
We, however, learned before leaving, that a portion of the
articles we had taken belonged to a man living on the
plantation as a tenant, who was supposed to have no
interest in the estate. We promptly returned to him all
we had taken.

We then went to another plantation, where we found
five more slaves, took some property and two white men.
We moved all slowly away into the territory for some
distance, and then sent the white men back, telling them
to follow us as soon as they chose to do so. The other
company freed one female slave, took some property, and,
as I am informed, killed one white man (the master), who
fought against the liberation.

Now for a comparison. Eleven persons are forcibly
restored to their natural and inalienable rights, with but
one man killed, and all "hell is stirred from beneath." It
is currently reported that the governor of Missouri has
made a requisition upon the governor of Kansas for the
delivery of all such as were concerned in the last named
"dreadful outrage." The marshal of Kansas is said to be

collecting a posse of Missouri [not Kansas] men at West Point in Missouri, a little town about ten miles distant, to "enforce the laws." All pro-slavery, conservative-free-state, and dough-face men and administration tools are filled with holy horror.

Consider the two cases, and the action of the administration party.

Respectfully yours,
John Brown.

About the 20th of January, John Brown started for Canada, by way of Nebraska, with his emancipated slaves, who were not safe from re-capture as long as they remained on United States soil. During their stay at Ossawattomie, their number was increased by the birth of a child, who was named "Captain John Brown."

This was Brown's final departure from Kansas. It appears likely that his sons left about the same time. They were fully identified with their father's plans, now nearly mature, and were pledged to assist him in carrying them out. Although he had entered so zealously into the struggle in Kansas, he had other and deeper projects in view, to the accomplishment of which he was powerfully stimulated by his experience of the lawless and cruel conduct of the abettors of slavery in that territory. Instead of wasting his strength on the outworks, he wished to strike a deadly blow at the citadel of slavery. The residence and exploits of Captain Brown in Kansas left an ineffaceable impression on the history and destiny of that territory. By encouraging the free-state settlers, and disheartening their enemies, they were mainly instrumental in bringing about the favourable turn in affairs which shortly afterwards took place, and which resulted in the reception of Kansas into the Union, as a free state, in January, 1861.

In order fully to realize the courageous and self-sacrificing spirit which animated him in this effort to secure their freedom to the "chattels" he had plucked from slavery, we must remember that the undertaking involved a tedious and difficult land journey of upwards of 2,500 miles, across the vast expanse of Iowa, Illinois, Indiana, and part of Michigan ; most of which states, though nominally free, were in great part inhabited by settlers hardly less hostile to the presence of abolitionists than of slaveholders. Besides, the Fugitive Slave Law being in full operation, his party was in constant danger of being betrayed by some of that numerous tribe of informers and kidnappers which that law has naturally produced.

A settler in Kansas, who accompanied Captain Brown and his party during the first five hundred miles of this journey, sent the following narrative of some of their adventures to Mrs. Child, the well known American authoress, to whom we are indebted for it :—

"On the 24th of January, 1859, Captain Brown came near to Lawrence, with his eleven emigrants from Missouri, and I joined him. We travelled, by the way of Topeka, northward through Nebraska. About

thirty-seven miles from Topeka we entered a vacant
log-cabin, belonging to an excellent man, who was a
warm friend of Captain Brown. Our party consisted
at this time only of the captain, myself, and a man
known by the name of Whipple in Kansas, but after-
ward as Stevens, at Harper's Ferry. Kagi and Tidd
had staid behind at Topeka, to procure provisions for
our journey, and our teamster had been sent back to
bring them along. While waiting for them to rejoin
us, we found ourselves surrounded by a band of human
blood-hounds, headed by the notorious deputy-marshal
of the United States, J. N. O. P. Wood. I afterwards
learned that he was put on our track by a traitor from
New Hampshire, named Hussey.

"Mr. Whipple lived alone in a small empty cabin
near the one we occupied. There had been heavy rains,
which produced a freshet; and one day he walked a
short distance from the cabin, to ascertain whether the
waters had subsided. Suddenly, eight of the marshal's
men came upon him, and asked him if he had seen any
negroes thereabout. He told them, if they would come
with him, he would show them some. He conducted
them to his cabin, where he had left his rifle. He came
out immediately, and pointed his rifle at the leader,
commanding him to surrender, which he did at once.
The other men put spurs to their horses, and rode off
as fast as possible. At that time, I was sole body-
guard of Captain Brown, the eleven fugitives, and the
prisoner who had surrendered. Whipple kept a sharp
look-out, acting as our sentry. We were detained at

this place about three days. At last our provisions arrived, and we were joined by a band of Topeka boys, who had walked thirty-seven miles in the night to aid us in our enterprise. We started on our journey. A short distance from our road was Muddy Creek. Marshal Wood, supposing our party must pass that way, stationed himself on the opposite side of the creek, with his eighty armed men. They had made careful preparations, well knowing that it was no joke to attack 'old John Brown.' Captain Brown had with him only twenty-three white men, all told. He placed them in double file in front of the emigrant waggons, and said, 'Now go straight at 'em, boys! They'll be sure to run.'

"In obedience to this order, they marched towards the creek; but, scarcely had the foremost entered the water, when the valiant United States marshal mounted his horse, and rode off in hot haste. His men followed as fast as possible; but they were not all as lucky as he was, in untying their horses from the stumps and bushes. The scene was ridiculous beyond description. Some horses were hastily mounted by two men. One man grabbed tight hold of the tail of a horse, trying to leap on from behind, while the rider was putting the spurs into his sides; so he went flying through the air, his feet touching the ground now and then. Those of our men who had horses followed them about six miles, and brought back with them four prisoners and five horses. Meanwhile, Captain Brown and the rest of his company succeeded in drawing the emigrant wagons through the creek, by means of long ropes. This battle of Muddy Creek was known ever after, in Kansas, by the name of ' The battle of the spurs.'

" When we resumed our journey, the captain did not think it prudent to allow the five prisoners to mount their horses, lest they should escape and bring a fresh party to attack us. So he told them they must walk ; but, as he meant them no unkindness, he would walk with them. They went on together, he talking with them all the way concerning the wickedness of slavery and the meanness of slave-hunting. He kept them with us all night. In the morning, he told them they might make the best of their way home, on foot. Their horses were retained from prudential motives, as it was obviously not for the safety of our coloured emigrants to have them return very speedily. The horses captured from Marshal Wood's posse were given to the brave Topeka boys who had walked so far to help us.

" As we passed through Nebraska City, we saw men at the corners of the streets, who looked very hard at us, but nobody molested us. Kagi visited his sister, and while he was there in bed, the marshal of Nebraska arrested his horse and carried it off. We heard that Marshal Wood was hidden in the city, but we saw nothing of him. We rested a week at Tabor, Iowa, and were hospitably entertained by friends of freedom there. A public meeting was called, and the captain told his story. Some of the people were not willing to endorse his bringing slaves out of Missouri. At

Grenely, Kagi delivered a lecture, and Captain Brown had a prayer-meeting at the congregational church. The audience manifested their sympathy by contributing twenty-five dollars to help on the emigrants. At Gooke settlement I parted from Captain Brown, and rode back to Lawrence, a distance of about five hundred miles, much of the way through mud up to the horse's knees. The captain and his company of emigrants arrived safely in Canada."

The following incidents respecting the four prisoners taken in "The Battle of the Spurs" are related by Mr. Redpath. There is a racy originality in the course pursued by Captain Brown to ensure the spiritual welfare of his captives. When Brown obliged them to dismount, and set the negroes on their horses, they gave vent to their vexation in some round oaths. He ordered them to be silent, as he would permit no blasphemy in his presence. They swore again. " Kneel !" said he, as, with stern earnestness, he drew his pistol. They knelt, and he ordered them to pray. They never swore again in his presence. On being released the following day, they asked Brown to restore their horses and weapons. "No," said he, gravely; "your legs will carry you as fast as you want to run ; you won't find any more old Browns between this and Atchison."

One of these men, after the capture of Brown at Harper's Ferry, spoke of him with the greatest admiration; and said that, "although evidently a monomaniac on the subject of slavery," he was an honest and brave man. On being jestingly advised to go into mourning for him, he said he might do so for many a worse man. This testimony from a kidnapper is not without value.

During this journey of nearly three months' duration, the liberated slaves and their benefactors were often closely followed, but the sight of Captain Brown's well-armed little party prevented an attack. They stopped at several villages, and were in general cordially received and treated with great kindness and hospitality. One of Brown's entertainers, who regarded him with the enthusiastic admiration which was afterwards so largely elicited by his subsequent demeanour, published at that time the following testimony respecting him:—

"Old Captain Brown of Kansas ! I have set my eyes on this old hero, feared by Missouri invaders, and loved as a father by the legions of liberty in Kansas. He had a company of twelve coloured people, en route for Canada, where I trust they are safe. In the family, simple-hearted as a child, he narrates stirring scenes, placing himself in the background of the picture; while an eye of the most determined expression I ever saw at once supplies what the modesty of the narrator has withheld as personal. He is the impersonation of firmness.

"Captain Brown avows his object to be to show the border ruffians that they have enough to do in taking care of slavery in Missouri, without making a foray on the people of Kansas to establish slavery there against the votes and wishes of the people. As God spares him, he says, he will 'deliver the poor that cry;' and does not conceal the fact that, in open day, he conducted out those who dreaded, next to death, a more southern prison house. Two companies of slave-hunters, headed by a marshal, looked upon them, but were not ready to lose their lives in a negro hunt. A reward of three thousand dollars by the governor of Missouri, with the value of his company as chattels, has made him quite a lion through the state of Iowa. The 'dirt-eating' democracy covet the reward, but keep at a good distance from the cold lead, and have no desire to be awed into silence and shame by one glance from the old hero, who feels that 'God will cover his head in the day of battle.' Stranger than fiction have been his escapes and exploits in Kansas. Combining the gentleness of a Christian, the love of a patriot, and the skill and boldness of a commander, whether ending his career in the quiet of home or in bloody strife, the freemen of Kansas will hallow his memory, and history will name him the Cromwell of our border wars.

"How unlike the old Brown sketched by fiendish hate is the man at your fireside!—his mouth unpolluted with tobacco, strong drinks abjured, regimen plain, conversation grave, and occupied with pleasant memories of other days. He drops a tear of gratitude on the mention of the practical kindness of ―――― to him in the hour of extremity. He recurs to the solid principles and hearty affection of Dr. Osgood of Springfield, on whose ministry he attended for many years. He had a lucrative occupation as wool-grower and dealer in Ohio,

and gained a medal as exhibitor of wool at the World's
Fair; and now finds himself in the 'wool business'
still, in a land where men find foes more dreaded than
the young Hebrew shepherd found in the beasts that
took a lamb out of the flock.

"Nothing seemed to excite him so much as an inti-
mation that oppression aroused a spirit of revenge. As
he spoke in public, there was no boasting, or display
of himself. The wrongs of Kansas, and the atrocities
of slavery, he pictured in a clear style, declaring that
it was 'nothing to die in a good cause, but an eternal
disgrace to sit still in the presence of the barbarities of
American slavery.' His logic, with all who were cap-
tious as to his course, was like a chain-shot argument;
yet he courted no discussion, being then occupied with
the safe escape of the eleven supposed chattels from
Missouri."

His host records the following sayings of Captain
Brown as having particularly arrested his attention at
this time :—"An old man should have more care to
end life well, than to live long."—"Duty is the voice
of God, and a man is neither worthy of a good home
here, or a heaven, that is not willing to be in peril for
a good cause!"—"The loss of my family and the troubles in Kansas have shattered my constitution, and I
am good for nothing to the world but to defend the
right, and that, by God's help, I have done, and will
do." This, in substance, and much more, was said in
reply to a wish which was expressed that he would
not return to Kansas, but seek that quiet with his

family which his health demanded. "He scouted the idea of rest while he held 'a commission direct from from God Almighty to act against slavery.' He claimed to be responsible for the wise exercise of his powers only, and not for the quality of certain acts. In thus taking away slaves out of Missouri, he declared that he would teach those 'living in glass houses not to throw stones,' and they should have more than they could do to keep slavery in Missouri, without extending it against the will of Kansas. The battle of 'Black Jack,' and others, he was free to say, he thought had scared Missouri, and that was General Lane's opinion. They did not report half the number killed, which they were ashamed to do, nor will it ever be known. I could repeat much that he said which showed a wonderful sagacity, and a bold, undaunted spirit. His whole demeanour was that of a well-bred gentleman, and his narratives were given with child-like simplicity. He feared nothing, 'for,' said he, 'any who will try to take me and my company are cowards, and one man in the right, ready to die, will chase a thousand. Not less than thirty guns have been discharged at me, but they only touched my hair.' "

In Chicago he sent his men in different directions, keeping Kagi and Stevens with him. A gentleman who conversed with him in that city thus writes :— "There is one thing he charged me to do when I last saw him. It is this :—'Do not allow any one to say I acted from revenge. I claim no man has a right to

9

revenge himself.   It is a feeling that does not enter into
my heart.   What I do, I do for the cause of human
liberty, and because I regard it as necessary.' "

The party reached Detroit, in Michigan, on the 12th
of March, and immediately crossed over to Canada.
There Captain Brown left the fugitives.   On being
subsequently asked what were his feelings when he
had landed them safely in Canada, his reply was,—
" Lord, permit now thy servant to die in peace, for
mine eyes have seen thy salvation.   I could not brook
the idea that any ill should befal them, or they be taken
back to slavery.   The arm of Jehovah protected us."

A Canadian gentleman, a few months later, thus
writes respecting the condition of Brown's protegés :—
" As everything relative to 'old John Brown' is now
interesting, I would inform your readers that I have
spent a few hours in Windsor, Upper Canada, with
seven of the twelve coloured Missourians who are now
residing in that place.   The other five are living about
nine miles in the country.   These make the twelve
persons taken by Brown last January into Canada.   As
various reports are afloat concerning them, I wish to
inform all parties that those living here are very industrious.   Two of the seven are men.   They 'team,' saw
wood, and 'job round.'   One, a boy about twelve,
helps around generally.   Two of the women, who were
field hands in Missouri last spring, on arriving at
Windsor, hired, for four dollars, an acre of land, and,
with a spade each, they actually spaded it, planted it
with corn and potatoes, and attended it well ; this crop

would challenge any crop I ever saw in Missouri, and is
not often beaten even in Kansas, where soil and climate
are superior to most portions of this world; their potatoes are very fine—all dug and put up in a secure.
manner in the garden back of their house for winter;
the corn, of which I brought some away, is beautiful.
One of their houses has a small garden attached; they
pay two dollars a month for this.   In this little garden
they have grown some very fine onions, carrots, parsnips,
and some very extraordinary cabbages; the cabbages are
taken up, put together, and covered thick with fodder
or straw, rather neatly packed.   They have ample sufficient corn, potatoes, &c., for winter.   As to meat, they
do without, till they have some fit to kill.   They have
three hogs growing finely, which they paid one dollar
each for, and feed them on what they collect in swill
from neighbours, &c.   As to clothing, they are neat,
with well-patched articles.   They informed me that,
after being here a short time, they were burned out,
losing all, or nearly all, of the useful articles given
them by friends on their way, while escorted by that
man whom they venerate.   While I read aloud the
sentence of Brown, with his speech, from the paper, to
them, O, how affecting to see their tears and hear their
sobs!   Two women declared, if it could be, they would
willingly die instead of their liberator.   A woman
among them remarked, if the Bible was true, John
Brown practised most of it here; so he would be
rewarded by 'Old Master,' up higher, with greater
happiness.   The father, mother, and three children in

9*

the country, work a farm on shares ; they have about sixteen acres of corn, potatoes, &c., part of which are theirs; and they are all anticipating the day when they can get a piece of land of their own."

Mr. Henry R. Smith, of Cleveland, Ohio, communicates the following additional information respecting these people, in a letter to Mrs. Child:—"I took a walk this morning to the humble abode of the eleven fugitives from Missouri, whom the immortal John Brown delivered from the house of bondage, last spring. The twelfth one, born on the way, is now a year old, and is thriving well. He is rightly named for his illustrious benefactor. When I rapped at the door, it was opened by a woman with sewing in her hand, who bade me welcome. A good supply of smoked hams and shoulders were hanging from the joists of their log-cabin. They all seem to be very industrious people. I went to see them three times ; once in fine autumn weather, once in the dead of winter, when the thermometer stood eight degrees below zero, and lastly on this beautiful morning of spring. On every occasion, I found them all hard at work. I wish you could hear this liberated eleven talk about Captain Brown. It would do your heart good."

After leaving Canada, Brown and his friend Mr. Kagi stopped at Cleveland, Ohio, from the 20th to the 30th March. An incident of their stay is thus related by Wendell Phillips:—"Prudence, skill, courage, thrift, knowledge of his time, knowledge of his opponents, undaunted daring in the face of the nation,—all these he had. He was the man who could leave Kansas and go into Missouri, take eleven men and give them liberty, and bring them off on the horses which he carried with him, and two which he took as tribute from their masters in order to facilitate escape. When he had passed his human protegés from the vulture of the United States to the safe shelter of the English lion,— this brave, frank, and sublime truster in God's right and absolute justice, entered his name, in the city of Cleveland, 'John Brown, of Kansas,' advertised these two horses for sale, and stood in front of the auctioneer's stand, notifying all bidders of the defect in the title. 'But,' he added, with nonchalance, when he told the story, 'they brought a very excellent price.'"

Our information respecting Brown's movements during the four succeeding months is extremely meagre. He was doubtless engaged in soliciting assistance and in making preparations for carrying out the enterprise he had so much at heart—an enterprise which we have now good reason to hope will be ultimately crowned with success, though not in the way anticipated by its projector. In the beginning of April he was laid up with an attack of ague in Ashtabula County, Ohio, probably at the residence of his eldest son, John, who was still suffering from the effects of the injuries inflicted on him when the prisoner of Captain Pate. He then visited Mr. Gerrit Smith at Peterboro'; and at Rochester he delivered an address in public, and enlisted among his adherents the brave negro, Shields Green, who was afterwards hanged for his participation in the affair at Harper's Ferry. In May we find Captain Brown in Boston, where he directed his attention to the manufacture of biscuits and beef meal, probably with a view to future military requirements. In June he completed the contract for pikes to which we have before referred, at Collinsville, Connecticut, paying three hundred dollars on account. He then returned to Ashtabula County.

It was at this time that the following letter was written by Brown's son Oliver, then aged about twenty, who fell by his father's side at Harper's Ferry a few months later, to his young wife, also since deceased. There is a simple pathos in its details which cannot fail to enlist the sympathies of our readers. The remark in the postscript shows considerable power of appreciation for so young a man.

OLIVER BROWN TO HIS WIFE.

West Andover, Ashtabula County, Ohio,
June 18th, 1859.

My dear wife: I write to let you know that we have arrived here sound and well, and in good spirits. We have met with great encouragement since we left home. We found John and his folks in good health. The frost has been much more severe here than at North Elba. Thousands of acres of wheat and rye are entirely ruined by it; the leaves on the maple and hickory trees are falling, as if it were Fall. The season is much more forward here; haying has commenced, and the grass is very good.

I send you a photograph of myself.   Oh, Martha, I would give everything if I could have your picture.   Do not fail of having it taken while I am gone, should you have an opportunity.   You don't know how I value that lock of hair.   There may yet be an opportunity to send a picture to me.   I send you two dollars, which I cannot be satisfied to keep.   I also send you a small book.

Heaven bless you, my dear Martha,

Your affectionate husband,

OLIVER BROWN.

P. S.   I have concluded to send you another copy of my picture, which is pasted upon a board and intended to be put into a frame for a wall picture.   These two you will please keep, as I may want some day to see how I looked when I was young.   I would send more for the rest of the family, but have not the means, as thirty cents is all the cash I can command.

I very much like the people here ; they are a liberal-minded, whole-souled people.   I am told that in no country in the world is there so great a proportion of "infidels;"* and also that it would be equally hard to find a country where there is so much comfort, thrift, intelligence, morality, and progressive and reform sentiment.   I look upon the development of such a people as the most important and encouraging fact I know of.   Much has the spirit of emigration done for all these western states ; it is the growing progressive spirit.   He certainly must be a very

* Many zealous opponents of slavery in the United States have withdrawn from the churches with which they had been connected, in consequence of the pro-slavery action of those bodies, and have hence been stigmatized as "infidels."   Such were probably those to whom Oliver Brown here alludes.

shallow observer and superficial reasoner who is ever cry-
ing over the folly of those who would move to better their
condition.   It was just such folly-stricken people who
have developed this whole western world, and are now
knocking the scales from the eyes of the conservative blind.

Again I am affectionately your husband,

OLIVER BROWN.

From Ohio, Brown went to Chambersburg, Pennsylvania, near the borders of Maryland, where he had a
depôt of arms and stores.   After remaining some days,
he proceeded, on the 30th of June, to Hagerstown in
Maryland, accompanied by his sons Watson and Oliver,
and by Mr. Anderson.   Their further movements are
thus related in a letter by a resident of this place:—

"John Brown, his two sons, and a Captain Anderson
spent a night here at the Washington House, in June,
and were taken to Harper's Ferry next day in a hack.
When here, I was struck with the long beard of one of
them, and called over to learn who they were and
where they came from.   Brown registered as 'Smith
and two sons, from western New York,' and told the
landlord that they had got tired of farming in that
region ; that the frosts had taken their crops for two or
three years ; that they were going to Virginia to look
out for a location for raising sheep and growing wool,
&c.   After looking around Harper's Ferry a few days,
and prowling through the mountains in search of mine-
rals, as they said, they came across a large farm with
three unoccupied houses; the owner, Dr. Booth Kennedy, having died in the spring.   These houses they

rented from the family till next March, and paid the
rent in advance ; and also purchased a lot of hogs from
the family for cash, and agreed to take care of the
stock until a sale could be had.   They did attend most
faithfully to them, and have all in first-rate order ;
they were gentlemen, and kind to everybody.   After
living there a few weeks, others joined them, until as
many as twelve were in these three houses ; and every
few days a stranger would appear and disappear again,
without creating the least surprise."

The Kennedy farm, where Brown and his confederates
took up their abode, was about five or six miles from
Harper's Ferry, on the Maryland side of the river.   In
the course of the summer the party was increased by
the arrival of his daughter Anne, a fine young woman
of fifteen, and Martha, the young wife of his son
Oliver.   These two females remained till the middle of
September, when they returned to North Elba.

A correspondent of one of the New York papers
gives the following particulars of their mode of life at
the Kennedy farm :—

" The house is located in the midst of a thickly settled neighbourhood, five or six families living within
hail, and the movements of the strangers were regarded with much curiosity.   They seemed to have no
settled purpose ; but a large number of boxes and
packages were sent to them by railroad, which they
carted home, and nearly every day one or more of them
paid a visit to the village.   They paid for everything
they wanted in hard cash, and were sociable and

friendly towards their neighbours. A great deal of their time appeared to be passed in hunting in the mountains, although they never brought home any game."

According to Cook's confession, " the greater part of the men kept out of sight during the day, for fear of attracting attention. The arms, munitions, &c. were carted from Chambersburg to the rendezvous. The spear-heads and guards came in strong boxes, and the shafts passed for fork-handles. They were put together by our men at the house, where most of them were afterwards found."

" During his residence at the Kennedy farm," writes one who lived there with him, " Brown used often to take his Bible, sit down on a stool in the corner near the door, read a chapter, and then make a prayer. He always did so in the morning. We never ate a meal at head-quarters until a blessing was asked on it."

We here give another letter from Oliver Brown; also three letters from his brother Watson, aged twenty-four; written during this sojourn near Harper's Ferry, to their respective wives residing at North Elba. They forcibly depict the tender characters of the writers, and the strength of those home affections whose claims they nevertheless freely sacrificed at what they felt to be the call of duty. Alas ! that two such brave, loving, and beloved young men should both have been laid in their bloody graves within a few days after the last of these letters was penned.

OLIVER BROWN TO HIS WIFE.—NO. II.

Home, October 9, 1859.

My dear Martha : Having opportunity to write you once more, I improve it with the greatest pleasure to myself and with the hope of pleasing you.   I arrived here two days sooner than father and Watson.   They have gone back once more.   We are all well at present.   You can hardly think how I want to see you, or how lonesome I was the day I left you.   That day I never shall forget. I passed some good resolutions on my way to New York. I mean to live up to them.   Nothing else could strengthen me to do the right so much as the thought of you.   It is when I look at your picture that I am wholly ashamed of my every meanness, weakness, and folly.   I would not part with that picture for anything on earth—but the original. I have made a morocco case for it, and carry it close around my body.   I am more and more determined every day to live a more unselfish life.

Now, Martha, you can hardly conceive my great anxiety about you in your present situation, and you will certainly allow me to suggest some ideas to you for your own good Let me ask you to try to keep up good, cheerful spirits. Take plenty of sleep and rest ; plenty of out-door exercise. Bathe often.   And finally, do read good books, such as Parker's Sermons and Combe's Constitution of Man.   These books will do much to keep you from being lonesome.

Finally, Martha, do try to enjoy yourself.   Make the most of everything.

Remember your affectionate husband,

OLIVER BROWN.

WATSON BROWN TO HIS WIFE.—NO. I.

Chambersburg, Sept. 3rd, 1859.

Dear Bell : You can guess how I long to see you only by knowing how you wish to see me. I think of you all day and dream of you at night. I would gladly come home and stay with you always, but for that which brought me here—a desire to do something for others, and not to live wholly for my own happiness. I am at home, five miles north of Harper's Ferry, in an old house on the Kennedy farm, where we keep some of our things. Four of us sleep here. I came here to be alone. I was at Chambersburg a few days ago, and wrote you a few lines from there. I am beginning to look for a letter from you.———It is now dark, and I am all alone. But I have some good company. I have just received your letter of August 30th, and you may well think I am glad to hear from you. You may kiss the baby a good many times every day for me. I am thinking of you and him all the time. Tell Salmon that I know better how to pity him for having to stay at home, than he does me for being away. Tell him to keep a stiff upper lip.

Bell, nothing but the object before me could keep me from you. It is hard for you, no doubt, and I hope it will not last long ; though I have no thought of backing out till I see the thing well a-going.

Give my respects to all, and answer this as soon as you can, and tell me all the news.

Yours for ever,

WATSON.

WATSON BROWN TO HIS WIFE.—NO. II.

Chambersburg or Harper's Ferry, Sept. 16th.

Dear wife : As I may not have an opportunity to write to you for some time, I improve this.

I received your letter of September 14th, the night the girls got home, which I was very glad to get. O, Bell, I do want to see you and the little fellow very much ; but I must wait. There was a slave near here whose wife was sold off south the other day, and he was found in Thomas Kennedy's orchard, dead, the next morning. Cannot come home so long as such things are done here. We have only two black men with us as yet, but expect more. One of these has a wife and seven children in slavery. I sometimes feel as though I could not make this sacrifice ; but what would I not want others to do, were I in their place ! I find that always to live at home and among one's friends is never to know how much we love them. Keep up good courage, in spite of the cold weather ; and keep the baby warm. Write often, as father directs ; and I will do as well as I can about writing. It does me good to have you say you think of me, although I know it.

Ever your husband,

WATSON BROWN.

———

WATSON BROWN TO HIS WIFE.—NO. III.

Chambersburg, Oct. 14th, 1859.

Dear wife : I am again here, and have another opportunity to write. We are all well here and at home. We leave here this afternoon or to-morrow for the last time.

You will probably hear from us very soon after getting this, if not before.

The weather is very fine here. We had a slight frost last Monday and Tuesday nights. We have some addition to our family since the girls left. We are all eager for the work and confident of success. There was another murder committed near our place the other day, making in all five murders and one suicide, within five miles of our place, since we have lived there ; they were all slaves too. Tell Salmon that we should be very glad of his company, but he must keep cool where he is, and be sure to write when he knows where to direct.

O, Bell, I would give a good deal for your picture. If you have an opportunity to get it taken, I wish you would, and send it to me.

Give my regards to all the friends, and keep up good courage ; there is a better day a-coming. I can but commend you to yourself and your friends if I should never see you again.

From your affectionate husband,
WATSON BROWN.

These letters show not only the character of the writers, but that of the entire family to which they belonged. Gentle and loving, but brave as lions—with hearts warm with all the domestic affections, yet embracing in their scope every suffering human being, they constituted a group with scarcely a counterpart in history.

After remaining some weeks at the Kennedy farm, Brown re-visited the north. On the 14th of October, he is believed to have been in Baltimore on his way back. On Saturday, the 15th, the confederates held a council, and next day they again met to discuss their plan of operations. Before they separated, Captain Brown thus addressed them :—

" And now, gentlemen, let me press one thing on your minds. You all know how dear life is to you, and how dear your lives are to your friends ; and, in remembering that, consider that the lives of others are as dear to them as yours are to you. Do not, therefore, take the life of any man if you can possibly avoid it ; but if it is necessary to take life in order to save your own, then make sure work of it."

On the evening of this day—Sunday, the 16th—" he took occasion," says Mr. Redpath, " to report himself at Harper's Ferry. The announcement was made so loudly that it reached every home in the North, and penetrated every cabin in the Southern plantations."

CHAPTER VI.

HARPER'S FERRY.—SEIZURE OF THE ARSENAL.—CAPTURE OF
SLAVEHOLDERS, AND LIBERATION OF SLAVES.—ARRIVAL
OF MILITIA.—SEVERAL OF BROWN'S PARTY KILLED.—THE
ARSENAL CARRIED BY A PARTY OF MARINES.—BROWN
WOUNDED AND TAKEN PRISONER.—DEATHS OF WATSON AND
OLIVER BROWN.—PANIC IN VIRGINIA.—VISIT OF GOVERNOR
WISE AND OTHERS, AND LONG CONVERSATION WITH CAP-
TAIN BROWN.

BEFORE we proceed with our narrative of the
events which succeeded, it may be well to give
the following description of the place where they occurred, in the words of a Virginian topographer.

"Harper's Ferry is situated in Jefferson County,
Virginia, at the confluence of the Potomac and Shenandoah rivers, on a point just opposite the gap through
which the united streams pass the Blue Ridge, on their
way toward the ocean. The Ridge here is about twelve
hundred feet in height, showing bare, precipitous cliffs
on either side of the river, and exhibiting some of the
most beautiful and imposing natural scenery to be found
in the country. The town was originally built on two
streets, stretching along a narrow shelf between the
base of the bluff and the rivers, meeting at the point at
nearly a right angle, and named respectively Potomac
and Shenandoah-streets. To accommodate its increasing
population, the town has straggled up the steep bluff,

and, in detached villages and scattered residences, occupies the level ground above—about four hundred feet above the streams.

"It has altogether a population of five thousand, is distant from Richmond one hundred and seventy-three miles, from Washington city fifty-seven miles by turnpike road, and from Baltimore eighty miles by rail. Here the Baltimore and Ohio railroad crosses the Potomac by a magnificent covered bridge, nine hundred feet long, and passes along Potomac-street westward, its track lying forty feet above the river. The Winchester and Harper's Ferry railroad, lying along Shenandoah-street, is connected with the Baltimore and Ohio at the bridge. Potomac-street is entirely occupied by the workshops and offices of the national armory, and its entrance is enclosed by a handsome gate and iron railing. Nearly at the angle of junction are the old arsenal buildings, where usually from one hundred thousand to two hundred thousand stand of arms are stored. The other buildings on the point and nearer the bridge are railroad offices, hotels, eating-houses, stores, shops, &c. Shenandoah-street contains stores and dwelling-houses for half a mile or more, when we come to Hall's rifle-works, situated on a small island in the Shenandoah river."

The spot was well adapted for Brown's purposes. He was familiar with the fastnesses and intricacies of the neighbouring mountains, which would afford protection to a guerilla force, with ample facilities for

10

defence, or for a rapid retreat before overwhelming numbers.

It had been the original intention of Captain Brown to seize the arsenal at Harper's Ferry on the night of the 24th of October, and to convey the arms deposited there into the mountains, with a number of the wealthier inhabitants of the vicinity as hostages, until they should redeem themselves by the liberation of an equal number of their slaves. We cannot now discover the reasons which determined him to strike the blow on the night of the 16th. This decision, however necessary it may have been, was unfortunate for the success of the enterprise; for the confederates from Canada, Kansas, New England, and the neighbouring free states, who had made their preparations to be present on the 24th, were unable to take part in the undertaking at this earlier date. Many who started with this object stopped midway; for the blow had already been struck, and the leader of the enterprise was a prisoner. The negroes, also, in the neighbouring counties, many of whom had promised to be in readiness for the 24th, were unprepared for the earlier attack; and, before they could act in concert—which they could do only by secret nocturnal meetings—the suspicions of their masters were aroused, and they were deprived of every chance of joining their friends.

The first movement of the confederates on entering Harper's Ferry, some time after dark, was to extinguish the lights of the town, and take possession of the armory buildings. This they accomplished without opposition or exciting alarm; although they took the three watchmen prisoners, and locked them up in the guard-house. The number of the confederates in the town was only twenty-two, of whom seventeen were whites, and five were of negro blood. But outside the town there were others (who afterwards succeeded in escaping), to whom was assigned the duty of cutting the telegraph wires, and tearing up the railroad track after the train had passed.

At half-past ten the watchman on the Potomac bridge was captured and imprisoned; and at midnight his successor, coming down to take his place, was challenged by Brown's sentinels, but succeeded in making his escape, a shot being fired at him from the bridge. He gave the alarm, but it produced no immediate action.

The eastward-bound railway train arrived at a quarter past one o'clock, and the conductor was made aware that the bridge was in the possession of armed men. The officers of the train and some of the passengers attempted to walk across, but, seeing the muzzles of four rifles resting on a railing, they prudently turned back. One man, who proved to be a negro porter, refusing to surrender, was shot in the back, and died next morning. About this time, some shots were exchanged between a clerk of the hotel and one or two of the confederates. The passengers in the train went into the hotel, and remained there in great alarm for four or five hours; for the conductor, although leave

10*

was given him at three o'clock to proceed with his train, refused to do so till it was light enough for him to see for himself that all was safe. Being satisfied on this point, the train proceeded on its way, Brown himself walking across the bridge with the conductor, to ensure a safe passage. It appears to have been an unwise concession to allow it to proceed; but it was consistent with his uniform desire to inflict as little damage as possible in the prosecution of his object. The train carried the news of the seizure of the arsenal through the country, and to Washington. The passengers, taking all the paper they could find, wrote accounts of what had happened, which they threw from the windows as the train rushed onward.

After Brown had obtained possession of the arsenal, he despatched a party under Stevens to the houses of Colonel Lewis Washington and a Mr. Alstadtt, with orders to make them prisoners, and to bring their slaves, horses, and arms to the arsenal. This party of six men arrived at Colonel Washington's shortly after midnight; they took him prisoner, seized his arms, horses and carriage, and liberated his slaves. On his way back to the arsenal, Stevens took Mr. Alstadtt and his son prisoners, and liberated the slaves on their estate.

"On entering the armory," said Colonel Washington, "I found some eight or ten persons who recognised me. We were seated together and conversing, when the old man, whom we found by this time to be Brown, after asking our names, said, 'It is now too dark to write, but when it is sufficiently light, if you have not paper and pens, I will furnish you, and I require that you shall each write to your friends to send a negro man a-piece as ransom.' "

At daylight every person who appeared in the street was taken prisoner, until they numbered between forty and fifty men. When any of them asked the object of their captors, the uniform answer was, "To free the slaves." One of the workmen belonging to the arsenal, seeing Stevens standing sentinel at the gate, asked him by what authority they had taken possession of the public premises. He replied, "By the authority of God Almighty."

The news soon spread through Harper's Ferry that the place was in the possession of abolitionists and slaves. A panic ensued, report magnifying the handful of invaders into an army. Brown and his sons Watson and Oliver, with Stevens and two others, occupied the inside of the armory grounds; Kagi, with Lee-man, Taylor, Anderson, and Copeland, held the lower part of the town and the rifle works; Cook, Owen Brown, Tidd, Merriam, and Coppock were stationed at the Kennedy farm and at a building called the school-house, where they had a supply of arms and ammunition; while the rest were posted as sentinels at the bridges, at the corners of the principal streets, and the public buildings.

Early in the morning, Captain Brown sent an order to the hotel called the Wager House for breakfast for forty-five men—his hostages and company. By eight o'clock the number of persons detained was over sixty. The first shot fired after daybreak was by a man named Turner, who fired at the guards as they were ordering two citizens to halt. Boerley, a grocer, fired the second shot : a bullet from a Sharpe's rifle instantly killed him. Some Virginians soon afterwards obtained possession of a room overlooking the armory gates, from which they fired at a party of sentinels, killing one, and mortally wounding Watson Brown.

The effect which these proceedings caused in the town is thus described by a Virginian writer :—

"As the sun rose upon the scene, the reported outrages and the bodies of the murdered men showed that, from whatever source the movement came, it was of a serious nature. Sentinels, armed with rifles and pistols, were seen guarding all the public buildings, threatening death, or firing at all who questioned or interfered with them ; and the savage audacity with which they issued their orders gave assurance that the buildings were occupied by large bodies of men. Messages were despatched to all the neighbouring towns for military assistance, while panic-stricken citizens seized such arms as they could find, and gathered in small bodies on the outskirts of the town, and at points remote from the works. All was confusion and mystery. Even the sight of several armed negroes among the strangers did not at once excite suspicion that it was an anti-slavery movement ; and the report of one of the captured slaves, confirmatory of the fact, was received with doubt and incredulity. Indeed, so averse was the public mind to the acceptance of this belief, that the suggestion was everywhere received with derision, and any other explanation adopted in preference."

During the whole forenoon the confederates had possession of the town. The prisoners were occasionally allowed to visit their families, under guard, in order to quiet their apprehensions. Had Brown now carried out his original plan, he might have retreated with his prisoners to the mountains without opposition. Two motives appear to have caused him to delay. He wished to convince the people that the prisoners would suffer no cruelty while in his hands ; and he also held on in the hope of being joined by the slaves when the night set in.

This delay, however, was fatal to his plans ; for half an hour after noon a detachment of one hundred militia arrived from the neighbouring town of Charlestown. Their movements are thus described by the officer who commanded them :—

" I proceeded, with the few troops we had under arms, on foot, to Harper's Ferry, where we arrived about twelve o'clock. I found the citizens in very great excitement. By this time the insurgents occupied all the lower parts of the town, had their sentinels posted on all the different streets, and had shot one of our citizens, and a negro man who had charge of the depôt on the Baltimore and Ohio railroad. I here formed two companies of the citizens, and placed them under the command of Captain Lawson Botts, and Captain John Avis. Their forces were variously estimated from three hundred to five hundred strong, armed with Sharpe's rifles and revolvers.

"I detached the Jefferson Guards, under the command of Captain Rowan, and ordered them to cross the Potomac river in boats, about two miles above Harper's Ferry, to march down on the Maryland side, take possession of the bridge, and permit no one to pass. This order was strictly executed. The command under Captain Botts was ordered to pass down the hill below Jefferson's Rock, and take possession of the Shenandoah bridge, to leave a strong guard at that point, and to march down to the Galt House, in the rere of the arsenal buildings, in which we supposed their men were lodged. Captain Avis's command was ordered to take possession of the houses directly in front of the arsenal. Both the above commands were promptly executed, which prevented any escape."

The first attack was made by the Charlestown Guards at the Shenandoah bridge. William Thompson was taken prisoner, unwounded, having just previously returned from the school-house. One of his companions was killed at the same time. The rifle works were then attacked, and, as only five persons were stationed inside, the building was soon carried. Kagi and his men attempted to cross the river, and four of them succeeded in reaching the rock in the middle of it. Here they renewed the fight, drawing on them the fire of two hundred Virginians, who fired at them from both sides of the river. Yet not one cried for quarter, or ceased to keep up the unequal contest, until the corpse of Kagi, riddled with balls, floated down the river, followed by one of his faithful black comrades, and Leary lay mortally wounded. Copeland, the unwounded survivor, seeing that the fight was over, yielded himself a prisoner; and, with Leary, who lingered twelve hours in agony, was taken to the town and imprisoned. At the same time, Leeman, the youngest of the party, was pursued, and tried to escape by swimming the river. A dozen shots were fired at him as he ran; he partially fell, but rose again, threw away his gun, drew his pistols and tried to shoot, but both of them snapped. He then unsheathed his bowie-knife, cut off his accoutrements, and plunged into the river. One of the Virginian militia waded in after him. Leeman turned round, threw up his hands, and cried, "Don't shoot!" Unheeding this appeal, the brutal Virginian fired his pistol in the poor young fellow's face, and blew it into pieces.

While the fight at the rifle-works was going on, Captain Avis and his company took possession of the houses around the armory buildings. As they were doing so, Captain Turner was shot dead by a sentinel at the arsenal gate. At the same time, Jem, one of Colonel Washington's slaves; a free negro, his companion; and Dangerfield Newby,* also a free man of colour and a native of the neighbourhood, who had a wife and nine children in slavery in the vicinity, were killed while

---

* Newby had been the slave of his own father, a Virginian, by whom he was emancipated.

fighting on the side of Captain Brown. "Jem fought like a tiger," said an eyewitness; and of Newby, another said, "He fought like the very devil." Negroes *can* fight.

Shortly after the death of Captain Turner, a stray shot killed Mr. Beckman, the mayor of the town, who rashly came within range of the rifles. In the course of this fight, Oliver Brown being shot, retreated inside of the gate, and died in a few minutes after his entrance.

At the request of Mr. Kitzmiller, one of John Brown's hostages, Stevens accompanied him out of the arsenal, to try to make terms for the benefit of the prisoners; yet, although he carried a flag of truce, he was shot down and carried off by the militia.

Thompson was then ordered to prepare for death by a number of young Virginian gentlemen, whose conduct on this occasion is a vivid illustration of the effects of slavery. They tried to murder him in the parlour where he was detained a prisoner, and were only prevented from doing so by a young lady throwing herself between their rifles and his body; she afterwards gave as her reason for interposing, that "she did'nt want to have the carpet spoiled!" The Virginians then dragged him to the bridge, and flung him off; shot him as he was falling, and riddled him with bullets as he was seen crawling at the base of the pier.

Another party of men now arrived from Martinsburg, and attacked the armory buildings both in front and rear. Seeing them coming from both sides in overwhelming numbers, Captain Brown, after exchanging volleys with them, retreated into the engine-house. The company that attacked the rear broke open some windows, and released eighteen of Brown's prisoners. The attacking party, numbering fifty men, then made an attempt to carry the engine-house, but were repulsed with the loss of two killed and six wounded.

During the day, re-inforcements were constantly arriving from the surrounding counties ; the telegraph wires and the railway tracks were being repaired ; and the cabinet at Washington, the governor of Virginia, and the city of Baltimore had ordered troops to hasten to the scene of the outbreak. The last militia force from Maryland arrived at five in the afternoon, when the arsenal buildings and the remnant of Brown's party were completely hemmed in by armed men. The united forces were placed under the command of Colonel Baylor. An offer made to him by Brown to liberate the hostages if his followers were allowed to cross the bridge unmolested, was refused. By this time, as the night had fallen, the firing ceased on both sides.

The result of the day's fight left the position of the confederates a desperate one. In the river floated the corpses of Kagi, Leeman, Taylor, and Thompson. Imprisoned and dangerously wounded, lay Stevens and Leary. Copeland was a captive. In the street lay the dead bodies of Newby and others. In the engine-house were the remains of Oliver Brown and Dauphin Thompson ; while Watson Brown lay wounded past hope of recovery. The only unwounded survivers in the engine-house were Captain Brown, Anderson, Coppock,

and Shields Green, the negro. Eight Virginian hostages and a few armed negroes were with them. In
the town there were fifteen hundred men under arms,
who guarded every approach. During the night, Colonel Lee, with ninety United States marines and two
pieces of artillery, arrived, and took up their position in
premises in immediate proximity to the engine-house.

The scene in Harper's Ferry is thus described by a
correspondent of the *Frederick Herald*, a Maryland
paper :—

"The dead lay on the streets and in the river, and
were subjected to every indignity that a wild and
madly excited people could heap upon them. Curses
were freely uttered against them, and kicks and blows
inflicted upon them. The huge mulatto that shot Mr.
Turner was lying in the gutter in front of the arsenal,
with a terrible wound in his neck ; and, though dead
and gory, vengeance was unsatisfied, and many, as they
ran sticks into his wounds or beat him with them,
wished that he had a thousand lives, that all of them
might be forfeited in expiation and avengement of the
foul deed he had committed. Leeman lay upon a rock
in the river, and was made the target for the practice
of those who had captured Sharpe's rifles in the fray.
Shot after shot was fired at him, and when tired of this
sport, a man waded out to where he lay, and set him
up in grotesque attitudes, and finally pushed him off,
when he floated down the stream. His body, and
that of Thompson, which was also in the water, were
subsequently brought on shore, as were all of them

except a few which were taken by the physicians. It may be thought that there was cruelty and barbarity in this ; but the public mind had been frenzied by the outrages of these men, who, being outlaws, were regarded as food for carrion birds, and not as human creatures."

Up to the close of Monday evening, John Brown had successfully maintained his position. Hemmed in by an overwhelming force, he never once faltered in his resolution, or exhibited the slightest sign of fear. One of the hostages said that during the live-long night his voice was heard continually repeating, "Are you awake, men ? Are you ready?" He conversed freely with Colonel Washington, and referred to his sons. He said he had not pressed them to join in the expedition, but did not regret their loss—they had died in a good cause.

At seven o'clock the preparations for an assault began. Lieutenant Stuart first held a parley with the besieged. He demanded an unconditional surrender, promising them protection from immediate violence, and a trial by law. Captain Brown refused all terms but those he had previously demanded, which were, substantially, that they should be permitted to march out with their men and arms, taking their prisoners with them; and to proceed unpursued to the second toll-gate, when they would free their prisoners ; the soldiers would then pursue them, and they would fight if they could not escape. Of course this was refused, and Lieutenant Stuart pressed upon Brown his desperate position, and insisted upon unconditional surrender, as the only course that was left to the insurgents.

To this Brown would not consent, and the signal for attack was given. The marines, headed by Major Russell and Lieutenant Green, advanced in two lines, one on each side of the door. Two powerful fellows sprang between the lines, and with heavy sledge hammers attempted to batter down the door ; it swung and swayed, but appeared to be secured within by a rope, the spring of which deadened the effect of the blows. They then took hold of a ladder, and, advancing at a run, brought it with tremendous effect against the door. At the second blow it gave way, and the marines immediately advanced to the breach. One of them fell. The firing from the interior was rapid and sharp, but the marines quickly poured in, the firing ceased, and the work was done. In the assault, two of the marines were disabled, and Anderson fell mortally wounded. Before the fight began, Brown, according to the testimony of Colonel Washington, urged his hostages to seek places of safety—to keep themselves out of harm's way ; while the crowd in the streets, judging the confederates by their own standard, supposed that they were killing them in cold blood. The moment the marines entered, Colonel Washington, who had borne himself with an intrepid coolness which excited the admiration of Captain Brown, sprang upon one of the engines, told his fellow-prisoners to hold up their hands that they might be recognized as non-combatants, and then pointed out Brown and his party to the soldiers.

Lieutenant Green, as soon as he saw Brown, although he was unarmed (according to the testimony of a Virginian), struck him in the face with his sabre, and knocked him down. Not content with this brutality, he repeated the blow several times, and a soldier ran a bayonet twice into the old man's prostrate body.

When the insurgents were brought out, they were greeted with execrations, and it needed all the precautions that had been taken to save them from immediate massacre. The crowd, nearly every man of which carried a gun, swayed with tumultuous excitement, and cries of " Shoot them! shoot them!" rang from every side. The appearance of the liberated prisoners, however, all of whom had escaped injury, changed the current of feeling, and prolonged cheers took the place of howls and execrations.

The lawn in front of the engine-house presented a dismal sight after the assault. There lay the bodies of two of those who were killed on the previous day, and five of the wounded. One of these was Anderson, now at the last gasp. One of the dead men was Captain Brown's son Oliver. Near him lay his brother Watson, mortally wounded. The old man himself presented a gory spectacle, as he lay upon the grass. He had a severe bayonet wound in his side, and his face and hair were clotted with blood. Two only of the prisoners, Edwin Coppock and Shields Green, were unhurt.

A short time after Captain Brown was brought out, he revived, and talked earnestly to those about him, defending his course, and replying to their questions substantially as follows :—

" Are you Captain Brown of Kansas ?"

" I am sometimes called so."

" Are you Ossawattomie Brown ?"

" I tried to do my duty there."

" What was your present object ?"

" To free the slaves from bondage."

" Were any other persons, but those with you now, connected with the movement ?"

" No."

" Did you expect aid from the North ?"

" No ; there was no one connected with the movement but those who came with me."

" Did you intend to kill people in order to carry your point ?"

" I did not wish to do so, but you forced us to it."

He urged that he had the town at his mercy, and could have burned it, and murdered the inhabitants, had such been his design. He had treated his prisoners with courtesy, and complained that he was struck down like a wild beast. He said it was no part of his purpose to seize the public arms. He had arms and ammunition enough re-shipped from Kansas. He only intended to make the first demonstration at this point, when he expected to receive a rapid increase of allies.

An examination of his wounds proved that they were not necessarily fatal. He expressed a desire to live, and to have a regular trial. In his pockets nearly three hundred dollars in gold were found. Several important papers in his possession were taken charge of by Colonel Lee, on behalf of the government.

Captain Brown and his dying son were then carried to the guardhouse, and Stevens was soon brought and laid down beside them on the floor. Poor Watson lingered in agony till morning, and died in the arms of Coppock, whose letter to Mrs. Brown respecting the death of her sons contains the following passage :—

" I was with your sons when they fell. Oliver lived but a very few moments after he was shot. He spoke no word, but yielded calmly to his fate. Watson was shot at ten o'clock on Monday morning, and died about three o'clock on Wednesday morning. He suffered much. Though mortally wounded at ten o'clock, yet at three o'clock Monday afternoon he fought bravely against the men who charged on us. When the enemy were repulsed, and the excitement of the charge was over, he began to sink rapidly. After we were taken prisoners, he was placed in the guardhouse with me. He complained of the hardness of the bench on which he was lying. I begged hard for a bed for him, or even a blanket, but could obtain none for him. I took off my coat, and placed it under him, and held his head in my lap, in which position he died, without a groan or struggle."

Some time after the capture, it was reported that Cook was in the mountains, a few miles off. Scouting parties went out in search of him, but returned unsuccessful. Amongst others who went on this mission were the Independent Greys of Baltimore. They discovered, in the "school-house," about a mile from Harper's Ferry, a large quantity of military stores, comprising 102 Sharpe's rifles, 12 pistols, 10 kegs of gunpowder, 23,000 rifle percussion caps, 100,000 pistol percussion caps, 13,000 Sharpe's rifle cartridges, 160 Sharpe's primers, 55 bayonets, 483 pikes, 12 reams of cartridge paper, and a variety of other articles. Of these they took possession, and packing them on a large new waggon of Brown's, to which they harnessed a pair of horses that were grazing in the enclosure, they conveyed their prize to the arsenal.   In the course of the day another party in search of Cook reached the Kennedy farm, which they found unoccupied. A fire was yet smouldering in the stove, and the place was littered with trunks and carpet-bags, which had been broken open ; indicating a recent hurried visit of the party stationed by Captain Brown in this neighbourhood. When they found that he was defeated and a prisoner, they probably called here in order to secure the means of supporting themselves in the mountains while attempting to escape to the free states. As we do not wish to break the thread of our narrative in this place, we shall defer some particulars of their adventures to a future chapter. Amongst other articles found at the farm was a large quantity of provisions and wearing apparel, besides letters, copies of the constitution drawn up by Captain Brown, and other documents, which the party making the search eagerly secured, hoping they would throw some light on the outbreak.

Meanwhile all Virginia was in alarm. Her militia forces were everywhere called out, all business was for the time suspended, and they who had boasted of the stability of a state of society based upon the institution of slavery now acknowledged its insecurity. At Washington the military force was increased, every precaution was taken to keep the negroes down, and it was currently reported from various districts of Virginia and Maryland, that a general stampede of slaves had taken place.

" The inhabitants," says a newspaper reporter, " are by no means easy in their minds as to the temper of the slaves and free negroes among them. Colonel Washington, who was one of old Brown's hostages, does not spend his nights at home, and we are assured that many other wealthy slaveholders, whose residences lie at a distance from those of their neighbours also regard it prudent to lodge elsewhere for the present. It has been ascertained that many negroes in the neighbourhood, who had been tampered with by Cook and others of Brown's gang, had, at least, cognizance of the plans of the marauders, if they did not sympathize with them. There is no doubt that Washington's negro coachman, Jim, who was chased into the river by citizens and drowned, had joined the rebels with a good will. A pistol was found on him, and he had his pockets filled with ball cartridges when he was fished out of the river. It is certain that Brown's party was considerably larger when the attack was made than he has acknowledged, or was at first supposed." Such

11*

were the few indications of sympathy among the slaves which struck terror to the hearts of the Virginians.

Governor Wise came down on Tuesday by the mid-day train, and visited the prisoners. As the following sketch of this interview is from the pen of a Virginian reporter, we are compelled to omit some passages disfigured by ebullitions of pro-slavery ferocity :—

" Accompanied by Andrew Hunter, Esq., a distinguished lawyer of Jefferson county, the governor presently repaired to the guard-room, where the two wounded prisoners lay, and there had a protracted and interesting conversation with the chief of the outlaws. Brown was lying upon the floor with his feet to the fire, and his head propped upon pillows on the back of a chair. His hair was a mass of clotted gore, so that I could not distinguish the original colour ; his eye, a pale blue or gray ; nose, Roman ; and beard, originally sandy, was white and blood-stained.

" A few feet from the leader lay Stevens, a fine-looking fellow, quiet, not in pain apparently, and conversing in a voice as full and natural as if he was unhurt. His hands, however, lay folded upon his breast in a child-like way, a position that I observed was assumed by all those who had died or were dying of their wounds. Only those who were shot stone-dead lay as they fell.

" Brown was frank and communicative, answering all questions without reserve, except such as might implicate his immediate associates not yet killed or taken. He avers that the small pamphlet, many copies of which were found on the persons of the slain, entitled " Provisional Constitution and Ordinances for the People of the United States," was prepared principally by himself, and adopted at a convention of abolitionists held about two years ago at Chatham, Canada West, where it was printed ; that, under its provisions, he was appointed 'commander-in-chief.' His two sons and Stevens were each captains, and Coppock was a lieutenant. They each had their commission, issued by himself.

" He avers that the whole number operating under this organization was but twenty-two, each of whom had taken the oath required by article xlviii.; but he confidently expected large reinforcements from Virginia, Kentucky, Maryland, North and South Carolina, and other slave states, besides the free states ; taking it for granted that it was only necessary to seize the public arms, and place them in the hands of the negroes and non-slaveholders, to recruit his forces indefinitely. In this calculation he reluctantly and indirectly admitted that he had been entirely disappointed.

" Concluding that the prisoner must be seriously weakened by his vigils and his wounds, the governor ordered some refreshment to be given him, and appointing a meeting on the following day, took his leave. As some of us lingered, the old man recurred again to his sons, of whom he spoke several times, asking if we were sure they were both dead. He was assured that it was so.

" 'How many bodies did you take from the engine-house ?' he asked.

" He was told, three.

" 'Then,' said he, quickly, 'they are not both dead; there were three dead bodies there last night.   Gentlemen, my son is doubtless living, and in your power.   I will ask for him what I would not ask for myself ; let him have kind treatment, for he is as pure and noble-hearted a youth as ever breathed the breath of life.'

" His prayer was vain.   Both his boys lay stark and bloody by the armory wall.

" I had observed Stevens holding a small packet in his folded hands, and feeling some curiosity in regard to it, it was handed to me.   It contained miniatures of his sisters ; one, a sweet girlish face of about fourteen, the other more mature, but pretty.   What strange reflec-tions these incidents awakened !   This old man craves a boon for his noble boys which neither pain nor death can bring him to ask for himself.   The other clasps to his dying breast a remembrance of his gentle sisters and his father's elm-shaded cottage, far away in peaceful Connecticut."

When Governor Wise, on his return to Richmond, appeared before the people, he thus expressed his opinion of Captain Brown :—

" They are themselves mistaken who take him to be a madman.   He is a bundle of the best nerves I ever saw, cut, and thrust, and bleeding, and in bonds.   He is a man of clear head, of courage, fortitude, and simple ingenuousness.   He is cool, collected, and indomitable,

and it is but just to him to say that he was humane to
his prisoners, as attested to me by Colonel Washington
and Mr. Mills, and he inspired me with great trust in
his integrity, as a man of truth. He is fanatic, vain, and
garrulous, but firm, and truthful, and intelligent. His
men, too, who survive, except the free negroes with
him, are like him. He professes to be a Christian in
communion with the Congregational Church of the
north, and openly preaches his purpose of universal
emancipation ; and the negroes themselves were to be
the agents, by means of arms, led on by white com-
manders. When Colonel Washington was taken, his
watch, and plate, and jewels, and money were demanded,
to create what they call a 'safety fund,' to compensate
the liberators for the trouble and expense of taking
away his slaves. This, by a law, was to be done with
all slaveholders. Washington, of course, refused to deliver up anything; and it is remarkable that the only
thing of material value which they took, besides his
slaves, was the sword of Frederick the Great, which
was sent to General Washington. This was taken by
Stevens to Brown, and the latter commanded his men
with that sword in this fight against the peace and
safety of Washington's native state ! He promised
Colonel Washington to return it to him when he was
done with it. And Colonel Washington says that he,
Brown, was the coolest and firmest man he ever saw in
defying danger and death. With one son dead by his
side, and another shot through, he felt the pulse of his
dying son with one hand and held his rifle with the

other, and commanded his men with the utmost composure, encouraging them to be firm, and to sell their lives as dearly as they could."

As soon as it was known that Captain Brown was not dead, and that three of his followers had been protected from the fury of the populace, four well-known members of the democratic party hastened to Harper's Ferry—to extort, if possible, confessions from the prisoners which might criminally implicate some of the champions of their political opponents, the republicans. A great object would be effected and a vast amount of "political capital" secured by the democrats, if it could be shown to the nation that any leading republicans were privy to such a daring onslaught on the slaveocracy, who were at that very juncture at the pinnacle of their influence in the United States ; being omnipotent with the President, Mr. Buchanan,* and having a

* When the Border Ruffians invaded Kansas, slaughtered her inhabitants in cold blood, and sacked her towns and settlements, the marauders were rewarded with appointments by the federal government.   The following instances are enumerated by the Albany *Evening Journal.*

S. W. Clark murdered a man named Barber in Kansas, by shooting him in the back.   For this practical illustration of modern democracy, he was made a purser in the navy.

James Gardiner, who co-operated with Clark in the murder of Barber, was appointed postmaster at Lawrence.

Jones headed the mob which sacked Lawrence.   He was paid off with a lucrative office in New Mexico.

Frederick Emery, one of the murderers of Phillips, at Leaven-

majority in the federal Senate and House of Representatives. These expectant visitors were two from the
south, namely, Mr. Wise, the governor of Virginia; and
Senator Mason, the author of the Fugitive Slave Law:
and two from the north, Mr. Johnson, a United States
marshal; and Mr. Vallandingham, a member of congress from Ohio.

Never did a recorded conversation produce a greater
change in public opinion. Before its publication Brown
was regarded by all, except those to whom he was intimately known, as a reckless fanatic, if not actually insane; while, after it, from every corner of the land,
came expressions of wonder and admiration, and, from
many quarters, there was no lack of outspoken sympathy and veneration. Brown lay on the floor, wounded
and a prisoner, surrounded by enemies, with the gallows
staring him in the face, and, whilst thus circumstanced,
he gave an answer as calm, clear, and collected to every
question that was put to him by his numerous interro-

worth, was compensated by the appointment of Receiver of the
Land Office at Ogden.

J. S. Murphy, who helped the assassination of Phillips, and
who was notoriously one of the gang by whom Hopps was scalped,
was made agent for the Pottawottamie Indians.

Rush Elmore, who made a persevering effort to assassinate
J. H. Kagi, was elevated to the office of United States District
Judge.

Russell and Waddell furnished teams and provisions to the
border ruffians who invaded Kansas and seized the ballot-boxes
in 1856. For this they have been given immense contracts by
the government.

gators, as if he had been sitting at home at North Elba, surrounded by his family. We give this remarkable conversation in full, from the report published at the time.

Mason.—Can you tell us who furnished money for your expedition?

Brown.—I furnished most of it myself. I cannot implicate others. It is by my own folly that I have been taken. I could easily have saved myself from it, fI had exercised my own better judgment rather than yielded to my feelings. I should have gone away, but I had thirty odd prisoners, whose wives and daughters were in tears for their safety, and I felt for them. Besides, I wanted to allay the fears of those who believed we came here to burn and kill. For this reason I allowed the train to cross the bridge, and gave them full liberty to pass on. I did it only to spare the feelings of those passengers and their families, and to allay the apprehension that you had got here in your vicinity a band of men who had no regard for life and property, nor any feeling of humanity.

Mason.—But you killed some people passing along the streets quietly.

Brown.—Well, sir, if there was anything of that kind done, it was without my knowledge. Your own citizens, who were my prisoners, will tell you that every possible means were taken to prevent it. I did not allow my men to fire, or even to return fire, when there was danger of killing those we regarded as innocent persons, if

I could help it. They will tell you that we allowed ourselves to be fired at repeatedly, and did not return it.

A bystander.—That is not so. You killed an unarmed man at the corner of the house, over there (at the water tank), and another besides.

Brown.—See here, my friend; it is useless to dispute or contradict the report of your own neighbours, who were my prisoners.

Mason.—If you would tell us who sent you here—who provided the means—that would be information of some value.

Brown.—I will answer freely and faithfully about what concerns myself; I will answer anything I can with honour, but not about others.

Vallandingham.—Mr. Brown, who sent you here?

Brown.—No man sent me here; it was my own prompting, and that of my Maker; or that of the devil, whichever you please to ascribe it to. I acknowledge no master in human form.

Vallandingham.—Did you get up the expedition yourself?

Brown.—I did.

Vallandingham.—Did you get up this document called a constitution?

Brown.—I did. They are a constitution and ordinances of my own contriving and getting up.

Vallandingham.—How long have you been engaged in this business?

Brown.—From the breaking out of the difficulties in

Kansas. Four of my sons had gone there to settle, and induced me to go. I did not go there to settle, but because of the difficulties.

Mason.—How many are engaged in this movement? I ask these questions for your own safety.

Brown.—Any questions that I can honourably answer, I will; not otherwise. So far as I am myself concerned, I have told everything truthfully. I value my word, sir.

Mason.—What was your object in coming?

Brown.—We came to free the slaves, and only that.

A young man (in the uniform of a volunteer company).—How many men in all had you?

Brown.—I came to Virginia with eighteen men besides myself.

A volunteer.—What in the world did you suppose you could do here in Virginia with that amount of men?

Brown.—Young man, I don't wish to discuss that question here.

A volunteer.—You could not do anything.

Brown.—Well, perhaps your ideas and mine on military subjects would differ materially.

Mason.—How do you justify your acts?

Brown.—I think, my friend, you are guilty of a great wrong against God and humanity—I say it without wishing to be offensive—and it would be perfectly right for any one to interfere with you so far as to free those you wilfully and wickedly hold in bondage. I do not say this insultingly.

Mason.—I understand that.

Brown.—I think I did right, and that others will do right who interfere with you, at any time, and all times. I hold that the golden rule, "Do unto others as you would that others should do unto you," applies to all who would help others to gain their liberty.

Lieutenant Stuart.—But you don't believe in the Bible?

Brown.—Certainly I do.

Vallandingham.—Where did your men come from? Did some of them come from Ohio?

Brown.—Some of them.

Vallandingham.—From the Western Reserve, of course! None came from southern Ohio?

Brown.—Oh, yes. I believe one came from Steuben-ville, down not far from Wheeling.

Vallandingham.—Have you been in Ohio this summer?

Brown.—Yes, sir.

Vallandingham.—How lately?

Brown.—I passed through to Pittsburg on my way, in June.

Vallandingham.—Were you at any county or state fair there?

Brown.—I was not there since June.

Mason.—Did you consider this a military organization in this paper? (Showing a copy of John Brown's constitution and ordinance). I have not yet read it.

Brown.—I did in some measure. I wish you would give that paper your close attention.

Mason.—You considered yourself the commander-in-chief of this provisional military force ?

Brown.—I was chosen, agreeably to the ordinance of a certain document, commander-in-chief of that force.

Mason.—What wages did you offer ?

Brown.—None.

Lieutenant Stuart.—"The wages of sin is death."

Brown.—I would not have made such a remark to you, if you had been a prisoner and wounded in my hands.

A bystander.—Did you not promise a negro in Gettysburg twenty dollars a month ?

Brown.—I did not.

A bystander.—He says you did.

Vallandingham.—Were you ever in Dayton, Ohio ?

Brown.—Yes, I must have been.

Vallandingham.—This summer ?

Brown.—No ; a year or two since.

Mason.—Does this talking annoy you at all ?

Brown.—Not in the least.

Vallandingham.—Have you lived long in Ohio ?

Brown.—I went there in 1805. I lived in Summit county, which was then Trumbull county. My native place is York state.*

Vallandingham.—Do you recollect a man in Ohio named Brown, a noted counterfeiter ?

Brown.—I do. I knew him from a boy. His father

---

* This must be a mistake of the reporter ; Brown was a native of Connecticut.

was Henry Brown, of Irish or Scotch descent. The family was very low.

Vallandingham.—Have you ever been in Portage County ?

Brown.—I was there in June last.

Vallandingham.—When in Cleveland, did you attend the Fugitive Slave Law convention there ?

Brown.—No. I was there about the time of the sitting of the court to try the Oberlin rescuers. I spoke there, publicly, on that subject. I spoke on the Fugitive Slave Law, and my own rescue. Of course, so far as I had any influence at all, I was disposed to justify the Oberlin people for rescuing the slave, because I have myself forcibly taken slaves from bondage. I was concerned in taking eleven slaves from Missouri to Canada, last winter. I think that I spoke in Cleveland before the convention. I do not know that I had any conversation with any of the Oberlin rescuers. I was sick part of the time I was in Ohio. I had the ague. I was part of the time in Ashtabula county.

Vallandingham.—Did you see anything of Joshua R. Giddings there ?[*]

Brown.—I did meet him.

Vallandingham.—Did you converse with him ?

---

[*] Mr. Giddings, for many years one of the ablest, most eloquent, and most courageous opponents of slavery in the United States House of Representatives, was especially obnoxious to the slave power. He was recently appointed United States Consul in Montreal by President Lincoln.

Brown.—I did.   I would not tell you, of course, anything that would implicate Mr. Giddings; but I certainly met with him, and had a conversation with him.

Vallandingham.—About that rescue case?

Brown.—Yes, I did.   I heard him express his opinion upon it very freely and frankly.

Vallandingham.—Justifying it?

Brown.—Yes, sir.   I do not compromise him, certainly, in saying that.

A bystander.—Did you go out to Kansas under the auspices of the Emigrant Aid Society?

Brown.—No, sir; I went out under the auspices of John Brown, and nobody else.

Vallandingham.—Will you answer this?   Did you talk to Giddings about your expedition here?

Brown.—No, sir! I won't answer that, because a denial of it I would not make; and to make an affidavit of it, I should be a great dunce.

Vallandingham.—Have you had any correspondence with parties at the north on the subject of this movement?

Brown.—I have had no correspondence.*

A bystander.—Do you consider this a religious movement?

Brown.—It is, in my opinion, the greatest service a man can render to his God.

A bystander.—Do you consider yourself an instrument in the hands of Providence?

---

* One report reads thus: the other omits the word " no,

Brown.—I do.

A bystander.—Upon what principle do you justify your acts ?

Brown.—Upon the golden rule. I pity the poor in bondage that have none to help them. That is why I am here ; it is not to gratify any personal animosity, or feeling of revenge, or vindictive spirit. It is my sympathy with the oppressed and the wronged, that are as good as you, and as precious in the sight of God.

A bystander.—Certainly. But why take the slaves against their will ?

Brown.—I never did.

A bystander.—You did in one instance, at least.

Stevens. (To the inquirer, interrupting Brown).—You are right, sir, in one case—(here he groaned with pain) —in one case, I know the negro wanted to go back. —(To Brown). Captain, the gentleman is right.

A bystander (To Stevens).—Where did you come from ?

Stevens.—I lived in Ashtabula county, Ohio.

Vallandingham.—How recently did you leave Ashtabula county ?

Stevens.—Some months ago. I never resided there any length of time. I have often been through there.

Vallandiugham.—How far did you live from Jefferson ?

Brown. (To Stevens).—Be very cautious, Stevens, about an answer to that ; it might commit some friend. I would not answer it at all.

Stevens, who had been moaning, as if the exertion of speaking was too much for him, seemed content to abide by the captain's advice. He turned on his side, and remained silent.

Vallandingham. (To Captain Brown).—Who are your advisers in this movement?

Brown.—I cannot answer that. I have numerous sympathizers throughout the entire north.

Vallandingham.—In northern Ohio?

Brown.—No more there than anywhere else—in all the free states.

Vallandingham.—But are you not personally acquainted in southern Ohio?

Brown.—Not very much.

Vallandingham. (To Stevens).—Were you at the convention last June?

Stevens.—I was.

Vallandingham. (To Captain Brown).—You made a speech there?

Brown.—I did, sir.

A bystander.—Did you ever live in Washington city?

Brown.—I did not. I want you to understand, gentlemen, that I respect the rights of the poorest and weakest of the coloured people, oppressed by the slave system, just as much as I do those of the most wealthy and powerful. That is the idea that has moved me, and that alone. We expected no reward except the satisfaction of endeavouring to do for those in distress —the greatly oppressed—as we would be done by.

The cry of distress, of the oppressed, is my reason, and the only thing that prompted me to come here.

A bystander.—Why did you do it secretly?

Brown.—Because I thought that necessary to success, and for no other reason.

A bystander.—And you think that honourable, do you? Have you read Gerrit Smith's last letter?

Brown.—What letter do you mean?

A bystander.—The *New York Herald* of yesterday, in speaking of this affair, mentions a letter in which he says, " that it is folly to attempt to strike the shackles off the slave by the force of moral suasion or legal agitation, " and predicts that the next movement made in the direction of negro emancipation will be an insurrection in the South.

Brown.—I have not seen a *New York Herald* for some days past ; but I presume, from your remarks about the gist of the letter, that I should concur with it. I agree with Mr. Smith, that moral suasion is hopeless.* I don't think the people of the slave states will ever consider the subject of slavery in its true light until some other argument is resorted to than moral suasion.

* In January, 1860, a committee was appointed, through the influence of the slaveholders, by the Senate of the United States, for the purpose of summoning witnesses, and making a thorough enquiry into every circumstance that could throw light upon Captain Brown's attempt at Harper's Ferry. Amongst these witnesses was a Mr. Arny, who was called three times before the committee on the 18th of January. He declared that the

12*

Vallandingham.—Did you expect a general rising of the slaves in case of your success ?

Brown.—No, sir ; nor did I wish it. I expected to gather strength from time to time ; then I could set them free.

Vallandingham.—Did you expect to hold possession here till then ?

Brown.—Well, probably I had quite a different idea. I do not know that I ought to reveal my plans. I am here a prisoner, and wounded, because I foolishly allowed myself to be so. You overrate your strength when you suppose I could have been taken if I had not

substance of his conversation with Brown, in 1858, in regard to his movements, was that Brown proposed to run off slaves from the South, so as to make that kind of property insecure. Arny testifies that he opposed this mode of interference with slavery. Brown said he disliked the "do nothing" policy of the abolitionists, and that they never would effect anything by their milk-and-water principles. As to the Republicans, Brown thought they were of no account, for they were opposed to meddling with slavery in the states where it existed. His doctrine was to free the slaves by the sword. Arny wanted to know how he reconciled that with his Quaker peace principles which he held when he first knew him, more than twenty years before. Brown said that the aggressions of slavery, the outrage and robbery perpetrated upon himself and members of his family, and the violation of law by Atchison and others in Kansas, from 1854 to that time, had convinced him that peace was but an empty word ; and he repeated his dislike to the Republican party and abolitionists, saying they were cravens—that they had refused to assist him. Arny testified that he declined to have anything further to do with his operations.

allowed it. I was too tardy, after commencing the open attack, in delaying my movements through Monday night, and up to the time I was attacked by the government troops. It was all occasioned by my desire to spare the feelings of my prisoners and their families, and the community at large.

Vallandingham.—Did you not shoot a negro on the bridge, or did not some of your party?

Brown.—I knew nothing of the shooting of the negro.

Vallandingham.—What time did you commence your organization over in Canada?

Brown.—It occurred about two years ago. If I remember right, it was, I think, in 1858.

Vallandingham.—Who was the secretary?

Brown.—That I would not tell if I recollected; but I do not remember. I think the officers were elected in May, 1858. I may answer incorrectly, but not intentionally. My head is a little confused by wounds, and my memory of dates and such like is somewhat confused.

Dr. Biggs.—Were you in the party at Dr. Kennedy's house?

Brown.—I was the head of that party. I occupied the house to mature my plans. I would state here that I have not been in Baltimore to purchase percussion caps.

Dr. Biggs.—What number of men was at Kennedy's?

Brown.—I decline to answer that.

Dr. Biggs.—Who lanced that woman's neck on the hill?

Brown.—I did.   I have sometimes practised in surgery, when I thought it a matter of humanity or of necessity—when there was no one else to do it ; but I have not studied surgery.

Dr. Biggs. (To the persons around).—It was done very well and scientifically.   These men have been very clever* to the neighbours, I have been told, and we had no reason to suspect them, except that we could not understand their movements.   They were represented as eight or nine persons ; on Friday there were thirteen.

Brown.—There were more than thirteen.

Questions were now asked by almost every one in the room.

Question.—Where did you get arms to obtain possession of the armory ?

Brown.—I bought them.

Question.—In what state ?

Brown.—That I would not state.

Question.—How many guns ?

Brown.—Two hundred Sharpe's rifles, and two hundred revolvers—what is called the Massachusetts Arms Company's revolvers—a little under the navy size.

Question.—Why did you not take that swivel you left in the house ?

Brown.—I had no occasion for it.   It was given to me a year or two ago.

A reporter.—I do not wish to annoy you ; but if you

---

* Clever, in America, means *kind, good-natured.*

have anything else you would like to say, I will report it.

Brown.—I do not wish to converse any more; I have nothing to say. I will only remark to these reporting gentlemen, that I claim to be here in carrying out a measure I believe to be perfectly justifiable, and not to act the part of an incendiary or ruffian ; but, on the contrary, to aid those suffering under a great wrong. I wish to say, furthermore, that you had better—all you, people of the south—prepare yourselves for a settlement of this question. It must come up for settlement sooner than you are prepared for it, and the sooner you commence that preparation, the better for you. You may dispose of me very easily. I am nearly disposed of now ; but this question is still to be settled—this negro question, I mean. The end of that is not yet. These wounds were inflicted upon me—both the sabre cut on my head, and the bayonet stabs in the different parts of my body—some minutes after I had ceased fighting, and had consented to surrender for the benefit of others, and not for my own benefit. [Several persons vehemently denied this statement. Without noticing the interruption, the Captain continued :] I believe the major here (pointing to Lieutenant Stuart) would not have been alive but for me. I might have killed him just as easy as I could kill a mosquito, when he came in ; but I supposed that he came in only to receive our surrender. There had been long and loud calls of surrender from us—as loud as men could yell—but in the confusion and excitement I suppose we were not heard.

I do not believe the major, or any one else, wanted to butcher us after we had surrendered.

An officer present here stated that special orders had been given to the marines not to shoot anybody ; but when they were fired upon by Brown's men, and one of them had been killed, and another wounded, they were obliged to return the compliment. Captain Brown insisted, with some warmth, that the marines fired first.

An officer.—Why did you not surrender before the attack ?

Brown.—I did not think it was my duty or interest to do so. We assured our prisoners that we did not wish to harm them, and that they should be set at liberty. I exercised my best judgment, not believing the people would wantonly sacrifice their fellow-citizens. When we offered to let them go upon condition of being allowed to change our position about a quarter of a mile, the prisoners agreed by vote among themselves to pass across the bridge with us. We wanted them only as a sort of guarantee for our own safety—that we should not be fired into. We took them, in the first place, as hostages, and to keep them from doing any harm. We did kill some men when defending ourselves ; but I saw no one fire except directly in self-defence. Our orders were strict not to harm any one not in arms against us.

Question.—Well, Brown, suppose you had every nigger in the United States, what would you do with them ?

Brown. (In a loud tone, and with emphasis).—Set them free, sir !

Question.—Your intention was to carry them off and free them ?

Brown.—Not at all.

A Bystander.—To set them free would sacrifice the life of every man in this community.

Brown.—I do not think so.

A bystander.—I know it. I think you are fanatical.

Brown.—And I think you are fanatical. " Whom the gods would destroy, they first make mad;" and you are mad.

Question.—Was your only object to free the negroes?

Brown.—Absolutely our only object.

A bystander.—But you went and took Colonel Washington's silver and watch.

Brown.—Oh, yes ; we intended freely to have appropriated the property of slaveholders, to carry out our object. It was for that, and only that; and with no design to enrich ourselves with any plunder whatever.

Question. Did you know Sherman in Kansas ? I understand you killed him.

Brown.—I killed no man except in fair fight. I fought at Black Jack, and at Ossawattomie ; and if I killed anybody, it was at one of those places.

During this conversation, the wounded prisoners lay stretched upon miserable pallets. Brown's long gray hair was matted and tangled, and his hands and clothes were smeared with blood, and begrimed with dirt—the effect of continued exposure to the smoke of powder. Yet his manner and conversation were courteous and affable, and he appeared to make a favourable impression upon his auditory. When Mr. Vallandingham returned to Ohio, he testified :—"It is vain to underrate either the man or the conspiracy. Captain John Brown is as brave and resolute a man as ever headed an insurrection, and, in a good cause, and with a sufficient force, would have been a consummate partisan commander. He has coolness, daring, persistency, the stoic faith and patience, and a firmness of will and purpose unconquerable. He is the farthest possible remove from the ordinary ruffian, fanatic, or madman. Certainly it was one of the best planned and best executed conspiracies that ever failed."

CHAPTER VII.

October 19th to November 2nd, 1859.

CAPTAIN BROWN AND HIS FELLOW-PRISONERS REMOVED TO
CHARLESTOWN JAIL.—EXAMINED BEFORE A PRELIMINARY
COURT.—THE GRAND JURY REPORT A TRUE BILL AGAINST
THEM.—BROWN ASKS FOR DELAY, WHICH IS REFUSED.—
THE TRIAL CONTINUES THROUGH FOUR DAYS.—HE IS
FOUND GUILTY.—HIS SPEECH IN COURT.—THE SENTENCE.

ON Wednesday, October 19th, after lying unattended
and bloody on the floor of the guardhouse for more
than thirty hours, interrogated by the curious, and insulted by the mob, the prisoners were conveyed under an escort of marines, to Charlestown, the county
town of Jefferson county, a few miles from Harper's
Ferry. They were accompanied by Governor Wise and
Mr. Hunter, and were lodged in jail under charge of
Captain Avis, to whom they were committed by a justice of the peace, on the oaths of Mr. Wise and two
others, "for feloniously conspiring with each other, and
other persons unknown, to make an abolition insurrection and open war against the commonwealth of Virginia," and for the additional crimes of murder, and
" conspiring with slaves to rebel and to make insurrection." On the same day a warrant was issued to the
sheriff, commanding him to summon eight justices of
the peace to hold a preliminary court of examination
on Tuesday, the 25th of October.

In the interval Captain Brown addressed the following letter to Judge Tilden of Massachusetts, applying for counsel for himself and his fellow prisoners.

CAPTAIN BROWN TO JUDGE TILDEN.

Charlestown, Jefferson Co., Oct. 22, 1859.
To the Hon. Judge Tilden.

Dear Sir : I am here a prisoner, with several sabre cuts on my head, and bayonet stabs in my body. My object in writing is to obtain able and faithful counsel for myself and fellow-prisoners, five in all, as we have the faith of Virginia, pledged through her governor, and numerous prominent citizens, to give us a fair trial. Without we can obtain such counsel from without the slave states, neither the facts in our case can come before the world, nor can we have the benefit of such facts as might be considered mitigating, in the view of others, upon our trial. I have money on hand here to the amount of two hundred and fifty dollars, and personal property sufficient to pay a most liberal fee to yourself, or any able man who will undertake our defence, if I can be allowed the benefit of said property. Can you, or some other good man, come on immediately, for the sake of the young men prisoners, at least ? My wounds are doing well.

Do not send an ultra-abolitionist.

Very respectfully yours,

JOHN BROWN.

P.S. The trial is set for Wednesday next, the 26th instant.

J. W. CAMPBELL, *Sheriff, Jefferson Co.*

On the appointed day the preliminary court assembled, Colonel Davenport presiding. At half-past ten o'clock in the forenoon, the prisoners were conducted from the jail under a guard of eighty armed men. Another military force was stationed around the court-house, which was bristling with bayonets on all sides.

Brown and Coppock were manacled together. The prisoners presented a pitiable sight when brought into court, Brown and Stevens being unable to stand without assistance. Brown had three sword-cuts in his body, and a sabre-cut on the head. Stevens had three balls in his head, two in his breast, and one in his arm ; he was also cut on the forehead. He seemed less injured than Brown, but looked haggard and depressed.

Charles B. Harding, attorney for Jefferson county, and Andrew Hunter, counsel for the state, appeared for the prosecution. The sheriff read the commitment of the prisoners, and the prosecuting attorney asked the court that counsel might be assigned them. The presiding magistrate then inquired if the prisoners had counsel. Captain Brown replied :—

" Virginians : I did not ask for quarter at the time I was taken. I did not ask to have my life spared. The governor of the state of Virginia tendered me his assurance that I should have a fair trial ; but under no circumstances whatever will I be able to attend to my trial. If you seek my blood, you can have it at any moment, without this mockery of trial.

" I have no counsel. I have not been able to advise with any one. I know nothing about the feelings of my fellow-prisoners, and am utterly unable to attend in any way to my own defence.   My memory don't serve me.   My health is insufficient, although improving.

" If a fair trial is to be allowed us, there are mitigating circumstances that I would urge in our favour. But if we are to be forced with a mere form—a trial for execution—you might spare yourselves that trouble. I am ready for my fate.   I do not ask a trial.   I beg for no mockery of a trial—no insult—nothing but that which conscience gives or cowardice would drive you to practise.

" I ask again to be excused from the mockery of a trial.   I do not know what the special design of this examination is.   I do not know what is to be the benefit of it to the commonwealth.   I have now little further to ask, other than that I may not be foolishly insulted, as only cowardly barbarians insult those who fall into their power."

Without paying the slightest attention to these remarks, the court assigned Charles J. Faulkner and Lawson Botts, both Virginians and pro-slavery men, as counsel for the defendants.

Harding.—(Addressing Brown). Are you willing to accept these gentlemen as counsel ?

Brown.—I wish to say that I have sent for counsel. I did apply, through the advice of some persons here, to some persons whose names I do not now recollect, to act as counsel for me ; and I have sent for other counsel, who have not had time to reach here, and have had no possible opportunity to see me. I wish for counsel, if I am to have a trial ; but if I am to have nothing but the mockery of a trial, as I said, I do not care anything about counsel. It is unnecessary to trouble any gentleman with that duty.

Harding.—You are to have a fair trial.

Brown.—I am a stranger here, and do not know the disposition or character of the gentlemen named. I have applied for counsel of my own, and doubtless could have them, if I am not, as I have said before, to be hurried to execution before they can reach here. But if that is the disposition that is to be made of me, all this trouble and expense can be saved.

Harding.—The question is, do you desire the aid of Messrs. Faulkner and Botts as your counsel ? Please to answer yes or no.

Brown.—I cannot regard this as an examination under any circumstances. I would prefer that they should exercise their own pleasure. I feel it as a matter of little account to me. If they had designed to assist me as counsel, I should have wanted an opportunity to consult with them at my leisure.

Mr. Harding then addressed each of the other prisoners separately, and each stated his willingness to be defended by the counsel named.

The court issued peremptory orders that the press should not publish detailed testimony, as it would render the getting of a jury before the circuit court impossible.

Eight witnesses were then examined, who testified to

the arrest of citizens, the occupation of the armory, the fight, the casualties of the conflict, and the self-avowed object of the liberators.   Kitzmiller admitted that Stevens was fired at and shot while under a flag of truce, with which, accompanied by the witness, and at his request, he had left the armory, to permit him to try to accommodate matters for the safety of the citizens detained there; that Brown, while the Virginian prisoners were in his power, treated them with great courtesy and respect; and repeatedly stated that his only object was to liberate the negroes, and that, to accomplish it, he was willing to fight.   The witnesses who were prisoners in the armory also testified that during the conflict they were requested by the confederates to keep themselves out of the fire of the marines.   At one stage of the proceedings, Stevens, weak from his wounds, appeared to be fainting, and a mattress was procured for him, on which he reposed during the remainder of the examination.   The prisoners were remanded to the circuit court for trial.

Hardly had the preliminary court adjourned, ere the circuit court met.   At two o'clock the grand jury were called, and charged by Judge Parker.   The preliminary court reported the result of their examination, and the grand jury retired with the witnesses.   At five o'clock they returned and asked to be discharged for the day.

On Wednesday, the 26th, they reassembled, and after a sitting of two hours reported a true bill against each of the prisoners.   First, for conspiring with negroes to produce insurrection ; second, for treason in the commonwealth ; and, third, for murder.

The prisoners were brought into court, accompanied by a body of armed men. Cannon were stationed in front of the court-house, and an armed guard were patrolling round the jail. Brown looked better to-day, his eye was not so much swollen. Stevens had to be supported, and reclined on a mattress on the floor of the court-room—unable to sit, and breathing with great difficulty. The prisoners were compelled to stand during the indictment, but they did so with difficulty. Stevens had to be supported by two bailiffs.

Before the indictment of the grand jury was read, Brown spoke as follows :—

"I do not intend to detain the court, but barely wish to say, as I have been promised a fair trial, that I am not now in circumstances that enable me to attend a trial, owing to the state of my health. I have a severe wound in the back, or rather in one kidney, which enfeebles me very much. But I am doing well, and I only ask for a very short delay of my trial, and I think I may get able to listen to it ; and I merely ask this that, as the saying is, 'the devil may have his due'— no more. I wish to say, further, that my hearing is impaired, and rendered indistinct, in consequence of wounds I have about my head. I cannot hear distinctly at all. I could not hear what the court has said this morning. I would be glad to hear what is said on my trial, and am now doing better than I could expect to do under the circumstances. A very short delay would do all I would ask. I do not presume to ask more than a very short delay, so that I may in some degree recover, and be able at least to listen to my trial, and hear what questions are asked of the citizens, and what their answers are. If that could be allowed me, I should be very much obliged."

Mr. Hunter said that the request was rather premature. The arraignment should be made, and this question could then be considered.

The court ordered the indictment to be read, so that the prisoner could plead guilty or not guilty, and it would then consider Mr. Brown's request.

The indictment was now read, and each of the prisoners pleaded "Not guilty," and demanded to have a separate trial. As soon as the prisoners had responded to the arraignment, Mr. Hunter rose and said, "The state elects to try John Brown first."

Mr. Botts said, "I am instructed by Brown to say that he is mentally and physically unable to proceed with his trial at this time. He has heard to-day that counsel of his own choice will be here, whom he will, of course, prefer. He only asks for a delay of two or three days. It seems to be but a reasonable request, and I hope the court will grant it."

After some conversation on this request, the court stated that, if physical inability were shown, a reasonable delay must be granted. As to the expectation of other counsel, that did not constitute a sufficient cause for delay, as there was no certainty about their coming. Under the circumstances in which the prisoners were situated, it was rational that they should seek delay. The brief period remaining before the close of the term of the court rendered it necessary to proceed as expeditiously as practicable, and to be cautious about granting delays. He would request the physician who had attended Brown to testify as to his condition.

The physician was called and swore that Brown was able to go on with the trial, and that he did not think his wounds were such as to affect his mind and recollection. The court accordingly refused to postpone the trial.

The afternoon sitting was occupied in obtaining a jury. The jailer was ordered to bring Brown into court. He found him in bed, from which he declared himself unable to rise. He was accordingly brought into court on a cot, which was set down within the bar. The prisoner lay most of the time with his eyes closed, and the counterpane drawn up close to his chin. The jury were then called and sworn. The court excluded those who were present at Harper's Ferry during the insurrection, and saw the prisoners perpetrating the act for which they were about to be tried. They were all from distant parts of the country, mostly farmers—some of them owning a few slaves. The examination was continued until twenty-four were decided by the court and counsel to be competent jurors. Out of these twenty-four, the counsel for the prisoners had a right to strike off eight, and then twelve were drawn by ballot out of the remaining sixteen.*

* As the above particulars are derived from the pens of southern reporters, they probably give no idea of the *manner* in which Brown's jury was impannelled. We shall, therefore, give a graphic account, by an eye-witness, of the calling of the jury who tried Edwin Coppock.

A stolid and heavy man stands up before the judge to answer the necessary questions. His countenance is lighted by the hope of getting a chance to give his voice against the prisoner. You can see this as plainly as if he told you.

Judge.—Were you at Harper's Ferry, sir, during these proceedings?

Juror.—No, sir.

Judge.—You are a freeholder of this county?

Juror.—Yes, sir.

Judge.—Have you heard the evidence in the other cases?

Juror.—(Eagerly.) Yes, sir.

Judge.—I mean, if you have heard the evidence, and are likely to be influenced by it, you are disqualified here. Have you heard much of the evidence?

Juror.—No, sir.

Judge.—Have you expressed any opinion as to the guilt of these parties?

Juror.—Yes, sir. (Eagerly again.)

Judge.—Are you, then, capable of judging this case according to the evidence, without reference to what you have before heard said?

Juror.—Yes, sir.

Judge.—Have you any conscientious scruples, which will prevent your finding this man guilty, because the death-penalty may be his punishment?

Juror.—Yes, sir. (Promptly.)

Judge.—I think you do not understand my question. I ask

Mr. Botts, as counsel for Brown, did not challenge a single juror, though many were open to objection. At five o'clock the prisoner was carried back to jail, and the court adjourned till next morning.

On Thursday morning, October 27th, the trial began. Brown was brought from jail, supported on either side, being too feeble to walk alone—and was laid down on his cot within the bar. The plea of insanity, advanced by some mistaken friends in the northern states, was brought forward before the jury were sworn, by the production of a telegram from Ohio. But Brown indignantly rejected the idea of putting in such a plea, and said, in continuation :—" I will add, if the court will allow me, that I look upon it as a miserable artifice and pretext of those who ought to take a different course in regard to me, if they took any at all, and I view it with contempt more than otherwise. Insane persons, so far as my experience goes, have but little ability to judge of their own sanity; and if I am insane, of course I should think I knew more than all the rest of the

you, if you would hesitate to find this man guilty, because he would be hung if you did ?

Juror looks puzzled, overcome by the abstract nature of the proposition.

Judge.—This man will be hung, if you find him guilty. Will that certainty of his being hung prevent you from finding him guilty, if the evidence convinces you he is so ?

Juror.—(Catching the idea.) No, sir—no, sir.

Judge.—Very well, sir ; you can take your seat as a juror.

world. But I do not think so. I am perfectly unconscious of insanity, and I reject, so far as I am capable,
any attempts to interfere on my behalf on that score."

The course taken by Brown this morning made it
evident that he sought no postponement for the mere
sake of delay. Yet, though he again asked for a sus-
pension of the proceedings in his case for one day only,
until a lawyer in Ohio to whom he had written, and
who had telegraphed a reply, should arrive in Charlestown, the court again refused to grant the request, and
ordered the examination to proceed. Mr. Hunter, in
opposing the request, expressed his belief that Brown
was less solicitous for a fair trial than to give to his
friends the time and opportunity to organize a rescue;
whilst Mr. Harding asserted that the prisoner was
merely shamming sickness—although he could not
stand unsupported for any length of time, and was
covered with wounds, not one of which had healed.

The following quotation from the telegraphic reports
of the Associated Press of the United States will give
us the clue to this indecent haste :—

"There is an evident intention to hurry the trial
through, and execute the prisoners as soon as possible
—fearing attempts to rescue them. It is rumoured
that Brown is desirous of making a full statement of
his motives and intentions through the press; but the
court has refused all access to reporters—fearing that
he may put forth something calculated to influence the
public mind, and to have a bad effect on the slaves.
The reason given for hurrying the trial is, that the

people of the whole country are kept in a state of excitement, and a large armed force is required to prevent attempts at rescue."

The jury were sworn, and the indictment was read. The court permitted the prisoner, while arraigned, to remain on his pallet. The indictment charged insurrection, treason, and murder. Brown pleaded, " Not guilty." Mr. Hunter then stated the facts he designed to prove by the evidence for the prosecution ; he reviewed the laws relating to the offences charged on the prisoner, and concluded by urging the jury to cast aside all prejudices, and give the prisoners a fair and impartial trial; and not to allow their hatred of abolitionists to influence them against those who had raised the black flag on the soil of Virginia.

Mr. Green, who had been requested by the court to act as assistant counsel for the prisoners in the absence of Mr. Faulkner, who had gone home, replied that,

1. To establish the charge of *treason*, it must be proven that the prisoner attempted to establish a separate and distinct government within the limits of Virginia, and the purpose also of any treasonable acts ; and this, not by any confessions of his own elsewhere made, but by two different witnesses for each and every act.

2. To establish the charge of a conspiracy with slaves, the jury must be satisfied that such conspiracy was effected within the state of Virginia, and within the jurisdiction of this court. If it was done in Maryland

this court could not punish the act. If it was done within the limits of the armory at Harper's Ferry, it was not done within the limits of this state, the government of the United States holding exclusive jurisdiction within the said grounds.

3. Over murder the court had no jurisdiction, if committed within the limits of the armory; and, in the case of Mr. Beckham, if he was killed on the railroad bridge, it was committed within the state of Maryland, which claims jurisdiction up to the armory grounds.

Mr. Botts supported these views. Mr. Hunter replied that the prisoner had attempted to break down the existing government of the commonwealth, and establish on its ruins a new government; he had usurped the office of commander-in-chief of this new government, and, together with his whole band, professed allegiance and fidelity to it; he represented not only the civil authorities of the state, but our own military; he is doubly, trebly, and quadruply guilty of treason. He was also guilty, on his own notorious confession, in advising conspiracy. In regard to the charge of murder, the proof will be, that this man was not only actually engaged in murdering our citizens, but that he was the chief director of the whole movement. No matter whether he was present on the spot or a mile off, he is equally guilty. Mr. Hunter further stated that the jurisdiction of Jefferson county in criminal offences committed at Harper's Ferry had been uninterrupted and unchallenged, whether they were committed on the government property or not.

In the afternoon session the examination of witnesses was commenced. The conductor of the railway train narrated the circumstances of its stoppage on the morning of Monday the 17th, and thus described his interview with Captain Brown :—" I met a man whom I now recognize as Coppock, and asked what they meant. He replied, 'We don't want to injure you or detain your train. You could have gone at three o'clock : all we want is to free the negroes.' I then asked if my train could now start, and went to the guard at the gate, who said, 'There is Captain Smith ; he can tell you what you want to know.' I went to the engine house, and the guard called Captain Smith. The prisoner at the bar came out, and I asked him if he was captain of these men. He replied he was. I asked him if I could cross the bridge, and he peremptorily responded, 'No, sir.' I then asked him what he meant by stopping my train. He replied, 'Are you the conductor on that train ?' I told him I was, and he said, " Why, I sent you word at three o'clock that you could pass.' I told him that, after being stopped by armed men on the bridge, I would not pass with my train. He replied, 'My head for it, you will not be hurt;' and said he was very sorry. It was not his intention that any blood should be spilled; it was bad management on the part of the men in charge of the bridge. I then asked him what security I would have that my train would pass safely, and asked him if he would walk over the bridge ahead of my train with me. He called a large, stout man to accompany him, and one of my passengers, Mr. McByrne, asked to accompany me ; but Brown ordered him to get into the train, or he would take them all prisoners in five minutes ; but it was advice more in the form of a threat. Brown accompanied me ; both had rifles. As we crossed the bridge, the three armed men were still in their places. When we got across, Brown said to me, ' You, doubtless, wonder that a man of my age should be here with a band of armed men ; but if you knew my past history, you would not wonder at it so much !' My train was then through the bridge, and I bade him good morning, jumped on my train, and left him. "

Colonel Washington was afterwards examined, and described his arrest. He testified that Captain Brown permitted his prisoners to keep in a safe position ; that he never spoke rudely or insultingly to them ; that he allowed them to go out to quiet their families by assuring them of their personal safety ; that he heard him direct his men, on several occasions, not to fire on an unarmed citizen ; and that he assured the captives they should be well treated, and none of their property destroyed.

This evidence ended the proceedings of the court on Thursday.

On Friday morning, October 28th, the examination of witnesses for the prosecution was resumed. Colonel

Washington stated that he heard Captain Brown frequently complain of the bad faith of the people in firing on his men when under a flag of truce ; " but he heard him make no threat, nor utter any vindictiveness against them."

Mr. Hunter then laid before the jury the printed constitution and ordinances of the provisional government, and a large bundle of letters and papers. He asked that the sheriff, who knew the handwriting of the prisoner, should be brought forward to identify it.

Brown.—I will identify any of my handwriting, and save all that trouble. I am ready to face the music.

Hunter.—I prefer to prove them by Mr. Campbell.

The bundle of letters was then opened. The handwriting of each was identified by Campbell ; and each letter was then handed to Brown, who said in a firm voice, " Yes, that is mine," as soon as he recognized his writing.

Mr. Ball, master machinist of the armory, one of the prisoners made by Brown, testified as to his arrest, stating : " I was conducted to Captain Brown, who told me his object was to free the slaves, and not to make war on the people ; that my person and my private property would be safe ; that his war was against the accursed system of slavery ; that he had power to do it, and would carry it out ; it was no child's play he had undertaken."

John Alstadtt testified to his having been taken from his farm by a party of men, who declared that their object was " to free the country from slavery." He also described his detention at the engine-house, and various incidents of the fight there.

Albert Grist described his arrest by a man armed with a spear on Sunday night, and his detention in the armory until he was dismissed by Captain Brown, after delivering a message to the conductor of the train. " Brown," he said, " declared that his object was to free the slaves. I told him there were not many there. He replied : ' The good book says, we are all free and equal.' "

At the afternoon session, Henry Hunter, a young man about twenty-two years of age (son of Andrew Hunter, Esq. who conducted the prosecution), was examined as to the murder of Thompson :—

Question.—Did you witness the death of this man Thompson ?

Answer.—I witnessed the death of one whose name I have been informed was Thompson.

Q.—The one who was a prisoner ?

A.—Yes, sir.

Q.—Well, sir, what were the circumstances attending it ?

A.—Do you ask my own connection with it, or simply a description of the circumstances ? Shall I mention the names ?

Mr. Andrew Hunter.—Every bit of it, Henry ; state all you saw.

Witness.—There was a prisoner confined in the parlour of the hotel, and after Mr. Beckham's death he was shot down by a number of us there belonging to this sharp-shooting band.

Mr. Andrew Hunter.—Will you allow him to state, before proceeding further, how he was connected with Mr. Beckham?

Mr. Green.—Certainly, sir.

Witness.—He was my grand-uncle, and my special friend—a man I loved above all others. After he was killed, Mr. Chambers and myself moved forward to the hotel for the purpose of taking the prisoner out and hanging him. We were joined by a number of other persons, who cheered us on in that work. We went up into the room where he was bound, with the undoubted and undisguised purpose of taking his life. At the door we were stopped by persons guarding the the door, who remonstrated with us, and the excitement was so great that persons who remonstrated with us at one moment would cheer us on the next. We burst into the room where he was, and found several around him, but they offered only a feeble resistance. We brought our guns down to his head repeatedly,—myself and another person,—for the purpose of shooting him in the room. There was a young lady there, the sister of Mr. Foulke, the hotel-keeper, who sat in this man's lap, covered his face with her arms, and shielded him with her person whenever we brought our guns to bear; she said to us, " For God's sake, wait, and let the law take its course." My associate shouted to kill him. " Let us shed his blood," were his words. All round were shouting, " Mr. Beckham's life was worth ten thousand of these vile abolitionists." I was cool about it, and deliberate ; my gun was pushed up by some one who seized the barrel, and I then moved to the back part of the room, still with purpose unchanged, but with a view to divert attention from me, in order to get an opportunity, at some moment when the crowd would be less dense, to shoot him. After a moment's thought, it occurred to me that it was not the proper place to kill him. We then proposed to take him out and hang him ; some portion of our band then opened a way to him, and, first pushing Miss Foulke aside, we slung him out of doors ; I gave him a push, and many others did the same ; we then shoved him along the platform and down to the trestle-work of the bridge ; he begged for his life all the time, very piteously at first. Before we took him out of the room, I asked the question what he came here for : he said their only purpose was to free the slaves or die ; then he begged, "Don't take my life —a prisoner;" but I put the gun to him, and he said, " You may kill me, but it will be revenged ; there are eighty thousand persons sworn to carry out this work." That was his last expression. We bore him out on the bridge with the purpose of hanging him ; we had no rope, and none could be found; it was a moment of wild excitement ; two of us raised our guns—which one was first I do not know—and pulled the trigger; before he had reached the ground, I suppose some five or six shots had been fired into his body ; he fell on the rail- road track, his back down to the earth, and his face up. We then went back for the purpose of getting another one (Stevens), but he was sick or wounded, and persons around him, and I persuaded them myself to let him alone. I said, " Don't let us operate on him, but go, around and get some more." We did this act with a purpose, thinking it right and justifiable under the circumstances, and fired and excited by the cowardly, savage manner in which Mr. Beckham's life had been taken.

Mr. Andrew Hunter.—Is that all, gentlemen ?

Mr. Botts.—Yes, sir.

Mr. Andrew Hunter (to the witness).—Stand aside.

This sworn statement of a cold-blooded murder, by one of the perpetrators, elicited not a word of condemnation from any journal in the southern states.

Several witnesses for the defence were then called, but none of them answered to their subpœnas. There was now no doubt that the trial would be closed at once ; for no earnest effort had been made, by the counsel for the defence, to compel the court to grant a brief delay ; when, unexpectedly, John Brown arose from his mattress and addressed the judge :—

" May it please the court ;—I discover that, notwithstanding all the assurances I have received of a fair trial, nothing like a fair trial is to be given me, as it would seem. I gave the names, as soon as I could get them, of the persons I wished to have called as witnesses, and was assured that they would be subpœnaed. I wrote down a memorandum to that effect, saying where these parties were; but it appears that they have not been subpœnaed, so far as I can learn. And now I ask, if I am to have anything at all deserving the name and shadow of a fair trial, that this proceeding be deferred until to-morrow morning; for I have no counsel, as I have before stated, on whom I feel I can rely; but I am in hopes counsel may arrive who will attend to seeing that I get the witnesses who are necessary for my defence. I am myself unable to attend to it. I have given all the attention I possibly could to it, but am unable to see or know about them, and can't even find out their names; and I have nobody to do any errands, for my money was all taken from me when I was sacked and stabbed, and I have not a dime. I had two hundred and fifty or sixty dollars in silver and gold taken from my pocket, and now I have no possible means of getting anybody to do my errands for me, and I have not had all the witnesses subpœnaed. They are not within reach, and are not here. I ask at least until to-morrow morning, to have something done, if anything is designed; if not, I am ready for anything that may come up."

Here the prisoner lay down again, drew his blanket over him, closed his eyes, and appeared to sink in tranquil slumber.

This bold speech, with its modest request (which was seconded by Mr. Hoyt,* who, we are told, "arose amid great sensation," and stated that other counsel would arrive to-night), shamed the Virginian advocates into an

---

* A young Boston lawyer, who arrived this day as a volunteer counsel for Captain Brown.

immediate resignation, and the court into an adjourn-
ment till the following morning.

In the course of this day, John E. Cook was committed to Charlestown jail; a reward for his apprehension had been offered by Governor Wise, and this
temptation had secured his capture in the free state of
Pennsylvania, where he had been hiding among the
mountains.

On Saturday, October 29th, the court assembled at
ten o'clock, when Captain Brown was brought in and
laid on his pallet. Mr. Samuel Chilton, of Washington, and Mr. Henry Griswold, of Ohio, appeared as additional counsel for the prisoner.

Mr. Chilton rose, and said that on his arrival in
Charlestown, after finding that the counsel whom he
had come to assist had retired from the case, he hesitated about undertaking it; it was only at the urgent
solicitation of the prisoner and his friends that he had
now consented to do so; but, not having had time to
read the indictment or the evidence already given, it
was impossible for him to discharge the full duty of a
counsel. Mr. Griswold was similarly situated. A
short delay—a few hours only—would enable them to
make some preparation.

The court refused to comply with this request, and
referred, with some asperity, to the recent speech of the
prisoner. "This term," said the judge, "will very
soon end; and it is my duty to endeavour to get
through with all the cases, if possible, in justice to the

prisoners, and in justice to the state. The trial must proceed."

The evidence for the defence was now proceeded with. The only portions of it which it is necessary for us to quote are those which refer to the object Brown had in view, and a few brief incidents of the conflict not elsewhere noted.

John P. Dangerfield deposed as follows :—" Was a prisoner in the hands of Captain Brown at the engine-house. About a dozen black men were there, armed with pikes, which they carried most awkwardly and unwillingly. During the firing they were lying about asleep, some of them having crawled under the engines. From the treatment of Captain Brown, he had no personal fear of him or his men during his confinement. Saw one of John Brown's sons shot in the engine-house ; he fell back, exclaiming, 'It's all up with me !' and died in a few moments. Another son came in and commenced to vomit blood ; he was wounded while out with Mr. Kitzmuller [carrying a flag of truce]. The prisoner frequently complained that his men were shot down while carrying a flag of truce. Brown promised safety to all descriptions of property except slave-property. After the first attack, Captain Brown cried out to surrender. Saw Brown wounded on the hip by a thrust from a sabre, and several sabre-cuts on his head. When the latter wounds were given, Captain Brown appeared to be shielding himself, with his head down, but making no resistance. The parties outside appeared to be firing as they pleased."

Major Mills, master of the armory, "was one of the hostages of Captain Brown in the engine-house. . . Brown's son went out with a flag of truce, and was shot. Heard Brown frequently complain that the citizens had acted in a barbarous manner. He did not appear to have any malicious feeling. His intentions were to shoot nobody unless they were carrying or using arms."

Brown here asked whether the witness saw any firing on his part that was not purely defensive.

Witness.—It might be considered in that light, perhaps; the balls came into the engine-house pretty thick.

A conversation here ensued between Captain Brown and Mr. Dangerfield, the former witness, as to the part taken by the prisoner in not unnecessarily exposing his hostages to danger. Mr. Dangerfield testified that his wife and daughter had been allowed to visit him unmolested; and that free verbal communication had been permitted with those outside. "We were treated kindly, but were compelled to stay where we didn't want to be."

Samuel Snider, the next witness, testified to the same effect; asserting that Brown honestly endeavoured to protect his hostages, and wished to make peace more for their sake than for his own personal safety.

Captain Simms, commander of the Frederick Volunteers, stated in evidence :—"Brown complained that his men were shot down like dogs, while bearing a flag of truce. I told him that they must expect to be shot down like dogs, if they took up arms in that way. Brown said he knew what he had to undergo when he came there. He had weighed the responsibility, and should not shrink from it. He said he had full possession of the town, and could have massacred all the inhabitants, had he thought proper to do so ; but, as he had not, he considered himself entitled to some terms. He said he had shot no one who had not carried arms. I told him that Mayor Beckham had been killed, and that I knew he was altogether un-armed. He seemed sorry to hear of his death, and said, ' I fight only those who fight me.' I saw Stevens at the hotel after he had been wounded, and shamed some young men who were endeavouring to shoot him as he lay in his bed, apparently dying. . . . I have no sympathy for the acts of the prisoner, but I regard him as a brave man."

Two other witnesses corroborated the foregoing evi-dence as to the courage and humanity of Brown, and the barbarity of the Virginians. The counsel for the defence here rested their case.

Mr. Chilton then asked for time to prepare his speech for the defence, saying that he had not had op-portunity to become sufficiently acquainted with the case to do so, and pleading that, the case being one of life and death, they ought not to be too precipitate.

The court here consulted with the jurors, who ex-pressed themselves very anxious to get home.

The judge said he was desirous to try this case precisely as he would try another, without any reference
at all to the feeling out of doors.

Mr. Hoyt declared that he was physically incapable
of speaking to-night, even if fully prepared. He had
worked very hard last night to get the law points,
until he fell unconscious from exhaustion and fatigue.
For the last five days and nights he had slept only ten
hours, and it seemed to him that justice to the prisoner
demanded the allowance of a little time in a case so
extraordinary in all its aspects as this.

The Court.—We may have the opening argument for
the prosecution to-night, at any rate.

Mr. Harding would not like to open the argument
now, unless the case was to be finished to-night. He
was willing, however, to submit the case to the jury
without a single word, believing they would do the
prisoner justice. The prosecution had been met not
only on the threshold, but at every step, with obstruc-
tions to the progress of the case. If the case was not
to be closed to-night, he would like to ask the same
indulgence for the other side, that he might collate the
notes of the evidence he had taken.

The judge inquired what length of time the defence
would require for argument on Monday morning. He
could then decide whether to grant the request or not.

After consultation, Mr. Chilton stated that there
would be only two speeches by himself and Mr. Griswold, not occupying more than two hours and a half in
all ; but the court ordered the prosecution to proceed,

as Mr. Hunter entered an earnest protest against delay. He then addressed the court at some length, and the trial was adjourned till Monday.

The court re-assembled early on Monday morning, the 31st of October, and Captain Brown was brought from prison, as usual between files of armed men, and laid down on his bed within the bar. He looked better than on the previous day. The court-room and every approach to it were densely crowded. The counsel on both sides addressed the jury at considerable length. Mr. Hunter wound up his speech for the prosecution with the following demand :—

"We therefore ask his conviction, to vindicate the majesty of the law. While we have patiently borne delays, as well here as outside in the community, in preservation of the character of Virginia, that plumes itself on its moral character, as well as physical, and on its loyalty and its devotion to truth and right, we ask you to discard anything else, and render your verdict as you are sworn to do. . . . Justice is the column upon which Deity sits. There is another column which represents its mercy. You have nothing to do with that."

The jury then retired, and, after an absence of three-quarters of an hour, returned into court with their verdict. At this moment the whole court-room, including even the space round the prisoner's couch within the bar, was thronged with a silent and attentive crowd. After recapitulating the offences set forth in the indictment, the clerk of the court said :—" Gentlemen of the jury, what say you ? Is the prisoner at the bar, John Brown, guilty, or not guilty?"

Foreman.—Guilty.

Clerk.—Guilty of treason, and conspiring and advising with slaves and others to rebel, and murder in the first degree ?

Foreman.—Yes.

Not the slightest sound was heard in the court as this verdict was thus returned and read. Not the slightest expression of elation or triumph was uttered from the hundreds present, who, a few minutes before, had joined in heaping threats and imprecations on the prisoner's head ; nor was this silence interrupted during the whole of the time occupied by the forms of the court. Brown himself said not even a word, but, as on previous days, turned to adjust his pallet, and then composedly stretched himself upon it.

Mr. Chilton moved an arrest of judgment, on account of errors both in the indictment and the verdict. However, counsel on both sides being too much exhausted to go on, the motion was ordered to stand over till the following day.

The 1st and 2nd of November were devoted to the trial of Edwin Coppock. On the second day, during the absence of the jury which was engaged on this case, Captain Brown was brought into court. He walked with much difficulty, and every movement appeared to be attended with pain, although his features did not betray it. It was late, and the gaslights gave an almost deathly pallor to his face. He seated himself near his counsel, and, after once resting his head upon his right hand, remained entirely motionless, and for a time appeared indifferent to all that passed, and unconscious of the execrations audibly whispered by some of the spectators. While the judge read his decision on the points of exception which had been submitted, Brown sat very firm, with lips tightly compressed. When the clerk directed him to stand and say why sentence should not be passed upon him, he rose and leaned slightly forward, his hands resting on the table. He spoke in a voice singularly gentle and mild, but somewhat hesitatingly, as if unprepared to speak at this time. It had been generally anticipated that all the prisoners would be condemned at the same time, and hence he had not expected to be sentenced so soon. His address was as follows :—

"I have, may it please the court, a few words to say. In the first place, I deny everything but what I have all along admitted—the design on my part to free the slaves. I intended certainly to have made a clear thing of that matter, as I did last winter, when I went into Missouri, and there took slaves without the snapping of a gun on either side, moved them through the country, and finally left them in Canada. I designed to have done the same thing again, on a larger scale.

That was all I intended.* I never did intend murder, or treason, or the destruction of property, or to excite

* Finding that what he said on this occasion, about his plan for liberating the slaves, had been misapprehended, Captain Brown addressed the following explanation to Mr. Hunter :—

Charlestown, Va., Nov. 22, 1859.

Andrew Hunter, Esq.

Dear Sir : I have just had my attention called to a seeming confliction between the statement I at first made to Governor Wise and that which I made at the time I received my sentence, regarding my intentions respecting the slaves we took about the Ferry. There need be no such confliction, and a few words of explanation will, I think, be quite sufficient. I had given Governor Wise a full and particular account of that ; and when called in court to say whether I had anything further to urge, I was taken wholly by surprise, as I did not expect my sentence before the others. In the hurry of the moment, I forgot much that I had before intended to say, and did not consider the full bearing of what I then said. I intended to convey this idea : that it was my intention to place the slaves in a condition to defend their liberties if they would, without any bloodshed, but not that I intended to run them out of the slave states. I was not aware of any such apparent confliction until my attention was called to it, and I do not suppose that a man in my then circumstances should be superhuman in respect to the exact purport of every word he might utter. What I said to Governor Wise was spoken with all the deliberation I was master of, and was intended for truth ; and what I said in court was equally intended for truth, but required a more full explanation than I there gave. Please make such use of this as you think calculated to correct any wrong impression I may have given.

JOHN BROWN.

or incite slaves to rebellion, or to make insurrection. I have another objection : and that is, it is unjust that I should suffer such a penalty. Had I interfered in the manner which I admit, and which I admit has been fairly proved (for I admire the truthfulness and candor of the greater portion of the witnesses who have testified in this case)—had I so interfered in behalf of the rich, the powerful, the intelligent, and so-called great, or in behalf of any of their friends, either father, mother, brother, sister, wife, or children, or any of that class, and suffered and sacrificed what I have in this interference, it would have been all right, and every man in this court would have deemed it an act worthy of reward rather than punishment.

"This court acknowledges, as I suppose, the validity of the law of God. I see a book kissed here which I suppose to be the Bible, or, at least, the New Testament. That teaches me that all things ' whatsoever I would that men should do unto me I should do even so to them.' It teaches me further, to ' remember them that are in bonds as bound with them.' I endeavoured to act up to that instruction. I say, I am yet too young to understand that God is any respecter of persons. I believe that to have interfered as I have done, as I have always freely admitted I have done, in behalf of His despised poor, was not wrong, but right. Now, if it is deemed necessary that I should forfeit my life for the furtherance of the ends of justice, and mingle my blood further with the blood of my children, and with the blood of millions in this slave country whose rights are

disregarded by wicked, cruel, and unjust enactments—
I submit : so let it be done.

"Let me say one word further. I feel entirely satisfied with the treatment I have received on my trial.
Considering all the circumstances, it has been more
generous than I expected. But I feel no consciousness
of guilt. I have stated from the first what was my
intention, and what was not. I never had any design
against the life of any person, nor any disposition to
commit treason, or excite slaves to rebel, or make any
general insurrection. I never encouraged any man to
do so, but always discouraged any idea of that kind.

"Let me say, also, a word in regard to the statement
made by some of those connected with me. I hear it
has been stated by some of them that I have induced
them to join me. But the contrary is true. I do not
say this to injure them, but as regretting their weakness. There is not one of them but joined me of his
own accord, and the greater part at their own expense.
A number of them I never saw, and never had a word
of conversation with, till the day they came to me, and
that was for the purpose I have stated.

"Now I have done."

Perfect quiet prevailed during the delivery of this
speech, and when it was concluded, the judge proceeded
to pass sentence. After a few preliminary remarks, he
stated that no doubt could exist of the guilt of the
prisoner, and sentenced him to be hanged by the neck
till he was dead, on Friday, the 2nd day of December.

CHAPTER VIII.

November, 1859.

THE ROUTE TO NORTH ELBA.— THE HOMESTEAD AND ITS ORNA-
MENTS.—THE FARM, AND WHY JOHN BROWN BOUGHT IT.—
THE FAMILY.—BROWN AMONG HIS CHILDREN.—HIS THEO-
LOGY.—HIS POLITICS.—THE CHARGE OF INSANITY.—PECU-
NIARY CONDITION OF THE FAMILY.

WE shall now lay before the reader, with a few unimportant omissions, Mr. Thomas Wentworth Higginson's deeply interesting narrative of his visit to the farm at North Elba, for the purpose of announcing to the family the progress of the trial, and escorting Mrs. Brown to Charlestown, Virginia. It should be premised that Mr. Higginson is a resident of Worcester, Massachusetts ; that he is a member of the American Anti-Slavery Society, and a well known abolitionist ; that he took a warm interest in the struggle in Kansas, which he had visited for the purpose of aiding the free-soil settlers ; and—though personally unknown to the family—had been for some time acquainted with Captain Brown, whom he greatly respected for his devoted and singleminded character :—

"The traveller into the enchanted land of the Adirondack has his choice of two routes, from Keeseville to the Lower Saranac Lake, where his out-door life is to begin. The one least frequented and most difficult should be selected, for it has the grandest mountain pass that the Northern states can show.   After driving twenty-two miles of mountain road from Keeseville, past wild summits bristling with stumps, and through villages where every man is black from the iron foundry or from the charcoal pit, your pathway makes a turn at the little hamlet of Wilmington, and you soon find yourself facing a wall of mountain, with only glimpses of one wild gap, through which you must penetrate. In two miles more you have passed the last house this side the Notch, and you then drive on over a rugged way, constantly ascending, with no companion but the stream which ripples and roars below.   Soon the last charcoal clearing is past, and thick woods of cedar and birch close around you—the high mountain on your right comes nearer and nearer, and close beside, upon your left, are glimpses of a wall, black and bare as iron, rising sheer for four hundred feet above your head.   Coming from the soft marble country of Vermont, and from the pale granite of Massachusetts, there seems something weird and forbidden in this utter blackness.   On your left, the giant wall now appears nearer—now retreats again; on your right foams the merry stream, breaking into graceful cascades—and across it the great mountain Whiteface, seamed with slides.   Now the woods upon your left are displaced by the iron wall, almost touching the road-side; against its steep abruptness scarcely a shrub can cling, scarcely a fern flutter—it takes your breath away; but five miles of perilous driving conduct you through it; and beyond this stern passway, this cave of iron, lie the lovely lakes and mountains of the Adirondack, and the homestead of John Brown.

"The Notch seems beyond the world, North Elba and its half-dozen houses are beyond the Notch, and there is a wilder little mountain road which rises beyond North Elba. But the house we seek is not even on that road, but behind it and beyond it; you ride a mile or two, then take down a pair of bars; beyond the bars, faith takes you across a half-cleared field, through the most difficult of wood-paths, and after half a mile of forest you come out upon a clearing. There is a little frame house, unpainted, set in a girdle of black stumps, and with all heaven about it for a wider girdle; on a high hill-side; forests on north and west,—the glorious line of the Adirondacks on the east, and on the south one slender road leading off to Westport, a road so straight that you could sight a United States marshal for five miles.

"There stands the little house, with no ornament or relief about it; it needs none, with the setting of mountain horizon. Yes, there is one decoration which at once takes the eye, and which, stern and misplaced as it would seem elsewhere, seems appropriate here. It is strange to see anything so old, where all the works of man are new! It is a mossy, time-worn tombstone—not marking any grave, nor set in the ground, but resting against the house, as if its time were either past or not yet come. Both are true—it has a past duty and a future one. It bears the name of Captain John Brown, who died during the Revolution, eighty-three years ago;

it was his tombstone, brought hither by his grandson, bearing the same name and title : the latter caused to be inscribed upon it, also, the name of his son, Frederick, 'murdered at Ossawattomie for his adherence to the cause of freedom' (so reads the inscription), and he himself has said for years that no other tombstone should mark his own grave.

"The farm is a wild place; cold and bleak. It is too cold to raise corn ; indeed, they can scarcely, in the most favourable seasons, obtain a few ears for roasting. Stock must be wintered for very nearly six months in every year. I was there on the first of November; the ground was snowy, winter had apparently begun, and it would last till near the middle of May. They never raise anything to sell off that farm, except a few fleeces. It was well, they said, if they raised their own provisions, and could spin their own wool for clothing.

"Do you ask why they lived in such a bleak spot ? With John Brown and his family there is a reason for everything, and it is always the same reason. The same purpose, nay, the selfsame project that sent John Brown to Harper's Ferry, sent him to the Adirondack.

"Twenty years ago, he made up his mind that there was an irrepressible conflict between freedom and slavery, and that in that conflict he must take his share. He saw at a glance, moreover, what the rest of us are only beginning to see, even now—that slavery must be met, first or last, on its own ground. The time has come to tell the whole truth now—that John Brown's whole Kansas life was the result of this self-imposed mission, not the cause of it. Let us do this man justice; he was not a vindictive guerilla, nor a maddened Indian; nor was he of so shallow a nature that it took the death of a son to convince him that right was right, and wrong was wrong. He had long before made up his mind to sacrifice every son he ever had, if necessary, in fighting slavery. If it was John Brown against the world, no matter; for, as his friend Frederick Douglass had truly said, "In the right, one is a majority." In this conviction, therefore, he deliberately determined, twenty years ago this summer, that at some future period he would organize an armed party, go into a slave state, and liberate a large number of slaves. Soon after, surveying professionally in the mountains of Virginia, he chose the very ground for his purpose. Visiting Europe afterwards, he studied military strategy for this purpose, even making designs, which I have seen, for a new style of forest fortification, simple and ingenious, to be used by parties of fugitive slaves when brought to bay. He knew the ground, he knew his plans, he knew himself; but where should he find his men? He came to the Adirondack to look for them.

"Ten years ago, Gerrit Smith gave to a number of coloured men tracts of ground in the Adirondack Mountains. The emigrants were grossly defrauded by a cheating surveyor, who, being in advance of his age, practically anticipated Judge Taney's opinion, that black men have no rights which white men are bound to respect. By his villany the colony was almost ruined in advance; nor did it ever recover itself;

though some of the best farms which I have seen in that region are still in the hands of coloured men. John Brown heard of this; he himself was a surveyor, and he would have gone to the Adirondack, or anywhere else, merely to right this wrong. But he had another object; he thought that among these men he should find coadjutors in his cherished plan. He was not wholly wrong, and yet he afterwards learned something more. Such men as he needed are not to be *found* ordinarily ; they must be *reared.* John Brown did not merely look for men, therefore ; he reared them in his sons. During long years of waiting and postponement, he found others ; but his sons and their friends, the Thompsons, formed the nucleus of his force in all his enterprises. What services the females of his family may have rendered, it is not yet time to tell. It is a satisfaction to think that he was repaid for his early friendship to these New York coloured men, by some valuable aid from freed slaves and fugitive slaves at Harper's Ferry; especially from Dangerfield Newby, who, poor fellow ! had a slave wife and nine slave children to fight for, all within thirty miles of that town.

" To appreciate the character of the family, it is necessary to know these things; to understand that they have all been trained from childhood on this one principle, and for this one special project. Five years before, when they first went to Kansas, the father and sons had a plan of going to Louisiana, trying this same project, and then retreating into Texas with the liberated slaves. Nurtured on it so long, for years sacrificing to it all the other objects of life, the thought of its failure never crossed their minds ; and it is an extraordinary fact that when the disastrous news first came to North Elba, the family utterly refused to believe it, and were saved from suffering by that incredulity till the arrival of the next weekly mail.

" I had left the world outside, to raise the latch of this humble door amid the mountains ; and now my pen falters on the threshold, as my steps did then. This house is a home of sacred sorrow.   How shall we enter it ?   Its inmates are bereft and ruined men and women, as the world reckons ; what can we say to them ?   Do not shrink ; you are not near the world ; you are near John Brown's household.   ' In the world ye shall have tribulation ; but be of good cheer : *they* have overcome the world.'

" Let me here pause a moment, and enumerate the members of the family.   John Brown was born in 1800, and his wife in 1816, though both might be supposed older than the ages thus indicated.   He has had in all twenty children—seven being the offspring of his first wife, thirteen of his second.   Four of each family are living—eight in all.   The elder division of the surviving family are John and Jason, both married, and living in Ohio ; Owen, unmarried, who escaped from Harper's Ferry, and Ruth, the wife of Henry Thompson, who lives on an adjoining farm at North Elba, an intelligent and noble woman.   The younger division consists of Salmon, aged twenty-three, who resides with his young wife in his mother's house, and three unmarried daughters, Anne (sixteen), Sarah (thirteen), and Ellen (five). In the same house dwell also the widows of the two slain sons—young girls, aged but sixteen and twenty. The latter is the sister of Henry Thompson, and of the two Thompsons who were killed at Harper's Ferry; they also lived in the same vicinity, and one of them also has left a widow. Thus complicated and intertangled is this genealogy of sorrow.

"All these young men went deliberately from North Elba for no other purpose than to join in this enterprise. 'They could not,' they told their mother and their wives, 'live for themselves alone;' and so they went. One young wife, less submissive than the others, prevailed on her husband to remain; and this is the only reason why Salmon Brown survives. Oliver Brown, the youngest son, only twenty, wrote back to his wife from Harper's Ferry in a sort of premonition of what was coming, 'If I can do a single good action, my life will not have been all a failure.'

"Having had the honour of Captain Brown's acquaintance for some years, I was admitted into the confidence of the family, though I could see them observing me somewhat suspiciously as I approached the door. Everything that was said of the absent father and husband bore testimony to the same simple, upright character. Though they had been much separated from him for the last few years, they all felt it to be a necessary absence, and had not only no complaint to make, but cordially approved it. Mrs. Brown had been always the sharer of his plans. 'Her husband always

15*

believed,' she said, 'that he was to be an instrument in
the hands of Providence, and she believed it too.'—
'This plan had occupied his thoughts and prayers for
twenty years.'—'Many a night he had lain awake, and
prayed concerning it.'—'Even now, she did not doubt,
he felt satisfied, because he thought it would be over-
ruled by Providence for the best.'   'For herself,' she
said, 'she had always prayed that her husband might
be killed in fight rather than fall alive into the hands
of slaveholders; but she could not regret it now, in
view of the noble words of freedom which it had been
his privilege to utter.'   When, the next day on the railway, I was compelled to put into her hands the newspaper containing the death warrant of her husband, I
felt no fear of her exposing herself to observation by
any undue excitement.   She read it, and then the tall,
strong woman bent her head for a few minutes on the
seat before us ; then she raised it, and spoke as calmly
as before.

"I thought that I had learned the lesson once for all
in Kansas, which no one ever learns from books of
history alone, of the readiness with which danger and
death fit into the ordinary grooves of daily life, so that
on the day of a battle, for instance, all may go on as
usual ; breakfast and dinner are provided, children are
cared for, and all external existence has the same
smoothness that one observes at Niagara, just above
the American Fall ; but it impressed me anew on visiting this household at this time.   Here was a family out
of which four noble young men had, within a fortnight,

been killed. I say nothing of a father under sentence
of death, and a brother fleeing for his life, but only
speak of those killed. Now, that word *killed* is a word
which one hardly cares to mention in a mourning household circle, even under all mitigating circumstances,
when sad unavailing kisses and tender funeral rites
have softened the last memories ; how much less here,
then, where it suggested not merely wounds, and terror,
and agony, but also coffinless graves in a hostile land,
and the last ignominy of the dissecting room.

" Yet there was not one of that family who could not
pronounce that awful word with perfect quietness ;
never, of course, lightly, but always quietly. For instance, as I sat that evening, with the women busily
sewing around me, preparing the mother for her sudden
departure with me on the morrow, some daguerreotypes
were brought out to show me, and some one said, 'This
is Oliver, one of those who were killed at Harper's
Ferry.' I glanced up sidelong at the young, fair-haired
girl, who sat near me by the little table—a wife at fifteen, a widow at sixteen ; and this was her husband,
and he was killed. As the words were spoken in her
hearing, not a muscle quivered, and her finger did not
tremble as she drew the thread. For her life had become too real to leave room for wincing at mere words.
She had lived through, beyond the word, to the sterner
fact, and having confronted *that*, language was an empty
shell. To the Browns, killing means simply dying—
nothing more ; one gate into heaven, and that one a
good deal frequented by their family ; that is all.

"There was no hardness about all this, no mere stoicism of will; only God had inured them to the realities of things. They were not supported by any notions of worldly honour or applause, nor by that chilly reflection of it, the hope of future fame. In conversing with the different members of this family, I cannot recall a single instance of any heroics of that description. They asked but one question after I had told them how little hope there was of acquittal or rescue—'Does it seem as if freedom were to gain or lose by this?' That was all.

"No; this family work for a higher prize than fame. You know it is said that in all Wellington's despatches you never meet with the word glory; it is always duty. In Napoleon's, you never meet with the word duty; it is always glory. The race of John Brown is of the Wellington type. Principle is the word I brought away with me as most familiar in their vocabulary. That is their standard of classification. A man may be brave, ardent, generous; no matter—if he is not all this from principle, it is nothing. The daughters, who knew all the Harper's Ferry men, had no confidence in Cook, because 'he was not a man of principle.' They would trust Stevens round the world, because 'he was a man of principle.' 'He tries the hardest to be good,' said Annie Brown, in her simple way, 'of any man I ever saw.'

"It is pleasant to add that this same brave-hearted girl, who had known most of her father's associates, recognized them all but Cook as being men of principle.

'People are surprised,' she said, 'at father's daring to invade Virginia with only twenty-three men; but I think if they knew what sort of men they were, there would be less surprise. I never saw such men.'

"Nothing impressed me more in my visit to the Brown family, and in subsequent correspondence with them, than the utter absence of the slightest vindictive spirit, even in words.

"The children spoke of their father as a person of absolute rectitude, thoughtful kindness, unfailing foresight, and inexhaustible activity. On his flying visits to the farm, every moment was used; he was 'up at three, a.m., seeing to everything himself,' providing for everything, and giving heed to the minutest points. It was evident that some of the older ones had stood a little in awe of him in their childish years. 'We boys felt a little pleased sometimes, after all,' said the son, 'when father left the farm for a few days.' 'We girls never did,' said the married daughter, reproachfully, the tears gushing to her eyes. 'Well,' said the brother, repenting, 'we were always glad to see him come back again; for if we did get more holidays in his absence, we always missed him.'

"In the midst of all their sorrow, their strong and healthy hearts could enjoy the record of his conversations with the Virginians, and applaud the keen, wise, simple answers which I read to them, selecting here and there from the ample file of newspapers I carried with me. When, for instance, I read the inquiry, 'Did

you go out under the auspices of the Emigrant Aid
Society?' and the answer was, 'No, sir; I went out
under the auspices of John Brown,' three voices eagerly
burst in with, 'That's true,' and 'That's so.' And
when it was related that the young Virginia volunteer
taxed him with the want of military foresight in bringing so small a party to conquer Virginia, and the
veteran imperturbably informed the young man that
probably their views on military matters would materially differ, there was a general delightful chorus of,
'That sounds just like father.' And his sublimer
expressions of faith and self-devotion produced no
excitement or surprise among them—since they knew
in advance all which we now know of him—and these
things only elicited, at times, a half-stifled sigh as they
reflected that they might never hear that beloved voice
again.

" References to their father were constant. This book
he had brought them; the one sitting room had been
plastered with the last money he sent; that desk, that
gun were his; this was his daguerreotype; and at last
the rosy little Ellen brought me, with reverend hands,
her prime treasure. It was a morocco case, enclosing a
small Bible; and in the beginning, written in the plain,
legible hand I knew so well, the following inscription,
which would alone, in its touching simplicity, have been
worthy the pilgrimage to North Elba to see :—

" This Bible, presented to my dearly beloved daughter
Ellen Brown, is not intended for common use, but to be

carefully preserved for her and by her, in remembrance of
her father (of whose care and attentions she was deprived
in her infancy, he being absent in the Territory of Kansas
from the summer of 1855.)

"May the Holy Spirit of God incline your heart, in
earliest childhood, 'to receive the truth in the love of it,'
and to form your thoughts, words, and actions by its wise
and holy precepts, is my best wish and most earnest prayer
to Him in whose care I leave you. Amen.

"From your affectionate father,

"JOHN BROWN.

"April 2, 1857."

"This is dated two years ago; but the principles
which dictated it were permanent. Almost on the eve
of his last battle, October 1, 1859, he wrote home to
his daughter Anne, in a letter which I saw, 'Anne, I
want you first of all to become a sincere, humble, and
consistent Christian—and then [this is characteristic]
to acquire good and efficient business habits. Save this
to remember your father by, Anne. God Almighty
bless and save you all.'

"John Brown is almost the only radical abolitionist
I have ever known, who was not more or less radical in
religious matters also. His theology was Puritan, like
his practice; and accustomed as we now are to see
Puritan doctrines and Puritan virtues separately exhibited, it seems quite strange to behold them combined
in one person again. He and his wife were regular
communicants of the Presbyterian Church: but it tried

his soul to see the juvenile clerical gentlemen who came into the pulpits up that way, and dared to call themselves Presbyterians—preachers of the gospel, with all the hard applications left out.· Since they had lived in North Elba, his wife said, but twice had the slave been mentioned in the Sunday services, and she had great doubts about the propriety of taking part in such worship as that. But when the head of the family made his visits home from Kansas, he commonly held a Sunday meeting in the little church, and the slave was mentioned pretty freely then.

"In respect to politics, Mrs. Brown told me that her husband had taken little interest in them since the election of Jackson, because he thought that politics merely followed the condition of public sentiment on the slavery question, and that this public sentiment was mainly created by actual collisions between slavery and freedom. Such, at least, was the view which I was led to attribute to him, by combining this fact which she mentioned with my own personal knowledge of his opinions. He had an almost exaggerated aversion to words and speeches, and a profound conviction of the importance of bringing all questions to a direct issue, and subjecting every theory to the test of practical application.

"I did not, of course, insult Mrs. Brown by any reference to the charge of insanity against her husband; but she alluded to it herself with surprise, and said if her husband were insane, he had been consistent in his insanity from the first moment she knew him.

"It is natural for those who read this narrative to ask, What is the pecuniary condition of this household? It is hard to answer, because the whole standard is different, as to such matters, in North Elba and in Massachusetts. The ordinary condition of the Brown family may be stated as follows :—They own the farm, such as it is, without incumbrance, except so far as unfelled forest constitutes one. They have ordinarily enough to eat of what the farm yields, namely, bread and potatoes, pork and mutton—not any great abundance of these, but ordinarily enough. They have ordinarily enough to wear, at least of woollen clothing, spun by themselves. But they have no money. When I say this I do not merely mean that they have no superfluous cash to go shopping with, but I mean almost literally that they have none. For nearly a whole winter, Mrs. Brown said, they had no money with which to pay postage, except a tiny treasury which the younger girls had earned for that express object, during the previous summer, by picking berries for a neighbour three miles off.

"The reason of these privations simply was, that it cost money to live in Kansas in adherence to the cause of freedom, but not so much to live at North Elba ; and therefore the women must stint themselves that the men might continue their Kansas work. But when the father came upon his visits, he never came empty-handed, but brought a little money, some plain household stores, flour, sugar, rice, salt fish ; tea and coffee they do not use. But what their standard of expense is, may be seen from the fact that Mrs. Brown seemed to speak as if her youngest widowed daughter was not totally and absolutely destitute, because her husband had left a property of five sheep, which would belong to her. These sheep, I found on inquiry, were worth, at that place and season, two dollars apiece : a child of sixteen, left a widow in the world, with an estate amounting to ten dollars ! The immediate financial anxieties of Mrs. Brown herself, seemed chiefly to relate to a certain formidable tax bill, due at new year's time ; if they could only weather that, all was clear for the immediate future. How much was it, I asked, rather surprised that that wild country should produce a high rate of taxation. It was from eight to ten dollars, she gravely said ; and she had put by ten dollars for that purpose, but had had occasion to lend most of it to a poor black woman, with no great hope of repayment. And one of the first things done by her husband, on recovering his money in Virginia, was to send her, through me, fifteen dollars, to make sure of that tax bill.

"I spent but one night at the house, and drove away with Mrs. Brown, in the early frosty morning, from that breezy mountain home, which her husband loved, (as one of them told me) ' because he seemed to think there was something romantic in that kind of scenery.' There was, indeed, always a sort of thrill in John Brown's voice, when he spoke of mountains. I never shall forget the quiet way in which he once told me that 'God had established the Alleghany Mountains from the foundation of the world, that they might one day be a refuge for fugitive slaves.' I did not then know that his own home was among the Adirondacks.

"Just before we went, I said something to Salmon Brown about the sacrifices of their family ; and he looked up in a quiet, manly way, which I shall never forget, and said briefly, 'I sometimes think that is what we came into the world for—to make sacrifices.' And I know that the murmuring echo of those words went with me all that day, as we came down from the mountains, and out through the iron gorge ; and it seemed to me that any one must be very unworthy the society which I had been permitted to enter, who did not come forth from it a wiser and a better man."

CHAPTER IX.

November, 1859.

MRS. BROWN ARRIVES IN BALTIMORE.—IS INDUCED TO RE-
TURN NORTHWARDS BEFORE REACHING CHARLESTOWN.—
HER STAY AT EAGLESWOOD, NEW JERSEY.—INTERVIEW WITH
MR. TILTON.—IS KINDLY RECEIVED IN PHILADELPHIA.—
CONVERSATION WITH MR. M'KIM RESPECTING CAPTAIN
BROWN.

MRS. BROWN pursued her journey for the purpose of visiting her husband in Charlestown jail. On reaching Baltimore, however, she was met by a message from Captain Brown, dated November 16th. It will be found in the collection of the letters written by him from prison, which we have grouped together in the next chapter. This letter is singularly calm, tender, and impressive, and is one of the most striking in the whole collection. In compliance with the conviction therein expressed, that, under such heartrending cir-cumstances, she had better defer an interview, at least for the present, Mrs. Brown returned northwards as far as Eagleswood, near Perth Amboy, in one of the most beautiful parts of the state of New Jersey.

Here she was the guest of Mr. and Mrs. Marcus Spring, who had proved themselves the kind friends of her husband ; and they were the better prepared to bid her welcome to their house, because Mrs. Spring had recently paid a visit to Captain Brown in prison, of

which many particulars will be found in our eleventh
chapter. This excellent pair are known to the English
public from the frequent mention of them by Miss
Fredrika Bremer in her account of her visit to the
United States. Mrs. Spring may claim an illustrious
parentage ; for her father, the late Arnold Buffum of
Massachusetts, was the first president and one of the
twelve original founders of the American Anti-slavery
Society, under the leadership of Mr. Garrison, in the
year 1833, at a time when it required an extraordinary
combination of high principle, moral courage, and faith
in the eventual triumph of the cause of justice and
humanity, to enable an American to become an abolitionist. Mr. Buffum, as his daughter testifies in a letter which lies before us, " suffered persecution, and saw
the faces of friends turned from him in consequence,
but he never swerved from the path he had chosen."

During Mrs. Brown's stay at Eagleswood, Mr. Theodore Tilton spent an evening in her company ; and, as
everything connected with Captain Brown and his
family was intensely interesting to the public of the
free states at that time, he sent the following communication to the *New York Independent*, a semi-religious
journal of vast circulation :—

" I conversed with her during the entire evening.
Ten minutes' acquaintance is enough to show that she
is a woman worthy to be the wife of such a man. She
is tall, large and muscular, giving the impression at first
sight of a frame capable of great strength and long en-

durance. Her face is grave and thoughtful, wearing, even in this hour of her trial, an expression of soberness rather than of sadness, as if, like her husband, she had long since learned how to suffer and be calm. Her manner is singularly quiet and retiring, although her natural simplicity and modesty cannot hide the evident force of character, and strength of will and judgment, which have fitted her so long to be a counsellor in her husband's enterprises, and a supporter in his trials. Notwithstanding the cares of her numerous family, and her many privations and struggles independent of household burdens, she still appears as fresh and hale as if she were only now in the prime and vigor of life.

"She alluded, with subdued though evident emotion, to the wounds of her husband, and to the loss of her two sons, Watson and Oliver, who fell in the struggle. But she made no such remark as that recently attributed to her, 'that four of her sons had already been slain, and she would be willing that all the rest of her family should be made a sacrifice, if necessary, to the cause of freedom.' These words, she said to me, could never possibly have fallen from her lips ; for she had already felt too many griefs to court any fresh sacrifices ; and she could not think, without pain, of any new death-stroke to her family. She would not shrink from any necessary trial or struggle when the hour came for it, but she could not look forward with composure to any further lessening of her family, already too sadly broken. She regretted that such a remark should have been put into her mouth, 'for,' as she observed, ' they were unmotherly words.' She said that she had been so long accustomed to sorrows that she had been trained to bear them. While living in Ohio, four of her children died from dysentery, within eleven days, three of whom were carried to the grave together on the same day ! She mentioned, in this connection, that her husband had always been a watchful nurse, and the chief caretaker of the children and of herself, during periods of sickness.

" I adverted, in alluding to Captain Brown's religious opinions, to the common report that he was an Old-School Presbyterian. She replied that he had been a church-member ever since he was a boy ; that he united at sixteen years of age with a Congregational Church in Hudson, Ohio ; and that on removing to Pennsylvania, thirty years ago, he transferred his membership to the Presbyterian Church, with which he had since remained connected. She said that the religious element of his character had always been the ruling motive of his life. He had always observed religious exercises in his household, with exemplary regularity. It had been for many years the custom of the family to read the Bible every morning, in regular course of chapters, each member reading in turn a verse. She said that her husband's familiarity with texts of Scripture was so great, that he could detect almost the slightest misquotation of any passage, and that if a portion of a verse in almost any part of the Bible were read or repeated to him, he could immediately repeat the remainder. His conversation frequently abounded with Scripture texts, and his letters were always filled with them.

16

" In his habits of living, his wife testified that he was always singularly self-denying. As an example, he never suffered himself or his family to wear expensive clothing. His standing admonition was, 'Let us save the money, and give to the poor.' The day before yesterday, when some clothes were sent from New York to Mrs. Brown, to go in a box to her husband, among the articles was a new coat of fine brown cloth, which, when it was shown to her, she immediately pronounced too gay for her husband to wear. It was accordingly sent back ; and last evening there came instead a coarser coat, which would better suit his taste, and which he might not think too good for him to put on ! He never in his life has used tobacco or ardent spirits, and never within the last few years has taken tea or coffee. His mode of living has been so rigidly temperate that, in Kansas, he would sometimes go for days with scarcely a mouthful of food, and suffer no faintness or exhaustion.

" I referred incidentally to the design upon Harper's Ferry as having been premeditated for two years ; to which she immediately replied, 'Not for two years, but for twenty ! He had been waiting twenty years for some opportunity to free the slaves ; we had all been waiting with him the proper time when he should put his resolve into action ; and, when at last the enterprise at Harper's Ferry was planned, we all thought that the time had now come. Mr. Brown was sanguine of success ; we all were equally confident ; he had no idea, nor had any of the family, that the experiment would result in defeat; we all looked to it as fulfilling the hopes of many years.' She shortly added, 'For he has borne the yoke of the oppressed, as if upon his own neck, for these thirty years.'

"She made several and repeated references to various newspaper accounts in which her husband's character had been misrepresented. She had been pained to see him described as a cruel man, for, she said, 'No man ever had a kinder heart; he is generous by nature; he has always aimed to impress his family with a spirit of benevolence; he has always taught his children to be unselfish—to act always for others before acting for themselves. His sympathies for the poor and the oppressed have always been too easily excited.'

"I enquired as to his habit of carrying fire-arms about his person. She said that since the many threatened attempts upon his life, during and since his efforts in Kansas, he had carried a revolver, but never before.

"Last evening I saw a letter from Captain Brown to his wife, dated November 8th. To the many overflowing expressions of his sympathy for his wife and children I do not feel at liberty to allude, further than to say that they are as warm, as tender, and as delicate as ever were written by a husband to a wife. They prove that his heart is not only as brave as a hero's, but as tender as a child's. During the evening, another letter came direct from the prison, dated November 10th. This fresh message was much briefer than the other, but of the same character, and in the same spirit.

"For several days past, until last evening, Mrs.

16*

Brown had been actively engaged, aided by some female friends, in preparing articles of clothing to be sent to her husband. A sewing machine had been busy at work from morning till night for two days. Last evening the box was packed, and this morning sent to the cars, containing shirts, stockings, pocket-handkerchiefs, a pair of easy slippers, some writing materials, two or three favourite books, and some preserved fruits and other delicacies. A great number of friends crowded around it, each anxious to add something before the cover was nailed on. From this scene Mrs. Brown retired, sobbing, to another part of the room, and for a few moments was unable to control her emotion, exclaiming, ' Poor man ! he will not need them long !' "

On the day after her meeting with Mr. Tilton, Mrs. Brown proceeded to Philadelphia, where she was received with every manifestation of kindness and sympathy by James and Lucretia Mott, eminent philanthropists, whose hearts and home have ever been open to the suffering and the oppressed. Mrs. Mott is widely known in the United States as an eloquent and dauntless advocate of the anti-slavery cause, and as a woman of extraordinary moral and intellectual endowments. During part of the time of her stay in Philadelphia, Mrs. Brown was the guest of Mr. J. Miller M'Kim, a correspondent of the *Anti-slavery Standard*. We extract the following particulars relative to the Brown family from his letter in that paper of the 28th

November, just before Mrs. Brown's farewell visit to her husband :—

"While much has been said—though not too much —of the heroism and nobility of soul of Captain John Brown it is not known as it ought to be that his wife and children have been distinguished in a large measure by the same characteristics. It has been my privilege, for most of the past week, to be an inmate of the same house with Mrs. Brown; and I must say, not only for myself but for those who have shared with me in the privilege, that the more we have seen of her, and the more we have learned, through her, of the rest of the family, the more we have been impressed in favour of them all.

"As for Mrs. Brown herself, she is just the woman to be the wife of the hero of Harper's Ferry. Stalwart of frame and strong in native intellect, she is imbued with the same religious faith, and her heart overflows with the same sympathies. Her bearing in her present distress is admirable. She is brave without insensibility, tender without weakness; and, though overwhelmed by the deepest sorrow, her sorrow is not as of one having no hope. Yet her hope is not that her husband will be reprieved, or have his sentence commuted, but that all he has done and is now doing will not only accrue to the benefit, but precipitate the triumph of the cause they have all had so much at heart. Absorbed by the great events that are passing before her, and apparently unconscious that she is an object of observation, her demeanor is marked by un-affected propriety and natural dignity.

"Mrs. Brown reads everything that is published concerning the great topic, and listens to everything that is said, with the keenest avidity. The daily papers are brought out in the evening, and read aloud ; her ears are open to every word, and her comments add much to their interest. Through the day she reads them all over and over again, and waits with impatience for the next that are to come. It was a great disap-pointment to her to be prevented from joining her husband in his prison, there to wait till the execution ; but she is fully convinced by what he has written, as well as by her own reflections, that it would not be best for her to do so. For the present, therefore, she is content to remain as near to him as possible, relying on post and telegraph to bring her word, without delay, of everything that may concern her. She is in the receipt of letters from him which afford her great comfort. In the last received he says :—' My mind is very tranquil, I may say joyous.' I wish your readers could have the pleasure, with us, of perusing these letters ; some of them are even more beautiful and touching than any that have yet been printed. Doubt-less they will all, ere long, be given to the public.

"When the letter of Mr. Brown to the Rev. Mr. Vaill of Litchfield was read to her, which it was, im-mediately after the paper came to hand containing it, she sat with form erect, and listened with deep but composed attention ; but when the reader came to the passage where he says, 'I have lost my two noble boys,' she dropped her head suddenly, as if pierced with an arrow, and for a while was overcome with emotion. She soon recovered herself, however, and, wiping her eyes and resuming her erect position, indicated that she was ready to hear the rest.

"She reads everything on the subject that comes within her reach—except the extracts from the *New York Observer*.* 'That paper,' she said the other evening, with more excitement of manner than is usual with her, 'I cannot abide. I can read all that the southern papers say, and all that is said in the *New York Herald*, but I cannot bear to read anything from the *New York Observer*.'

"From facts stated and remarks incidentally made by Mrs. Brown in conversation, it is evident that entire harmony has prevailed in their large and diversified family circle. Mr. Brown's ascendancy over them all is very great, and in him they are bound together as a unit. They cherish his religious faith, and accord fully

---

* This disgust with the *New York Observer* is shared by all the opponents of slavery in the United States, and wherever else that newspaper is known. The *Observer*, as a "religious" paper, is an exponent of the opinions of the Old School Presbyterians. It is bitterly opposed to all interference with American slavery, to abolitionism of whatever shade, and to all attempts to limit or restrain the power of the slaveholders. It never misses an opportunity to vilify or misrepresent the abolitionists. The Rev. Samuel Irenæus Prime, one of the editors, is the author of a little book called "the Power of Prayer," which has had a prodigious circulation on both sides of the Atlantic.

in his views of duty. All the children, from the eldest son down to the daughter of sixteen, have been ready to take their lives in their hands, and brave any peril, if by so doing they could rescue the slave from his oppressor. Six of the family—the father and three sons, and two others connected with them by marriage —were among the party who led the forlorn hope at Harper's Ferry; and some who remained behind found it cost more self-denial to do so than was called for by those who went.

"Captain Brown, though born to command and bound to be obeyed, was a tender husband and a kind and gentle father. 'When I have been ill,' said Mrs. Brown, 'he has always been nurse; unless,' she added, 'he was compelled to be absent.' 'For two weeks together he has sat up, night after night, just to keep alive the fire, fearing, if he were to lie down and go soundly to sleep, it would go out, and I should thereby take cold.' 'Many and many a time has he bid me good-bye, hardly able to speak for his tears, saying that he might never see me again.'

"Such has been the character of Captain Brown, as seen in his domestic relations. His children, it appears, were, in this respect, essentially like him. 'The last time Watson went away,' said Mrs. Brown, 'after he came out from taking leave of his wife, he sobbed so loud that he could be heard in every part of the house. Their infant was only two weeks old, and you may suppose it was very hard for them to part under such circumstances. And it was the same way,' she added, 'with Oliver and his wife, only that Oliver's grief was more quiet than Watson's.'

"Mrs. Brown represents her son Oliver as having been a youth of more than common promise. He was 'in advance of his years—a deep thinker—much like his father.' When near Harper's Ferry, last summer, he was much impressed by certain tragic circumstances which there occurred, and he wrote home to his sister that he could not think of abandoning his work so long as such things were going on. 'If,' said he, in that letter, 'only one good action is done in a lifetime, it is enough to show that life is not altogether a failure.'

"In the rearing of his family, Captain Brown had great regard to their religious interests. His library consisted chiefly of the Bible, Baxter's Saints' Rest, Bunyan's Pilgrim's Progress, and Doddridge's Rise and Progress of Religion in the Soul. The Bible, with which his letters show him to be perfectly familiar, he was in the practice of reading 'in course,' as were his fathers before him. The custom of hearing the family, every Sunday afternoon, repeat the 'Catechism,' he did not keep up, regarding it as more burdensome than profitable; but he substituted therefor the recitation of the Ten Commandments. These, all the family, old and young, were required to repeat every Sunday as regularly as the day came round. 'After which,' said Mrs. Brown, 'he usually talked to them; speaking sometimes half an hour, sometimes an hour, sometimes two hours, just as he or they might seem interested.'

"Captain Brown inculcated a practical, not a formal

or a sentimental, religion. 'First pure, then peaceable,' was his idea of Christianity. Love for God was to be shown by good-will to men. In a letter written home not long since, he requested that little Ellen, their youngest child, a girl of five years, might be taught a certain couplet which all the rest had learned by heart as they grew up. 'But,' said Mrs. Brown, 'his request was not necessary, for Ellen had already learned it from the other children.' The lines were these :

> " Count that day lost whose low descending sun
> Views from thy hand no worthy action done."

" The wives of Watson and Oliver, as well as the wife of Captain Brown, were in the fullest sympathy with their husbands, and, from all that appears, have borne their parts with equal bravery and heroism. Captain Brown incidentally bears testimony to this, in part at least, when he says, in one of his recent letters to his wife :—'The sacrifices which *you* and I have made (underscoring the word 'you') ' I do not regard as at all too great.' Mrs. Brown speaks of her daughters-in-law—Isabella and Martha, the wives respectively of Watson and Oliver—with warm commendation.

" From all this—and you need not be assured that in these statements I have adhered as close as may be to the simple verity—I think you will agree with me that Captain Brown, in the generosity and nobleness of his character, does not stand alone in his family. He has a wife meet for such a husband, and children worthy of their father."

CHAPTER X.

OCTOBER 31st—DECEMBER 2nd, 1859.

CAPTAIN BROWN'S LETTERS FROM PRISON :—1. TO HIS FAMILY
AT NORTH ELBA.—2. TO MRS. L. M. CHILD, BOSTON.—3. TO
A QUAKER LADY, RHODE ISLAND.—4. TO HIS FAMILY AT
NORTH ELBA.—5. TO HIS HALF-BROTHER JEREMIAH.—
6. TO AN UNKNOWN FRIEND.—7. TO THE REV. H. L. VAILL.
8. TO MRS. BROWN AT BALTIMORE.—9. TO MR. MUSGRAVE,
JUN.—10. TO MRS. BROWN.—11.—TO HIS CHILDREN AT
NORTH ELBA.—12. TO HIS SONS IN OHIO.—13. TO REV. MR.
MCFARLAND.—14. EXTRACT.—15. TO MR. HOYT.—16. TO
MRS. BROWN AT PHILADELPHIA.—17. TO MR. HYATT.—
18. TO A YOUNG LADY.—19. TO JUDGE TILDEN.—20. TO
MR. SEWALL, BOSTON.—21. TO REV. MR. MILLIGAN, PENN-
SYLVANIA.—22. TO HIS FAMILY AT NORTH ELBA.—23. TO
MR. FORMAN.

I.—TO HIS FAMILY AT NORTH ELBA.

Charlestown, Jefferson County, Virginia,
October 31, 1859.

My dear wife and children, every one :

I suppose you have learned before this, by the
newspapers, that two weeks ago to-day we were fighting
for our lives at Harper's Ferry; that during the fight
Watson was mortally wounded, Oliver killed, William
Thompson killed, and Dauphin slightly wounded ; that on
the following day I was taken prisoner, immediately after
which I received several sabre-cuts in my head and bayo-
net-stabs in my body. As nearly as I can learn, Watson
died of his wound on Wednesday the second, or on Thursday the third day after I was taken. Dauphin was killed

when I was taken, and Anderson, I suppose, also. I have
since been tried, and found guilty of treason, &c., and of
murder in the first degree. I have not yet received my
sentence. No others of the company with whom you were
acquainted were, so far as I can learn, either killed or
taken. Under all these terrible calamities, I feel quite
cheerful in the assurance that God reigns, and will over-
rule all for his glory and the best possible good. I feel no
consciousness of guilt in the matter, nor even mortification
on account of my imprisonment and irons; and I feel perfectly assured that very soon no member of my family will
feel any possible disposition to "blush on my account."
Already dear friends at a distance, with kindest sympathy,
are cheering me with the assurance that posterity at least
will do me justice. I shall commend you all together,
with my beloved, but bereaved daughters-in-law, to their
sympathies, which I have no doubt will soon reach you.
I also commend you all to Him "whose mercy endureth
for ever"—to the God of my fathers, "whose I am, and
whom I serve." "He will never leave you or forsake
you," unless you forsake him. Finally, my dearly beloved,
be of good comfort. Be sure to remember and to follow
my advice, and my example too, so far as it has been
consistent with the holy religion of Jesus Christ, in which
I remain a most firm and humble believer. Never forget
the poor, nor think anything you bestow on them to be
lost to you, even though they may be black as Ebedmelech,
the Ethiopian eunuch, who cared for Jeremiah in the pit
of the dungeon, or as black as the one to whom Philip
preached Christ. Be sure to entertain strangers, for
thereby some have * * * "Remember them that are in
bonds as bound with them." I am in charge of a jailor
like the one who took charge of "Paul and Silas;" and

you may rest assured that both kind hearts and kind faces are more or less about me, whilst thousands are thirsting for my blood. "These light afflictions, which are but for a moment, shall work out for us a far more exceeding and eternal weight of glory." I hope to be able to write you again. My wounds are doing well. Copy this, and send it to your sorrow-stricken brothers, Ruth, to comfort them. Write me a few words in regard to the welfare of all. God Almighty bless you all, and make you "joyful in the midst of all your tribulations." Write to John Brown, Charlestown, Jefferson County, Virginia, care of Captain John Avis. Your affectionate husband and father,

JOHN BROWN.

Nov. 3, 1859.

P.S.—Yesterday, Nov. 2, I was sentenced to be hanged on Dec. 2nd next. Do not grieve on my account. I am still quite cheerful. God bless you. Yours ever,

JOHN BROWN.

2.—TO MRS. LYDIA MARIA CHILD.

[No date.]

Mrs. L. Maria Child,

My dear friend, (such you prove to be, though a stranger,) your most kind letter has reached me, with the kind offer to come here and take care of me. Allow me to express my gratitude for your great sympathy, and at the same time to propose to you a different course, together with my reasons for wishing it. I should certainly be greatly pleased to become personally acquainted with one so gifted and so kind ; but I cannot avoid seeing some ob-

jections to it, under present circumstances. First, I am
in charge of a most humane gentleman, who, with his
family, have rendered me every possible attention I have
desired, or that could be of the least advantage ; and I am
so far recovered from my wounds as no longer to require
nursing. Then, again, it would subject you to great personal inconvenience and heavy expense, without doing me
any good.

Allow me to name to you another channel through which
you may reach me with your sympathies much more effectually. I have at home a wife and three young daughters
—the youngest but little over five years old, the oldest
nearly sixteen. I have also two daughters-in-law, whose
husbands have both fallen near me here. There is also
another widow, Mrs. Thompson, whose husband fell here.
Whether she is a mother or not, I cannot say. All these,
my wife included, live at North Elba, Essex County, New
York. I have a middle-aged son, who has been, in some
degree, a cripple from his childhood, who would have as
much as he could well do to earn a living. He was a most
dreadful sufferer in Kansas, and lost all he had laid up.
He has not enough to clothe himself for the winter comfortably. I have no living son, or son-in-law, who did not
suffer terribly in Kansas.

Now, dear friend, would you not as soon contribute fifty
cents now, and a like sum yearly, for the relief of those
very poor and deeply afflicted persons, to enable them to
supply themselves and their children with bread and very
plain clothing, and to enable the children to receive a common English education ? Will you also devote your own
energies to induce others to join in giving a like amount
or any other amount, to constitute a little fund for the `
purpose named ?

I cannot see how your coming here can do me the least good; and I am quite certain you can do me immense good where you are. I am quite cheerful under all my afflicting circumstances and prospects; having, as I humbly trust, "the peace of God, which passeth all understanding," to rule in my heart. You may make such use of this as you see fit. God Almighty bless and reward you a thousand fold.

Yours, in sincerity and truth,

JOHN BROWN.

3.——TO A QUAKER LADY, RHODE ISLAND.

Charlestown, Jefferson County, Virginia,
Tuesday, 1st November, 1859.

My dear friend, E. B. of Rhode Island :

Your most cheering letter of the 27th October is received, and may the Lord reward you a thousand fold for the kind feeling you express toward me ; but more especially for your fidelity to the "poor that cry, and those that have no help." For this I am a prisoner in bonds. It is solely my own fault, in a military point of view, that we met with our disaster. I mean, that I mingled with our prisoners, and so far sympathized with them and their families, that I neglected my duty in other respects. But God's will, not mine, be done. You know that Christ once armed Peter, so also in my case I think he put a sword into my hand, and there continued it so long as he saw best, and then kindly took it from me ; I mean, when I first went to Kansas. I wish you could know with what cheerfulness I am now wielding the "sword of the spirit," on the right hand and on the left. I bless

God that it proves "mighty to the pulling down of strong holds." I always loved my Quaker friends, and I commend to their kind regard my poor, bereaved, widowed wife, and my daughters and daughters-in-law, whose husbands fell at my side. One is a mother, and the other is likely to become so soon. They, as well as my own sorrow-stricken daughter, are left very poor, and have much greater need of sympathy than I, who, through Infinite Grace and the kindness of strangers, am "joyful in all my tribulations."

Dear sister, write them at North Elba, Essex County, New York, to comfort their sad hearts. Direct to Mary A. Brown, wife of John Brown. There is also another— a widow—wife of Thompson, who fell with my poor boys in the affair at Harper's Ferry, at the same place.

I do not feel conscious of guilt in taking up arms; and had it been in behalf of the rich and powerful, the intelligent, the great—as men count greatness—of those who form enactments to suit themselves, and corrupt others or some of their friends, that I interfered, suffered, sacrificed, and fell, it would have been doing very well. But enough of this.

These light afflictions, which endure for a moment, shall work out for me a far more exceeding and eternal weight of glory. I would be very grateful for another letter from you. My wounds are healing. Farewell. God will surely attend to his own cause in the best possible way and time, and he will not forget the work of his own hands.

Your friend,

JOHN BROWN.

4.—TO HIS FAMILY AT NORTH ELBA.

Charlestown, Jefferson Co., Virginia,
8th November, 1859.

Dear wife and children, every one,

I will begin by saying that I have in some degree recovered from my wounds, but that I am quite weak in my back, and sore about my left kidney. My appetite has has been quite good most of the time since I was hurt. I am supplied with almost everything I could desire to make me comfortable, and the little I lack (some articles of clothing, which I lost) I may perhaps soon get again. I am, besides, quite cheerful, having, as I trust, the peace of God, which "passeth all understanding," to "rule in my heart," and the testimony (in some degree) of a good conscience that I have not lived altogether in vain. I can trust God with both the time and the manner of my death, believing, as I now do, that for me at this time to seal my testimony for God and humanity with my blood, will do vastly more towards advancing the cause I have earnestly endeavoured to promote, than all I have done in my life before. I beg of you all meekly and quietly to submit to this, not feeling yourselves in the least degraded on that account. Remember, dear wife and children all, that Jesus of Nazareth suffered a most excruciating death on the cross as a felon, under the most aggravating circumstances. Think also of the prophets and apostles, and Christians of former days, who went through greater tribulations than you or I; and try to be reconciled. May God Almighty comfort all your hearts, and soon wipe away all tears from your eyes. To Him be endless praise. Think, too, of the crushed millions who "have no comforter." I charge you

17

all never in your trials to forget the griefs of "the poor that cry, and of those that have none to help them."

I wrote most earnestly to my dear and afflicted wife not to come on for the present, at any rate. I will now give her my reasons for doing so. First, it would use up all the scanty means she has, or is at all likely to have, to make herself and children comfortable hereafter. For let me tell you that the sympathy that is now aroused in your behalf may not always follow you. There is but little more of the romantic about helping poor widows and their children, than there is about trying to relieve poor "niggers." Again, the little comfort it might afford us to meet again would be dearly bought by the pains of a final separation. We must part, and, I feel assured, for us to meet under such dreadful circumstances would only add to our distress. If she comes on here, she must be only a gazing stock throughout the whole journey, to be remarked upon in every look, word, and action, and by all sorts of creatures, and by all sorts of papers throughout the whole country. Again, it is my most decided judgment that in quietly and submissively staying at home, vastly more of generous sympathy will reach her, without such dreadful sacrifice of feeling as she must put up with if she comes on. The visits of one or two female friends that have come on here have produced great excitement, which is very annoying, and they cannot possibly do me any good. O Mary, do not come; but patiently wait for the meeting of those who love God and their fellow-men, where no separation must follow. "They shall go no more out forever." I greatly long to hear from some one of you, and to learn anything that in any way affects your welfare. I sent you ten dollars the other day. Did you get it? I have also endeavoured to stir up Christian friends to visit and write to you in your deep affliction.   I have no doubt that some of them, at least, will heed the call.   Write to me, care of Captain John Avis, Charlestown, Jefferson County, Virginia.

"Finally, my beloved, be of good comfort."   May all your names be "written in the Lamb's book of life"—may you all have the purifying and sustaining influence of the Christian religion—is the earnest prayer of your affectionate husband and father,

JOHN BROWN.

P.S. I cannot remember a night so dark as to have hindered the coming day, nor a storm so furious or dreadful as to prevent the return of warm sunshine and a cloudless sky.   But, beloved ones, do remember that this is not your rest, that in this world you have no abiding place or continuing city.   To God and his infinite mercy I always commend you.—J. B.

Nov. 9.

5.—TO HIS HALF-BROTHER JEREMIAH.

Charlestown, Jefferson Co., Virginia,
Nov. 12, 1859.

Dear brother Jeremiah,

Your kind letter of the 9th instant is received, and also one from Mr. Tilden, for both of which I am greatly obliged.   You enquire, "Can I do anything for you or your family?"   I would answer that my sons, as well as my wife and daughters, are all very poor, and that anything that may hereafter be due me from my father's

17*

estate I wish paid to them, as I will endeavour hereafter to describe, without legal formalities to consume it all. One of my boys has been so entirely used up, as very likely to be in want of comfortable clothing for the winter. I have, through the kindness of friends, fifteen dollars to send him, which I will remit shortly. If you know where to reach him, please send him that amount at once, as I shall remit the same to you by a safe conveyance. If I had a plain statement from Mr. Thompson of the state of my accounts with the estate of my father, I should then better know what to say about that matter. As it is, I have not the least memorandum left me to refer to. If Mr. Thompson will make me a statement, and charge my dividend fully for his trouble, I would be greatly obliged to him. In that case you can send me any remarks of your own. I am gaining in health slowly, and am quite cheerful in view of my approaching end, being fully persuaded that I am worth inconceivably more to hang, than for any other purpose. God Almighty bless and save you all.

Your affectionate brother,
JOHN BROWN.

P. S. Nov. 13.—Say to my poor boys never to grieve for one moment on my account ; and should many of you live to see the time when you will not blush to own your relation to old John Brown, it will not be more strange than many things that have happened. I feel a thousand times more on account of my sorrowing friends than on my own account. So far as I am concerned, I " count it all joy." " I have fought the good fight," and have, as I trust, " finished my course." Please show this to any of my family you may see. My love to all ; and may God, in his infinite mercy, for Christ's sake, bless and save you all.

Your affectionate brother,

J. BROWN.

6.—TO AN UNKNOWN FRIEND.

Charlestown, Jefferson County, Virginia,
November 15, 1859.

My dear sir,

Your kind mention of some things in my conduct here which you approve is very comforting indeed to my mind. Yet I am conscious that you do me no more than justice. I do certainly feel that through divine grace I have endeavoured to be " faithful in a very few things," mingling with even these much of imperfection. I am certainly " unworthy even to suffer affliction with the ' people of God ;'" yet in infinite grace he has thus honoured me. May the same grace enable me to serve him in a " new obedience," through my little remainder of this life, and to rejoice in him forever. I cannot feel that God will suffer even the poorest service we may any of us have rendered him or his cause to be lost or in vain. I do feel, " dear brother," that I am wonderfully " strengthened from on high."

May I use that strength in " showing his strength unto this generation," and his power to every one that is to come. I am most grateful for your assurance that my poor, shattered, heart-broken " family will not be forgotten." I have long tried to recommend them to " the God of my fathers." I have many opportunities for faithful plain dealing with the more powerful, influential, and intelligent classes in this region, which, I trust, are not entirely misimproved. I humbly trust that I firmly believe that "God reigns," and I think I can truly say, "Let the earth rejoice." May God take care of his own cause, and of his own great name, as well as of those who love their neighbours. Farewell!

Yours, in truth,
JOHN BROWN.

7.—TO REV. MR. VAILL, LITCHFIELD, CONNECTICUT.

Charlestown, Jefferson County, Virginia,
November 15, 1859.

Rev. H. L. Vaill,

My dear, steadfast friend, your most kind and most welcome letter of the 8th instant reached me in due time.

I am very grateful for all the good feeling you express, and also for the kind counsels you give, together with your prayers in my behalf. Allow me here to say, that notwithstanding "my soul is amongst lions," still I believe that "God in very deed is with me." You will not, therefore, feel surprised when I tell you that I am "joyful in all my tribulations;" that I do not feel condemned of Him whose judgment is just, nor of my own conscience. Nor do I feel degraded by my imprisonment, my chain, or prospect of the gallows. I have not only been, though utterly unworthy, permitted to "suffer affliction with God's people," but have also had a great many rare opportunities for "preaching righteousness in the great congregation." I trust it will not all be lost. The jailer, in whose charge I am, and his family and assistants, have all been most kind ; and, notwithstanding he was one of the bravest of all who fought me, he is now being abused for his humanity. So far as my observation goes, none but brave men are likely to be humane to a fallen foe. Cowards prove their courage by their ferocity. It may be done in that way with but little risk.

I wish I could write you about a few only of the interesting times I here experience with different classes of men—clergymen among others. Christ, the great Captain of liberty as well as of salvation, and who began his mission, as foretold of him, by proclaiming it, saw fit to take from me a sword of steel after I had carried it for a time ; but he has put another in my hand ("the sword of the Spirit,") and I pray God to make me a faithful soldier wherever he may send me—not less on the scaffold than when surrounded by my warmest sympathizers.

My dear old friend, I do assure you I have not forgotten our last meeting, nor our retrospective look over the route by which God had then led us ; and I bless his name that he has again enabled me to hear your words of cheering and comfort, at a time when I, at least, am on the "brink of Jordan." See Bunyan's Pilgrim. God in infinite mercy grant us soon another meeting on the opposite shore. I have often passed under the rod of Him whom I call my Father ; and certainly no son ever needed it oftener ; and yet I have enjoyed much of life, as I was enabled to discover the secret of this somewhat early. It has been in making the prosperity and happiness of others my own ; so that really I have had a great deal of prosperity. I am very prosperous still, and looking forward to a time when "peace on earth and good-will to men" shall everywhere prevail ; I have no murmuring thoughts or envious feelings to fret my mind. "I'll praise my Maker with my breath."

Your assurance of the earnest sympathy of the friends in my native land is very grateful to my feelings; and allow me to say a word of comfort to them.

As I believe most firmly that God reigns, I cannot believe that anything I have done, suffered, or may yet suffer, will be lost to the cause of God or of humanity. And before I began my work at Harper's Ferry, I felt assured that in the worst event it would surely pay. I often expressed that belief, and can now see no possible cause to alter my mind. I am not as yet, in the main, at all disappointed. I have been a good deal disappointed as it regards myself, in not keeping up to my own plans; but I now feel entirely reconciled even to that; for God's plan was infinitely better, no doubt, or I should have kept to my own. Had Samson kept to his determination of not telling Delilah wherein his great strength lay, he would probably have never overturned the house. I did not tell Delilah; but I was induced to act very contrary to my better judgment; and I have lost my two noble boys and other friends, if not my two eyes.

But "God's will, not mine, be done." I feel a comfortable hope that, like that erring servant of whom I have just been writing, even I may, through infinite mercy in Christ Jesus, yet "die in faith." As to both the time and manner of my death, I have but very little trouble on that score, and am able to be, as you exhort, "of good cheer."

I send through you my best wishes to Mrs. W. and her son George, and to all dear friends. May the God of the poor and oppressed be the God and Saviour of you all.

Farewell, till we meet again.

Your friend, in truth,

JOHN BROWN.

8.—TO MRS. BROWN, AT BALTIMORE.

Charlestown, Jefferson Co., Virginia,
16th November, 1859.

My dear wife,

I write you in answer to a most kind letter of November 13th, from dear Mrs. Spring. I owe her ten thousand thanks for her kindness to you particularly, and more especially than for what she has done and is doing in a more direct way for me personally. Although I feel grateful for every expression of kindness or sympathy towards me, yet nothing can so effectually minister to my comfort as acts of kindness done to relieve the wants or mitigate the sufferings of my poor, distressed family. May God Almighty and their own consciousness be their eternal rewarders. I am exceedingly rejoiced to have you make the acquaintance and be surrounded by such choice friends as I have long known some of those to be with whom you are staying, by reputation. I am most glad to have you meet with one of a family (or I would rather say of two families) most beloved and never to be forgotten by me. I mean dear, gentle ———. Many and many a time have she, her father, mother, brother, sisters, uncle, and aunt, like angels of mercy, ministered to the wants of myself and of my poor sons, both in sickness and in health. Only last year I lay sick for quite a number of weeks with them, and was cared for by all as though I had been a most affectionate brother or father. Tell her that I ask God to bless and reward them all for ever. "I was a stranger, and they took me in." It may possibly be that ——— would like to copy this letter, and send it to her home. If so, by all means let her do so. I would write them if I had the power.

" Now, let me say a word about the effort to educate our daughters. I am no longer able to provide means to help towards that object, and it therefore becomes me not to dictate in the matter. I shall gratefully submit the direction of the whole thing to those whose generosity may lead them to undertake it in their behalf, while I give anew a little expression of my own choice respecting it. You, my wife, perfectly well know that I have always expressed a decided preference for a very plain, but perfectly practical, education for both sons and daughters. I do not mean an education so very miserable as that you and I received in early life, nor as some of our children enjoyed. When I say plain but practical, I mean enough of the learning of the schools to enable them to transact the common business of life, together with that thorough training in good business habits which best prepares both men and women to be useful though poor, and to meet the stern realities of life with a good grace. You well know that I always claimed that the music of the broom, wash-tub, needle, spindle, loom, axe, scythe, hoe, flail, &c. should first be learned at all events, and that of the piano, &c. afterwards. I put them in that order, as most conductive to health of body and mind ; and for obvious reasons, that, after a life of some experience and much observation, I have found ten women as well as ten men who have made their mark in life right, whose early training was of that plain, practical kind, to one who had a more popular and fashionable early training. But enough of this.

Now, in regard to your coming here : If you feel sure that you can endure the trials and the shock, which will be unavoidable if you come, I should be glad to see you once more ; but when I think of your being insulted on the road, and perhaps while here, and of only seeing your wretchedness made complete, I shrink from it. Your composure and fortitude of mind may be quite equal to it all; but I am in dreadful doubt of it. If you do come, defer your journey till about the 27th or 28th of this month. The scenes which you will have to pass through on coming here will be anything but those you now pass, with tender-hearted friends and kind faces to meet you everywhere. Do consider the matter well before you make the plunge. I think I had better say no more on this most painful subject. My health improves a little; my mind is very tranquil, I may say joyous, and I continue to receive every kind attention that I have any possible need of. I wish you to send copies of all my letters to all our poor children. What I write to one must answer for all, till I have more strength. I get numerous kind letters from friends in almost all directions, to encourage me to " be of good cheer," and I still have, as I trust, " the peace of God to rule in my heart." May God, for Christ's sake, ever make his face to shine on you all.

Your affectionate husband,

JOHN BROWN.

— —

9.—TO MR. MUSGRAVE, JUN. NORTHAMPTON, MASS.

Charlestown, Jefferson Co., Virginia,
Nov. 17, 1859.

My dear young friend,

       I have just received your most kind and welcome letter of the 15th inst., but did not get any other from you. I am under many obligations to you and to your father, for all the kindness you have shown me, especially since my disaster. May God and your own con-

sciences ever be your rewarders. Tell your father that I
am quite cheerful—that I do not feel myself in the least
degraded by my imprisonment, my chains, or the near
prospect of the gallows. Men cannot imprison, or chain,
or hang the soul. I go joyfully in behalf of millions that
"have no rights" that this great and glorious, this Christian republic is "bound to respect." Strange change in
morals, political as well as Christian, since 1776! I look
forward to other changes to take place in God's good time,
fully believing that the "fashion of this world passeth
away."

Farewell! May God abundantly bless you all.

Your friend,
JOHN BROWN.

10.—TO MRS. BROWN.

Charlestown, Jefferson County, Virginia,
November 21st, 1859.

My dear wife,

Your most welcome letter of the 13th instant I
got yesterday. I am very glad to learn from yourself that
you feel so much resigned to your circumstances, so much
confidence in a wise and good Providence, and such composure of mind in the midst of all your deep afflictions.
This is "just as it should be ;" and let me still say, "Be
of good cheer," for we shall soon "come out of all our
great tribulations," and very soon (if we trust in Him)
"God shall wipe away all tears from our eyes." Soon
"we shall be satisfied when we are awake in His likeness." There is now here a source of much disquietude to
me, viz. the fires which are almost of daily and nightly

occurrence in this immediate neighbourhood. Whilst I well know that no one of them is the work of our friends, I know at the same time that by more or less of the inhabitants we shall be charged with them, the same as with the ominous and threatening letters to Governor Wise. In the existing state of public feeling, I can easily see a further objection to your coming here at present; but I did not intend saying another word to you on that subject. Why will you not say to me whether you had any crops mature this season? If so, what ones? Although I may never more intermeddle with your worldly affairs, I have not yet lost all interest in them. A little history of your success or of your failures I should very much prize; and I would gratify you and other friends some way, were it in my power. I am still quite cheerful, and by no means cast down. I "remember that the time is short." The little trunk and all its contents, so far as I can judge, reached me safe. May God reward all the contributors! I wrote you under cover to our excellent friend Mrs. Spring on the 16th instant. I presume you have it before now. When you return, it is most likely the Lake will not be open; so you must get your ticket at Troy for Moreau Station, or Glens Falls (for Glens Falls, if you can get one), or get one for Vergennes in Vermont, and take your chance of crossing over on the ice to Westport. If you go soon, the route by Glens Falls to Elizabethtown will probably be the best. I have just learned that our poor Watson lingered with his wound until Wednesday about noon of the 19th of October. Oliver died near my side in a few moments after he was shot. Dauphin died the next morning after Oliver and William were killed, viz. Monday. He died almost instantly- was by my side. William was shot by several persons. Anderson was killed with Dauphin.

Keep this letter to refer to. God Almighty bless and keep you all.

Your affectionate husband,
JOHN BROWN.

Dear Mrs. Spring, I send this to your care, because I am at a loss where it will reach my wife.

Your friend, in truth,
J. BROWN.

11.—TO HIS CHILDREN AT NORTH ELBA.

Charlestown, Jefferson Co., Virginia,
November 22nd, 1859.

Dear children all,

I address this letter to you, supposing that your mother is not yet with you. She has not yet come here ; as I have requested her not to do at present, if at all. She may think it best for her not to come at all. She has (or will), I presume, written you before this. Annie's letter to us both, of the 9th, has but just reached me. I am very glad to get it, and to learn that you are in any measure cheerful. This is the greatest comfort I can have, except that it would be to know that you are all Christians. God in mercy grant you all may be so. That is what you all will certainly need. When and in what form death may come is of but small moment. I feel just as content to die for God's eternal truth, and for suffering humanity's, on the scaffold as in any other way ; and I do not say this from any disposition to " brave it out." No;

I would readily own my wrong, were I in the least convinced of it. I have now been confined over a month,
with a good opportunity to look the whole thing as "fair
in the face," as I am capable of doing; and I now feel
it most grateful that I am counted, in the least possible
degree, worthy to suffer for the truth. I want you all
to "be of good cheer." This life is intended as a season of training, chastisement, temptation, affliction, and
trial, and the "righteous shall come out of" it all. Oh,
my dear children! let me again entreat you all to "forsake
the foolish, and live." What can you possibly lose by such
a course? "Godliness with contentment is great gain, having the promise of the life that now is, and of that which
is to come." "Trust in the Lord, and do good, so shalt
thou dwell in the land; and verily thou shalt be fed." I
have enjoyed life much; why should I complain on leaving
it? I want some of you to write me a little more particularly about all that concerns your welfare. I intend to
write you as often as I can. "To God and the word of his
grace I commend you all."

Your affectionate father,
JOHN BROWN.

12.—TO HIS SONS JOHN AND JASON, IN OHIO.

Charlestown, Jefferson Co., Virginia,
Nov. 22, 1859.

Dear children,

Your most welcome letters of the 16th instant
I have just received, and I bless God that he has enabled
you to bear the heavy tidings of our disaster with so much
seeming resignation and composure of mind. That is ex-

actly the thing I have wished you all to do for me—to be
cheerful and perfectly resigned to the holy will of a wise
and good God.   I bless his most holy name that I am, I
trust, in some good measure able to do the same.   I am
even "joyful in all my tribulations," ever since my confinement, and I humbly trust that " I know in whom I
have trusted."   A calm peace, perhaps like that which
your own dear mother* felt in view of her last change,
seems to fill my mind by day and by night.   Of this
neither the powers of "earth or hell" can deprive me.   Do
not, dear children, any of you grieve for a single moment
on my account.   As I trust my life has not been thrown
away, so I also humbly trust that my death shall not be
in vain.   God can make it to be a thousand times more
valuable to his own cause than all the miserable service,
at best, that I have rendered it during my life.   When I
was first taken, I was too feeble to write much; so I wrote
what I could to North Elba, requesting Ruth and Anne
to send you copies of all my letters to them.   I hope they
have done so, and that you, Ellen,† will do the same with
what I may send to you, as it is still quite a labour for me
to write all that I need to.   I want your brothers to know
what I write, if you know where to reach them.   I wrote
Jeremiah, a few days since, to supply a trifling assistance,
fifteen dollars, to such of you as might be most destitute.‡
I got his letter, but do not know as he got mine.   I hope
to get another letter from him soon.   I also asked him to
show you my letter.   I know of nothing you can any of

* His first wife.
† Wife of John Brown.
‡ He here covertly alludes to his son Owen, then destitute and
in hiding, after his escape from Harper's Ferry.

you now do for me, unless it is to comfort your own hearts, and cheer and encourage each other to trust in God, and Jesus Christ whom he hath sent.   If you will keep his sayings, you shall certainly " know of his doctrine whether it be of God or no."   Nothing can be more grateful to me than your earnest sympathy, except it be to know that you are fully persuaded to be Christians.   And now, dear children, farewell for this time.   I hope to be able to write you again.   The God of my father take you for his children.

Your affectionate father,

JOHN BROWN.

13.—TO REV. MR. MCFARLAND, WOOSTER, OHIO.

Jail, Charlestown, Wednesday, Nov. 23, 1859.
Rev. McFarland—Dear friend,

Although you write to me as a stranger, the spirit you show towards me and the cause for which I am in bonds makes me feel towards you as a dear friend.   I would be glad to have you or any of my liberty-loving ministerial friends here, to talk and pray with me.   I am not a stranger to the way of salvation by Christ.   From my youth I have studied much on that subject, and at one time hoped to be a minister myself ; but God had another work for me to do.   To me it is given, in behalf of Christ, not only to believe on him, but also to suffer for his sake.   But, while I trust that I have some experimental and saving knowledge of religion, it would be a great pleasure to me to have some one better qualified than myself to lead my mind in prayer and meditation, now that my time is so near a close.   You may wonder, are there no ministers

of the gospel here? I answer, No. There are no ministers of Christ here. These ministers who profess to be
Christian, and hold slaves or advocate slavery, I cannot
abide them. My knees will not bend in prayer with them,
while their hands are stained with the blood of souls. The
subject you mention as having been preaching on, the day
before you wrote to me, is one which I have often thought
of since my imprisonment. I think I feel as happy as
Paul did when he lay in prison. He knew, if they killed
him, it would greatly advance the cause of Christ; that
was the reason he rejoiced so. On that same ground " I
do rejoice, yea, and will rejoice." Let them hang me; I
forgive them, and may God forgive them, for they know
not what they do. I have no regret for the transaction
for which I am condemned. I went against the laws of
men, it is true; but "whether it be right to obey God or
men, judge ye." Christ told me to remember them that
are in bonds as bound with them, to do towards them as
I would wish them to do towards me in similar circumstances. My conscience bade me do that. I tried to do
it, but failed. Therefore I have no regret on that score.
I have no sorrow either as to the result, only for my poor
wife and children. They have suffered much, and it is
hard to leave them uncared for. But God will be a husband to the widow, and a father to the fatherless.

I have frequently been in Wooster; and if any of my
old friends from about Akron are there, you can show
them this letter. I have but a few more days, and I feel
anxious to be away, "where the wicked cease from troubling, and the weary are at rest." Farewell.

Your friend, and the friend of all friends of liberty,

JOHN BROWN.

14.—EXTRACT.

November 24th.

I have had many interesting visits from pro-slavery persons, almost daily, and I endeavour to improve them faithfully, plainly, and kindly. I do not think I ever enjoyed life better than since my confinement here. For this I am indebted to Infinite Grace, and kind letters from friends from different quarters. I wish I could only know that all my poor family were as composed and as happy as I. I think nothing but the Christian religion could ever make anyone so composed.

> " My willing soul would stay
> In such a frame as this."

JOHN BROWN.

15.—TO MR. HOYT, BOSTON.

Charlestown, Jefferson County, Virginia,
November 24, 1859.

George H. Hoyt, Esq.

Dear sir, your kind letter of the 22nd instant is received. I exceedingly regret my inability to make you some other acknowledgment for all your efforts in my behalf than that which consists merely in words ; but so it is. May God and a good conscience be your continual reward. I really do not see what you can do with me any further. I commend my poor family to the kind remembrance of all friends, but I well understand that they are not the only poor in our world. I ought to begin to leave off saying ' our world.' I have but very little idea of the charges made against Mr. Griswold, as I get to see

18*

but little of what is afloat. I am very sorry for any wrong that may be done him; but I have no means of contradicting anything that may be said, not knowing what he said. I cannot see how it should be any more dishonourable for him to receive some compensation for his expenses and service, than for Mr. Chilton, and I am not aware that any blame is attached to him on that score.* I am getting more letters constantly than I well know how to answer. My kind friends appear to have very wrong ideas of my condition, as regards replying to all the kind communications I receive.

Your friend, in truth,
JOHN BROWN.

———

16.—TO MRS. BROWN AT PHILADELPHIA.

[Before Mrs. Brown started from Philadelphia for Charlestown, she received a letter from her husband, dated November 25, in which, after referring to the circumstance that she was then staying under the hospitable roof of Mrs. Lucretia Mott, he continues :—]

. . . I remember the faithful old lady well, but presume she has no recollection of me. I once set myself to

* Mr. Chilton, Brown's southern lawyer, demanded a fee of one thousand dollars, which was paid out of the fund contributed for his family and cause in the New England states. Mr. Griswold accepted a fee of two hundred and fifty dollars, for travelling expenses and services, from Captain Brown personally, supposing that he was a man of independent fortune. For receiving this fee, Mr. Griswold was denounced in the democratic papers, while not one of them printed a word against the Maryland lawyer.

oppose a mob at Boston, where she was. After I interfered, the police immediately took up the matter, and
soon put a stop to mob proceedings. The meeting was, I
think, in Marlborough-street church, or hotel, perhaps.
I am glad to have you make the acquaintance of such old
"pioneers" in the cause. I have just received from Mr.
John Jay, of New York, a draft for fifty dollars for the
benefit of my family, and will enclose it made payable to
your order. I have also fifteen dollars to send to our
crippled and destitute unmarried son ; when I can, I intend to send you, by express, two or three little articles
to carry home. Should you happen to meet with Mr.
Jay, say to him that you fully appreciate his great kindness both to me and my family. God bless all such friends.
It is out of my power to reply to all the kind and encouraging letters I get ; I wish I could do so. I have been
so much relieved from my lameness for the last three or
four days, as to be able to sit up to read and write pretty
much all day, as well as part of the night; and I do assure
you and all other friends that I am quite busy, and none
the less happy on that account. The time passes quite
pleasantly, and the near approach of my great change is
not the occasion of any particular dread.

I trust that God, who has sustained me so long, will not
forsake me when I most feel my need of fatherly aid and
support. Should he hide his face, my spirit will droop
and die ; but not otherwise, be assured. My only anxiety
is to be properly assured of my fitness for the company of
those who are "washed from all filthiness," and for the
presence of him who is infinitely pure. I certainly think
I do have some "hunger and thirst after righteousness."
If it be only genuine, I make no doubt I "shall be filled."
Please let all our friends read my letters when you can ;

and ask them to accept of it as in part for them. I am inclined to think you will not be likely to succeed well about getting away the bodies of your family; but should that be so, do not let that grieve you. It can make but little difference what is done with them.

You can well remember the changes you have passed through. Life is made up of a series of changes, and let us meet them in the best manner possible. You will not wish to make yourself and children any more burdensome to friends than you are really compelled to do. I would not.

I will close this by saying that, if you now feel that you are equal to the undertaking, do exactly as you feel disposed to do about coming to see me before I suffer. I am entirely willing.

Your affectionate husband,
JOHN BROWN.

17.—TO MR. THADDEUS HYATT.

Charlestown, Jefferson Co. Virginia,
November 27, 1859.

Thaddeus Hyatt, Esq.—My dear sir,

Your very acceptable letter of the 24th instant has just been handed to me. I am certainly most obliged to you for it, and for all your efforts in behalf of my family and myself. . . . . Your effort, at any rate, takes from my mind the greatest burden I have felt since my imprisonment, to feel assured that, in some way, my shattered and broken-hearted wife and children would be so far relieved as to save them from great physical suffering. Others may have devised a better way of doing it. I had no advice in regard to it, and felt very grateful to know, while I was yet living, of almost any active measure being taken. I hope no offence is taken at yourself or me in the matter. I am beginning to familiarize my mind with new and very different scenes. Am very cheerful.

Farewell, my friend.

JOHN BROWN.

18.—TO A YOUNG LADY.

Charlestown, Jefferson Co., Virginia,
Nov. 27, 1859.

My dear Miss ——,

Your most kind and cheering letter of the 18th instant is received. Although I have not been at all low-spirited or cast down in feeling since being imprisoned and under sentence, which I am fully aware is soon to be carried out, it is exceedingly gratifying to learn from friends that there are not wanting in this generation some to sympathize with me and appreciate my motive, even now that I am whipped.* Success is in general the standard of all merit. I have passed my time here quite cheerfully; still trusting that neither my life nor my death will prove a total loss. As regards both, however, I am liable to mistake. It affords me some satisfaction to feel conscious of having at least tried to better the condition of those who are always on the under-hill side, and am in hope of being able to meet the consequences without a murmur. I am endeavouring to get ready for ano-

---

* The word *whipped* is commonly used in the United States in the sense of *subdued, defeated.*

ther field of action, where no defeat befalls the truly brave. That God reigns, and most wisely, and controls all events, might, it would seem, reconcile those who believe it, to much that appears to be very disastrous. I am one who tried to believe that, and still keep trying. Those who die for the truth may prove to be courageous at last ; so I continue "hoping on," till I shall find that the truth must finally prevail. I do not feel in the least degree despondent or degraded by my circumstances, and I entreat my friends not to grieve on my account. You will please excuse a very poor and short letter, as I get more than I can possibly answer. I send my best wishes to your kind mother, and to all the family, and to all the true friends of humanity. And now, dear friends, God be with you all, and ever guide and bless you.

Your friend,
JOHN BROWN.

19.—TO JUDGE TILDEN, OF MASSACHUSETTS.

Charlestown, Jefferson Co., Virginia,
Monday, Nov. 28, 1859.

Hon. D. R. Tilden,—My dear sir,

Your most kind and comforting letter of the 23rd instant is received. I have no language to express the feelings of gratitude and obligation I am under for your kind interest in my behalf ever since my disaster.

The great bulk of mankind estimate each other's actions and motives by the measure of success or otherwise that attends them through life. By that rule I have been one of the worst and one of the best of men. I do not claim to have been one of the latter; and I leave it to an impar-

tial tribunal to decide whether the world has been the
worse or the better of my living and dying in it. My
present great anxiety is to get as near in readiness for a
different field of action as I well can, since being in a
good measure relieved from the fear that my poor, broken-
hearted wife and children would come to immediate want.
May God reward a thousand-fold all the kind efforts made
in their behalf. I have enjoyed remarkable cheerfulness
and composure of mind ever since my confinement; and it
is a great comfort to feel assured that I am permitted to
die for a cause; not merely to pay the debt of nature—as
all must. I feel myself to be most unworthy of so great
distinction. The particular manner of dying assigned to
me gives me but very little uneasiness. I wish I had the
time and the ability to give you, my dear friend, some
little idea of what is daily, and, I might almost say,
hourly passing within my prison walls ; and, could my
friends but witness only a few of those scenes, just as
they occur, I think they would feel very well reconciled
to my being here, just what I am, and just as I am. My
whole life before had not afforded me one half the opportunity to plead for the right. In this, also, I find much
to reconcile me to both my present condition and my immediate prospect. I may be very insane, and I am so if
insane at all. But, if that be so, insanity is like a very
pleasant dream to me. I am not in the least degree conscious of my ravings, of my fears, or of any terrible
visions whatever ; but fancy myself entirely composed ;
and that my sleep, in particular, is as sweet as that of a
healthy, joyous little infant. I pray God that he will
grant me a continuance of the same calm but delightful
dream, until I come to know of those realities which
eyes have not seen, and which ears have not heard. I

have scarce realized that I am in prison or in irons at all. I certainly think I was never more cheerful in my life.

I intend to take the liberty of sending by express, to your care, some trifling articles for those of my family who may be in Ohio, which you can hand to my brother Jeremiah when you may see him, together with fifteen dollars I have asked him to advance to them. Please excuse me so often troubling you with my letters, or any of my matters. Please also remember me most kindly to Mr. Griswold, and to all others who love their neighbours. I write Jeremiah to your care.

Your friend, in truth,

JOHN BROWN.

20.—TO MR. SAMUEL E. SEWALL, OF BOSTON.

Charlestown, Jefferson County, Virginia,
November 29, 1859.

S. E. Sewall, Esq.· —My dear sir,

Your most kind letter of the 24th instant is received. It does, indeed, give me pleasure and the greatest encouragement to know of any efforts that have been made in behalf of my poor and deeply afflicted family. It takes from my mind the greatest cause of sadness I have experienced during my imprisonment here. I feel quite cheerful, and ready to die. I can only say, for want of time, may the God of the oppressed and the poor, in great mercy, remember all those to whom we are so deeply indebted. Farewell.

Your friend,

JOHN BROWN.

21.—TO THE REV. MR. MILLIGAN, PENNSYLVANIA.

Charlestown, Jefferson Co. Virginia,
29th Nov., 1859.

My dear Covenanter (Rev. A. M. Milligan,)*

Dear Friend : notwithstanding I now get daily more than three times the number of kind letters I can possibly answer, I cannot deny myself the satisfaction of saying a few words to a stranger whose feelings and whose judgment so nearly coincide with my own. No letter, of a great number I have got to cheer, encourage, and advise me, has given more heart-warming satisfaction or better counsel than your own. I hope to profit by it ; and I am greatly obliged for this your visit to my prison. It really seemed to impart new strength to my soul, notwithstanding I was very cheerful before. I trust, dear brother, that God, in infinite grace and mercy, for Christ's sake, will "neither leave me nor forsake me," till "I have shewed his power to this generation, and his strength to every one that is to come." I would most gladly commune further as we journey on ; but I am so near the close of mine that I must break off, however reluctant.

Farewell, my faithful brother in Christ Jesus. Farewell.

Your friend,
JOHN BROWN.

* The Covenanters, a small religious body, holding highly Calvinistic tenets, are the only sect in the United States who maintain a thoroughly consistent testimony against slavery. They not only refuse to hold slaves, but decline all political action, on the ground of the inherent constitutional complicity of the federal government with the slave system.

22.—HIS LAST LETTER TO HIS FAMILY.

Charlestown Prison, Jefferson Co., Virginia,
November 30, 1859.

My dearly beloved wife, sons and daughters, every one :

As I now begin what is probably the last letter
I shall ever write to any of you, I conclude to write to all
at the same time.   I will mention some little matters particularly applicable to little property concerns in another
place.

I recently received a letter from my wife, from near
Philadelphia, dated Nov. 22, by which it would seem that
she was about giving up the idea of seeing me again.   I
had written to her to come on if she felt equal to the undertaking, but I do not know that she will get my letter in
time.   It was on her own account chiefly that I asked her
to stay back.   At first I had a most strong desire to see her
again, but there appeared to be very serious objections ;
and should we never meet in this life, I trust that we shall
in the end be satisfied it was for the best, at least, if not
most for her comfort.   I enclosed in my last letter to her
a draft of fifty dollars from John Jay, made payable to her
order.   I have now another to send her, from my excellent
old friend Edward Harris, of Woonsocket, Rhode Island,
for one hundred dollars, which I shall also make payable
to her order.

I am waiting the hour of my public murder with great
composure of mind and cheerfulness, feeling the strong
assurance that in no other possible way could I be used to
so much advantage to the cause of God and of humanity,
and that nothing that either I or all my family have sacrificed or suffered will be lost.   The reflection that a wise
and merciful as well as just and holy God rules not only

the affairs of this world, but of all worlds, is a rock to set
our feet upon under all circumstances—even those more
severely trying ones in which our own feelings and wrongs
have placed us. I have now no doubt but that our seeming disaster will ultimately result in the most glorious success. So, my dear, shattered, and broken family, be of
good cheer, and believe and trust in God with all your
heart and with all your soul, for he doeth all things well.
Do not feel ashamed on my account, nor for one moment
despair of the cause, or grow weary of well doing. I bless
God I never felt stronger confidence in the certain and
near approach of a bright morning and glorious day than
I have felt, and do now feel, since my confinement here.
I am endeavouring to return, like a poor prodigal as I am,
to my Father, against whom I have always sinned, in the
hope that he may kindly and forgivingly help me, though
a very great way off.

O, my dear wife and children, would to God you could
know how I have been travailing in birth for you all, that
no one of you may fail of the grace of God through Jesus
Christ; that no one of you may be blind to the truth and
glorious light of his Word, in which life and immortality
are brought to light. I beseech you, every one, to make
the Bible your daily and nightly study, with a childlike,
honest, candid, teachable spirit of love and respect for
your husband and father.

And I beseech the God of my fathers to open all your
eyes to the discovery of the truth. You cannot imagine
how much you may soon need the consolations of the Christian religion. Circumstances like my own, for more than
a month past, have convinced me, beyond all doubt, of our
great need of some theories treasured up when our prejudices are excited, our vanity worked up to the highest

pitch.   O, do not trust your eternal all upon the boisterous ocean, without even a helm or compass to aid you in steering.   I do not ask of you to throw away your reason.   I only ask you to make a candid, sober use of your reason.

My dear young children, will you listen to this last poor admonition of one who can only love you ?   O, be determined at once to give your whole heart to God, and let nothing shake or alter that resolution.   You need have no fears of regretting it.   Do not be vain and thoughtless, but sober-minded ; and let me entreat you all to love the whole remnant of our once great family.   Try and build up again your broken walls, and to make the utmost of every stone that is left.   Nothing can so tend to make life a blessing as the consciousness that your life and example bless and leave you the stronger.   Still, it is ground of the utmost comfort to my mind to know that so many of you as have had the opportunity have given some proof of your fidelity to the great family of man.   Be faithful unto death; from the exercise of habitual love to man, it cannot be very hard to love his Maker.

I must yet insert the reason for my firm belief in the divine inspiration of the Bible, notwithstanding I am, perhaps, naturally sceptical ; certainly not credulous.   I wish all to consider it most thoroughly when you read that blessed book, and see whether you cannot discover such evidence yourselves.   It is the purity of heart, filling our minds as well as work and actions, which is everywhere insisted on, that distinguishes it from all the other teachings, that commends it to my conscience.   Whether my heart be willing and obedient or not, the inducement that it holds out is another reason of my conviction of its truth and genuineness.   But I do not here omit this my last argument on the Bible, that eternal life is what my soul is panting after this moment. I mention this as a reason for endeavouring to leave a valuable copy of the Bible, to be carefully preserved in remembrance of me, to so many of my posterity, instead of some other book at equal cost.

I beseech you all to live in habitual contentment with moderate circumstances and gains of worldly store, and earnestly to teach this to your children and children's children after you, by example as well as precept. Be determined to know by experience, as soon as may be, whether Bible instruction is of divine origin or not. Be sure to owe no man anything, but to love one another. John Rogers wrote to his children, "Abhor that arrant whore of Rome." John Brown writes to *his* children to abhor, with undying hatred also, that sum of all villanies—slavery. Remember, he that is slow to anger is better than the mighty, and he that ruleth his spirit than he that taketh a city. Remember, also, that "they that be wise shall shine," and "they that turn many to righteousness, as the stars forever and ever."

And now, dearly beloved family, to God and the word of his grace I commend you all.

Your affectionate husband and father,

JOHN BROWN.

***

23.—TO MR. JAMES FORMAN.

Charlestown Prison, Jefferson County, Virginia,
December 1, 1859.

My dear friend,

I have only time to say I got your kind letter of the 26th November, this evening. Am very grateful for all the good feeling expressed by yourself and wife.   May God abundantly bless and save you all.   I am very cheerful, in hopes of entering on a better state of existence in a few hours, through infinite grace in " Christ Jesus my Lord."   Remember the "poor that cry," and "them that are in bonds as bound with them."

Your friend as ever,

JOHN BROWN.

24.—HIS WILL.

Charlestown, Jefferson County, Virginia,
December 1, 1859.

I GIVE to my son John Brown, jun., my surveyor's compass and other surveyor's articles, if found; also my old granite monument, now at North Elba, New York, to receive upon its two sides a further inscription, as I will hereafter direct; said stone monument, however, to remain at North Elba so long as any of my children and my wife may remain there as residents.

I give to my son Jason Brown my silver watch, with my name engraved on inner case.

I give to my son Owen Brown my double-spring opera-glass, and my rifle gun (if found), presented to me at Worcester, Massachusetts.   It is globe-sighted and new. I give also to the same son fifty dollars in cash, to be paid him from the proceeds of my father's estate, in consideration of his terrible sufferings in Kansas, and his crippled condition from his childhood.

I give to my son Solomon Brown fifty dollars in cash, to be paid him from my father's estate, as an offset to the first two cases above named.

I give to my daughter Ruth Thompson my large old Bible, containing the family record.

I give to each of my sons, and to each of my other daughters, my son-in-law Henry Thompson, and to each of my daughters-in-law, as good a copy of the Bible as can be purchased at some bookstore in New York or Boston, at a cost of five dollars each in cash, to be paid out of the proceeds of my father's estate.

I give to each of my grandchildren that may be living when my father's estate is settled, as good a copy of the Bible as can be purchased, as above, at a cost of three dollars each. All the Bibles to be purchased at one and the same time, for cash, on the best terms.

I desire to have fifty dollars each paid out of the final proceeds of my father's estate to the following named persons, to wit: To Allen Hammond, Esq., of Rockville, Tolland County, Connecticut, or to George Kellogg, Esq., former agent of the New England Company at that place, for the use and benefit of that company. Also, fifty dollars to Silas Havens, formerly of Lewisburg, Summit County, Ohio, if he can be found; also, fifty dollars to a man of Storck County, Ohio, at Canton, who sued my father in his lifetime, through Judge Humphrey and Mr. Upson of Akron, to be paid by J. R. Brown to the man in person, if he can be found. His name I cannot remember. My father made a compromise with the man by taking our house and lot at Manneville. I desire that any remaining balance that may become my due from my father's estate may be paid in equal amounts to my wife, and to each of my children, and to the widows of Watson and Oliver Brown, by my brother.

JOHN BROWN.

JOHN AVIS, witness.

19

CHAPTER XI.

VISIT FROM JUDGE RUSSELL AND WIFE.—CALMNESS AND COU-
RAGE OF THE PRISONER.—VISIT FROM MRS. MARCUS SPRING
AND HER SON.—TESTIMONY OF A PREJUDICED WITNESS.—
APPEAL FOR WRIT OF ERROR REFUSED.—CAPTAIN BROWN
REJECTS THE AID OF PROSLAVERY DIVINES.—REPORT OF
HIS CONVERSATION WITH COLONEL SMITH.—HIS INSCRIPTION
IN A BIBLE.—HIS FAREWELL INTERVIEW WITH MRS. BROWN.

CAPTAIN BROWN was imprisoned in the jail of
Charlestown for forty-two days. From his commitment on the 19th of October till the 7th of November,
no clean clothing was given to him; he wore fetters on
his legs, and he lay in his blood-stained garments, as
he had fallen at Harper's Ferry. His conduct while
in prison was in keeping with his brave and constant
character. He never swerved in his faith, nor faltered
in the presence of any man.

We shall here give a selection from the notices of his
life in prison which were published at the time. They
vividly portray the dignity and cheerfulness of his
demeanour, and his unfailing confidence in the goodness of the cause to which his life was devoted.

On the 2nd November, the day on which sentence
was pronounced, Judge Russell of Boston and his wife
arrived in Charlestown, and had a long interview with
Captain Brown, which appeared to give him much

gratification. A gentleman who was admitted to see the prisoner on the same day, informs us that "Brown is as comfortably situated as any man can be in a jail. He has a pleasant room, which is shared by Stevens, whose recovery remains doubtful. He has opportunities of occupying himself by writing and reading. His jailer, Avis, was of the party who assisted in capturing him. Brown says that Avis is one of the bravest men he ever saw, and that his treatment is precisely what he should expect from so brave a fellow. Avis is a just and humane man. He does all for his prisoners that his duty allows him to. I think he has a sincere respect for Brown's undaunted fortitude and fearlessness. Brown is permitted to receive such visitors as he desires to see. He states that he welcomes every one, and that he is preaching, even in jail, with great effect, upon the enormities of slavery, and with arguments which every body fails to answer. His wounds, excepting one cut on the back of the head, have all now healed without suppuration, and the scars are scarcely visible. He attributes his very rapid recovery to his strictly abstemious habits through life. He is really a man of imposing appearance, and neither his tattered garments, the rents in which were caused by sword cuts, nor his scarred face, can detract from the manliness of his mien. He is always composed, and every trace of disquietude has left him."

To a newspaper correspondent who visited him at this time he spoke in praise of Captain Avis. Seeing

19*

that one of the deputy jailers was present, he added,
" I don't say this to flatter; it isn't my way. I say it
because it is true." He adds, " Brown appears perfectly
fearless in all respects—says that he has no feeling
about death on a scaffold. He speaks highly of his
medical attendants, but rejects the offered counsel of
all ministers who believe that slavery is right. He
will die as fearlessly as he lived."

A reporter who had access to the cell on November
3rd, states that " Brown's cheerfulness never fails him.
He converses with all who visit him in a manner so
free from restraint and with so much unconcern, that
none can doubt his real convictions of self-approval.
His daring courage has strongly impressed the people,
and I have more than once heard public avowals of
admiration of his fearlessness, in spite of ominous mur-
murs of disapprobation from bystanders. A telegraphic
despatch, dated Boston, was this morning received
from T. W. Higginson. It said, 'John Brown's wife
wishes to go on and see him. Can you obtain permission for her?' This was answered affirmatively; but
when the matter was mentioned to Brown, he directed
that this message should be immediately sent: 'Do
not, for God's sake, come here now. John Brown.'"

The same reporter adds :—" You, at a distance, can
hardly form an impression of the rage for vengeance
which is felt by the citizens of this place. When Brown
was in court on trial, there were always faces burning
with hatred hanging over him, fiercely watching every

movement that he made. In the event of an attempt to rescue, which has been the great fear all along, the jailers have been instructed to shoot him. The populace are resolute in their determination that their victims shall never be taken from them, and it does not seem that this determination is to be shaken by any expedient. Brown's own ideas on the subject are characteristic. He tranquilly says, ' I do not know that I ought to encourage any attempt to save my life. I am not sure that it would not be better for me to die at this time. I am not incapable of error, and I may be wrong ; but I think that perhaps my object would be nearer fulfilment if I should die. I must give it some thought.' There is no insincerity about this, you may be sure. Brown does not value his life ; or, at least, is wholly unmoved at the prospect of losing it. He was never more firm than at this moment. The only compunctions he expresses are in relation to his management at Harper's Ferry, by which he lost not only himself, but sacrificed his associates. He sometimes says that if he had pursued his original plan of immediate escape to the mountains, he could never have been taken, for he and his men had studied the vicinity thoroughly, and knew it a hundred times better than any of the inhabitants. It was, he says, his weakness in yielding to the entreaties of the prisoners, and thus delaying his departure, that ruined him. ' It was the first time,' are his own words, 'that I ever lost command of myself, and now I am punished for it.'"

On the 5th of November, Mrs. Marcus Spring, of Perth Amboy, New Jersey, accompanied by her son, arrived in Charlestown to visit Captain Brown, and found much difficulty in obtaining permission to see him. Next day, however, they were admitted to his cell, which was also occupied by Stevens. She describes the prison as a large brick building which seemed to have been formerly used as a dwelling-house. The prisoners occupied a room on the ground floor, about sixteen feet square, opening with a single door into a long gallery, and lighted by a small window defended by heavy double bars. They were lying on their beds when Mrs. Spring and her son entered. Captain Brown rose to receive his guests, and stood a few moments leaning against the bedstead, lying down again immediately from weakness. His visitors were struck with the cheerfulness of his expression and the calmness of his manner.

Mrs. Spring said to him, "I expected Mrs. Child would be here to introduce me ; I am sorry not to find her, for her presence would make this room brighter for you!"

He smiled and replied, "I have written to her the reasons why she should not come ; but she was very kind—very kind ! * * * * The reason why I did not wish her or my wife to come, was lest they would be harassed and annoyed, and that on this account I would be troubled myself."

Mrs. Spring thus continues her account of the interview :—"Between Mr. Brown and his jailer there has grown up a most friendly feeling. Captain Avis, who is too brave to be afraid to be kind, has done all he could for the prisoners, and been cursed accordingly. Still their condition was very cheerless, and Mr. Brown was in the same clothes in which he was taken. A cloth under his head was much stained with blood from a still open wound. It was hard for me to forget the presence of the jailer (I had that morning seen his advertisement of 'fifty negroes for sale');* but I soon lost all thought of him in listening to Mr. Brown, who spoke at once of his plans and his failure. Twenty years he has laboured, and waited, and suffered; and at last he believed the time of fulfilment had come. But he failed; and instead of being free on the mountains, strong to break every yoke and let the oppressed go free, he was shorn of his strength, with prison walls about him. 'But,' he said, 'I do not now reproach myself; I did what I could.'

"I said, 'The Lord often leads us in strange ways.'

"'Yes,' he answered, 'and I think I cannot now better serve the cause I love so much than to die for it; and in my death I may do more than in my life.'

"A pleasant smile came over his face when I exclaimed, 'Then you will be our martyr!' I continued, 'I want to ask one question for others, not for myself: Have you been actuated by any feeling of revenge?'

---

* We have been informed that Captain Avis was not a slave-dealer, as this would imply. As keeper of a jail in a southern state, he had charge of slaves kept for sale, and signed his name as jailer to the advertisements.

" He raised his head, and gave me a surprised look ; then, lying back, he answered slowly, but firmly, ' I am not conscious of having had a feeling of the kind. No; not in all the wrong done to me and my family in Kansas have I had a feeling of revenge.'

" ' That would not sustain you now,' I remarked.

" ' No, indeed,' he replied quickly ; ' but I sleep as peacefully as an infant ; or, if I am wakeful, glorious thoughts come to me, entertaining my mind.' Presently he added, ' The sentence they have pronounced against me did not disturb me in the least; it is not the first time that I have looked death in the face.'

" ' It is not the hardest thing for a brave man to die,' I answered ; ' but how will it be in the long days before you, shut up here ? If you can be true to yourself in all this, how glad we shall be !'

" ' I cannot say,' he responded ; ' but I do not believe I shall deny my Lord and Master, Jesus Christ ; and I should do so, if I denied my principles against slavery. Why, I preach against it all the time—Captain Avis knows I do.' The jailer smiled, and said, ' Yes.'

" We spoke of those who, in times of trial, forgot themselves ; and he said, ' There seems to be just that difference in people ; some can bear more than others, and not suffer so much. I have been through all kinds of hardships, and do not mind them.'

" My son remarked it was a great thing to have confidence in one's own strength.

" ' I do not mean to say that,' was his answer ; ' it

is only a constitutional difference, and I have been trained to hardships. But,' he added, smiling, 'I have one unconquerable weakness : I have always been more afraid of being taken into an evening party of ladies and gentlemen, than of meeting a company of men with guns.'

" I think he is still more afraid of giving trouble to others. He seems to me to be purely unselfish, and in all that he has done to have never thought of himself, but always of others. In a noble letter to his wife, which I brought away with me, he entreats his ' dear wife and children, every one, never in all your trials forget the poor that cry, and him that hath none to help him.' I never saw a person who seemed less troubled or excited, or whose mind was less disturbed and more clear. His remarks are pointed, pithy and sensible. He is not in the least sentimental, and seems to have singularly excellent common-sense about every thing. While he was talking to me with the deepest solicitude of his family, the rabble, ever hanging about the court-house and prison, fearful that we were plotting treason inside, became restless. The sheriff was frightened, and called the jailer, so that I had only a moment to speak to Stevens, and to say farewell to Mr. Brown, who stood up to take leave of us, saying, ' The Lord will bless you for coming here.' There was, I learned afterwards, an angry mob outside the jail, but I did not see it. In a moment we reached the hotel, and at once recorded all we could remember of this interesting visit. That night there were rumours of an attack on the jail, and it was thought best that I should not repeat my visit.*

* The circumstances attending the espionage upon strangers sometimes afforded much amusement. The following dialogue. which took place in the court-house yard, Charlestown, between a stranger and one of the inhabitants, furnishes an illustration :—

Stranger (to Virginian).—What are you staring at ?

Virginian.—I am staring at you.   What are you doing in this town ?

Stranger.—What am I doing ?   I'm minding my business, and that's as much as any one man can do, I reckon.

Virginian.—What is your business ?

Stranger.—Minding my business, I tell you.

Virginian.—You know there is great excitement here.

Stranger.—I don't know, and I am darned if I want to know.

Virginian.—Come, tell me where you are from ?

Stranger.—I'm from Georgia.

Virginian.—You are not a native of Georgia ?

Stranger.—No, but my wife is ; that's enough for you.

Virginian.—Do you know Governor Wise ?

Stranger.—No, nor I don't want to know him.

Virginian.—Do you know President Buchanan ?

Stranger.—Yes, sir'ee ; I do know James Buchanan. · I take off my hat to President Buchanan, and he takes off his to me ; and he says to me, " How do you do ?" and I say, " Very well, President."

Virginian.—Do you know Brown ?

Stranger.—I know nothing of Brown or Wise either.

Virginian.—Well, I must know your business ; what is it ?

Stranger.—Do you want to know ?

Virginian.—Yes.

Stranger. (putting his hand into a capacious pocket and pulling out a half-pint bottle of medicine)—Well, this is my business : to get fifty cents for this bottle of medicine, which cures cramps,

" But the evening before we left Charlestown, a telegram announced to me that Mrs. Brown was in Philadelphia ; and I was anxious, therefore, to have another
interview with her husband. In the morning I sent
for the judge, who went with us to the prison-door.
Mr. Brown was sitting at the table, where he had just
finished a letter to his wife and a note to me. He
looked better, and brighter, and happier than at my
first visit, and Stevens also looked better. The old
man said little except about his family, whom he com--
mended to the kindness of good people."

A correspondent of the *New York Herald*[*] testifies
to the character and courage of the prisoner :—" A person visiting Brown in jail, and seeing him for the first
time, with an estimate formed of the man from his
conduct during the trial and the speeches there delivered
by him, would find his pre-conceived opinions rapidly
disappear before the subject of them. It is true that,

scalds, bruises, rheumatism, mumps, measles, affections in the
jaw, and other complaints too numerous to tote up, I reckon.

Here a former purchaser of the medicine bore testimony to the
genuineness of the article, upon which the vendor launched forth
upon its various merits. This, however, did not save him from
visiting the interior of the jail, where he was detained a short time
and ordered to clear out upon his parole. The next morning the
stranger obeyed the injunction.

[*] This unscrupulous newspaper, edited by James Gordon Ben-
nett, is notorious as the mouthpiece of the pro-slavery democracy,
—the " northern men with southern principles."

acting under excitement, and from the consciousness
that he was surrounded by his enemies, Brown frequently indulged in irascible remarks, feeling somewhat
secure in the protection of the law whose victim he
must be; while, at the same time, he dared, and indeed
seemed to court, the worst his foes could do, thinking
perhaps that he might escape the slower and more
vengeful process of the law. In this state of feeling,
sensitive as an enthusiast in giving to the world the
motives of an act which, to his own diseased mind, was
great and good, but which the world must condemn,
he claimed with petulance and impatience those delays
in the administration of the law which neither his
crimes nor the circumstances of the court could fairly
admit of. His object in this was, as he himself said,
to give the world a fair opportunity of judging of his
motives. If this opportunity was to be denied him, a
summary quietus from one of the Sharpe's rifles in the
hands of his enemies was all he next most desired.
Now that he has received at the hands of justice and
fair play all the delay that he could possibly hope for
—a trial protracted over five days—with the fullest
publicity given to the statements of those witnesses
who testified most directly and generously to his humanity to his prisoners in the armory at Harper's Ferry, he
is satisfied, and awaits the result with that calm firmness which is the sure characteristic of a brave man.

"What Brown was most anxious to establish in the
eyes of the world, during the trial, was his claim to
being considered humane and merciful from his con-

duct to his prisoners. Whatever good quality a man possesses in a marked degree he is most anxious to have acknowledged at a time when circumstances point the other way; and so it was with Brown. Though his deeds in the Kansas border wars did not entitle him to be considered either as humane, or as averse to the shedding of blood, certainly his prisoners at Harper's Ferry had no fault to find with him on that score. They frankly acknowledged his humanity and courtesy towards them. At all events, the opinions formed of the man from the darker features of his life would fade before the influence of a personal interview with him in prison. Now that his fate has been decided by the just and proper process of law, he feels resigned to it. He no longer indulges in complaints and invectives. He rarely adverts to his trial; but whenever he does, he pays a tribute to all concerned—judge, counsel, and witnesses. He speaks freely upon all subjects but one, and that is, the death of his sons. From his taciturnity he has been adjudged as entirely callous as to the fate of his sons and the other unfortunate victims of his mad enterprise; but this is a very great mistake.

" Brown frequently indulges in amusing narratives of his encounters with his border enemies of Kansas and Missouri. He related to me that upon one occasion he had succeeded in running away with a party of slaves from Missouri, but that he was so hotly pursued that some stratagem was necessary to prevent them from being overtaken, in the event of which a severe fight and consequent sacrifice of life must be the result. To avoid this, Brown himself left the track of the retreating party, and, having completely disguised himself, joined the pursuers as an amateur. With them he remained a day and a night, entering into their counsels, and so effectually controlling their motions that he turned them off the right track, and gave his friends an opportunity to escape. The old man laughed as he recalled the scene, and said, 'I never was good at a disguise, but that time I deceived several of the party who had seen and known me before.' With all who come in a kindly spirit to visit him, Brown is exceedingly free and open. He esteems such as friends, and seems to view their leave-taking with regret. But these visits are but as angels' visits, for the jealousy and suspicion with which the people of Charlestown regard all who are likely to feel for and sympathize with the prisoner, keep barred the prison doors. It is not so, however, in regard to those about whose earnest hostility to all abolition movements there is no doubt entertained. They enter in flocks, and gape, and stare, and follow the jailer in and out. He is in the same cell with Stevens, at whose bedside he is constantly found sitting, with the Bible (just closed as the visitor enters) placed upon his knees. This is the Bible he always carried with him. It was found after the final attack and recapture in the armory at Harper's Ferry, and was restored by some kind person to its owner in captivity. It is almost needless to say that Brown awaits death with that resignation and tranquillity which disarm the dreaded phantom of all terror."

The correspondent of a republican paper, writing under date of November 8th, informs us that "Brown's conversation is singularly attractive. His manner attracts every one who approaches him, and while he talks he reigns. The other prisoners venerate him. Stevens sits in his bed, usually with his face away from the window, and listens all day to 'the Captain's' words, seldom offering a syllable except when called upon. Sometimes he gets a little excited, and springs forward to make clear some point about which 'the Captain' is in doubt; but his five bullets, in head and breast, weigh him down, and he is soon exhausted. As for the other men—Copeland, Green, and Coppock—they are always sending messages to 'the Captain,' assuring him that 'it was not they who confessed, and he mustn't growl at them, but at Cook.' I cannot forget hearing Brown express himself on the subject of the threatening anonymous letters that have been received by Governor Wise relating to his case. 'Well, gentlemen,' he said, 'I tell you what I think of them. They come from no friends of mine. I have nothing to do with such friends. Why, gentlemen, of all the things in the world that I despise, anonymous letters are the worst. If I had a little job to do, I would sooner take one-half of the men I brought down here to help me, than as many of these fellows as could fill all Jefferson County, standing close upon every inch. If I don't get out of this jail before such people as they take me out, I shan't go very soon."

During all this time, Brown daily received large numbers of letters. All anonymous notes he burned without reading. He replied to as many of the others as he had time to answer. Amongst other visitors, two militia companies called to see him—the Continentals and the Fredericksburg Guards. He received them cordially, but objected "to be made a monkey show of." He told the Continentals that he had seen their uniform on the border during the war between the United States and England, in the year 1812.

On the 16th of November, Captain Brown's counsel appealed against the judgment of the court, and petitioned for a writ of error, chiefly on the ground of an omission in the treason count; pleading that it was not proved that at the time of committing the acts charged as treason, he was a citizen of the state of Virginia, or even of the United States. But the five judges of the Supreme Court of Appeals unanimously confirmed the decision of the Jefferson County Court, and declined to hear Brown's counsel in the matter.

Captain Brown had frequent calls from the Virginian clergy. Mr. Lowry, an old neighbour who visited him, says that one of the pro-slavery divines of Virginia called to pray with him. The prisoner asked him if he was ready to fight, if necessity required it, for the freedom of the slave. On his answering in the negative, Brown said he would thank him to retire from his cell; that his prayers would be an abomination to his God. To another clergyman he said that he would not insult his God by bowing down with any one who had the blood of the slave upon his skirts.

A correspondent of the *Baltimore American* informs us that "Captain Brown refuses to receive any ministers who countenance slavery, telling them to go home and read their Bibles. Rev. Alfred Griffith had an interview with him a few days since, which lasted for nearly an hour, principally on the subject of slavery. They quoted Scripture to sustain their views, and had quite a clashing time of it; but neither was able to convince the other of the correctness of his peculiar doctrines."

Another reporter says that "Brown was visited yesterday by the Rev. Mr. March of the Methodist Episcopal Church. This gentleman having advanced an argument in favor of the institution of slavery as it now exists, Brown replied, 'My dear sir, you know nothing about Christianity; you will have to learn the A B C in the lesson of Christianity, as I find you are entirely ignorant of the meaning of the word. Of course I respect you as a gentleman, but it is as a heathen gentleman.'"

In speaking of the Pottawattomie executions, and of his being accused of having killed the ruffians, he assured Mr. Lowry that the charge needed no refutation from him. "Time and the honest verdict of posterity," added he, "will approve of every act of mine to prevent slavery from being established in Kansas. I never shed the blood of a fellow-man, except in self-de-

fence or in promotion of a righteous cause." Mr. Lowry
adds: "During our conversation, the martial music (for
Governor Wise was reviewing some soldiers outside the
prison) made a great noise, and, thinking it must annoy
him, I asked him if it did not. 'No,' said he; 'it is
inspiring!'"

On the 24th, the militia colonel hitherto in command was superseded by General Taliaferro, and martial
law was proclaimed. The telegraph was seized by the
government of Virginia, every train that entered the
state was searched and put under guard, and the passport system was put in force for the first time in the
history of the Union.

The next record of Captain Brown's prison life,
although from the reporter of a pro-slavery paper,
bears internal evidence of truthfulness.

Colonel Smith, of the Virginia Military Institute,
paid a visit to the prisoner, in company with Mr. O.
Jennings Wise, a son of Governor Wise. After their
interview the reporter asked many questions of one of
the officers of the jail who had been present, and he
gives his replies, as follows:—

Reporter.—Did Colonel Smith question Brown as to
whether he had any desire to have a clergyman to ad-
minister to him the consolations of religion?

Officer.—Yes, he did; but Brown said he did not
recognise any slaveholder, lay or clerical, or any man
sympathizing with slavery, as a Christian. He gave the

same reason yesterday for his refusal to accept the services of some clergymen who called upon him. He also said he would as soon be attended to the scaffold by blacklegs or robbers of the worst kind, as by slaveholding ministers, or ministers sympathizing with slavery; and that if he had his choice, he would prefer being followed to the scaffold by barefooted, barelegged, ragged negro children, and their old gray-headed slavemother, than by a clergyman of this character. He would feel, he said, much prouder of such an escort, and he wished he could have it.

Reporter.—Has he said anything on the subject of religion to the clergymen who have called upon him?

Officer.—Yes, he argues with them; but winds up frequently by telling them that they, and all slaveholders and sympathizers with slavery, have far more need of prayers themselves than he has, and he accordingly advises them to pray for themselves and exhibit no concern about him. While making these remarks, he requests that he would not be understood as designing to offer any insult.

Reporter.—Does his health seem impaired by the anxiety which he must necessarily feel in view of his impending fate?

Officer.—No, sir; he looks much better to-day than he did at any period since his imprisonment. He eats his meals regularly, and seems to be in better spirits this morning than he has been for ten days.

Reporter.—What is generally the character of the letters sent to him?

20*

Officer.—They are generally letters of sympathy and condolence.

Reporter.—Does he receive any assuring him of a purpose to rescue him ?

Officer.—Yes ; several. These, however, are mostly anonymous, and he invariably commits them to the flames. I have observed him throwing them into the fire upon finding them to be anonymous. Recently he reads no anonymous letter. Any communication, how-ever, applauding him as a martyr to the anti-slavery cause, he carefully files away. Referring to his execu-tion, during his conversation with Mr. O. J. Wise and Colonel Smith, he said he was not to be executed, but publicly murdered.

Reporter.—Is he aware that he will not be permitted to make any speech from the scaffold ?

Officer.—Yes, he is; and when informed of the fact, he said he did not care about saying anything on that occasion.

Another visitor states that in all his conversation he showed the utmost gentleness and tranquillity, and a quiet courtesy which contrasted strongly with the bearing of some of his visitors.

A few days before his death he presented a Bible to a merchant of Charlestown, who had been kind to him. It had this inscription on the fly-leaf :—

" With the best wishes of the undersigned, and his sincere thanks for many acts of kindness received. There is no com-mentary in the world so good in order to a right understanding of this Blessed Book as an honest, child-like, and teachable spirit.

JOHN BROWN.

" Charlestown, 29th Nov., 1859."

On the opposite page was written :—

" John Brown.   The leaves were turned down and marked by him while in prison at Charlestown, Virginia.   But a small portion of those passages, which in the most positive terms condemn oppression and violence, are marked."

" Many hundred passages," writes the correspondent of a southern paper, " which can by any possibility of interpretation be tortured into a support of his peculiar theory, are carefully marked, both by having the corner of the pages turned over, and by being surrounded by heavy pencil marks."

During her stay in Philadelphia, Mrs. Brown wrote to Governor Wise, asking him for the bodies of her sons Watson and Oliver, and of her husband after his execution.   He sent her the requisite orders for their delivery to her, which she received on the evening of Monday, the 28th of November.   One who was present when this communication reached Mrs. Brown says, " It annihilated in an instant the last hope of her heart.   She had said she had no hope.   In that terrible moment she learned how tenaciously she had grasped the shadow of one.   Strong soul as she is, she was overwhelmed by the surges of her grief; and who could comfort her ?   But she has sources of strength which the world knows not of, and they have never failed her, and never will. She is never so unnerved that she would save her husband's life, were it possible, by a mean or wicked act. It was delightful to hear the quiet, matter of course way in which she said, when a gleam of hope had fallen on her heart from the report that a case of insanity might be made out, 'But I couldn't say, if I were called upon, that my husband was insane—even to save his life ; because he wasn't ;' as if the utterance of an untruth were a natural as well as a moral impossibility to her."

Mrs. Brown having received a letter from her husband, leaving her at liberty to visit him if she felt equal to it, she immediately decided to go, and on the evening of Wednesday, the 30th, she arrived at Harper's Ferry, accompanied by two gentlemen from Philadelphia. Her intention was to proceed with them to Charlestown early next day ; but when the morning came, a despatch arrived from head-quarters, directing the officers on duty to detain Mrs. Brown and her friends until further orders. An official correspondence by telegraph was then carried on for several hours between Charlestown, Richmond, and Harper's Ferry, which ended in a message from General Taliaferro, saying that he had sent a file of dragoons to escort Mrs. Brown, but not her companions.

On this day great preparations were making in Charlestown for the approaching execution, and the military display by which it was to be accompanied. These arrangements were watched with intense public interest, but their attraction ended at once when, at noon, the knowledge that John Brown's wife was expected became general. At one o'clock, twenty-five of a cavalry corps—the Black Horse Rangers—surrounded the carriage in which Mrs. Brown was to be brought, and, with much clashing of arms and glittering display, the procession departed. At four o'clock the return of the cavalcade was announced, and in an instant the road to the jail was thronged with hundreds of eager gazers. For a brief time the way was obstructed, and the carriage and escort paused before the head-quarters of the commander-in-chief, while a body of troops cleared the way, and formed a hollow square reaching from the carriage to the jail. As soon as all was ready, the cavalcade passed on, and the grief-stricken woman arrived at the jail between double rows of bayonets and thickly planted pieces of artillery.

Mrs. Avis, in pursuance of orders, took Mrs. Brown into a private room, where her person was searched for concealed weapons. In the mean time Captain Brown had been informed of his wife's arrival by General Taliaferro, who asked how long he wished the interview to last.

"Not long," said Captain Brown; "three or four hours will do."

"I am very sorry, Captain Brown," said the general, "that I cannot oblige you. Mrs. Brown must return to-night to Harper's Ferry."

"Well," answered Brown, "I ask nothing of you, sir; I beg nothing from the state of Virginia. Carry

out your orders, general, that is enough. I am content."

Mrs. Brown was led into the cell by the jailer. Her
husband rose as she entered, and received her in his
arms. For some minutes they stood speechless, Mrs.
Brown resting her head on her husband's breast, and
clasping his neck. At length they sat down and conversed. To Captain Avis, who was the only witness of
the sorrowful scene, we are indebted for the following
particulars of the interview.

Brown spoke first. "Wife, I am glad to see you."

"My dear husband, it is a hard fate."

"Well, well! cheer up, cheer up, Mary. We must
all bear it in the best manner we can. I believe it is
all for the best."

"Our poor children—God help them!"

"Those that are dead to this world are angels in
another. How are all those still living? Tell them
their father died without a single regret for the course
he has pursued—that he is satisfied he is right in the
eyes of God and of all just men."

Mrs. Brown then spoke of their remaining children
and their home. Brown's voice, as he alluded to the
bereavements of his family, was broken with emotion.

Mrs. Brown observed the chain about the ankles of
her husband. To avoid its galling his limbs, he had
put on two pairs of woollen socks. Mrs. Brown said
she was desirous of procuring the chain as a family
relic. She had already at her home the one with which
the limbs of John Brown, jun., were inhumanly shack-

led in Kansas, and in which he was goaded on by the border ruffians until he was mad, and the chain had worn through his flesh to the bone. Captain Brown said he had himself asked that his chain should be given to his family, but had been refused.

The conversation then turned upon matters of business which Brown desired to have arranged after his death. He gave his wife all the letters and papers which were needed for this purpose, and read to her his will (which had been drawn up for him by Mr. Hunter) carefully explaining every portion of it.

Subsequently he requested his wife to make a denial of a statement which had gained publicity, that he had said in his interview with Governor Wise that he had been actuated by feelings of revenge. He denied that he had ever made such a statement; or that any such base motives had ever influenced him.

After this conversation they supped together. This occupied only a few minutes. Their last sorrowful meal being concluded, and the time approaching at which they must part, Mrs. Brown asked to be permitted to speak to the other prisoners. But General Taliaferro's orders forbade this, though Captain Avis expressed a willingness to permit her to see them, even at the risk of violating orders. She declined to see them under these circumstances.

Brown again touched upon business affairs, until an order was received from Taliaferro, saying that the interview must terminate. Brown then said, " Mary, I hope you will always live in Essex County. I hope you will be able to get all our children together, and impress the inculcation of right principles on each succeeding generation. I give you all the letters and papers which have been sent me since my arrest. I wish you also to take all my clothes that are here, and carry them home. Goodbye, goodbye. God bless you!"

Mrs. Brown was then escorted back to Harper's Ferry, and arrived there, greatly exhausted, at nine o'clock in the evening.

CHAPTER XII.

DECEMBER 2ND—DECEMBER 8TH, 1859.

THE EXECUTION.—THE BODY DELIVERED TO CAPTAIN BROWN'S
FRIENDS.—JOURNEY OF THE FUNERAL PARTY TO NORTH
ELBA.—AFFECTING RECEPTION BY THE FAMILY.—FUNERAL
SERVICES.—MR. M'KIM'S ADDRESS, RELATING THE EVENTS
OF THE LAST FEW DAYS.—HE READS A LETTER FROM EDWIN
COPPOCK TO MRS. BROWN, AND CAPTAIN BROWN'S LAST
INSTRUCTIONS TO HIS FAMILY.—REMARKS FROM WENDELL
PHILLIPS.—THE INTERMENT.—BROWN'S PERSONAL APPEAR-
ANCE, HIS TEMPERAMENT, AND CHARACTER.

THE sun rose clear and bright on the second of
December. A haze, that presently veiled it, soon
disappeared, and ere the hour appointed for the execution not a cloud was to be seen. On the previous evening the timber for the scaffold had been removed from
the enclosure of the new Baptist church, to a field
about half a mile distant from the jail. At seven o'clock
the carpenters began to erect it. It was about six feet
high, twelve wide, and fifteen or eighteen in length. A
hand-rail extended around three sides and down the
flight of steps. On the other side were stout uprights,
with a cross beam, which was supported by strong
braces. In the centre of the cross beam was an iron
hook, from which the rope was suspended.

At eight o'clock the troops began to arrive on the
ground. Horsemen in scarlet jackets were posted
around the field at distances of fifty feet apart, and a

double line of sentries was stationed farther in. The first companies of infantry and cavalry having taken their position, the artillery arrived, with a huge brass cannon, which was so placed that, in the event of an attempted rescue, the prisoner might be blown to shreds by the heavy charge of grape-shot it contained. Other cannon were placed so as to sweep the jail and every approach to it. From eight o'clock till ten the military were in constant motion. The extent of the precautions taken may be inferred from the fact that the lines of pickets and patrols encircled the field of death for fifteen miles, that over five hundred troops were posted about the scaffold, and that nearly three thousand militia were on the ground. In fact, the arrangements made by the state of Virginia to prevent a rescue in the case of the old farmer of North Elba, were not exceeded by those which were taken by the commonwealth of England when Charles the First was brought to the block at Whitehall. There were not more than about four hundred private citizens present; for the fear of a servile insurrection, or of an anti-slavery invasion, had kept them at home to guard against surprise.

Captain Brown rose at daybreak, resumed his correspondence with undiminished energy, and continued to write till half-past ten o'clock, when the sheriff, jailer, and assistants entered, and told him that he must prepare to die. The sheriff bade him farewell in his cell, Brown thanking him for his kindness. He was then conducted to the cell of the two negroes, Shields Green and John Copeland, whom he charged to "stand up like men, and not betray their friends." He then took leave of John E. Cook and Edwin Coppock, who were in another cell, chained together; and afterwards of Aaron D. Stevens, who had been his prison companion, but was removed to another cell the evening before, preparatory to Mrs. Brown's visit. "Goodbye, Captain," said Stevens; "I know you are going to a better land." Brown replied, "I know I am." He did not visit the prisoner Albert Hazlitt, as he said he had no knowledge of him.

At eleven o'clock he left the jail, his face wearing an expression of serenity and cheerfulness. As he stepped out of the door, a negro woman stood near with her child in her arms. They were of the despised race for whose sake he had sacrificed so much, and was now about to lay down his life. He paused for a moment, stooped, and kissed the child tenderly.* As he passed

---

* This incident has been commemorated by Mrs. Child in the following lines :—

THE HERO'S HEART.

A winter sunshine, still and bright,
The Blue Hills bathed with golden light,
And earth was smiling to the sky,
When calmly he went forth to die.

Infernal passions festered there,
Where peaceful Nature looked so fair ;
And fiercely, in the morning sun,
Flashed glittering bayonet and gun.

along, another black woman ejaculated, "God bless
you, old man ; I wish I could help you, but I cannot."
He heard her, and as he looked at her, a tear stood in
his eye.

The vehicle in which Captain Brown was conveyed
to the scaffold was a furniture wagon. On the front
seat, beside the driver, sat Mr. Saddler, the undertaker.
In the box was the coffin, made of walnut, enclosed in
a poplar box with a flat lid, in which the coffin and·
remains were to be transported to the north. Brown

> The old man met no friendly eye,
> When last he looked on earth and sky ;
> But one small child, with timid air,
> Was gazing on his silver hair.
>
> As that dark brow to his up-turned,
> The tender heart within him yearned ;
> And, fondly stooping o'er her face,
> He kissed her for her injured race.
>
> The little one, she knew not why
> That kind old man went forth to die ;
> Nor why, 'mid all that pomp and stir,
> He stooped to give a kiss to *her*.
>
> But Jesus smiled that sight to see,
> And said, "He did it unto *me!*"
> The golden harps then sweetly rang,
> And this the song the angels sang :—
>
> "Who loves the poor doth love the Lord !
> Earth cannot dim thy bright reward ;
> We hover o'er yon gallows high,
> And wait to bear thee to the sky."

took his seat by Captain Avis, and the wagon proceeded, surrounded by an escort of several companies of cavalry.

From the time of leaving the jail until he mounted the gallows' stairs he wore a smile upon his countenance, and his keen eye took in every detail of the scene. There was no blenching, nor the remotest approach to cowardice nor nervousness. As he was leaving jail, when asked if he thought he could endure his fate, he said, " I can endure almost anything but parting from friends; that is very hard." On the road to the scaffold he said, in reply to an inquiry, " It has been a characteristic of mine, from infancy, not to suffer from physical fear. I have suffered a thousand times more from bashfulness than from fear."

" I was very near the old man," writes an eye witness, "and scrutinized him closely. He seemed to take in the whole scene at a glance ; and he straightened himself up proudly, as if to set the soldiers an example of a soldier's courage. The only motion he made, beyond a swaying to and fro of his body, was that same patting of his knees with his hands that we noticed throughout his trial and while in jail. As he came upon an eminence near the gallows, he cast his eye over the beautiful landscape, and followed the windings of the Blue Ridge Mountains in the distance. He looked up earnestly at the sun, and sky, and all about, and then remarked, 'This is a beautiful country. I have not cast my eyes over it before—that is, while passing through the field.'"

" You are a game man, Captain Brown," said Mr. Saddler.

" Yes," he said, " I was so trained up ; it was one of the lessons of my mother ; but it is hard to part from friends, though newly made."

" You are more cheerful than I am, Captain Brown," was the reply.

" Yes," said he, " I ought to be."

The sun shone with splendour as the escort came up, and afar off could be seen the gleaming muskets and bayonets of the guard which surrounded the prisoner. On the field the several companies glittered with the same sparkle of guns and trappings ; and the gay colours of their uniforms came out in strong relief with the winter tints of field and forest. To the east and south the splendid mass of the Blue Ridge loomed against the sky and shut in the horizon. All nature seemed at peace, and the shadow of the approaching solemnity seemed to have been cast over the soldiers, for not a sound was to be heard but their solemn measured tread, as the column came slowly up the road, and passed to their station.

As the procession entered the field, the prisoner, as if surprised at the absence of the people, remarked, " I see no citizens here—where are they ?"

" The citizens are not allowed to be present—none but the troops," was the reply.

" That ought not to be," said he, " citizens should be allowed to be present as well as others."

Having arrived at the scaffold, the troops composing

the escort took up their assigned positions, but the immediate body guard remained as before, closely surrounding the wagon. They finally opened ranks to let the prisoner pass out; when, with the assistance of two men, he descended from the vehicle. Mr. Hunter and Mr. Mayor Green were standing near. " Gentlemen, good-bye," said Captain Brown in an unfaltering tone ; and then, with firm step and erect form, he calmly walked past jailer, sheriff, and officers, and mounted the scaffold steps. As he quietly waited the necessary arrangements, he surveyed the scene unmoved, looking principally in the direction of the people in the far distance. " There is no faltering in his step," writes an eye-witness, " but firmly and erect he stands amid the almost breathless lines of soldiery that surround him. With his pinioned right arm he takes the slouched hat from his head, and casts it upon the platform by his side." " I know," said another witness, " that every one within view was greatly impressed with the dignity of his bearing. I have since heard southerners say that his courageous fortitude filled them with amazement."

The hour had now come, and the sheriff approached him. Taking leave of Captain Avis, he said : " I have no words to thank you for all your kindness to me."

His elbows and ankles were pinioned, the white cap was drawn over his eyes, and the rope adjusted around his neck.

" Captain Brown," said the sheriff, " you are not standing on the drop. Will you come forward?"

21

"I can't see, gentlemen," was his reply in a firm voice, "you must lead me."

The sheriff, leading his prisoner forward to the centre of the drop, said, "Shall I give you a handkerchief, and let you drop it as a signal?"

"No; I am ready at any time; but do not keep me needlessly waiting."

This was the last of John Brown's requests to Virginia; and it was refused. Instead of permitting the execution to be at once consummated, the proceedings were checked by the martial order, "Not ready yet;" and the mockery of a vast military display. For ten minutes at least, under the orders of the commanding officer, the troops marched and countermarched, now advancing towards the gallows, now turning about in sham defiance of an imaginary enemy.

Each moment seemed an hour, and some of the people murmured, "Shame! shame!" At last the order was given, the rope was severed with a hatchet, and the trap fell.

After the body had hung for twenty minutes, the Charlestown physicians went up and made their examination, and after them the military surgeons, the prisoner being executed by the civil power with military assistance. At length it was ordered to be cut down, the authorities being quite satisfied that their dreaded enemy was dead. It was lifted upon the scaffold and placed in the coffin; the guard closed in around the wagon, the cavalry led the van, and the mournful procession moved off.

The body of Captain Brown was delivered to Mr. James Miller M'Kim and Mr. Hector Tyndale, the companions of Mrs. Brown, at Harper's Ferry, a few hours after the execution. The party proceeded by the morning train next day (Saturday) to Baltimore, and thence to Philadelphia, where they arrived shortly after noon. Here they had intended to remain until Monday, partly in order that Mrs. Brown might have time for repose, after the terrible ordeal through which she had passed. But the mayor of the city met them on their arrival at the terminus, and peremptorily insisted that the body should be sent forward by the next train for New York. He declared that such was the state of excitement in the city, of enthusiasm among the admirers of Brown, and of curiosity among the public generally, that it would be impossible, if the body should remain, to preserve that order which the decencies of the occasion and a proper regard for the feelings of the widow required. As he avowed his purpose to enforce his determination, if necessary, by the whole force of the police, and even of the military, Mrs. Brown and her companions could not do otherwise than comply. It is probable that political considerations had their influence on his mind. He may have deemed it inexpedient to let the south see how strong and irrepressible was the admiration for Captain Brown among the people of Philadelphia.

A large crowd had collected in anticipation of the arrival of the body, but they were dispersed by the police, and the coffin was transferred without delay

21*

from the railway car to a wagon, and conveyed to the train for New York, where it arrived at seven o'clock in the evening. Here it was prepared for interment, and placed in a new coffin. The friends of the slave in New York had expected that some time would be afforded in that city for a public demonstration of respect to the remains ; but as it was the earnest desire of Mrs. Brown that her children and grandchildren should look upon his features once more, while they were still life-like, it was decided to proceed without unnecessary delay. Accordingly, early on Monday morning, the party pursued their journey by the Hudson River railroad, reaching the town of Troy at two in the afternoon, where they stopped at the American House, at which Captain Brown had been in the habit of staying when in Troy, and which he had mentioned to his wife as a suitable resting place when on her way home. Many of the most respectable inhabitants called to express their sympathy.

Starting at four o'clock p.m. the party reached Rutland, Vermont, about ten; there they remained until five next morning, when they resumed their journey, and in the evening stopped at Vergennes, where the hotel was crowded by sympathizing visitors. Carriages were shortly provided to convey the party to the shore of Lake Champlain. A procession was formed, and all moved forward amid the tolling of bells. Arrived at the bridge over Otter Creek, a distance of about a third of a mile, the gentlemen composing the procession halted, and, forming themselves into a double line and uncovering their heads, allowed the body, with the stricken widow and her friends, to pass through; after which they took leave. It was a spontaneous and affecting tribute.

At the lake shore a boat was in readiness, which landed the party close by the town of Westport. Mrs. Brown was now among the friends and familiar acquaintances of her husband, every kindness that the occasion called for was freely bestowed, and her companions, too, shared in the good will which was manifested towards her. Without delay conveyances were provided, and the little cortege was soon on its way to Elizabethtown, where they were to tarry for the night. A heavy rain was falling, and the snow was disappearing so fast that it had been deemed best to substitute wheel-carriages for sleighs. On reaching Elizabethtown, Mr. Adams, sheriff of the county, offered the court-house as a place in which to deposit the body for the night. This offer was accepted, and in a few minutes a procession was formed, and the body was borne to its temporary resting-place. The house was soon filled by the leading residents of the town, who found it hard to realize that their old friend and fellow-citizen, whom they had known so well and respected so highly, had actually been put to death.

The party were now within twenty-five miles of their destination. But the road lay over a mountain, and was well-nigh impassable; so that, short as was the distance, it would take the whole of the following day to accomplish the journey. Mr. Henry Adams, a son of the sheriff, volunteered to start off in the night, with a swift horse, to notify the family of their approach. Six young men undertook to sit up all night in the courthouse as a guard over the body.

At daylight on Wednesday the journey was re-sumed. The roads were found to be even worse than was anticipated, so that they did not arrive at the town of Keene, a distance of eight miles, until ten o'clock. Here Mr. Norton, an old friend of Captain Brown, wel-comed them most hospitably. So reluctant had he been to believe that the fatal sentence would be executed, that he was quite overcome by the sight of the coffin of his venerated friend and neighbour. After partaking of refreshment, the party again started. Slowly they climbed the mountain pass, and as slowly descended the other side. The sun had set by the time they reached North Elba, and it was dark when they approached their destination. As they drew nigh, they were met by friends of the family carrying lanterns, who had been waiting all the afternoon in anxious expectation, and, unable to bear the suspense, had set out to meet them. By these they were conducted in silence to the house. At length the carriage which bore Mrs. Brown stopped at the door. She alighted with difficulty, being much agitated. Instantly there was a sharp, low cry of "Mother!" and, in answer, another in the same tone of mingled agony and tenderness, "O! Anna!" and the mother and daughter were locked in a long embrace. Then followed the same scene with the next daughter, Sarah; then Ellen, the little girl of five, was brought forward, and another burst of anguish ensued; lastly came the daughter-in-law, Oliver Brown's widow. It was a scene entirely beyond description. When the agitation had somewhat subsided, the strangers were introduced, emotion was put under restraint—an accustomed task with these people—and all was quiet. The evening meal had been ready for some time, and the family and guests took their seats. Supper was soon despatched, for no one was much disposed to eat.

Shortly afterwards Mrs. Brown announced to Mr. McKim and Mr. Phillips* that the family were gathered in another room, waiting anxiously to hear the recital of what had happened; and the guests were invited to join them. Besides the members of the family we have already mentioned, there were present Salmon Brown, the only surviving son of Mrs. Brown,

---

* Mr. Wendell Phillips had joined Captain Brown's funeral party, probably at New York. This gentleman is the most widely known and the most influential of the American abolitionists, with the single exception of Mr. Garrison. His eminence in this respect is due to the entire consecration of his splendid eloquence, in which he is surpassed by none of his countrymen, if by any living orator, to the object of the American Anti-Slavery Society—which is, to convince the American people that the maintenance of chattel slavery and of free institutions under one government is impossible, and that one or the other must give way. In pursuance of this aim he has known neither fear nor favour. His life has been repeatedly in danger from popular violence in the city of Boston, and he has also been threatened with popular ovations. Such is the exquisite charm of his eloquence, that a southern editor declared that he was "an infernal machine set to music."

an intelligent-looking and handsome young man of twenty-three; Ruth Thompson, Captain Brown's daughter by his first wife ; and other connections of the family.   Isabella, the widow of Watson Brown, was unavoidably absent on this occasion.

Mr. McKim, at Mrs. Brown's request, briefly related all that had happened of particular interest to them from the time of their mother's arrival in Philadelphia, on the 12th of November, up to that moment.   He told how she had been put under his charge by Mr. Higginson, with a request that he would aid her in making her way to Virginia ; how he had accompanied her to Baltimore ; that, arriving there, she had been met by a letter from her husband, requesting her not to proceed ; that she had returned the same day to Philadelphia, and (with the exception of a few days spent at Eagleswood, New Jersey) remained there with sympathizing friends, till the near approach of the day fixed for the execution.   He told them of their mother's letter to Governor Wise, asking for the remains of her husband and sons, when all should be over ; of the Governor's answer, which, at his request, Mr. Phillips then read, with the order also to General Taliaferro ; of the letter she had received from Mr. Brown, saying he was now willing she should come to see him, if she thought herself equal to the task ; and of her setting out accordingly, accompanied by Mr. Tyndale, himself, and Mrs. M'Kim.   He then described the journey to Baltimore ; the difficulty experienced there till they produced Governor Wise's letter as a passport ; the painful delay at Harper's Ferry, and the assurances that had been given them that the respectable people of Virginia did not approve, but strongly condemned it. He made no comments on the refusal of General Taliaferro to allow either of Mrs. Brown's companions to accompany her to Charlestown; nor on the limitation of the interview with her husband to a space of little more than two hours. He was careful in his relation to say nothing that would needlessly add to their distress. He told them as much as he could recall of what had been related to him of their father's last hours, and lingered, evidently to their great gratification, over anecdotes which he had heard illustrative of his bravery and other noble qualities.

When Mr. McKim had finished, Mr. Phillips took up the theme, and in the tenderest and most beautiful manner pursued it, till all tears were wiped away. A holy joy seemed gradually to dispel all grief, and a becoming filial and conjugal pride to reconcile these stricken ones to their loss. It was now late, and the prospect of the duties and trials of the morrow admonished the party that some of them had need of rest.

The house in which the family live is a frame building, such as is common in that part of the country. It has four rooms on the first floor, and corresponding space above. The company was comparatively large, but ample accommodations were found for them all. On opening the front door next morning, a glorious landscape appeared. Directly opposite, apparently within a few miles, but really much further off, looms up a rugged chain of the Adirondack mountains; broken, jagged, massive, and wonderfully picturesque. Off to the left stands, in solitary grandeur, the towering pyramid called "White Face"—deriving its name from the colour of the rocks on its summit. The Saranac and Ausable rivers flow at each side of it; and just at its base is Lake Placid, a sheet of water famed through all this country of fine lakes for its exquisite beauty. On the right is to be seen, in the distance, the peak of Mount Marcy; and, still more remote, Macintyre, the loftiest pinnacle of the Adirondack range.

Captain Brown had expressed a desire that his body should be laid in the shadow of a rock, not far from his house. This rock stands about fifty feet from the house; it is about eight feet in height, and from fifteen to twenty feet square, and is a picturesque object.

The funeral was to take place this day, December 8th, at one o'clock, and by that time the neighbours were gathered, and all were ready. The services commenced with a hymn which had been a great favourite with Captain Brown, and with which, it was said, he had successively sung all his children to sleep :—

> BLOW ye the trumpet, blow ;
> 　The gladly solemn sound
> Let all the nations know
> 　To earth's remotest bound ;
> 　　The year of jubilee is come ;
> 　　Return, ye ransom'd sinners, home.

Jesus, our great High Priest,
  Has full atonement made ;
Ye weary spirits, rest ;
  Ye mournful souls, be glad :
    The year of jubilee is come ;
    Return, ye ransom'd sinners, home.

Extol the Lamb of God,
  The all-atoning Lamb ;
Redemption by his blood
  Through all the world proclaim.
    The year of jubilee is come ;
    Return, ye ransom'd sinners, home.

Ye slaves of sin and hell,
  Your liberty receive ;
And safe in Jesus dwell,
  And blest in Jesus live :
    The year of jubilee is come ;
    Return, ye ransom'd sinners, home.

Ye who have sold for nought
  Your heritage above,
Receive it back unbought,
  The gift of Jesus' love :
    The year of jubilee is come ;
    Return, ye ransom'd sinners, home.

The gospel trumpet hear,
  The news of heavenly grace ;
And, saved from earth, appear
  Before your Saviour's face.
    The year of jubilee is come ;
    Return, ye ransom'd sinners, home.

This hymn, which was sung to the good old tune of
Lenox, will be at once recognized by all who know any-

thing about the old-fashioned sacred music. The air has a stirring, half-military ring, and the words are redolent of liberty. Its themes are "jubilee," "ransom," &c. and it seems to blow the trumpet of freedom.

After the hymn an impressive prayer was offered by the Rev. Mr. Young of Burlington, Vermont, and Mr. McKim then addressed the company. He said that if he were to consult his own feelings he would prefer to remain silent; but it was due to these weeping widows, these bereaved children, these sorrowing friends and neighbours, that he should say something in honour of the hero whose body was to-day to be laid in the dust—something for the comfort of those whose hearts had been broken, and whose hearth-stones were left desolate. What could he say of a man whom they had known better than he? He had not the privilege of a personal acquaintance with Mr. Brown. He had never looked on his face 'till it was cold in death. But he had become acquainted with him by the developments of the last few weeks. How he honoured, loved, and admired him, words could not express. To stand under his roof and aid in his burial was the greatest honour that had ever been vouchsafed him. That John Brown was a brave, magnanimous, truthful, consistent man, rested not on the testimony of admiring friends, but was freely conceded by his open enemies. He had enjoyed, as they knew, the privilege of accompanying Mrs. Brown on her sacred and solemn mission to Virginia. He had witnessed the respect and the expressions of sympathy with which she was met by the best classes of people from the time she crossed the slave border 'till the time of her return.   In Baltimore, on the railway, at Harper's Ferry—wherever she went —southern men treated her with respect, and comforted her by stories of her husband and her children, illustrative of their bravery and consistency.   A blunt officer, with epaulettes on his shoulders, had said, in the presence of a promiscuous group at the Harper's Ferry hotel; "I'll tell you what my opinion is of Brown ; he's one of that kind of men that God Almighty does not put many of above ground."   Another officer, equally high in command, and one of the most thoroughly pro-slavery Virginians that he met during his visit, took him aside, the night before he left, and said, " I do not like to make the request of Mrs. Brown at such a time as this, but I desire very much to get from her some little memento of Captain Brown—his autograph, or some other like relic ; any trifle that she could give me I should greatly value."   And not only had he heard most ample testimony borne at the south to the bravery and uprightness of the leader in that extraordinary undertaking, but similar testimony to the same qualities on the part of his sons.   Oliver Brown, Watson Brown, Dauphin Thompson, William Thompson, all were attested to be—with the exception of this one act, the assault on Harper's Ferry—without reproach, as well as without fear.   And it is due to those who are in prison, to say that they too are worthy of a tribute on this occasion.   Of Copeland and Green he had heard nothing while at Harper's Ferry. This was eulogy. They belonged to the oppressed and hated race, and if anything could be said to their disadvantage, it would have been heard ere this. As for Edwin Coppock, a letter which he held in his hand would illustrate his character. It was brought to Mrs. Brown, at Harper's Ferry, by the bearer of Captain Brown's remains. Mr. M'Kim then read the letter.

FROM EDWIN COPPOCK TO MRS. BROWN.

Charlestown Jail, Virginia,
December —, 1859.

Mrs. John Brown—Dear Madam,

I was very sorry that your request to see the rest of the prisoners was not complied with. Mrs. Avis brought me a book whose pages are full of truth and beauty, entitled " Voices of the True-Hearted," which she told me was a present from you. For this dear token of remembrance, please accept my many thanks.

My comrade, J. E. Cook, and myself, deeply sympathize with you in your sad bereavement. We were both acquainted with Anna and Martha. They were to us as sisters, and as brothers we sympathize with them in this dark hour of trial and affliction.

I was with your sons when they fell. Oliver lived but a very few moments after he was shot. He spoke no word, but yielded calmly to his fate. Watson was shot at ten o'clock on Monday morning, and died about three o'clock on Wednesday morning. He suffered much. Though mortally wounded at ten o'clock, yet at three o'clock Monday afternoon he fought bravely against the men who charged on us. When the enemy were repulsed, and the excitement of the charge was over, he began to sink rapidly.

After we were taken prisoners, he was placed in the guard-house with me. He complained of the hardness of the bench on which he was lying. I begged hard for a bed for him, or even a blanket, but could obtain none for him. I took off my coat and placed it under him, and held his head in my lap, in which position he died, without a groan or struggle.

I have stated these facts, thinking that they may afford to you, and to the bereaved widows they have left, a mournful consolation.

Give my love to Anna and Martha, with our last farewell.

Yours truly,

EDWIN COPPOCK.

There was much weeping during the reading of this letter.

Some of Captain Brown's friends, continued Mr. McKim, speak as though they regarded the result at Harper's Ferry as a disaster. Disastrous in some respects it was, but in no respect a failure. Mr. Brown said, in one of his last letters, "The Captain of my salvation, who is also the Captain of Liberty, has taken away my sword of steel, and put into my hands the sword of the Spirit." This is well said, like all his utterances. With his sword of steel he struck the hollow shell of southern society, political and social, and revealed its emptiness. He made such developments of the weakness, imbecility, and utter powerlessness of a slaveholding commonwealth, in an emergency, as are certain to result in the extinction of the whole slave system. He has "builded better than he knew." He did much better than if he had established, as it would appear was his purpose, an armed exodus of fugitive slaves. He did infinitely better than if he had organized—which certainly was not his purpose—an insurrection.

In selecting the place for the grave, they had followed the instructions given by Mr. Brown to his wife in their last interview; and in a paper written on the morning of his execution, he gave the following directions for an inscription on his tombstone :—

TO BE INSCRIBED ON THE OLD FAMILY MONUMENT AT
NORTH ELBA.

OLIVER BROWN, born ———, 1839, was killed at Harper's Ferry, Virginia, November 17, 1859.

WATSON BROWN, born ———, 1835, was wounded at Harper's Ferry, November 17, and died November 19, 1859.

(My wife can fill up the blank dates as above.)

JOHN BROWN, born May 9, 1800, was executed at Charlestown, Virginia, December 2, 1859.

He also added the following codicil to his will :—

Charlestown, Jefferson Co., Virginia,
December 2, 1859.

It is my desire that my wife have all my personal property not previously disposed of by me ; and the entire use of all my landed property during her natural life ; and that after her death, the proceeds of such land be equally divided between my then living children ; and that what would be a child's share be given to the children of each of my two sons who fell at Harper's Ferry, and that a child's share be divided among the children of my now living children who may die before their mother (my present beloved wife). No formal will can be of use when my express wishes are made known to my dutiful and beloved family.

JOHN BROWN.

My dear wife :

I have time to enclose the within and the above, which I forgot yesterday, and to bid you another farewell. " Be of good cheer," and God Almighty bless, save, comfort, guide, and keep you to the end.

Your affectionate husband,
JOHN BROWN.

The addendum, said the speaker, was undoubtedly the last work of the brave man's pen. Note his sublime composure ! He speaks as though he was about starting on a journey !

Mr. McKim concluded with exhortations to the family and friends to be comforted ; assuring them that by their sacrifices they had made large contributions to the cause of freedom and humanity, that in this respect their position was an honourable one, and that the hearts of tens of thousands beat in the deepest sympathy with them.

Wendell Phillips then spoke as follows :—

22

" How feeble words seem here !   How can I hope to
utter what your hearts are full of ?   I fear to disturb
the harmony which his life breathes round this home.
One and another of you, his neighbours, say, ' I have
known him five years,' ' I have known him ten years.'
It seems to me as if we had none of us known him.
How our admiring, loving wonder has grown, day by
day, as he has unfolded trait after trait of earnest,
brave, tender, Christian life !   We see him walking
with radiant, serene face to the scaffold, and think, what
an iron heart, what devoted faith !   We take up his
letters, beginning ' My dear wife and children, every
one'—see him stoop on his way to the scaffold and kiss
that negro child—and this iron heart seems all tenderness.   Marvellous old man !   We have hardly said it
when the loved forms of his sons, in the bloom of young
devotion, encircle him, and we remember he is not alone;
only the majestic centre of a group.   Your neighbour
farmer went, surrounded by his household, to tell the
slaves there were still hearts and right arms ready and
nerved for their service.   From this roof, four; from a
neighbouring one, two ; to make up the score of heroes.
And these weeping children and widows seem so lifted
up and consecrated by long, single-hearted devotion to
his great purpose, that we dare to remind them how
blessed they are in the privilege of thinking that in the
last throbs of those brave young hearts, which lie buried
on the banks of the Shenandoah, thoughts of them mingled with love to God and hope for the slave.   He has
abolished slavery in Virginia.   You may say this is too

much. Our neighbours are the last men we know. The hours that pass us are the ones we appreciate the least. Men walked Boston streets when night fell on Bunker's Hill, and pitied Warren, saying, 'Foolish man! Thrown away his life! Why didn't he measure his means better?' We see him standing colossal that day on that blood-stained sod, and severing the tie that bound Boston to Great Britain. That night George III. ceased to rule in New England. History will date Virginian emancipation from Harper's Ferry. True, the slave is still there. So, when the tempest uproots a pine on our hills, it looks green for months—a year or two. Still, it is timber, not a tree. Thus has John Brown loosened the roots of the slave system.

"Surely such a life is no failure. How vast the change in men's hearts! Insurrection was a harsh, horrid word to millions a month ago. John Brown went a whole generation beyond it, claiming the right for white men to help the slave to freedom by arms. Harper's Ferry was no single hour, standing alone—taken out from a common life ; it was the flowering of fifty years of single-hearted devotion. He must have lived wholly for one great idea, when these who owe their being to him and those whom love has joined group so harmoniously around him, each accepting serenely his and her part. I feel honoured to stand under such a roof. Hereafter you will tell children standing at your knees, ' I saw John Brown buried—I sat under his roof.'

"God make us all worthier of him whose dust we lay among these hills he loved. Here he girded himself and went forth to battle. Fuller success than his heart ever dreamed God has granted him. He sleeps in the blessings of the crushed and the poor, and men believe more firmly in virtue, now that such a man has lived. Standing here, let us thank God for a firmer faith and fuller hope."

Another hymn was then sung, during which the coffin was placed on a table before the door, with the face exposed, so that all could see. It looked almost as natural as in life—far more so than that of an ordinary corpse. There was a flush on the face, and nothing of the usual paleness of death.

Mr. Phineas Norton, who acted as the friend of the household on the occasion, invited all the neighbours who desired to do so, to come and take a last look. They went forward as invited, and took their final leave of all that remained of their cherished friend; and then the family followed. It was a touching sight to see those widows, the eldest still in the prime of life, and the younger ones in its opening bud, deprived of their natural companions, leaning, as they stood round the coffin, on the arms of strangers.

Then followed the short procession from the house to the grave. First came Mrs. Brown, supported by Mr. Phillips; the widow of Oliver Brown, followed, leaning on the arm of Mr. McKim, who, in his other hand, held that of the little girl Ellen ; next came the widow of Watson Brown, supported by the Rev. Mr. Young; and after them the widow of William Thompson, lean-

ing on the arm of one of the family. Salmon Brown
and his sisters followed, with Henry Thompson, and
his wife Ruth, John Brown's eldest daughter; then
Roswell Thompson and his wife, the aged parents who
had lost two of their sons at Harper's Ferry; and lastly
the friends and neighbours. As the body was lowered
into the grave, a gush of grief burst from the family,
and the Rev. Mr. Young repeated aloud :—" I have
fought a good fight; I have finished my course; I have
kept the faith; henceforth there is laid up for me a
crown of righteousness, which the Lord, the Righteous
Judge, shall give me ; and not to me only, but unto all
that love his appearing ;" which words he followed
with the benediction :—

" May the grace of our Lord Jesus Christ, the blessing of God our Father, and the Communion of the
Holy Spirit, be with us, and abide with us all, now and
for ever. Amen."

The words seemed to fall like balm on all who heard
them. The sobs were hushed, and the family and
friends retired from the grave, leaving the remains of
the loved one to their last repose.

———

We shall conclude this narrative with a few extracts
respecting the personal appearance, temperament, and
moral characteristics of Captain Brown.

Osborne P. Anderson informs us that when Captain Brown visited Chatham, Canada, in April, 1858, he made a profound impression upon those who saw or became acquainted with him. His long white beard, his thoughtful and reverend brow and physiognomy, his sturdy, measured tread, as he walked about in his coat of plain brown cloth, with other garments to match, revived to those honoured with his acquaintance and knowing his history the memory of a Puritan of the most exalted type.

Mrs. Lydia Maria Child, in a letter to the *New York Tribune*, describes a remarkable bust of John Brown which she had lately seen in the studio of Mr. Brackett, an eminent sculptor in Boston. In her account of the circumstances under which the sculptor was induced to select Brown as a subject of his art, an impressive idea is conveyed of his presence and demeanour :—

" It is fortunate that he chanced to meet John Brown in the streets of Boston several months before his brave bearing at Harper's Ferry had made him world-famous. The expression of the face and the carriage of the head attracted his artistic eye. He said to himself, ' There's a head for a sculptor.' He looked after him earnestly, and went back in order to pass him again. Upon inquiring who it was, he was told, ' That is old John Brown of Kansas.' The strong impression then made on his mind had much to do with his subsequent desire of going to Virginia for the purpose of modelling his head. When the artist returned, his soul was so completely absorbed in his work, that John Brown was continually before him, in the dreams of the night and the mental visions of the day. He read attentively all his writings and sayings, in order to become thoroughly imbued with his character. With such concentration of thought, perhaps it is not extraordinary that he should have produced an excellent likeness. In Brackett's bust of Brown, the character of the man looks through the features wonderfully. Any good judge that examines it, without knowing whom it was intended to portray, would say, ' There is a man of strong will and lofty courage ; kindly of heart, and religious to the very core of his being.' A Boston gentleman, who had lived very much in Europe, exclaimed, ' It is singularly like Michael Angelo's Moses !' Other visitors have also observed this resemblance. But Mr. Brackett has never seen Michael Angelo's Moses, nor any representation of it. In fact, the similarity is merely in character. It is the sublime expression, the air of moral grandeur, which connects the two in the imagination of the spectator. An artist who was extremely hostile to Brown, after looking at this magnificent head, exclaimed with an oath, " He ought to be ashamed of himself, for making all the rest of us look so mean !"

The Rev. La Roy Sunderland of Boston, in a letter published about the time of Brown's death, says that, having been acquainted with him for many years, he had excellent opportunities for knowing him, and that, in the combination of firmness, courage, and the power of enduring pain, he excelled all the men he ever knew. He seemed not to know the emotion of fear, and to possess more firmness than fifty average men. On one occasion, in order to test the reality of an experiment in which he suspected collusion, Brown submitted himself to a painful test which prevented him from sleeping for three nights, and which he bore with an amazing power of endurance. Mr. Sunderland's concluding testimony has been amply justified by the event:—"The degree of courage manifested by John Brown made him the extraordinary man he was; and this, combined with his integrity of character, drew from Governor Wise the testimony that he was 'honest, truthful, and sincere.' Posterity will do justice to the memory of this martyr to democratic slavery. Men never pause to parley over the errors of those who are 'honest, truthful, and sincere,' and who manifest the rare qualities which combined in the character of John Brown. He was not insane, he was not a monomaniac, (insane on one subject), nor was he moved by a feeling of revenge. Those who speak of him in this manner, do not know the man. Instead of being revengeful, he was humane, even to his own detriment, as may be shown from numerous incidents in his career. And, above all, he was a hero, whose manly bearing and courage has struck terror into the hearts of American tyrants, from which they can never recover. John Brown was never so really alive or so efficient in action as now, and hence it is that the Moloch of slavery trembles, and stands aghast from the fear of what the memory of that 'honest, truthful, sincere,' and brave old man, will yet do for the liberation of the slaves."

An American writer who had no sympathy with Brown's uncompromising hostility to slavery, and was therefore the less likely to be influenced by admiration for his self-sacrificing enthusiasm, has portrayed him in these vigorous terms :—

"He had elements of character which, under circumstances favourable to their proper development and right direction, would have made him one of the greatest men that ever lived. Napoleon himself had no more blind and trusting confidence in his own destiny and resources ; his iron will and unbending purpose were equal to those of any man, living or dead ; his religious enthusiasm and sense of duty were earnest and sincere, and not excelled by those of Oliver Cromwell or any of his followers ; while no danger could for a moment alarm or disturb him. Though doubtless his whole nature was subject to and almost constantly, for the last three or four years, pervaded by the deepest excitement, his exterior was always calm and cool. His manner, though conveying the idea of a stern and self-sustaining man, was yet gentle and courageous, and marked by frequent and decided manifestations of kindness ; and it can probably be said of him with truth, that, amid all his provocations, he never perpetrated an act of wanton or unnecessary cruelty. He was scrupulously honest, moral, and temperate, and never gave utterance to a boast. Upon one occasion, when one of the ex-governors of Kansas said to him that he was a marked man, and that the Missourians were determined, sooner or later, to take his scalp, he straightened himself up, with a glance of enthusiasm and defiance in his gray eye, and said, ' Sir, the angel of the Lord will camp round about me.' "

And Mr. Garrison, while claiming that every reference to him should be as respectful and as appreciative as to any of the patriots to whom civilized nations do homage, pithily remarks that Brown " was of such stuff as the Waldenses and Albigenses, the Scotch covenanters, the Smithfield martyrs, the Mayflower pilgrims were composed ; apparently as true to his convictions of duty toward God as any man who ever walked the earth before him. He perilled all that was dear to him, not to achieve liberty for himself, or those of his own complexion, but to break the fetters of a race 'not colored like his own,' most wickedly abhorred, universally proscribed, and subjected to a bondage full of unutterable woe and horror."

CHAPTER XIII.

DECEMBER, 1859—MARCH, 1860.

ENUMERATION OF THE CONFEDERATES AT HARPER'S FERRY.— COPELAND, GREEN, COOK, AND COPPOCK CONDEMNED TO DIE.—NOTICES OF COPELAND AND GREEN.—THEIR EXECUTION.—NOTICE OF COOK.—ESCAPE OF COOK, TIDD, OWEN BROWN, BARCLAY COPPOCK, AND MERRIAM FROM HARPER'S FERRY.—CAPTURE OF COOK.—COOK'S CONFESSION.—COOK AND EDWIN COPPOCK IN PRISON.—THEY ATTEMPT TO BREAK JAIL, BUT ARE ARRESTED.—EXECUTION OF COOK AND EDWIN COPPOCK.—FUNERAL OF COOK.—COOK'S PARTING VERSES TO HIS WIFE.—FUNERAL OF EDWIN COPPOCK.—NOTICE OF ALBERT HAZLITT.— OSBORNE ANDERSON AND HAZLITT FLY FROM HARPER'S FERRY.—HAZLITT IS ARRESTED, BUT ANDERSON MAKES GOOD HIS ESCAPE.—NOTICE OF STEVENS. —STEVENS AND HAZLITT RECEIVE SENTENCE.—STEVENS IN PRISON.—EXECUTION OF STEVENS AND HAZLITT.—STEVENS' LETTERS FROM PRISON.—FUNERAL OF STEVENS AND HAZLITT.

OF Captain Brown's confederates in the attempt at Harper's Ferry, his sons Watson and Oliver, his trusted lieutenant and companion in arms, John Henry Kagi,* Dauphin (or Adolphus) Thompson, Stewart Taylor, and three men of African descent, namely, Sherrard Lewis Leary, Dangerfield Newby, and Jeremiah Anderson, were killed during the struggle. William H. Leeman and William Thompson were cruelly murdered

---

* "Of the men who came to Chatham with Captain Brown, no one was greater in the essentials of true nobility of character and

—the first while swimming in the river, and Thompson while an unarmed prisoner. John Copeland and Shields Green, both men of colour, John E. Cook, Edwin Coppock, Aaron Dwight Stevens, and Albert Hazlitt, were taken prisoners, tried at Charlestown, found guilty, and executed. And Owen Brown, Barclay Coppock, Charles P. Tidd, Francis Jackson Merriam, and Osborne P. Anderson, a coloured man, succeeded in effecting their escape. The last named was the only one of the party actually engaged in fighting at Harper's Ferry who got off safely.

We propose in the present chapter to give some particulars respecting the character and previous history of the six brave young men who within a few short

executive skill than John H. Kagi, the confidential friend and adviser of the old man, and second in position in the expedition : no one was held in more deserved respect. Kagi was, singularly enough, a Virginian by birth, and had relatives in the region of the Ferry. He left home when a youth, an enemy to slavery, and brought as his gift-offering to freedom three slaves, whom he piloted to the north. His innate hatred of the institution made him a willing exile from the State of his birth, and his great abilities, natural and acquired, entitled him to the position he held in Captain Brown's confidence. He discoursed elegantly and fluently, wrote ably, and could occupy the platform with greater ability than many a man known to the American people as famous in these respects. John Brown appreciated him, and, to his men, his estimate of John Henry was a familiar theme. Kagi's bravery, his devotion to the cause, his deference to the commands of his leader, were most nobly illustrated in his conduct at Harper's Ferry."—*Anderson's Narrative.*

weeks or months followed their leader to the gallows. And as two of their number, Cook and Hazlitt, escaped from Harper's Ferry, in the first instance, along with their more fortunate confederates who eventually eluded pursuit, some account of the adventures of these latter fugitives will be included in the narrative.

COPELAND, GREEN, COOK, AND EDWIN COPPOCK CONDEMNED TO DIE.

It was hoped by many in the free states, that after the execution of Captain Brown Virginia would be satisfied with inflicting an imprisonment, more or less protracted, on the six prisoners who still remained in Charlestown jail. But it soon became evident that this hope was vain, and that the law would be unflinchingly carried out. In about a week after the death of their leader, Copeland, Green, Cook, and Coppock were brought up to receive sentence.

Of the trials of Coppock, Copeland, and Green we have been able to learn nothing except that the men were found guilty. That of Cook, which took place on the 9th of November, 1859, was sharply contested. The intense hatred which the people of that part of Virginia bore to him, far exceeding that felt towards any of the other prisoners, and the magnitude of the preparations for the defence, combined to excite an unusual interest in the progress of his case. He was defended by five counsel, led by his brother-in-law, Mr. Willard, Governor of Indiana, who exerted themselves to the utmost to get up a feeling in his favour. One of these, Mr. Voorhies, addressed the jury with great power, almost admitting the guilt of Cook, but appealing to their political prejudices by throwing the blame on the republican party and the abolitionists, and beseeching mercy, or at least a recommendation to mercy, on the plea of his client's facile character.

Mr. Andrew Hunter followed for the prosecution, with directness, force, and success, for, after being out about an hour, the jury returned a verdict such as had been returned against Copeland and Green, namely, not guilty of treason, but guilty of the remaining counts— for conspiracy with slaves to rebel and murder. Cook received the verdict without any exhibition of emotion.

On the following day at about eleven o'clock the hall began to fill; and by the time the prisoners were ready to receive sentence, it was crowded to the full extent of its capacity. The prisoners having been severally asked if they had anything to say previous to listening to their sentence of death, Coppock spoke as follows :—

" The charges that have been made against me are not true. I never committed any treason against the state of Virginia. I never made war upon it. I never conspired with anybody to induce your slaves to rebel, and I never even exchanged a word with one of your servants. What I came here for, I always told you. It was to run off slaves into a free state, and liberate

them there.   This is an offence against your laws, I admit, but I never committed murder.   When I escaped
to the engine-house, and found the captain and his
prisoners surrounded there, I saw no way of deliverance
but by fighting a little.   If anybody was killed on that
occasion, it was in a fair fight.   I have, as I said, committed an offence against your laws, but the punishment for that offence would be very different from what
you are going to inflict on me now.   I have no more
to say."

Green and Copeland, when called upon to answer,
said nothing.   When Cook's turn came, he spoke in a
hesitating, nervous manner, saying, in substance, that
he had not come to commit treason or murder, but
merely in pursuance of orders from his commander-in-
chief, with a design to liberate slaves.   As to the sword
and pistols of George Washington, taken from Lewis
Washington's house, he said they were seized by order
of Brown, not for purposes of robbery, but for the sake
of the moral effect that their possession might afford in
case of a war of liberation.   At the conclusion of his
speech, Judge Parker pronounced sentence of death, in
a manner showing genuine emotion and pity—feelings
which did not seem to be shared by his hearers.

NOTICES OF COPELAND AND GREEN.

John A. Copeland was a light-complexioned mulatto,

and was about twenty-four years of age at the time of his death. A few years before he had resided at Oberlin, in Ohio, and was one of those who assisted in the rescue of a fugitive slave at that place, from the hands of a United States marshal, under circumstances which created great excitement at the time, and led to the imprisonment of several of the citizens who were engaged in it. One of these, Professor Peck of Oberlin College, testifies that, although of incomplete education and a man of few words, Copeland was brave and energetic, and was much respected.

Shields Green was a full-blooded negro, and was but twenty-two years of age. He had a good countenance, and a sharp, intelligent face. He was a native of Rochester, New York, where, as we have before mentioned, he became acquainted with Captain Brown during the preceding summer. Osborne P. Anderson, in his "Narrative of Events at Harper's Ferry," thus describes him :—"The most inexorable of our party, a very Turco in his hatred of the stealers of men, a braver man never lived than Shields Green."

EXECUTION OF COPELAND AND GREEN.

Their execution took place on Friday, the 16th of December, a fortnight after the death of their leader. At half-past twelve o'clock, General Taliaferro, having given orders for them to prepare for death, took his departure with his staff of twenty-five officers, to join the main body of the troops on the field. The military then formed in a hollow square around the jail, and an open wagon, containing the coffins of the prisoners, drew up in front, with a carriage to convey Sheriff Campbell and his deputies. The crowd of citizens and strangers was very great—at least five times as numerous as on the occasion of Captain Brown's execution. The religious ceremonies in the cell of the prisoners were very impressive, and were conducted by the Rev. Mr. North of the Presbyterian, and the Rev. Henry Waugh of the Methodist Episcopal Church. The *Baltimore Sun* says, " A few moments before leaving the jail, Copeland said, ' If I am dying for freedom, I could not die for a better cause—I had rather die than be a slave !' "

Shortly before eleven o'clock, the prisoners, accompanied by the sheriff and Rev. Mr. North, appeared at the jail door, and with their arms pinioned moved slowly forward toward the vehicle in waiting for them. They were helped into the wagon, and took their seats on their coffins without looking to the right or left. The escort now set forward, the wagon being closely flanked on either side by a company of riflemen in double file. In ten minutes it stopped at the foot of the gallows. The prisoners mounted the scaffold with a firm step, and were immediately joined by Sheriff Campbell. They were accompanied by the Reverend Messrs. Waugh, North, and Lehr, to whom they bade an affectionate farewell, and expressed the hope of meeting them in heaven. After a brief prayer the caps were drawn over their heads and the ropes affixed around their necks.

23

Governor Wise took pains to spread a report that Copeland and Green had evinced a craven fear in their last hours ; which is flatly denied by credible witnesses. A military officer in charge on the day of the execution says, " I had a position near the gallows, and carefully observed all. I can truly say I never witnessed more firm and unwavering fortitude, more perfect composure, or more beautiful propriety, than were manifested by young Copeland to the last ;" and Professor Monroe of Oberlin, who was also present on the occasion, testifies to Green's manly conduct, his patient and heroic endurance in prison, and his pious, courageous, and consistent deportment as he stood on the fatal gallows. During the few moments they thus stood, Copeland remained quiet, but Green was engaged in earnest prayer up to the last moment.

The relatives and friends of Copeland in Ohio made the most earnest efforts to secure his body for Christian burial, but without effect. Governor Wise assured Mr. Beecher, the mayor of Oberlin, that the body should be delivered by General Taliaferro to any white citizen who was authorized to demand it. A southern gentleman, known to be strongly pro-slavery in sentiment, being furnished with the requisite order, proceeded to Charlestown for the purpose. On his arrival he was ushered into the presence of Taliaferro, but on presenting his letters he was put under arrest, and detained for twelve hours, when he was permitted to return to Washington. A correspondent of the *Cincin-*

nati Gazette, who was present at the execution of Copeland and Green, says that the bodies, which had been placed in poplar coffins and buried almost immediately after their death, were allowed to remain in the ground but a few moments, when they were taken up and deliverered to the students of Winchester medical college for dissection.

———

COPELAND'S LETTERS FROM PRISON.

The following touching letters, written by Copeland in prison,—one of them on the very day of his execution,—give such an insight into his character and feelings under his appalling circumstances, and are so full of pathetic interest, that we insert them at length.

JOHN COPELAND TO HIS BROTHER.

Charlestown, Virginia, Dec. 10, 1859.

My dear brother,

I now take my pen to write you a few lines to let you know how I am, and in answer to your kind letter of the 5th instant. Dear brother, I am, it is true, so situated at present as scarcely to know how to commence writing; not that my mind is filled with fear, or that it has become shattered in view of my near approach to death. Not that I am terrified by the gallows, which I see staring me in the face, and upon which I am so soon to stand and suffer death for doing what George Washington, the so-called father of this great but slavery-cursed

23*

country, was made a hero for doing, while he lived, and when dead, his name was immortalized, and his great and noble deeds in behalf of freedom taught by parents to their children. And now, brother, for having lent my aid to a general no less brave, and engaged in a cause no less honorable and glorious, I am to suffer death. Washington entered the field to fight for the freedom of the American people—not for the white man alone, but for both black and white. Nor were they white men alone who fought for the freedom of this country. The blood of black men flowed as freely as that of white men. Yes, the very first blood that was spilt was that of a negro. It was the blood of that heroic man (though black he was), Crispus Attucks. And some of the very last blood shed was that of black men. To the truth of this, history, though prejudiced, is compelled to attest. It is true that black men did an equal share of the fighting for American independence, and they were assured by the whites that they should share equal benefits for so doing. But, after having performed their part honorably, they were by the whites most treacherously deceived—they refusing to fulfil their part of the contract. But this you know as well I do, and I will therefore say no more in reference to the claims which we, as colored men, have on the American people.

It was a sense of the wrongs which we have suffered that prompted the noble but unfortunate Captain Brown and his associates to attempt to give freedom to a small number, at least, of those who are now held by cruel and unjust laws, and by no less cruel and unjust men. To this freedom they were entitled by every known principle of justice and humanity, and for the enjoyment of it God created them. And now, dear brother, could I die in a more noble cause? Could I, brother, die in a manner and

for a cause which would induce true and honest men more
to honor me, and the angels more readily to receive me to
their happy home of everlasting joy above? I imagine
that I hear you, and all of you, mother, father, sisters and
brothers, say—"No, there is not a cause for which we,
with less sorrow, could see you die." Believe me when I
tell you, that though shut up in prison and under sentence
of death, I have spent some very happy hours here. And
were it not that I know that the hearts of those to whom
I am attached by the nearest and most endearing ties of
blood-relationship—yea, by the closest and strongest ties
that God has instituted—will be filled with sorrow, I
would almost as lief die now as at any time, for I feel that
I am now prepared to meet my Maker.

Dear brother, I want you, and all of you, to meet me in
heaven. Prepare your souls for death. Be ready to meet
your God at any moment, and then, though we meet no
more on earth, we shall meet in heaven, where parting is
no more. Dear William and Fred, be good boys—mind
your mother and father—love and honor them—grow up
to be good men, and fear the Lord your God. Now, I
want you, dear brothers, to take this advice and follow it;
remember, it comes from your own brother, and is written
under most peculiar circumstances. Remember it is my
dying advice to you, and I hope you will, from the love
you have for me, receive it.

You may think I have been treated very harshly since
I have been here, but it is not so. I have been treated
exceedingly well—far better than I expected to be. My
jailor is a most kind-hearted man, and has done all he
could, consistent with duty, to make me and the rest of
the prisoners comfortable. Captain John Avis is a gentleman who has a heart in his bosom as brave as any other.

He met us at the Ferry, and fought us as a brave man would do. But since we have been in his power, he has protected us from insult and abuse which cowards would have heaped upon us. He has done as a brave man and gentleman only would do. Also one of his aids, Mr. John Sheats, has been very kind to us, and has done all he could to serve us. And now, Henry, if fortune should ever throw either of them in your way, and you can confer the least favour on them, do it for my sake.

Give my love to all my friends. And now, my dear brothers, one and all, I pray God we may meet in heaven.

Good bye. I am now, and shall remain, your affectionate brother,

JOHN A. COPELAND.

————

J. A. COPELAND TO HIS PARENTS, BROTHERS, AND SISTERS.

Charlestown Jail, Virginia, Dec. 16, 1859.
Dear father, mother, brothers Henry, William and Freddy, and sisters Sarah and Mary :

The last sabbath with me on earth has passed away. The last Monday, Tuesday, Wednesday and Thursday that I shall ever see on this earth have now passed by. God's glorious sun, which he has placed in the heavens to illuminate this earth—whose warm rays make man's home on earth pleasant—whose refulgent beams are watched for by the poor invalid, to enter and make, as it were, a heaven of the room in which he is confined-—I have seen declining behind the western mountains for the last time. Last night, for the last time, I beheld the soft bright moon as it rose, casting its mellow light into my felon's cell, dissipating the darkness, and filling it with that soft pleasant light which causes such thrills of joy to all those in like circumstances with myself. This morning, for the last time, I beheld the glorious sun of yesterday rising in the far-off east, away off in the country where our Lord Jesus Christ first proclaimed salvation to man ; and now, as he rises higher and his bright light takes the place of the pale, soft moonlight, I will take my pen for the last time, to write you who are bound to me by those strong ties—yea, the strongest that God ever instituted—the ties of blood and relationship. I am well both in body and in mind. And now, dear ones, if it were not for those feelings I have for you—if it were not that I know your hearts will be filled with sorrow at my fate, I could pass from this earth without a regret. Why should you sorrow ? Why should your hearts be racked with grief ? Have I not everything to gain, and nothing to lose by the change ? I fully believe that not only myself, but also all three of my poor comrades who are to ascend the same scaffold—(a scaffold already made sacred to the cause of freedom by the death of that great champion of human freedom, Captain John Brown,) are prepared to meet our God.

I am only leaving a world filled with sorrow and woe, to enter one in which there is but one lasting day of happiness and bliss. I feel that God, in his mercy, has spoken peace to my soul, and that all my numerous sins are forgiven.

Dear parents, brothers, and sisters, it is true that I am now in a few hours to start on a journey from which no traveller returns. Yes, long before this reaches you, I shall, as I sincerely hope, have met our brother and sister who have for years been worshiping God around his throne —singing praises to him, and thanking him that he gave his Son to die that they might have eternal life. I pray daily and hourly that I may be fitted to have my home with them, and that you, one and all, may prepare your souls to meet your God ; that so, in the end, though we meet no more on earth, we shall meet in heaven, where we shall not be parted by the demands of the cruel and unjust monster, slavery.

But think not that I am complaining, for I feel reconciled to meet my fate. I pray God that his will be done, not mine.

Let me tell you that it is not the mere fact of having to meet death which I should regret, (if I should express regret, I mean,) but that such an unjust institution should exist as the one which demands my life, and not my life only, but the lives of those to whom my life bears but the relative value of zero to the infinite. I beg of you, one and all, that you will not grieve about me ; but that you will thank God that he spared me to make my peace with him.

And now, dear ones, attach no blame to any one for my coming here, for not any person but myself is to blame.

I have no antipathy against any one. I have freed my mind of all hard feelings against every living being, and I ask all who have any thing against me to do the same.

And now, dear parents, brothers and sisters, I must bid you to serve your God, and meet me in heaven.

I must with a very few words close my correspondence with those who are the most near and dear to me : but I hope, in the end, we may again commune, never more to cease.

Dear ones, he who writes this will in a few hours be in this world no longer. Yes, these fingers which hold the pen with which this is written will, before to-day's sun has reached his meridian, have laid it aside forever, and this poor soul have taken its flight to meet its God.

And now, dear ones, I must bid you that last, long, sad farewell. Goodbye, father, mother, Henry, William, and Freddy, Sarah and Mary ! Serve your God, and meet me in heaven.

Your son and brother to eternity.
JOHN A. COPELAND.

NOTICE OF COOK.

John E. Cook had lived, some years before, in the neighbourhood of Harper's Ferry, part of the time engaged as teacher in a school. He afterwards went to Kansas, and there made the acquaintance of Captain Brown in the summer of 1856, shortly after the skirmish at Black Jack. After the convention at Chatham in May, 1858, he returned to the neighbourhood of Harper's Ferry, and married there. He was well known in that part of the country, and regarded as an intelligent man and opposed to slavery, though he was not so outspoken on the subject as to excite suspicion. He was a brave man, of good impulses, but possessing no great firmness of character.

ESCAPE OF COOK, TIDD, OWEN BROWN, BARCLAY COPPOCK, AND F. J. MERRIAM FROM HARPER'S FERRY.

We are informed by Cook, in his confession written

in jail, that on Monday—the day after the seizure of Harper's Ferry—whilst Charles P. Tidd was sent, by Captain Brown's orders, for a second wagon-load of arms to the Kennedy farm, he was himself left at the school-house with one of the negroes, to guard the arms which were there. "A short time after the departure of Tidd," he continues, "I heard a good deal of firing, and became anxious to know the cause, but my orders were strict to remain at the school-house and guard the arms, and I obeyed the orders to the letter. About four o'clock in the evening C. P. Tidd came with the second load. I then took one of the negroes with me, and started for Harper's Ferry. I met a negro woman a short distance below the school-house, who informed me they were fighting hard at the Ferry. I hurried on till I came to the lock kept by George Hardy, about a mile above the bridge, where I saw his wife and Mrs. Elizabeth Reed, who told me that our men were hemmed in, and that several of them had been shot. I expressed my intention to get to them. Mrs. Reed begged me not to go down to the Ferry. She said I would be shot. I told her I must make an attempt to save my comrades, and passed on down the road. A short distance below the lock I met two boys whom I knew, and they told me that our men were all hemmed in by troops from Charlestown, Martinsburg, Hagerstown, and Shepherdstown. The negro who was with me had been very much frightened at the first report we received; and as the boys told me the troops were coming up the road after us soon, I

sent him back to inform Tidd, while I hastened down
the road.   After going down opposite the Ferry, I
ascended the mountain in order to get a better view of
the position of our opponents.   Our party were completely surrounded; and as I saw a body of men on
High-street firing down upon them—they were about
half a mile distant from me—I thought I would draw
their fire upon myself; I therefore raised my rifle, took
the best aim I could, and fired.   It had the desired
effect, for the very instant the party returned it.   Several shots were exchanged.   I then passed down to the
lock-house, went down the steps to the lock, where I
saw William McGreg, and questioned him in regard to
the troops on the other side.   He told me that the
bridge was filled by our opponents, and that all our
party were dead but seven—that two of them were shot
while trying to escape across the river.   He begged
me to leave immediately.   After questioning him in
regard to the position and number of the troops, and
from what source he received his information, I bade
him good-night, and started up the road at a rapid
walk.   I stopped at the house of an Irish family at
the foot of the hill, and got a cup of coffee and some
eatables. · I was informed by them that Captain Brown
was dead; that he had been shot about four o'clock in
the afternoon.   At that time I believed that report to
be true.   I went on up to the school-house, and found
the shutters and door closed.   I then started up the
road toward Captain Brown's house [the Kennedy
farm].   I saw a party of men coming down the road;

when within about fifty yards, I ordered them to halt; they recognized my voice and called me. I found them to be Charles P. Tidd, Owen Brown, Barclay Coppock, F. J. Merriam, and a negro who belonged to Washington or Alstadtt. They asked me the news, and I gave the information that I received at the canal lock, and on the road. It seemed that they thought it would be sheer madness to attempt a rescue of our comrades, and it was finally determined to return to the house of Captain Brown. Here we got a few articles which would be necessary, and then went over into the timber on the side of the mountain, a few yards beyond the house where the spears were kept. Here we lay down and went to sleep. About three o'clock in the morning one of our party awakened, and found that the negro had left us. He immediately aroused the rest of the party, and we concluded to go to the top of the mountain before light. Here we remained for a few hours, and then passed over to the other side of the mountain, where we waited till dark, and then crossed the valley to the other range beyond."

We continue the adventures of the fugitives in the words of Osborne P. Anderson :—

"Having heard, through some means, that the con-flict was against the insurgents, they provided themselves with food, blankets, and other necessaries, and then took to the mountains. They were fourteen days making the journey to Chambersburg. The weather was extremely bad the whole time; it rained, snowed, blew, and was freezing cold ; but there was no shelter for the fugitive travellers, one of whom, F. J. Merriam, was in poor health, lame, and physically slightly formed. H was, however, greatly relieved by his companions, who did everything possible to lessen the fatigue of the journey for him. The bad weather and their destitution made it one of the most trying journeys it is possible for men to perform. Sometimes they would have to lie over a day or two for the sick, and when fording the streams, as they had to do, they carried th sick over on their shoulders.

"They were a brave band, and any attempt to arrest them in a body would have been a most serious undertaking, as all were well armed, could have fired some forty rounds apiece, and would have done it, without any doubt whatever. The success of the Federal officers consisted in arresting those unfortunate enough to fall into their clutches singly. In this manner did poor Hazlitt and John E. Cook fall into their power.

"Starvation several times stared Owen Brown's party in the face. They would search their pockets over and over for some stray crumb that might have been overlooked in the general search, for something to appease their gnawing hunger, and pick out carefully, from among the accumulated dirt and medley, even the smallest crumb, and give it to the comrade least able to endure the long and biting fast.

" John E. Cook became completely overcome by this hungry feeling. A strong desire to get salt pork took possession of him, and against the remonstrances of his comrades, he ventured down from the mountains to Montalto, Pennsylvania, fourteen miles from Chambersburg, in quest of it. He was arrested by Daniel Logan and Clegget Fitzhugh, and taken before Justice Reisher. Upon examination, a commission signed by Captain Brown, marked No. 4, being found upon his person, he was committed to await a requisition from Governor Wise, and finally, as is well-known, was surrendered to Virginia, where he was tried, after a fashion, condemned, and executed.

"Owen Brown, and the other members of the party, becoming impatient at Cook's prolonged absence, began to suspect something was wrong, and moved at once to a more retired and safer position. Afterwards they went to Chambersburg, and stopped in the outskirts of the town for some days, communicating with but one person, directly, while there. Through revelations made by Cook, it became unsafe in the neighbourhood, and they left, and went some miles from town, when Merriam took the cars for Philadelphia, thence to Boston, and subsequently to Canada. The other three travelled on foot to Centre County, Pennsylvania, when Barclay Coppock separated from them, to take the cars, with the rifles of the company boxed up in his possession. He stopped at Salem, Ohio, a few days, and then went to Cleveland, to Detroit, and over into Canada, where, after remaining for a time, he proceeded westward. Owen Brown and C. P. Tidd went to Ohio, where the former spent the winter. The latter, after a sojourn, proceeded to Massachusetts."

CAPTURE OF COOK.

A correspondent of the *New York Tribune*, writing from Chambersburg, informs us that in order to ascertain the truth of the various rumours with reference to Cook's capture, he called on Squire Reisher, the justice before whom the fugitive was brought, and asked for permission to copy the evidence produced in the case. The magistrate stated that the testimony had not been committed to writing, but that he would repeat the substance of the evidence of Logan and Fitzhugh—the men by whom Cook had been betrayed, in expectation of the reward of two thousand dollars offered by the governor of Virginia. The following is Mr. Reisher's statement :—

" I was in my office, about eight o'clock, when two men came in and asked me to go down with them to the Franklin hotel. They said they had a man whom they supposed to be Captain Cook. I told them they should bring him up here before me to my office.— They said there were a great many persons there, and likely to be considerable excitement, and I had better go up with them to see him. I went there, and found this man supposed to be Cook, with a room full of persons and several outside. I told him that there were accusations to be preferred against him of a very serious nature, and informed him of his rights, put him on his legal guard, and told him he was not obliged to say anything which would criminate himself. He looked haggard, and I told them to give him something to eat.

They did so. There were at the time about forty persons in the room. They brought food, and he ate so heartily that I thought the poor fellow had not eaten anything for some time. I asked his accusers what grounds they had to suspect this man to be Captain Cook. They stated that he had come out of the mountains, and asked for some salt meat; he said he had been hunting in the mountains, and had got out of provisions. Fitzhugh saw a man called Logan, who is a rough kind of a man, and made signs to him to keep with him. Logan let on he had a store up the road, and that he would give him some salt meat. Fitzhugh winked at Logan, and whispered that he believed this was Cook, when Logan put his hand on his shoulder and said, 'You are my prisoner.' Logan said that Cook sprang up like a wire-trap, and thrust his hand into his pocket. Logan caught him by the arm, and held on. Logan is a strong, active man, and yet both of them could hardly get him to the ground. They then took away his arms. He had a pistol and campaign knife—which is a knife with a fork and spoon. The pistol was a five-inch revolver, with six barrels, and finely finished. It was fully loaded and capped. After having secured him, they took him down to the house to get something to eat; told him that they pitied his case very much; that he might get clear; that his best course was to go before a magistrate, enter bail, and then, to use Logan's word, 'skeet' or escape. Logan rather got Cook persuaded that he was friendly to him. Finding the excitement increasing, I appointed a special police of six, and had Cook conducted to my office. I there repeated the advice I had given him at the tavern, to put him on his legal guard—when he said that if such was the law, he chose to remain quiet, and not answer any question. I then swore the accusers. Fitzhugh was the first witness, and repeated his statements made at the tavern."

The reporter inquired where these men captured Cook.

"At Mount Alto," the justice replied, "near Hughes's foundries."

"The hardest place in this country," said a bystander. "They are the hardest people in this section there—just such folks as would delight to do such actions. Cook could not have chosen a worse locality in all this state than that neighbourhood. If he had gone by the North Mountain, he would have easily escaped."

"I then asked Fitzhugh," said the magistrate, "if he had made any offer or promise of reward to the prisoner. He denied having made any other than that to go before a magistrate would be the easiest way to get off. After being sworn, Logan was asked if Cook had made any declaration with regard to who he was. Logan hesitated. The question was repeated. He hesitated again. The question was again put. We waited for some time for an answer. I told him he was bound to tell the truth, and the whole truth, with reference to any conversation he had had with Cook. Logan said, if he must, he must, but that he did not like it. To my mind," said Squire Reisher, " when he was making

2+

this statement, he wanted to tell all; but not in the presence of Cook. Logan then stated that the prisoner had told him that he was Captain Cook. Cook had being standing behind my chair all the time thus far, but now he rather pressed himself forward, and looked at Logan just as a dead man might look. Logan cringed beneath his look. Logan further stated that Cook confessed having been at Harper's Ferry. Here the counsel for Cook made some objections, and spoke disrespectfully of Logan. [Logan had the reputation of being a slave-catcher]. The witness seemed rather to get cross with the counsel, and in proof of one statement, pulled out of his pocket a commission made out to Cook by John Brown. Here Logan fairly cringed under the look Cook gave him as he pulled out this paper."

" Yes, he betrayed Cook—the scoundrel!" said a bystander who was present while Mr. Reisher was giving this information.

"Logan," continued the magistrate, "said that this was the commission he took from Cook. He then read the commission. It was signed by Brown as commander-in-chief, and I think it was countersigned by Kagi. It was a printed commission : one line of letters, in the form of an arrow, was very peculiar ; I could not read it ; I never saw such letters before. After hearing this testimony, I thought the evidence was sufficient to authorize me to hold the prisoner over to answer. I committed him to prison that night. In the short time

I was with him, I thought him a gentleman. There was a great deal of candour about him. He is evidently a very brave man."

Cook's captors behaved with cruelty as well as baseness. Not content with having him at their mercy, after disarming and overpowering him they loaded him with irons to bring him to town. His offered word of honour and entreaties were impotent to prevent this indignity.

Cook's conduct in prison at Chambersburg was in keeping with his bearing in court. He refused to answer all questions, and when addressed as Mr. Cook, or when inquiries were cunningly proposed to him about Harper's Ferry, he merely said that he had not admitted that he was Cook. He asked for books, and spent the day in reading. There was a general feeling of pity for him. His coolness, his unassuming but undaunted demeanour, elicited universal admiration. He was taken to Charlestown on the 28th October, and committed to jail.

COOK'S CONFESSION.

While in Charlestown jail, Cook drew up his confession, at the instance of his relative, Governor Willard, in the hope of procuring a pardon. But his death was already determined on, even had he made any important revelations, which does not appear to have been the case. He gave the names of some well known northern gentlemen as being in connection with Captain

24*

Brown, and to some extent privy to his plans; and some of these were in consequence obliged to keep out of the way for a time; but no proof appeared against them, and the matter was not followed up. In reference to some errors of statement in this confession, O. P. Anderson remarks :—" It is not my intention to dwell upon the failings of John E. Cook. That he departed from the record, as familiar to John Brown and his men, every one of them 'posted' in the details of their obligations and duties, well knows; but his very weakness should excite our compassion. He was brave —none could doubt that; and life was invested with charms for him which his new relation as a man of family tended to intensify; and charity suggests that the hope of escaping his merciless persecutors, and of being spared to his friends and associates in reform, rather than treachery to the cause he had espoused, furnishes the explanation."

COOK AND EDWIN COPPOCK IN PRISON.—THEY BREAK JAIL,
BUT ARE ARRESTED.

John E. Cook and Edwin Coppock were visited on the day before their execution, by several presbyterian and methodist ministers. Mr. Butler, a member of the Society of Friends, from Ohio, by whom Coppock had been reared, had an affecting interview with him. A paternal uncle of Coppock, also from Ohio, paid him a visit which lasted more than an hour. He seemed in great distress at the tragic fate which awaited his nephew.

At a quarter past eight o'clock on the same evening, Charlestown was thrown into commotion by the report of a rifle under the wall of the jail, followed by several shots from the vicinity of the guard-house, in close proximity. The military were called to arms, and the excitement was intense. In a few minutes the streets and avenues of the town were in possession of armed men, and it was with some difficulty that the cause of the turmoil could be ascertained. The sentinel stationed near the jail reported that at a quarter past eight o'clock he observed a man on the jail wall. He challenged him, and, receiving no answer, fired. Another head was also seen above the wall, but he retreated as soon as the first had been fired at. The man on the top of the wall seemed at first determined to jump down, but the sentinel declared his intention of impaling him on his bayonet, and he then retreated into the jail-yard with Coppock, and both gave themselves up without further resistance. Cook afterwards said that if he could have got over and disabled the guard, he would have made his escape. The Shenandoah mountains are within ten minutes run of the jail-wall ; and had he reached them, with his thorough knowledge of the mountains, his arrest would have been difficult, especially as but few of the military could have followed him during the night. They had succeeded after two weeks' labour, whenever alone, and at night when the bed-clothing muffled the sound of the saw (which they had

made out of an old knife) in cutting through their iron
shackles, so that they could take them off whenever
they had their other work completed. They had also
made a sort of chisel out of an old bed-screw, with which
they succeeded in removing the plaster from the wall,
and then brick after brick, until a space sufficient for
them to pass through was opened, requiring only the
removal of the outer brick.   The part of the wall on
which they operated was behind the bed on which they
slept ; and the bed, being pushed against the wall,
completely hid their work from view. The bricks they
took out were concealed in the drum of the stove, and
the dirt and plaster removed in the course of their work
were placed between the bed-clothes. They acknowledged that they had been at work a whole week in
making the aperture in the wall through which they
hoped to escape.

Their cell being on the first floor, the aperture was
not more than five feet above the pavement of the
yard, and, when freed from their shackles, their access
to the yard was easy.   Here, however, there was a
smooth brick wall about fifteen feet high. This difficulty was soon overcome with the aid of the timbers of
the scaffold on which Captain Brown was hung, and
which were intended also for their own execution.
They placed these against the wall, and then succeeded
in reaching the top, from which they could easily have
dropped to the other side, had not the vigilance of the
sentinel on duty checked their movements. They were
arrested in the jail-yard by General Taliaferro and the

officer of the day, who rushed to the jail the moment the alarm was given.

Cook, after his capture, said that they had done the best they could, that life was as sweet to them as to any one else, and that they had planned it for ten days. They had set down Tuesday night for the attempt, but it was deferred on account of not wishing to compromise Governor Willard, who was in town that night. Cook said to a gentleman who addressed him, that he most fully believed slavery to be a sin, that it would be abolished in Virginia in less than ten years, and that by the people of Virginia. He was prepared to die in such a cause, and thought he had done nothing to regret so far as principle was concerned. Coppock said the affair was not ended yet; that they had friends at the north who would not rest satisfied till they had been avenged.

EXECUTION OF COOK AND EDWIN COPPOCK.

The bodies of Copeland and Green having been brought back to the jail shortly before noon on Friday, (Dec. 16th), notice was given to Cook and Coppock that their time was approaching—only one hour longer being allowed them. The military movements, similar to those at the first execution, were repeated; and the wagon, with two more coffins, was standing at the door at half-past twelve o'clock. The same military escort was in readiness, while the closing religious ceremonies

were progressing in the cell. The prisoners were re-
served and rather quiet, but they joined fervently in
the services.

Previous to their departure for the scaffold, the prisoners were engaged in the entrance, washing their feet and
putting on their under-clothing. Captain Avis said
that if they had anything to say they could do so then,
in the presence of fifteen or twenty persons. Cook
replied that he was grateful for the kindness shown
him by Sheriff Campbell, the jailer, and the guards;
to the ministers who had manifested such interest in
his welfare, as well as to the citizens generally for their
kindness to him. He then gave directions in regard to
one or two articles; a breastpin, which he did not
take off then, nor at the scaffold, he wished to be
given to his wife—or to his boy, if he lived. Inside his
shirt, on the left side, were a daguerreotype and a lock of
his son's hair, which he wished to be given to his wife.
Both requested that their arms should not be pinioned
tight enough to stop the circulation of the blood, which
was complied with.

During these proceedings, Coppock was struggling
to keep down his emotion, and Cook was striving to
be calm. Mr. Butler remarked that "it was hard to
die;" to which Coppock responded, "It is the parting
from friends, not the dread of death, that moves us."
On the way down stairs they were allowed to enter
the cell of Stevens and Hazlitt, and bid them farewell.
They shook hands cordially, and Cook said to Stevens,
"My friend, good bye." Stevens said, "Good bye,

cheer up ; give my love to my friends in the other world." Both then shook hands with Hazlitt, and bade him "good bye," but did not call him by name. On leaving the jail, Cook recognized and bowed to several gentlemen. The prisoners ascended the scaffold with a determined firmness that was scarcely surpassed by Captain Brown. A brief prayer was offered up by one of the clergymen, the ropes were adjusted, and the caps drawn over their faces. Coppock, at this point, turned towards Cook, and stretched forth his hand as far as possible. At the same time Cook said, "Stop a minute—where is Edwin's hand?" They then shook hands cordially, and Cook said, "God bless you." The calm and collected manner of both was very marked. After the rope was adjusted, Cook exclaimed, "Be quick—as quick as possible," which was also repeated by Coppock.

After hanging for about half an hour, both bodies were taken down and placed in black walnut coffins, which were afterwards enclosed in boxes of poplar wood for transmission by railway. The remains of Cook were accompanied by Governor Willard of Indiana, Mr. Voorhies, Secretary of State of Indiana, and Dr. Stanton—all relatives of the deceased—to Williamsburg, Wayne County, Indiana, where they arrived on the morning of Sunday, December 18th.

FUNERAL OF COOK.

Some idea of the power of pro-slavery influence in

controlling the action of religious bodies in the United
States may be formed from the fact, that when Mr.
Croly, the brother-in-law of Cook, applied to the Consistory of the Lee Avenue Church for permission to
have the services performed at that edifice, (as the deceased was once a Sunday school teacher in the Lee
Avenue school,) the request was denied; and Mr.
Croly then advised with the Rev. Dr. Porter, of the
Fourth Street Church, who at once consented to preach
the funeral discourse, and made arrangements for the
ceremony. The Consistory also giving their consent,
it was supposed that all was arranged, until Friday
night; when Dr. Porter was informed that such re-
strictions had been imposed upon the services as rendered it impossible that they could take place at that
church. Under these circumstances, Mr. Croly decided
to accept the offer of a friend to have the services performed at his house.

The funeral was held on Tuesday morning, and a large
number of persons assembled in the street before the
house. The body, embalmed and placed in a rosewood
coffin—which had been substituted for that in which
it was brought from Charlestown—was exposed in the
front hall. The face was much discoloured, but the
features and the firm expression were well preserved, as
was shown by a photograph that lay on the coffin. The
blonde hair and moustache were the most lifelike features. The services were conducted by the Rev. Mr.
Caldicott, and other ministers; the father and sisters
of the deceased, as well as his wife, and her brother

Governor Willard, being present. The Rev. Mr. Caldicott, after reading impressive portions of Scripture, said that he thought they had abundant evidence that the departed was a child of God. It had been incorrectly reported that he was a wayward, disobedient child. The mourning father testified that it was not so—that John was a loving, affectionate son. True, he left his friends, but he never forgot them, or ceased to yearn after their society, and he never lost his love for the Christian religion. Mr. Caldicott then read Cook's last letters, and closed by an affectionate address to the mourners. The body was buried at the Cypress Hill Cemetery.

COOK'S FAREWELL VERSES TO HIS WIFE.

One of Cook's last acts in this world was to write an affectionate letter to his wife and child, enclosing the following verses :—

> If upon this earth we're parted,
>   Never more to meet below,
> Meet me, O thou broken-hearted !
>   In that world to which I go.
>
> In that world where time unending
>   Sweeps in glory bright along,
> Where no shadows there are blending,
>   And no discord in the song ;
>
> Where the Saviour's flocks are resting
>   By the river bright and fair,
> And immortal glory cresting,
>   Every head that enters there ;

Where the anthem loud is pealing
    Songs of praise to Him alone ;
Where the seraph bands are kneeling
    'Mid the radiance of the Throne.

There at last I hope to meet thee,
    Never, never more to part ;
In those happy bowers to greet thee,
    Where no farewell tears shall start.

And again in heaven united,
    'Mid those fair Elysian bowers,
We'll perfect the love we plighted
    In this darkened world of ours.

Then look forward to that meeting,
    Which shall know no blight or woe—
That eternal joyous greeting,
    'Mid Elysium's endless flow.

FUNERAL OF EDWIN COPPOCK.

The body of Edwin Coppock was forwarded for
interment to a cemetery near New Garden, Columbiana
County, Ohio. It was removed a few days after to
Salem, his native place, the principal town in the same
county. The *Anti-Slavery Bugle* states that on Friday,
December the 23rd, the body was taken to the town
hall, so that all who wished to look upon it might
have the opportunity. Every seat was speedily filled,
and for more than three hours a continuous stream of
citizens and strangers passed into the hall, pausing a
moment to look on the body, and then leaving by

another door from that at which they entered.   The
number in attendance was variously estimated ; some
accounts placing it at about five or six thousand, and
others stating that it was considerably greater.   All
having had an opportunity of looking upon the deceased,
a touching prayer was made by James A. Thome, of
Cleveland ; and, after a few remarks by the same
speaker, the funeral procession was formed.   First came
the relatives and intimate friends of the deceased; next,
the coloured people, in behalf of whose race his life had
been given ; then the friends of freedom, who wished
to honour one who had fallen in its defence.

The family of Edwin Coppock belonged to the Society
of Friends, or Quakers.   He lost his father when about
seven years old, and was then placed by his mother
under the care of her friend Mr. Butler, in whose
family he remained eight years.   During the imprisonment of Coppock, Mr. Butler addressed a letter to the
Salem *Republican,* in reply to some calumnious stories
which had been circulated respecting his former ward.
In this communication he testifies that, during the time
the lad was under his charge, " there was nothing particular to remark in point of character, except that he
gave evidence of an unusually strong will in trying to
carry out his own views, and that he was very fearless,
never manifesting anything like cowardice in times of
danger, or by night.   He was a very industrious and
careful boy, more careful and particular that everything
was kept in its proper place on the farm and about the
buildings, and to have his work done well and in the

given time, than is common for boys of his age." In 1850 he removed with his mother to the state of Iowa, and some years afterwards emigrated into the territory of Kansas. At the time of his death Edwin Coppock was about twenty-four years of age ; he was of middle height, his hair was brown, and his complexion dark.

NOTICE OF ALBERT HAZLITT.

Of Albert Hazlitt little is known with certainty— not even his true name, which is believed to have been Harrison. He was one of the youngest of Captain Brown's companions, and remarked, while in prison, that on the day of his execution, March 16th, his age would be exactly twenty-two years, twenty-two weeks, and twenty-two days. He was of a serious and thoughtful disposition, courageous, and fond of adventure. In a letter written the day before his death, he said, " I am willing to die in the cause of liberty. If I had ten thousand lives, I would willingly lay them all down for the same cause. My death will do more good than if I had lived."

Hazlitt was born in Indiana County, Pennsylvania, and went to Kansas in the spring of 1857. He soon became engaged in the defence of the free-state cause, and proved himself a brave and efficient soldier. In the winter of 1858–'59, when J. H. Kagi was in command in southern Kansas, Hazlitt was an officer under him, and displayed the utmost coolness and daring.

He was tall, slender and active, of nervous sanguine temperament, with small and sharp oval features, very fair hair, and florid complexion. He was esteemed among his comrades as an honest, upright, intelligent man, and a genial companion.

ANDERSON AND HAZLITT FLY FROM HARPER'S FERRY.

Osborne P. Anderson thus narrates the escape of himself and Hazlitt from Harper's Ferry, and the subsequent arrest of Hazlitt :—

"Of the six men assigned a position in the arsenal by Captain Brown, four were either slain or captured ; and Hazlitt and myself, the only ones remaining, never left our position until we saw, with feelings of intense sadness, that we could be of no further avail to our commander, he being a prisoner in the hands of the Virginians. We therefore, upon consultation, concluded it was better to retreat while it was possible, as our work for the day was clearly finished, and gain a position where in the future we could work with better success than to recklessly invite capture and brutality at the hands of our enemies. We travelled up the Shenandoah along the railroad, and overtook one of the citizens. He was armed, and had been in the fight in the afternoon. We took him prisoner, in order to facilitate our escape. He submitted without resistance, and quietly gave up his gun. From him, we learned substantially of the final struggle at the rifle factory, where the noble

Kagi commanded. The number of citizens killed was, according to his opinion, much larger than either Hazlitt or I had supposed, although we knew there were a great many killed and wounded together. He said there must be at least seventy killed, besides wounded. Hazlitt had said there must be fifty, taking into account the defence of the three strong positions. I do not know positively, but would not put the figure below thirty killed, seeing many fall as I did, and knowing the 'dead aim' principle upon which we defended ourselves. One of the southern published accounts, it will be remembered, said twenty citizens were killed, another said fifteen. At last it got narrowed down to five, which was simply absurd, after so long an engagement. We had forty rounds apiece when we went to the Ferry, and when Hazlitt and I left, we had not more than twenty rounds between us. The rest of the party were as free with their ammunition as we were, if not more so. We had further evidence that the number of dead was larger than published, from the many that we saw lying dead around.

" When we had gone as far as the foot of the mountains, our prisoner begged us not to take his life, but to let him go at liberty. He said we might keep his gun ; he would not inform on us. Feeling compassion for him, and trusting to his honour, we suffered him to go, when he went directly into town, and finding every thing there in the hands of our enemies, he informed on us, and we were pursued. After he had left us, we crawled or climbed up among the rocks in the mountains, some hundred yards or more from the spot where we left him, and hid ourselves, as we feared treachery, on second thought. A few minutes before dark, the troops came in search of us. They came to the foot of the mountains, marched and counter-marched, but never attempted to search the mountains; we supposed from their movements that they feared a host of armed enemies in concealment. Their air was so defiant, and their errand so distasteful to us, that we concluded to apply a little ammunition to their case, and having a few cartridges on hand, we poured from our excellent position in the rocky wilds, some well-directed shots. It was not so dark but that we could see one bite the dust now and then, when others would run to aid them instantly, particularly the wounded. Some lay where they fell, undisturbed, which satisfied us that they were dead. The troops returned our fire, but it was random shooting, as we were concealed from their sight by the rocks and bushes. Interchanging of shots continued for some minutes, with much spirit, when it became quite dark, and they went down into the town. After their return to the Ferry, we could hear the drum beating for a long time; an indication of their triumph, we supposed. Hazlitt and I remained in our position three hours, before we dared venture down.

"When we descended from the rocks, we passed through the back part of Harper's Ferry on the hill, down to the railroad, proceeding as far as the saw-mill on the Virginia side, where we came upon an old boat tied up to the shore, which we cast off, and crossed the

25

Potomac. The Maryland shore once gained, we passed along the tow-path of the canal for some distance, when we came to an arch, which led through under the canal, and thence to the Kennedy Farm, hoping to find something to eat, and to meet the men who had been stationed on that side. When we reached the farm-house, all our expectations were disappointed. The old house had been ransacked and deserted, the provisions taken away, with every thing of value to the insurgents. Thinking that we should fare better at the school-house, we bent our steps in that direction. The night was dark and rainy, and after tramping for an hour and a half, at least, we came up to the school-house. This was about two o'clock in the morning. The school-house was packed with things moved there by the party the previous day, but we searched in vain, after lighting a match, for food, our great necessity, or for our young companions in the struggle. Thinking it unsafe to remain in the school-house, from fear of oversleeping ourselves, we climbed up the mountain in the rear of it, to lie down till daylight.

" It was after sunrise some time when we awoke in the morning. The first sound we heard was shooting at the Ferry. Hazlitt thought it must be Owen Brown and his men trying to force their way into the town, as they had been informed that a number of us had been taken prisoners, and we started down along the ridge to join them. When we got in sight of the Ferry, we saw the troops firing across the river to the Maryland side with considerable spirit. Looking closely, we saw, to our surprise that they were firing upon a few of the coloured men, who had been armed the day before by our men at the Kennedy Farm, and stationed down at the school-house by C. P. Tidd. They were in the bushes on the edge of the mountains, dodging about, occasionally exposing themselves to the enemy. The troops crossed the bridge in pursuit of them, but they retreated in different directions. Being further in the mountains, and more secure, we could see without personal harm befalling us. One of the coloured men came towards us where we were, when we hailed him, and inquired the particulars. He said that one of his comrades had been shot, and was lying on the side of the mountains ; that they thought the men who had armed them the day before must be in the Ferry. That opinion, we told him, was not correct. We asked him to join with us in hunting up the rest of the party, but he declined, and went his way.

" While we were in this part of the mountains, some of the troops went to the school-house, and took possession of it. On our return along up the ridge, from our position, screened by the bushes, we could see them as they invested it. Our last hope of shelter, or of meeting our companions, now being destroyed, we concluded to make our escape north. We started at once, and wended our way along until dark, without being fortunate enough to overtake our friends, or to get anything to eat. As may be supposed, from such incessant activity, and not having tasted a morsel for forty-eight hours, our appetites were exceedingly keen.

25*

So hungry were we, that we sought out a cornfield under cover of the night, gathered some of the ears, (which by the way were pretty well hardened,) carried them into the mountains, our fortunate resource, and, having matches, struck fire, and roasted, and feasted.

" During our perilous and fatiguing journey to Pennsylvania, and for some time after crossing the line, our only food was corn roasted in the ear, often difficult to get without risk, and seldom eaten but at long intervals. As a result of this poor diet and the hard journey, we became nearly famished, and very much reduced in bodily strength. Poor Hazlitt could not bear the privations as I could; he was less inured to physical exertion, and was of rather slight form, though inclined to be tall. With his feet blistered and sore, he held out as long as he could, but at last gave out, completely broken down, ten miles below Chambersburg. He declared it was impossible for him to go further, and begged me to go on, as we should be more in danger if seen together in the vicinity of the towns. He said, after resting that night, he would throw away his rifle, and go to Chambersburg in the stage next morning, where we agreed to meet again. The poor young man's face was wet with tears when we parted. I was loth to leave him, as we both knew that danger was more imminent than when in the mountains around Harper's Ferry. At the latter place, the ignorant slaveholding aristocracy were unacquainted with the topography of their own grand hills;—in Pennsylvania, the cupidity of the pro-slavery classes would induce them to seize a stranger on

suspicion, or to go hunting for our party, so tempting
to them is the bribe offered by the slave power. Their
debasement in that respect was another reason why we
felt the importance of travelling at night, as much as
possible.

————

HAZLITT IS ARRESTED, BUT OSBORNE ANDERSON MAKES GOOD HIS ESCAPE.

" The next day, Hazlitt went boldly into Chambersburg, carrying his blanket, rifle and revolver, and proceeded to the house where Kagi had boarded. The reward was then out for John E. Cook's arrest, and, sus-
pecting him to be Cook, Hazlitt was pursued. He was
chased from the house where he was by the officers,
dropping his rifle in his flight. When he got to Car-
lisle, so far from receiving kindness from the citizens of
his native State,—he was from Northern Pennsylvania,
—he was arrested and lodged in jail, given up to the
authorities of Virginia, and executed by them ; his
identity, however, never having been proven before the
court.

" After leaving young Hazlitt," continues Anderson,
" I travelled on as fast as my disabled condition would
admit of, and got into Chambersburg about two hours
after midnight. I went cautiously, as I thought, to the
house of an acquaintance, who arose and let me in.
Before knocking, however, I hid my rifle a little distance
from the house. My appearance caused my friend to

become greatly agitated. Having been suspected of complicity in the outbreak, although he was in ignorance of it till it happened, he was afraid that, should my whereabouts become known to the United States Marshal, he would get into serious difficulty. From him I learned that the Marshal was looking for Cook, and that it was not only unsafe for me to remain an hour, but that any one they chose to suspect would be arrested. I represented to him my famished condition, and told him I would leave as soon as I should be able to eat a morsel. After having despatched my hasty meal, and while I was busy filling my pockets with bread and meat, in the back part of the house, the United States Marshal knocked at the front door. I stepped out at the back door to be ready for flight, and while standing there, I heard the officer say to my friend, " You are suspected of harboring persons who were engaged in the Harper's Ferry outbreak." A warrant was then produced, and they said they must search the house. These Federal hounds were watching the house, and, supposing that whoever had entered was lying down, they expected to pounce upon their prey easily. Hearing what I did, I started quietly away to the place where I left my arms, gathered them up, and concluded to travel as far as I could before daylight. When morning came, I went off the road some distance to where there was a straw stack, where I remained throughout the day. At night, I set out and reached York, where a good Samaritan gave me oil, wine and raiment. From York, I wended my way to the Pennsylvania railrord.   I took the train at night at a convenient station, and went to Philadelphia, where great kindness was extended to me; and from there I came to Canada, without mishap or incident of importance.   To avoid detection when making my escape, I was obliged to change my apparel three times, and my journey over the railway was at first in the night-time, I lying in concealment in the day-time."

NOTICE OF AARON D. STEVENS.

Aaron Dwight Stevens was born at Norwich, Connecticut, where his aged father, Mr. Aaron Stevens, (who is choir-leader in Mr. Arms's Congregational Church,) still resides.   He lost his mother at an early age.   On the day before his execution he reached his twenty-ninth year.   His personal appearance was in no small degree prepossessing.   A photograph taken in his cell represents a face remarkable for an intelligent, amiable, and benevolent expression.   He had large blue eyes, and auburn hair and beard.   About six feet in height, and finely proportioned, with erect carriage, a quick action and generous soul, he was fitted for a leader in perilous enterprises.   His head was large, and his voice like a bugle.   He was noted among his friends for the animation, and oftentimes the brilliancy, of his conversational powers ; he was a favourite in social companies as a singer.   His father says of him :—" My son had one of the finest bass voices I ever heard."

He was of a kind and sympathetic nature, which led him always to take the side of the innocent and the wronged. Any specially kind act from friend or stranger would move him to tears. Writing from prison to a person who had befriended him during his sufferings, he said :—" I believe I shall be killed with kindness sooner than in any other way." His active and daring spirit early induced him to leave home. At eighteen years of age he joined the American army, and was employed as a dragoon. He saw considerable service in New Mexico and the Rocky Mountains, among the Indian tribes. In the spring of 1855, an officer of his company committed a brutal and unjustifiable assault upon a fellow-soldier; and the injustice fired Stevens so that he struck down his cowardly superior. For this he was brought in chains to Fort Leavenworth, Kansas, and was there confined. Knowing that the result of the court-martial would be a sentence of death, Stevens succeeded in freeing himself of his fetters, and breaking from jail. He fled to Topeka, and took a piece of land in the vicinity, under the assumed name of Whipple. When the difficulties in Kansas broke out, he joined the free-state forces, and was elected colonel of a regiment. His military knowledge, strength, and intrepidity made him a general favourite. He was one of the best drill-masters in the free-state ranks ; and we have seen him acting in this capacity in Ohio, in the winter of 1857–1858, when training Captain Brown's volunteers for the projected enterprise at Harper's Ferry.

Stevens at first supported the doctrine of making Kansas a free white state, excluding coloured people, whether bond or free—an inhuman policy, originating in the cruel prejudices generated by slavery. We even find him at this time using all his eloquence—of course unsuccessfully—to induce Mr. Redpath to restore to bondage two fugitive slaves who had taken refuge in his camp, in order to prove to Missouri that it was not for the slave but for the white man that the free-state men of Kansas were fighting. This circumstance is in strong contrast with the hearty assistance which Stevens afterwards gave to Captain Brown in the rescue of the eleven slaves from Missouri, and at Harper's Ferry; and shows what progress his sentiments and convictions had made in the interim. He was regarded by Captain Brown as one of his most reliable men. He headed the party that captured the slaveholders and released the slaves on the night of the outbreak at Harper's Ferry, and on Monday he had charge of the ground in front of the arsenal gate. In the afternoon of that day he was shot down while bearing a flag of truce; receiving six bullets, some of which he carried to his grave.

STEVENS AND HAZLITT RECEIVE SENTENCE.

We have not been able to obtain any particulars of the trial of Stevens and Hazlitt. On the 14th of February they were brought into court to receive sentence.

Being asked whether they had anything to say why sentence should not be passed upon them, Stevens replied :—

"May it please the court, I have a few words to say. Some of the testimony given against me was untrue. One of the witnesses stated that I said, 'Let us kill the —— of —— and burn the town.' To those who know me it is useless to make a denial of this charge, but I deny here, before God and man, ever having made such a proposition. I wish to say I am entirely satisfied with the conduct of my counsel, Mr. Sennott. I think he did all in his power in my behalf. I desire also to return my thanks to the officers who have had charge of me, for their universal kind treatment, and to my physician for the services rendered me whilst suffering from my wounds. When I think of my brothers slaughtered and sisters outraged, my conscience does not reprove me for my actions. I shall meet my fate manfully."

Hazlitt then spoke as follows :—

"I have a few words to say. I am innocent of the charge on which I have been convicted. I deny ever having committed murder, or ever having contemplated murder, or ever having associated with anyone with such intentions. Some of the witnesses here have sworn to things which I deny, and which were positively false. But I forgive them all. I have been treated kindly since my confinement—much better than I had expected—and I must say I think much better of Virginia.

I wish also to return my thanks to the counsel who have so ably defended me; they have done more in my behalf than northern counsel could possibly have done. I repeat, I am innocent of murder, but I am prepared to meet my fate."

Judge Kenny, after some prefatory remarks, which he uttered with deep emotion, proceeded to sentence each of them to be hanged publicly on Friday, the 16th of March.

STEVENS IN PRISON.

Stevens' sister, Mrs. Pierce of Norwich, visited him in Charlestown jail, and had repeated interviews with him during the eight days preceding his execution. Before her first entrance into the cell, Captain Avis considerately removed the chains from the prisoner's feet, that he might not be unnecessarily reminded of the discomfort of his confinement.

" I asked my brother," says Mrs. Pierce, " what was his intention in going to Harper's Ferry."

" It was for good," he replied ; " it was to help my fellow-men out of bondage. *You* know nothing of slavery—*I* know a great deal. It is the crime of crimes. I hate it more and more, the longer I live. Even since I have been lying in this cell, I have heard the cryings of slave-children torn from their parents." He said that during his imprisonment a woman had been sold in the jail, and separated from her husband and three children.

During one of Mrs. Pierce's visits, a Virginian who called to see the prisoners told them that the slaves at the south were in a better condition than the poor people of the north. " I am poor myself," replied Stevens, " but I never yet saw the day, in all my life, when I would have exchanged liberty for riches."

On another occasion his sister asked if he had been roused to a bitter or revengeful spirit, under his wounds and during his imprisonment ; to which he replied— " No ; for I believe I can truly say that I love every man, woman, and child on earth; I can forgive the man who hangs me. When we went to Harper's Ferry, we had no intention to injure a single human being ; our design was to free the slaves without bloodshed, just as we did in Missouri ; we carried rifles and pikes only for self-defence, and to inspire, by the appearance of military force, a fear of resisting us in our project. I think no man was killed by any of our party until after I was shot down while bearing a flag of truce. Some of the Virginians were killed by their own party, in mistake. As for myself, I did not shed a single drop of blood except from my own wounds."

" I am glad," he said, after a reference by his sister to the great pain he had suffered, " I am glad that I did not die of my wounds; for I believe that my execution upon the gallows will be a better testimony for truth and liberty."

His sister sang with him several hymns, among which his favourites were the following :

> " Joyfully, joyfully, onward we move ;"
> " To-day the Saviour calls ;"
> " We're travelling home to heaven above."

His moral courage under his trial and in view of death is clearly manifested in his numerous letters written in prison. The following extracts are not unlike the best sayings in the letters of Captain Brown : —" I wish you a long life, and a happy one, and in your last days the thought of having helped the world forward instead of back."—" I hope your soul is so strong that sorrow cannot find a lodging there. I am cheerful and happy, patiently awaiting the fate of man —death."—" I could bear all the sorrow of the world, if I had it on my shoulders."—" It makes my soul overflow with sorrow to see men with great talents use them in defending what is both a curse to themselves and to all mankind."—" I have had a glorious time with my sister here : she is such a bundle of nerves, that I am almost ashamed of myself when compared with her. There is no greater joy on earth, for me, than to see a noble woman; for in her I see more of God than in anything else." " I hope you will always, as you love yourself, as you love woman, as you love man, as you love God, work with hands, head, and heart for the happiness of all mankind."

The near approach of the day of execution seemed to

have but little effect on the prisoners, and during the last few days they were unusually cheerful, Stevens declaring it was his wish to be free, and that he desired the day for his execution to arrive.

On the afternoon before the fatal day, a new visitor was admitted as a welcome guest into the cell—Miss Jennie Dunbar, an intelligent and amiable young woman from Ohio—who had just been to Richmond on a fruitless errand to Governor Letcher, (successor to Governor Wise,) to plead for the prisoner's life. Her coming was not unexpected by Stevens, for frequent letters had passed between them, of such a character as had served to strengthen a friendship which was only confirmed by separation and misfortune. The prisoner regretted that she had lost so much of the remaining precious time, by going a useless journey to fall on her knees before the unpitying governor of an unpitying state. She had buoyed herself up with the hope of obtaining a pardon until she entered the governor's office in the Capitol; "But," said she, "the moment I looked into his eye, I saw that there was nothing in him to which I could make an appeal." It is sufficient to say that she was coldly received and coldly dismissed. Indeed the governor had already taken the pains to say that he could not save the prisoner's life ; and that he would not, if he could. Many influential northern pro-slavery men also besought Governor Letcher to pardon Stevens, assuring him that he would thus promote the democratic interest, while the execution of the unfortunate prisoner, unnecessary as it was to southern security, would feed the flame of anti-slavery excitement in the free states. But the appeal was in vain. Nothing less than the death of everyone of those concerned with John Brown in the effort to give liberty to the slaves would satisfy the vindictive spirit of Virginia.

EXECUTION OF STEVENS AND HAZLITT.

On the morning of Friday, the day of execution, the prisoners, with Mrs. Pierce, Miss Dunbar, and a brother of Hazlitt, breakfasted together. Mrs. Pierce, on entering the cell, was so overcome by the sudden thought of this being her last visit to her brother, that she hastily retired until she could return with more composed feelings. Miss Dunbar burst into tears, but was soon calmed by her friend's greater cheerfulness of spirits. The interview was brief, at Stevens's own request. At an hour which he himself had previously appointed, a carriage was driven to the jail to convey the visitors away from the town before the preparations for the execution began.

At eleven o'clock the field on which the scaffold was erected was occupied by a large number of spectators, a still larger number, however, remaining in town to accompany the sad procession. The military made a magnificent display. At ten minutes to twelve o'clock the prisoners made their appearance on the field, escorted by three companies of military. They walked to the scaffold.   Hazlitt was in advance, and ascended the steps with an easy, unconcerned air, followed by Stevens.   Both seemed to survey with perfect indifference the large mass of persons in attendance, and neither gave the least sign of fear.   A short time was spent by them in taking an affectionate leave of the sheriff, jailer, and jail-guard.   Just before the caps were drawn over their heads, they embraced and kissed each other. Both these young men followed the example of their leader in declining the ministrations of the clerical champions of slavery.

STEVENS' LETTERS FROM PRISON.

At a large and respectable meeting held in Boston on the day of their execution, and with immediate reference to it, the following letters, written in prison by Stevens, were read to the audience.   The first was addressed to friends in Ohio, and was written on the day subsequent to the execution of his comrades, Cook, Coppock, Copeland, and Green.

AARON D. STEVENS TO HIS FRIENDS IN OHIO.

Charlestown, Virginia, Dec. 17, 1859.

Dear friends,

With deep feelings of love, I sit to write you a few lines, hoping they will find you yet living, and in good health.   I suppose you have heard all about the sad affair at Harper's Ferry.   It appears that I am the only one now left, and I expect to follow them ere long to that brighter world where we shall again meet; and what joy it will be to meet with those who have suffered and died for the human family! I was pretty badly shot, up at the Ferry, receiving six wounds—two in my head, two in my breast, one in my face, and one through my left arm. Three of them were slight, and three of them pretty severe, but I am well now as ever, except my face. One side of it is paralyzed, and my lower jaw, the loss of which is hard—so that I cannot grind up my food very fine. I feel very cheerful and happy. Of course, it is rather disagreeable to be confined to so narrow limits and wear chains, but I forget all about it when thinking how many are suffering so much more than this. At times, my heart feels like bursting with sorrow for the crimes and sufferings of the human family, and if I could help to wash away that suffering, I would give ten thousand lives, if I had them to give. Four of the men passed off yesterday to the spirit land, through the mercy of Virginia. They were cheerful, and met their fate like men. Captain Brown was as cheerful on the morning of his execution as ever I saw him. I shall remember you for your many acts of kindness to the end of time. * * * Good-bye!

Yours for the good of all,
AARON D. STEVENS.

TO THE SAME.

Charlestown, Virginia, Dec. 27, 1859.

There are some good men here, but the curse of slavery has killed or blurred the most noble part of their souls. Oh, how I wish they could look through the eyes of my soul, and see the evils of oppression! I know it would make them sick to look at it. We must live and learn. It was little we thought, when we saw each other last, that I should be in a Virginia prison for treason, murder, &c., but such is life. I am as cheerful and contented as you could expect—ready to meet anything that comes. It is true that I should like to live yet awhile, for I have just got old enough to see how to live.

TO THE SAME.

Charlestown, Virginia, Feb. 17, 1860.

My dear friends,

I sit down once more to write you before I go to the spirit's home, which will be on the 16th, very probably, of March, as that is the day set by the court, and I have not much hope that the governor will commute my sentence. I do not think the people, as a general thing, want to see us hanged, but they think the law must be maintained. There are many very good feeling people about here, and I have been treated very kindly by the better classes generally. I am very cheerful and happy, and ready to die at a moment's warning, if needs be, although I should like to live as long as 'most anybody. I do not want you to worry in the least about me, for if I go to the other world, I shall be better off than I could be here. * * * Oh! I should like to see you all once more, but it will be but a few years, compared with eternity, before we shall meet in the spirit land, and that meeting will wash away all sorrow of parting here.

> " Truth is for the open ear,
> Hush and listen! hark and hear!"

Remember me most kindly to all inquiring friends. I should like to hear from you if you have time.

Yours in the the bonds of love, and for justice to all mankind, through all eternity,

AARON D. STEVENS.

FUNERAL OF STEVENS AND HAZLITT.

In accordance with an arrangement made with the prisoners before the day of execution, and with the assent of the executive of Virginia, the bodies of Stevens and Hazlitt were conveyed to Eagleswood, Perth Amboy, to the house of Mr. Marcus Spring, where the funeral services took place. Mr. Aaron Stevens and Mrs. Lydia Pierce, the father and sister of Aaron D. Stevens, Mr. Meech, his uncle, of Griswold, Connecticut, and Miss Dunbar were present. No relative of Hazlitt attended. The Rev. Hiram P. Arms, of Norwich, Connecticut, pastor of the church of which the father of young Stevens is a member, conducted the religious services. The house of Mr. Spring was crowded by the residents of Eagleswood, (including the teachers and scholars connected with the school of Theodore D. Weld,) and by citizens of Perth Amboy. The services commenced with singing the hymn,

"Come unto me and I will give you rest."

Rev. Mr. Arms then read selections from the Scriptures, and delivered an appropriate address He said that he had known Aaron D. Stevens only as a boy, at which

26*

period of his life he was noted for the promptness and zeal with which he always espoused the cause of the weak and the defenceless. It was this trait of his character, no doubt, that led him to hate slavery, and made him willing to unite with John Brown in an effort to break the chains of its victims. Mr. Arms having offered an appropriate prayer, Mr. Theodore Tilton of New York made an address, in which the topics suggested by the occasion were handled with a power that stirred every heart. Mrs. Spring then read some very interesting extracts from letters written by Stevens during his incarceration, showing that he considered it an honour to die in the cause of liberty, and that his last days were cheered by the hope of a blessed immortality. The exercises were concluded with the hymn,

" Nearer, my God, to thee."

The bodies of the dead, followed by nearly all the residents of the place, were then borne to the Eagleswood cemetery, where they were interred side by side, near the graves of James G. Birney and Arnold Buffum.

THE END.

APPENDIX A.

THE following letter, addressed to the editors of the *Boston Traveller* by Mr. R. J. Hinton, formerly the correspondent of that paper in Kansas, appeared under the head of " A Defence of the Memory of John Brown." It is a reply to statements which were made by the pro-slavery papers during Brown's imprisonment, with a view to fix upon him the responsibility of the death by Lynch law of a number of border ruffians at Pottawattomie, which has been repeatedly referred to in the preceding pages.

December 3, 1859.

To the Editors of the *Boston Traveller*,

In your issue of yesterday, you have an article under the caption of " Documents relating to John Brown," by which a wrong impression is given to the public. Will you allow me to present a few points which you, in common with the press generally, have overlooked in reference to the *ex parte* statements now being raked out of the ashes of the past? As for nearly four years I have been your correspondent in Kansas, I may ask the privilege now desired, and trust that the confidence I hope to have merited in endeavouring faithfully to give the facts of Kansas history will stand me in need in the remarks I shall make.

The affidavits alluded to by you have been published in the *Herald of Freedom*. The same have also been re-published in the *Post* of this city. They can be found in the report of the Congressional Kansas Investigating Committee. They were not, however, taken before the full session of that body, but were concocted at Westport, Missouri, by General Whitefield and Mr. Oliver, the pro-slavery member of the Commission, who abundantly proved during that investigation his desire to make out a good case against the free-state men.

Again—the statements made in those affidavits are entirely different from those first made by the women* when they arrived at Westport, after the killing at Pottawatomie Creek. This can and will be proven. But the affidavits are not such as would be received as evidence in any court of law. A fifth-rate practitioner could tear them all to pieces as far as they go to show that John Brown had anything to do with the homicides. But one of the parties testifies to having seen John Brown in the neighbourhood on the night of the deed. That man says the captain called at one of the houses on the creek a short time before these men were kill-ed, and from that it is inferred that John Brown did the deed.

One of the actors in that affair, now dead, gave me in the sum-mer of 1856 a description of it, the causes of the deed, and the manner in which it was done ; and from that statement, which has been verified by all the inquiries that have been made since, there is no hesitation on my part in declaring that Captain John Brown was not at the scene, nor a participator in the righteous act by which five ruffians were sent to their account.

It is inferred in your article that Doyle was a peaceable citizen, though a pro-slavery man. Let me say that in Kansas no one presumes to make such a statement. He not only was a pro-slavery man, but a ruffian of the most malignant stamp. All of those killed were members of an active gang of ruffians who made their head-quarters in that vicinity. Doyle was engaged with others in a fiendish attempt to outrage the persons of Captain Brown's daughter, (the wife of Henry Thompson,) and of his daughter-in-law, the wife of one of Brown's sons.

Wilkinson was a member of that body of usurpers which, under the name of legislature, passed a code of laws that have since become a by-word and a hissing among the nations, for bar-barity and tyranny. He came to Kansas a professed free-state man, tried to get the nomination from that party, and, failing that, took position with the border ruffians. At Shawnee Mis-

---

* The wives of the Doyles.

sion, he, with another of the same stamp, one Chapman, was universally despised by the Missourians, who made use of them as fit tools for our enslavement. Every member of that usurping body deserved death at the hands of an outraged people. Wilkinson was a leading member of the same gang with Doyle and Sherman.

Another point is inferred in your article, and that is that the Pottawattomie homicides were the first acts of the kind, and that therefore the doers of the deed were the aggressors. Turn back to history. Wilkinson, Doyle, and the others were killed on the night of the 24th of May, 1856. Three days before, the city of Lawrence had been sacked by Buford's ruffians. Five months before, 2,000 Missourians lay around that place, thirsting for the blood of the people. For months the territory had been in a state of civil war. Dow of Hickory Point, Collins of Doniphan, R. P. Brown of Easton, Jones of the Wakarusa, Robert Barber and Stewart of Lawrence, had all of them been assassinated by the men with whom Doyle and Wilkinson acted. These men had, in conjunction with others, stolen John Brown's cattle and those of his sons and neighbours, and otherwise injured the anti-slavery people of that settlement. At the time, these men were engaged in a conspiracy to drive out the Browns, Partridges, and others on the creek, and their own sudden death alone prevented its being carried out. The stories of mutilating the bodies are false, an invention probably of the editor of the *Herald of Freedom*, who endeavours to outdo Virginia in attempts to blacken the character of the Cromwellian soul which yesterday returned unto its God.

You state that, after this affair at Pottawattomie, John Brown lost the confidence of the free-state leaders in Kansas. Let me state a few facts, which will possibly put a different face on the matter.

Charles Robinson, the present republican candidate for governor of Kansas, wrote a letter some time after this affair to John Brown, which fully endorsed his course, and praised him highly, as being beneficial to the cause. In that same summer, he, with other prominent free-state men, consulted with John Brown, endorsing plans for defensive operations submitted by him, and furthermore signed orders on the Central Committee of Safety for money and equipments, with which to make John Brown's company more effective.

I myself was a witness to scenes which show directly that John Brown had the confidence of the free-state leaders in Kansas.

On the first Sunday in September, 1856, a council of war was held in Lawrence, which was attended by General James H. Lane, Adjutant-General Marcus J. Parrott, General Charles H. Branscomb, Colonels Harvey, Cracklin, Samuel Walker, Joel K. Grover, and a large number of the principal officers and citizens of the free-state volunteers and party.

Captain John Brown appeared on the street, for the first time after his heroic defence of Ossawattomie, a few days before. His arrival created a sensation, and the council immediately sent a message to him to attend. They were very urgent, but the old Spartan did not like talk. His reply was,—" If the general had any work to do, he would do it, but he would not come to the council." He was in the room a short time, but left with the remark, " All talk and no cider—great cry and little wool."

The first time I saw Captain Brown was in the emigrant camp at Plymouth, on the northern border. I know that he was consulted by Colonel Dickie, and the officers of the train. During that campaign, General Lane several times urged the Captain to act with him as second in command. This was done with the concurrence of the free-state men generally. On the 13th of September, 1856, when 2,700 ruffians appeared in front of Lawrence, Captain Brown again made his appearance. At that time—and I state what I know—he was solicited by all the prominent citizens to take charge of the defence. Among these were G. W. Brown, the editor who now attempts to slander John Brown.

These are facts which politicians cannot blink. I am not a politician, and therefore dare to honour and vindicate John

Brown, a man whom I love and reverence beyond all others who laboured for the cause of freedom in Kansas.

In closing, let me say that John Brown told me he was not a participator in the Pottawattomie homicides. John Brown was incapable of uttering a falsehood. I would take his word against the oaths of a million of Doyles.

R. J. HINTON.

APPENDIX B.

Letters and Extracts of Letters which passed between John Brown and some members of his family from 23rd January, 1839, to 9th September, 1859, inclusive.

I.—JOHN BROWN TO HIS FAMILY,

New Hartford, Connecticut, 23 Jan., 1839.

* * * * I have felt distressed to get my business done and return, ever since I left home, but know of no way consistent with duty but to make thorough work of it while there is any hope. Things now look more favourable than they have, but I may still be disappointed. We must all try to trust in Him who is very gracious and full of compassion and of almighty power; for those that do will not be made ashamed. Ezra the prophet prayed and afflicted himself before God, when himself and the captivity were in a straight, and I have no doubt you will join with me under similar circumstances. Don't get discouraged, any of you, but hope in God, and try all to serve him with a perfect heart.

2.—TO THE SAME.

Ripley, Virginia, 27th April, 1840.

* * * * I like the country as well as I expected, and its inhabitants rather better; and I have seen the spot where, if it be the will of Providence, I hope one day to live with my family.

* Then living at Franklin Mills, Portage County, Ohio.

*   *   *   Were the inhabitants as resolute and industrious as the northern people, and did they understand how to manage as well, they would become rich, but they are not generally so. They seem to have no idea of improvement in their cattle, sheep, or hogs, nor to know the use of enclosed pasture fields for their stock, but spend a large portion of their time in hunting for their cattle, sheep, and horses, and the same habit continues from father to son.   *   *   *   By comparing them with the people of other parts of the country, I can see new and abundant proof that knowledge is power. I think we might be very useful to them on many accounts, were we so disposed. May God in mercy keep us all, and enable us to get wisdom, and with all our getting or losing to get understanding.

Affectionately yours,

JOHN BROWN.

————

3.—TO HIS WIFE.

Springfield, (Mass.), March 7, 1844.

My dear Mary,

    It is once more Sabbath evening, and nothing so much accords with my feelings as to spend a portion of it conversing with the partner of my own choice, and the sharer of my poverty, trials, discredit, and sore afflictions; as well as of what of comfort and seeming prosperity has fallen to my lot for quite a number of years. I would you should realize that, notwithstanding I am absent in body, I am very much of the time present in spirit. I do not forget the firm attachment of her who has remained my fast and faithful affectionate friend, when others said of me, "Now that he lieth, he shall rise up no more."   *   *   *

*   *   *   *   *   I now feel encouraged to believe that my absence will not be very long. After being so much away, it seems as if I knew pretty well how to appreciate the quiet of home. There is a peculiar music in the word, which a half-year's absence in a distant country would enable you to understand. Millions there are who have no such thing to lay claim to. I feel considerable regret by turns that I have lived so many years, and have in reality done so little to increase the amount of human happiness. I often regret that my manner is no more kind and affectionate to those I really love and esteem ; but I trust my friends will over-look my harsh, rough ways, when I cease to be in their way as an occasion of pain and unhappiness.

In imagination I often see you in your room with Little Chick, and that strange Anna. You must say to her, that father means to come before long and kiss somebody.

I will close by saying, that it is my growing resolution to endeavour to promote my own happiness by doing what I can to render those about me more so. If the large boys do wrong, call them alone into your room, and expostulate with them kindly, and see if you cannot reach them by a kind but powerful appeal to their honour. I do not claim that such a theory accords very much with my practice ; I frankly confess it does not ; but I want your face to shine, even if my own should be dark and cloudy.

You can let the family read this letter, and perhaps you may not feel it a great burden to answer it, and let me hear all about how you get along.

Affectionately yours,

JOHN BROWN.

———

4.—TO THE SAME.

Springfield, 29th November, 1846.

Dear Mary, * * * Your letter dated the 20th was received last night, and afforded me a real though a mournful satisfaction. That you had received, or were to receive a letter from either John or Jason, I was in perfect ignorance of, till you informed me ; and I am glad to learn that, wholly uninfluenced by me, they have shown a disposition to afford you all the comfort in your deep affliction which the nature of the case would admit of. Nothing is scarcely equal with me, to the satisfaction of seeing that one portion of my remaining family are not disposed to exclude from their sympathies and their warm affections another portion. I accept it is one of the most grateful returns that can be made to me, for any care or exertions on my part to promote either their present or their future well-being; and while I am able to discover such a feeling, I feel assured that, notwithstanding God has chastised us often and sore, yet He has not himself entirely withdrawn from us, nor forsaken us utterly. The sudden and dreadful manner in which He has seen fit to call our dear little Kitty to take her leave of us, is, I need not tell you, how much on my mind; but before Him I will bow my head in submission, and hold my peace. * * * I have sailed over a somewhat stormy sea for nearly half a century, and have experienced enough to teach me thoroughly that I may most reasonably buckle up and be prepared for the tempest. Mary, let us try to maintain a cheerful self-command while we are tossing up and down, and let our motto still be, Action, Action; as we have but one life to live.

Affectionately yours,

JOHN BROWN.

———

5.—TO HIS WIFE.

Springfield, Mass., November 28th, 1850.

Dear wife,

* * Since leaving home, I have thought that under all the circumstances of doubt attending the time of our removal, and the possibility that we may not remove at all, that I had perhaps encouraged the boys to feed out the potatoes too freely. * * * I want to have them very careful to have no hay or straw wasted; but I would have them use enough straw for bedding the cattle to keep them from lying in the mire. I heard from Ohio a few days since; all were then well. It now seems that the Fugitive Slave Law was to be the means of making more

abolitionists than all the lectures we have had for years. It really looks as if God had his hand on this wickedness also. I, of course, keep encouraging my colored friends to "trust in God, and keep their powder dry." I did so to-day at thanksgiving meeting publicly. * * * While here, and at almost all places where I stop, I am treated with all kindness and attention; but it all does not make home. I feel lonely and restless, no matter how neat and comfortable my room and bed, nor how richly loaded may be the table; they have very few charms for me, away from home. I can look back to our log-cabin at the centre of Richfield, with a supper of porridge and johnny-cake, as to a place of far more interest to me, than the Massasoit [hotel] of Springfield. But "there's mercy in every place."

6.—TO THE SAME.

"Springfield, Mass. 17th Jan., 1851.

Dear wife,

     * * Since the sending off to slavery of Long from New York, I have improved my leisure hours quite busily with colored people here, in advising them how to act, and in giving them all the encouragement in my power. They very much need encouragement and advice, and some of them are so alarmed that they tell me they cannot sleep on account of either themselves, or their wives and children. I can only say I think I have been enabled to do something to revive their broken spirits. I want all my family to imagine themselves in the same dreadful condition. My only spare time being taken up (often, till late hours at night) in the way I speak of, has prevented me from the gloomy, home-sick feelings which had before so much oppressed me; not that I forget my family at all. * * * I wrote Owen last week that if he had not the means on hand to buy a little sugar, to write Mr. Cutting of Westport to send out some. I conclude you have got your belt before this. I could not manage to send the slates for the boys, as I intended, so they must be provided for some other

way. * * * Say to the little girls that I will run home the
first chance I get ; but I want to have them learn to be a little
more still.   May God in infinite mercy bless and keep you all, is
the unceasing prayer of

Your affectionate husband,

JOHN BROWN.

7.—TO HIS WIFE.*

Boston, Mass., Dec. 22nd, 1851.

Dear Mary,

 * * * There is an unusual amount of very interesting
things happening in this and other countries at present, and no
one can foresee what is yet to follow.   The great excitement produced by the coming of Kossuth, and the last news of a new revolution in France, with the prospect that all Europe will soon
again be in a blaze, seem to have taken all by surprise.   I have
only to say in regard to those things, I rejoice in them ; from the
full belief that God is carrying out his eternal purpose in them all.
I hope the boys will be particularly careful to have no waste of
any kind of feed ; for I am strongly impressed with the idea that
a long severe winter is before us.

8.—TO THE SAME.

Utica, New York, 27th Dec. 1852.

 * * * I seem to be pretty much over the effects of the
ague, except as to my sight, which is some impaired, and which
will not probably ever become much better.   I made a short visit
to North Elba, and left them all well ; and very comfortable, one
week ago to-day. * * .* The colored families appear to be
doing well, and to feel encouraged.   They all send much love to
you.   They have constant preaching on the sabbath ; and in-

* Then at Akron, Summit County, Ohio.

telligence, morality, and religion appear to be all on the advance. Our old neighbours appear to wish us back. I can give no particular instructions to the boys, except to take the best of care of everything ; not forgetting their own present and eternal good. If any young calves come that are nice ones, I want them to be well looked after ; and if any very mean ones, I would have them killed at once. I am much pleased to get so good an account from the boys, and from Anne and Sarah.

9.—TO THE SAME.

Boston, Mass., 16th Jan. 1853.

Dear wife,

I have the satisfaction to say that we have at last got to trial ; and that I now hope that a little more than another week will terminate it. Up to this time our prospects appear favourable. * * * I have no word for the boys except to say I am very glad to hear they are doing so well ; and that every day increases my anxiety that they all will decide to be wise and good ; and I close by saying that such is by far my most earnest desire for you all.

Your affectionate husband,
JOHN BROWN.

10.—TO HIS FAMILY.*

Syracuse, 28th June, 1855.

Dear wife and children,

I reached here on the first day of the convention, and I have reason to bless God that I came ; for I have met with a most warm reception from all, so far as I know ; and, except by a few sincere, honest, peace-friends, a most hearty approval of my intention of arming my sons and other friends in Kansas. I received to-day donations amounting to a little over sixty dollars

* Then at North Elba, New York.

—twenty from Gerrit Smith, five from an old British officer ; others giving smaller sums with such earnest and affectionate expressions of their good wishes as did me more good than money even.　John's two letters were introduced, and read with such effect, by Gerrit Smith, as to draw tears from numerous eyes in the great collection of people present.　The convention has been one of the most interesting meetings I ever attended in my life ; and I made a great addition to the number of warm hearted and honest friends.　I would have given anything to have had you all present to witness these scenes.　*　*　*

Your affectionate husband and father,

JOHN BROWN.

11.— TO HIS FAMILY.

Ossawattomie, Kansas Territory, 23rd Nov. 1855.

Dear wife and children, all,

　　　Ruth's letter to Henry, saying she was about moving, and dated 23rd October (I think) was received by last week's mail.　We were all glad to learn again of your welfare ; and as to your all staying in one house, I can see no possible objection, if you can only be well agreed ; and try to make each other as comfortable as may be.　Nothing new of account has occurred amongst us since I wrote.　Henry, Jason, and Oliver are unable to do much yet ; but appear to have but little ague now.　The others are all getting middling well.　We have got both families so sheltered that they need not suffer hereafter ; have got part of the hay (which had lain in cocks) secured ; made some progress in preparation to build a house for John and Owen ; and Salmon has caught a prairie wolf in the steel trap.　We continue to have a good deal of cold stormy weather—rains with severe winds, and forming into ice as they fall ; together with cold nights that freeze the ground considerably.　"Still God has not forsaken us ;" and we get "day by day our daily bread ;" and I wish we all had a great deal more of gratitude to mingle with our undeserved blessings. Much suffering would be avoided by people settling in Kansas, were they aware that they would need plenty of warm clothing, and light warm houses as much as in New Hampshire or Vermont; for such is the fact. Since Watson wrote, I have felt a great deal troubled about your prospects of a cold house to winter in; and since I wrote last I have thought of a cheap ready way to help it much at any rate. Take any common straight-edged boards; and run them from the ground up to the eaves, barn fashion; not driving the nails in so far but that they may easily be drawn,—covering all but doors and windows as close as may be in that way; and breaking joints, if need be. This can be done by anyone, and in any weather not very severe; and the boards may afterwards be mostly saved for other uses. I think much, too, of your kind of widowed state; and I sometimes allow myself to dream a little of again some time enjoying the comforts of home; but I do not dare to dream much. May God abundantly reward all your sacrifices for the cause of humanity; and a thousandfold more than compensate your lack of worldly connections. We have received two newspapers you sent us, which were indeed a rich treat; shut away as we are from the means of getting the news of the day. Should you continue to direct them to some of the boys, after reading, we shall prize them much.

Your affectionate husband and father,

JOHN BROWN.

12.—TO THE SAME.

Ossawattomie, Kansas Territory, 1st Feb. 1856.

Dear wife and children, every one,

Your and Watson's letters to the boys and myself of December 30th and January 1st, were received by last mail. * * * Salmon and myself are so far on our way home from Missouri, and only reached Mr. Adair's last night. They are all well, and we know of nothing but all are well at the boys' shanties.

The weather continues very severe; and it is now nearly six weeks that the snow has been almost constantly driven (like dry sand) by the fierce winds of Kansas. Mr. Adair has been collecting ice of late from the Osage river, which is nine and a half inches thick of clear, solid ice, formed under the snow. By means of the sale of our horse and wagon, our present wants are tolerably well met; so that if health is continued to us, we shall not probably suffer much. The idea of again visiting those of my dear family at North Elba is so calculated to unman me, that I seldom allow my thoughts to dwell upon it; and I do not think best to write much about it. Suffice it to say that God is abundantly able to keep both us and you; and in him let us all trust. We have just learned of some new and shocking outrages at Leavenworth; and that the free-state people there have fled to Lawrence, which place is again threatened with an attack. Should that take place, we may soon again be called upon to "buckle on our armour;" which, by the help of God, we will do : when I suppose Henry and Oliver will have a chance. My judgment is, that we shall have no general disturbance until warmer weather. I have more to say, but not time now to say it. So farewell for this time. Write.

Your affectionate husband and father,

JOHN BROWN.

13.—TO HIS FAMILY.

Ossawattomie, Kansas Territory, 6th Feb. 1856.

Dear wife and children; every one,

       * * * Thermometer on Sunday and Monday at 28 to 29 below zero. Ice in the river, in the timber, and under the snow, eighteen inches thick this week. On our return to where the boys live, we found Jason again down with the ague, but he was some better yesterday. Oliver was also laid up by freezing his toes,—one great toe so badly frozen that the nail has come off. He will be crippled for some days yet. Owen has one foot some

frozen.   We have middling tough times (as some would call them)
but have enough to eat, and abundant reasons for the most un-
feigned gratitude.   It is likely that when the snow goes off, such
high water will prevail as will render it difficult for Missouri to
invade the territory; so that God by his elements may protect
Kansas for some time yet.   *   *   *   Write me as to all your
wants for the coming spring and summer.   I hope you will all be
led to seek God "with your whole heart;" and I pray him in
mercy to be found of you.   All mail communications are entirely
cut off here by the snow-drifts; so that we get no news whatever
this week.   *   *   *

14.—TO THE SAME.

Brown's Station, Kansas Territory, 7th April, 1856.
Dear wife and children; every one,

       *   *   *   Since I wrote last, three letters have been re-
ceived by the boys from Ruth and Watson, dated March 5th and
9th.   The general tone of those letters I like exceedingly.   We
do not want you to borrow trouble about us; but trust us to the
care of " Him who feeds the young ravens when they cry."   *   *
* We have no wars as yet; but we still have abundance of
" rumours."   We still have frosty nights ; but the grass starts a
little.   There are none of us complaining much just now; all
being able to do something.   John has just returned from Topeka,
not having met with any difficulty ; but we hear that preparations
are making in the United States court for numerous arrests of free-
state men.   For one, I have no desire (all things considered) to
have the slave power cease from its acts of aggression.   " Their
foot shall slide in due time."   No more now ; may God bless and
keep you all.

                    Your affectionate husband and father.

27*

15.—TO HIS FAMILY.

Ossawattomie, Kansas Territory, 17th April, 1856.

Dear wife and children; every one,

I have just opened a letter from Watson to Oliver, and seen one from Ruth to Henry, both dated 26th March, by which I learn of your health, and also of your straitened circumstances. I must say in regard to the last, that while my heart is sorely grieved at your trials, I think that you are to be blamed for not frankly writing to me more about your situation before you got on to your last loaf of bread; as I might and should have sent you a little help sooner, had I known your real need. * * * You may look for something before long. * * * Let me just say that I hope God will inspire you all with some degree of trust and confidence in Him; and that you may all learn to exercise fortitude in times of darkness and difficulty. How do you think I have been enabled to carry my load for many years? I will answer,—"Hitherto the Lord hath been my helper." If you get short again for a small amount of provisions, might you not, Watson, work out a few days and earn a little to keep you along until you can get help from other sources? "I have been young and now am old; yet have I not seen the righteous forsaken, nor his seed begging bread." May you all learn to cast your cares on God, "for he careth for you." The committee of Congress are said to have arrived in Kansas, and much good it is believed will grow out of their coming. We trust it may be so; but at all events God will take care of his own cause. The trees begin to leave out a little, and the grass to grow—which we hope will soon come to visit you; and that green may in some measure take the place of blue. Can think of but little more to add but my earnest desire for your happiness; and the constant ringing in my ears of the despairing cry of millions whose woes none but God knows. "Bless the Lord, O my soul, for he hears."

16.—TO HIS WIFE.

Springfield, Mass., 31st March, 1857.

Dear wife,

Your letter of the 21st is just received. I have only to say, as regards the resolution of the boys to "learn and practise war no more,"—that it was not at my solicitation that they engaged in it at the first; and that while I may perhaps feel no more love of the business than they do, still I think there may be possibly in their day that which is more to be dreaded; if such things do not now exist. * * * I have just got a long letter from Mr. Adair [Kansas.] All middling well, March 11th; but had fears of further trouble after a while.

Your affectionate husband,

JOHN BROWN.

17.—TO THE SAME.

Hudson, Ohio, 27th May, 1857.

Dear wife and children; every one,

* * * I have got Salmon's letter of the 19th instant, and am much obliged for it. There is some prospect that Owen will go on with me. If I should never return, it is my particular request that no other monument be used to keep me in remembrance, than the same plain old one that records the death of my grandfather and son; and that a short story, like those already on it, be told of John Brown the fifth, under that of grandfather. I think I have several good reasons for this. I would be glad that my posterity should not only remember their parentage, but also the cause they laboured in. I do not expect to leave these parts under four or five days; and will try to write again before I go off. I am much confused in mind, and cannot remember what I wish to write. May God abundantly bless you all. * * *

Your affectionate husband and father,

JOHN BROWN.

18.—TO HIS FAMILY.

Wassonville, Iowa, 17th July, 1857.

Dear wife and children ; every one

Since I last wrote I have made but little progress ; having teams and waggons to rig up and load, and getting a horse hurt pretty bad. Still we shall get on just as well and as fast as Providence intends, and I hope we may all be satisfied with that.   We hear of but little that is interesting from Kansas. It will be a great privilege to hear from home again ; and I would give anything to know that I should be permitted to see you all again in this life.   But God's will be done.   To his infinite grace I commend you all.

Your affectionate husband and father,

JOHN BROWN.

19.—TO THE SAME.

Tabor, Fremont Co., Iowa, 12th Sept. 1857.

Dear wife and children ; every one,

It is now nearly two weeks since I have seen anything from home, and about as long since I wrote. * * * We get nothing very definite from Kansas yet, but think we shall in the course of another week.   * * * Got a most kind letter yesterday from Mr. F. B. Sanborn ; also one from Mr. B. ———, where Oliver was living. You probably have but little idea of my anxiety to get letters from you constantly ; and it would afford me great satisfaction to learn that you all regularly attend to reading your Bibles, and that you are all punctual to attend meetings on sabbath days.   I do not remember ever to have heard any one complain of the time he had lost in that way.

Your affectionate husband and father,

JOHN BROWN.

20.—TO HIS WIFE.

New York, 2nd March, 1858.

My dear wife,

I received yours of the 17th February yesterday; was very glad of it, and to know that you had got the ten dollars safe. I am having a constant series of both great encouragements and discouragements; but am yet able to say, in view of all, "Hitherto the Lord hath helped me." I shall send Salmon something as soon as I can; and will try to get you the articles you mention. I find a much more earnest feeling among the colored people than ever before; but that is by no means universal. On the whole, the language of Providence to me would certainly seem to say, Try on. I flatter myself that I may be able to go and see you again before a great while; but I may not be able. I long to see you all. * * * May God abundantly bless you all. No one writes me but you.

21.—TO HIS FAMILY.

Tabor, Iowa, 10th Feb. 1859.

Dear wife and children; all,

I am once more in Iowa, through the great mercy of God. Those with me, and other friends, are well. I hope soon to be at a point where I can learn of your welfare, and perhaps send you something beside my good wishes. I suppose you get the common news. May the God of my fathers be your God.

[No signature.]

[The above is the entire letter. His company was the eleven slaves whom he brought from Missouri to Canada safely.]

22.—RUTH THOMPSON TO JOHN BROWN.

North Elba, July 20th, 1856.

My dear father,

* * * The reception of your letters made us all both glad and sorrowful. Glad to hear that all were alive, but

exceedingly sorry to hear that any of our friends were taken prisoners, or wounded, or sick. This was indeed sad intelligence, and we still live as we did for the last six weeks, in dreadful suspense. What the next news will be makes us almost sick at heart. But we hope for the best. We have seen for some time accounts of trouble in Kansas, that you were obliged to live in a cave to keep away from the ruffians, that two of your sons were taken prisoners, one of whom feigned insanity, (as they called it), and last that you had fallen into the hands of the border ruffians (or what might prove the same thing, the federal authority of Kansas). But last week's papers published the trial of John Brown, jun. by the Bogus court, who had been called Captain Brown, which we all supposed to be you, not knowing that John was captain of a company. We here, and at ninety-five, take the New York *Weekly Times*, which gives us a great deal of Kansas news. It denounces in strong terms the conduct of the administration in reference to Kansas difficulties. Last week's paper gave a description of the horrible treatment of John and Jason and the other prisoners who were taken to Tecumseh. It says that it was a scene which has no parallel in a republican government. You have no doubt heard all the particulars from Jason if you have seen him. We supposed that Frederick was the one the paper spoke of as feigning insanity. This was taken from a St. Louis paper; but the *Times* said it was John, and was "caused by his inhuman treatment." Oh! my poor afflicted brother, what will become of him? Will it injure his reason for life? We hope not, but have great anxiety for him, and we sympathize most deeply with Wealthy.* It is dreadful. I can hardly endure the thought. We felt afraid that if it was Frederick, it would kill him; but we pray that he may escape any such trouble, and that John will entirely recover. I cannot be thankful enough that my dear husband so narrowly escaped being killed, and Salmon also. I cannot attribute it to anything but the merciful preserva-

---

* Wealthy Brown was the wife of John Brown, jun.

tion of God, that their lives and the lives of all our dear friends were spared. It is a comforting thought that "the Lord careth for us." I feel great confidence in your skill in taking care of the sick and wounded, and that you will do all in your power for their comfort. I wish John and Jason had been in your company. You must have had very exciting times at the battle you fought, before it was over. I should hardly have thought twenty-three men would have laid down their arms to so small a company. But "might was with the right" at that time. How mean it was in Colonel Sumner not to give up his prisoners after you gave up yours. But such conduct is all we need expect from Pierce or any of his officials. The Kansas bill has passed the Senate. Gerrit Smith has had his name put down for ten thousand dollars towards starting a company of one thousand men to Kansas. We are constantly hearing of companies starting, but do not hear of their getting through without trouble. I do hope there will be better times there before long. You can hardly imagine how anxious we feel for you and all of our friends there. We trust that the Lord will be with you, and deliver you from the hands of your enemies. "Happy is he that hath the God of Jacob for his help, whose hope is in the Lord his God ; which made heaven and earth, the sea, and all that therein is ; which keepeth truth for ever ; which executeth judgment for the oppressed ; which giveth food to the hungry. The Lord looseth the prisoners. The Lord openeth the eyes of the blind. The Lord raiseth them that are bowed down. The Lord loveth the righteous." We think of you all in your trials, and we should have written oftener, but we did not get any letters from any of you; and thought if we did write, you would not get ours. We are all well, but feel sad and lonesome. It has been very dry this summer ; until quite lately it has rained considerable. Mother and Watson will write you soon, I think. Watson tried to write the next morning after getting your letters, and commenced a letter; but said he could not collect his thoughts enough to write. I have not felt fit for writing or doing anything for more than a week, but I know

I ought to write to you. Do write as often as you can. I should have been very glad to have got even word from Henry, but I suppose he was not able. Am sorry to hear that Owen, Salmon, and Oliver were sick with fever; hope they are better. Father Thompson's folks all sympathize with you all in your affliction. That the Lord would deliver and keep you all, is the prayer of your affectionate daughter,

RUTH THOMPSON.

23.· -RUTH THOMPSON TO JOHN BROWN.

North Elba, Feb. 20, 1858.

My dear father,

Your letter of January 3rd we received this week, it having lain in the office a week. Oliver went to the office and got our news; there were two letters for me, but the post-master did not give him yours. We did not get it this week in time to answer it, or we should have done so immediately. I am sorry for such a delay. We were rejoiced to hear that you were so near us, and we hope that you can visit us yet before leaving York state. It really seems hard that we cannot see you when you have been gone so long from home, yet we are glad that you still feel encouraged. Dear father, you have asked me rather of a hard question. I want to answer you wisely, but hardly know how. I cannot bear the thought of Henry leaving me again, yet I feel that I am selfish. When I think of my poor, despised sisters, that are deprived of both husband and children, I feel deeply for them ; and were it not for my little children, I would go most anywhere with Henry, if by going I could do them any good. What is the place you wish him to fill ? How long would you want him ? Would my going be of any service to him or you ? I should be very glad to be with him, if it would not be more expense than what good we could do. I say *we ;* could I not do something for the cause ?

Henry's feelings are the same that they have been ; he says, "Tell father that I think he places too high an estimate on my qualifications as a scholar, and tell him I should like much to see him." I wish we could see you, and then we should know better what to do, but will you not write to us and give us a full explanation of what you want him to do ?   *   *   *

Please write often.   Your affectionate daughter,

RUTH THOMPSON.

24.—OLIVER BROWN TO THE FAMILY AT NORTH ELBA.

Parts Unknown,* Sep. 9th, 1859.

Dear mother, brother, and sisters,

Knowing that you all feel deeply interested in persons and matters here, I feel a wish to write all I can that is encouraging, feeling that we all need all the encouragement we can get while we are travelling on through eternity, of which every day is a part. I can only say that we are all well, and that our work is going on very slowly but we think satisfactorily. I would here say, that I think there is no good reason why any of us should be discouraged, for if we have done but one good act, life is not a failure. I shall probably start home with Martha and Anna about the last of this month. Salmon, you may make any use of the sugar things you can next year. I hope you will all keep a stiff lip, a sound pluck, and believe that all will come out right in the end. Nell, I have not forgotten you, and I want you should remember me. Please, all write. Direct to John Henrie, Chambersburgh, Pennsylvania.

Believe me your affectionate son and brother,

OLIVER SMITH.†

* Near Harper's Ferry.

† When in that neighbourhood, the Browns took the name of Isaac Smith and sons.

APPENDIX C.

The following memorandum respecting the friendly reception of
Brown and his party of fugitive slaves from Missouri was
found among his papers, and appears to have been drawn up,
the heading included, for publication in the newspapers of
the vicinity. It reached the editor too late for insertion in its
proper place in the " Life," but is worthy of preservation on
account of its matter-of-fact tenor, and the total absence of self-
glorification :—

RECEPTION OF BROWN AND PARTY AT GRINNELL, IOWA.

1. Whole party and teams kept for two days free of cost.
2. Sundry articles of clothing given to the captives.
3. Bread, meat, cakes, pies, &c. prepared for our journey.
4. Full houses for two nights in succession, at which meetings
   Brown and Kagi spoke, and were loudly cheered and fully
   endorsed. Three congregational clergymen attended the
   meeting on Sabbath evening (notice of which was given
   out from the pulpit) ; all of them took part in justifying our
   course, and in urging for contributions in our behalf.

   There was no dissenting speaker present at either meeting. Mr. Grinnell spoke at length, and has since laboured
   to procure us a free and safe conveyance to Chicago ; and
   effected it.
5. Contributions in cash amounting to twenty-six dollars and
   fifty cents.
6. Last, but not least, public thanksgiving to Almighty God
   offered by Mr. Grinnell in behalf of the whole company,
   for his great mercy and protecting care, with prayers for
   a continuance of those blessings.

   As the action of Tabor friends has been published in the
   newspapers by some of her people, as I suppose, would

not friend Gaston or some other friend give publicity to
all the above.

Respectfully your friend,

JOHN BROWN.

Springdale, Iowa, 26th Feb., 1859.

P.S.—Our reception among the Quaker friends here has been
most cordial.

———◆———

APPENDIX D.

The following extract from Osborne P. Anderson's " Narrative
of Events at Harper's Ferry " gives some particulars of the
way in which Brown and his confederates spent their time at
the Kennedy Farm, and of the circumstances which precipitated
the attack upon Harper's Ferry.

Kennedy Farm, in every respect an excellent location for business as "head-quarters," was rented at a cheap rate, and men and
freight were sent thither.   Owen, Watson, and Oliver Brown
took their position at head-quarters, to receive whatever was sent.
These completed the arrangements.   The captain laboured and
travelled night and day, sometimes on old Dolly, his brown mule,
and sometimes in the wagon.   He would start directly after night,
and travel the fifty miles between the Farm and Chambersburg
by daylight next morning ; and he otherwise kept open communication between head-quarters and the latter place, in order that
matters might be arranged in due season.

The Farm is located in Washington County, Maryland, in a
mountainous region, on the road from Chambersburg ; it is in
a comparatively non-slaveholding population, four miles from

Harper's Ferry ; yet, during three weeks of my residence there, no less than four deaths took place among the slaves ; one, Jerry, living three miles away, hung himself in the late Dr. Kennedy's orchard, because he was to be sold South, his master having become insolvent.   The other three cases were homicides ; they were punished so that death ensued immediately, or in a short time.   It was the knowledge of these atrocities, and the melancholy suicide named, that caused Oliver Brown, when writing to his young wife, to refer directly to the deplorable aspect of slavery in that neighbourhood.

At Harper's Ferry there was no milk and water sentimentality —no offensive contempt for the negro, while working in his cause ; the pulsations of each and every heart beat in harmony for the suffering and pleading slave.   I thank God that I have been permitted to realize to its furthest, fullest extent the social harmony of an anti-slavery family, carrying out to the letter the principles of its ante-type, the anti-slavery cause.   In John Brown's house, and in John Brown's presence, men from widely different parts of the continent met and united into one company, wherein no hateful prejudice dared intrude its ugly self—no ghost of a distinction found space to enter.

To a passer-by, the house and its surroundings presented but indifferent attractions.   Any log tenement of equal dimensions would be as likely to arrest a stray glance.   Rough, unsightly, and aged, it was only those privileged to enter and tarry for a long time, and to penetrate the mysteries of the two rooms it contained—kitchen, parlour, dining-room below, and the spacious chamber, attic, store-room, prison, drilling-room, comprised in the loft above—who can tell how we lived at Kennedy Farm.

Every morning, when the old man was at home, he called the family around, read from his Bible, and offered to God most fervent and touching supplications for all flesh ; and especially pathetic were his petitions in behalf of the oppressed.   I never heard John Brown pray that he did not make strong appeals to God for the deliverance of the slave.   This duty over, the men went to the loft, there to remain all the day long ; few only could be seen about, as the neighbours were watchful and suspicious. It was also important to talk but little among ourselves, as visitors to the house might be curious. Besides the daughter and daughter-in-law, who superintended the work, some one or other of the men was regularly detailed to assist in the cooking, washing, and other domestic work.

The principal employment of the prisoners, as we severally were, when compelled to stay in the loft, was to study Forbes' Manual, and to go through a quiet, though rigid drill, under the training of Captain Stevens, at some times. At others, we applied a preparation for bronzing our gun barrels—discussed subjects of reform —related our personal history ; but when our resources became pretty well exhausted, the ennui from confinement, imposed silence, &c., would make the men almost desperate. At such times neither slavery nor slaveholders were discussed mincingly. We were, while the ladies remained, often relieved of much of the dullness growing out of restraint by their kindness. As we could not circulate freely, they would bring in wild fruit and flowers from the woods and fields. We were well supplied with grapes, paw-paws, chestnuts, and other small fruit, besides bouquets of fall flowers, through their thoughtful consideration.

During the several weeks I remained at the encampment, we were under the restraint I write of through the day ; but at night we sallied out for a ramble, or to breathe the fresh air, and enjoy the beautiful solitude of the mountain scenery around, by moonlight.

Captain Brown loved the fullest expression of opinion from his men, and not seldom, when a subject was being severely scrutinized by Kagi, Oliver, or others of the party, the old gentleman would be one of the most interested and earnest hearers. Frequently his views were severely criticised, when no one would be in better spirits than himself. He often remarked that it was gratifying to see young men grapple with moral and other important questions, and express themselves independently; it was evidence of self-sustaining power.

About ten days before the capture of the Ferry, Captain John Brown and Kagi went to Philadelphia, on business of great importance. On their way home, at Chambersburg, they met young F. J. Merriam, of Boston. Several days were spent at Chambersburg, when Merriam left for Baltimore, to purchase some necessary articles for the undertaking. John Copeland and Sherrard Lewis Leary reached Chambersburg on the 12th of October, and on Saturday, the 15th, at daylight, they arrived, in company with Kagi and Watson Brown. In the evening of the same day, F. J. Merriam came to the Farm.

Saturday, the 15th, was a busy day for all hands. The chief and every man worked busily, packing up, and getting ready to remove the means of defence to the school-house, and for further security, as the people living around were in a state of excitement, from having seen a number of men about the premises a few days previously. Not being fully satisfied as to the real business of " I. Smith & Sons" after that, and learning that several thousand stand of arms were to be removed by the government from the Armory to some other point, threats to search the premises were made against the encampment. A tried friend having given information of the state of public feeling without, and of the intended process, Captain Brown and party concluded to strike the blow immediately, and not, as at first intended, to await certain reinforcements from the north and east, which would have been in Maryland within one and three weeks. Could other parties, waiting for the word, have reached head-quarters in time for the outbreak when it took place, the taking of the Armory, engine-house, and rifle factory would have been quite different. But the men at the Farm had been so closely confined, that they went out about the house and farm in the day-time during that week, and so indiscreetly exposed their numbers to the prying neighbours, who thereupon took steps to have a search instituted in the early part of the coming week. Captain Brown was not seconded in another quarter as he expected at the time of the action, but could the fears of the neighbours have been allayed for a few days, the disappointment in the former respect would not have had much weight.

On Sunday morning, October 16th, Captain Brown arose earlier than usual, and called his men down to worship. He read a chapter from the Bible, applicable to the condition of the slaves and our duty as their brethren, and then offered up a fervent prayer to God to assist in the liberation of the bondmen in that slaveholding land. The services were impressive beyond expression. Every man there assembled seemed to respond from the depths of his soul, and throughout the entire day a deep solemnity pervaded the place. The old man's usually weighty words were invested with more than ordinary importance, and the countenance of every man reflected the momentous thought that absorbed his attention within.

In the evening, before setting out to the Ferry, he gave his final charge, in which he said, among other things :—" And now, gentlemen, let me impress this one thing upon your minds. You all know how dear life is to you, and how dear your life is to your friends. And in remembering that, consider that the lives of others are as dear to them as yours are to you. Do not, therefore, take the life of any one, if you can possibly avoid it ; but if it is necessary to take life in order to save your own, then make sure work of it."

APPENDIX E.

Extracts from Speeches, Letters, Sermons, and Leading Articles by eminent American writers respecting Captain John Brown and the attack on Harper's Ferry.

REV. GEORGE B. CHEEVER, D.D.

* From a sermon entitled "The Martyr's Death and the Martyr's Triumph," delivered on the 4th of December, 1859, from Matt. x. 27, 28:—"What I tell you in darkness, that speak ye in light, and what ye hear in the ear, that preach ye on the housetops; and fear not them which kill the body, but are not able to kill the soul; but rather fear Him who is able to destroy both soul and body in hell."

NEARLY two hundred and fifty years ago, in the end of the stormy winter month of December, a little frail vessel was tossing on the waves of the Atlantic near the New England coast. In the cabin of that vessel, before she touched the land, a great covenant of principle was transacted, which grew out of their church covenant, " As the Lord's free people, to walk in all his ways made known, or to be made known to them, according to their best endeavours, WHATEVER IT MIGHT COST THEM."

One of the few men in the cabin of the Mayflower who took upon themselves that covenant, and in so doing laid the foundations of a state of freedom among men by allegiance to God, was named Peter Brown. It is now nearly two hundred and fifty years since that signature, and what amazing changes have passed upon the world ! This Western continent filled with more millions than in that little company there were men ; but millions so diverse in character from theirs, so little consecrated and instructed by their example, so disobedient, indeed, to the supreme Divine law to which they promised a sole eternal loyalty, that in the middle of this third century after the Mayflower landed, a lineal descendant of Peter Brown rises up, and is publicly hanged for carrying into effect the principles of that Mayflower compact, that covenant of obedience to just and equal laws, obedience to God and his Word as supreme, and disobedience to man's authority, if requiring aught that God has in his law forbidden.

Two great passages in God's Word shone before him like a star, occupied his being like presiding angels, like flames of fire, like a chariot of flame, in which, at length, his whole nature having been occupied with their fulfilment, he ascended from the scaffold to the great cloud of witnesses. One of these passages was from the New Testament, "Remember them that are in bonds, as bound with them." The other from the Old, "If thou forbear to deliver them that are drawn unto death, and those that are ready to be slain ; if thou sayest, behold we knew it not; doth not He that pondereth the heart consider it, and He that keepeth thy soul, doth not He know it? and shall He not render to every man according to his works?" Commissioned by such words, John Brown grew onward to the sphere of character and duty for which God had appointed him. The same influence in kind came upon him as upon Jeremiah, the same concentration and intensifying of Divine revelation in one direction, as always happens when God pleases, and when, for His own great purposes, He will discipline and prepare a man for himself, to bear the reproach among men of being a fanatic,—a man of one idea. "From above He hath sent fire into my bones. His word was in my heart as a burning fire shut up in my bones, and I was weary with forbearing, and I could not stay."

With an eye single against the iniquity of Slavery in law and in practice, John Brown, trusting in God, has thrown himself into this conflict, a martyr even unto death. By his death, in the train of his daring opposition against this infinite unrighteousness in law, in government, and in society, the whole country is stirred to its foundations.

If John Milton were on earth, he would show you that as clearly as God ever sent Ehud against Eglon and his tyranny, so clearly, and much more, was John Brown commissioned against

28*

this tyranny of Slavery, and against the State and the laws that uphold it. And though the man might mistake as to the manner and method of the protest, yet that it is God's protest is as true as that it is God's Providence. And the kind of instrument that God has taken for this work is a most plain and sacred indication that it is from Him. For many years the man had walked with God; he had trained up his family in God's fear; he had maintained the family altar, and all the sanctities, the instructions, the careful observant discipline of a household piety. He had been a man of strict, known, undoubted integrity. He was a man whose conscientious sense of right and wrong was as a flame of fire, where in common men it was merely a spark in sluggish embers. His sensitiveness to injustice was extreme—injustice against others ; the iron entered into his own soul. He was accustomed, with great steadfastness and holy principle, to rebuke profaneness and wickedness in high or low. In the midst of his trial, wounded and lying on his cot, when he heard the oaths of some in the court-room round about him, he would raise himself upon his elbow, and calmly say, " Gentlemen, can you not compass this business without swearing ? " Just so with all under his command ; both by example and teaching he endeavoured to inculcate obedience to the precepts of religion.

He had learned from a child the sacredness and dignity of human nature under whatever skin, and as an old man on the verge of eternity could say, with the simplicity of a child and the majesty of an angel, " I am yet too young to understand that God is any respecter of persons."

He had long been a student of God's word. He made it the man of his counsel, and sought the guidance of God's spirit in pondering its sacred pages. He seems to have been familiar with every part of it ; but by God's own peculiar guidance of his mind and heart, was baptized especially with the fire of its benevolence against oppression, and its sacred sympathy in behalf of the oppressed. His tender sympathies and practical charities abounded towards the poor and needy. An apprentice of his relates the following anecdote of his benevolence. "Having heard that a poor man with a large family was suffering for the necessaries of life, he sent me to his house to inform him that John Brown would sell him provisions on credit. He came at once and got about thirty dollars worth, agreeing to pay in work the next summer ; but with summer came other calls for his labor than the payment of old debts ; so he came to Brown and frankly told him his situation, and that it would be impossible to pay as agreed upon. The noble old man said to him, ' Go home and take care of your family, and let me hear no more about this debt. *It is a part of my religion to assist those in distress, and to comfort those that mourn.' "*

A course of years in the practice of such virtues indicates the man of God, even if his profession of religion had not been known and read of all. " For by their fruits ye shall know them, for men do not gather grapes of thorns, nor figs of thistles ; but every good tree bringeth forth good fruit, while a corrupt tree bringeth forth evil fruit."

He was a man of prayer. He walked with God even amidst surrounding violence. He was once, it was said, early in life, that is, at the beginning of his Christian career, destined to the ministry, and there is nothing that we know of in his life, amidst the pursuits to which he was turned aside from such preparation and such a vocation, inconsistent with the baptism of God's Spirit for the ministration of the Gospel. On the contrary, in one great point of fitness for that work, he seems to have been always growing ; increasing in the knowledge of the Word of God, in a reverential submission to it, in a sense and living experience of it as fire and power, for thus God evidently was training him.

Now with these developments of character, these possessions of grace, under these many years of discipline, this specimen of God's fireworks is suddenly touched into a flame, and rises out of obscurity into a light that fills the whole atmosphere, and turns the eyes of the spectators of a whole nation to scan the spectacle. This man of God breaks out in the most daring venture against the most consolidated, remorseless, powerful, all-conquering system of iniquity, that any civilized country ever saw or endured; breaks out in an act that, while some declare by God's Word to be the venture of a man in God's behalf, doing God's work against the vastest of human crimes, others declare to be the act of a madman; others the hallucination of a good man; others the crime of a man possessed with a devil.

But amidst all the hazards and disasters of the outbreak, he is the same man that he ever has been, and after the conflict, amidst his wounds, amidst his enemies, overpowered, apparently unsuccessful, he is as calm and confident as ever in God, and in the justice and sacredness of the cause he has undertaken. And after the disastrous failure of his enterprise, in his prison, through all the mockery of his trial and sentence, and in all his words, speeches, letters, in all his intercourse with men, in all his deportment, he is the same man as before; the same Christian man confiding in God. He is still seen walking with God, and God does not desert him. Nay, the evidences of the presence and power of God's Spirit in his heart brighten and increase, till they are sublime, attractive, wonderful. He speaks and writes with an almost superhuman simplicity, dignity, calmness, and depth of feeling; a restraint, an absence of all rhetoric, ostentation, and false emotion; a transparency of character, a profound thoughtfulness, a peace of mind, a trust in God, quite impossible to be assumed in such a position, at such an hour,—quite impossible, indeed, ever under such circumstances to be palmed off, and credit gained for them, by a self-deluded man, or a wicked man and an impostor.

After the battle is over,—after this mighty crime, as some call it, for which he is sentenced to death,—in the soiled and tattered garments bathed in blood, chained, reviled, hated, he appears greater than ever, more manifestly the Christian hero, in possession of the spirit of love and of power and of a sound mind. And thus daily he is seen preparing for death, and daily God is with him. Manifestly God was with him—with him to the end

—with him, maintaining his confidence in the justice of his cause and the righteousness of his effort, even unto death—the righteousness of the very act for which he was to die. God was with him so sustaining, as to enable him to feel and to say that he willingly gave himself to the sentence of the law, counting it a privilege to be permitted to die in behalf of the outcast race for which he had endeavoured to live, and for whose deliverance he had ventured with death in view.

An outcast race! And John Brown felt and knew that what he did for them he was doing for his Saviour. Under sentence of death for an action in their behalf, he could say that he considered himself "worth inconceivably more to be hung in this cause" than to be disposed of in any other way; and "could wait the hour of his public murder with great composure of mind and cheerfulness, feeling the strong assurance that in no other possible manner could he be used to so much advantage to the cause of God and of humanity."

When has there been in the world any thing like this? It has properly been remarked, in regard to the brightest names in the historic records of self-sacrificing patriotism, in the pages of the struggles for liberty, that their ventures were for their own country, kindred, homes, every thing; and if ye love them that love you, what thank have ye? If ye salute your brethren only, or defend your own caste, do not even the publicans so? But this self-sacrifice of John Brown was for a despised and hated race, condemned to perpetual slavery. It is a sublime and solitary instance in all modern history. A man in his senses, in an age of prudential wisdom worshipped as religion—in an age of self interest and expediency—when the world is full of priests and Levites, ecclesiastical, political, social, passing by on the other side—offers himself in the service of a despised, rejected, down-trodden caste, pursues his purpose for twenty years, watches for opportunities to strike some mighty blow of deliverance, and at length, thinking that God had given him the hour, goes forth to suffer unto death for slaves—for negroes.

Now, I say that under such circumstances, John Brown has all the characteristics of a martyr, and his death is a martyr's death. The false accusations, the prejudice and hatred, the reigning religion and law against him, the abuse, the present ignominy and shame, the apparent failure of his life, and defeat of all his plans, and perfect triumph of his enemies—all these things are essential circumstances of martyrdom, as a just cause and spirit are its qualities. Success never can make a martyr, never could canonize one, and those who determine the moral quality of an action or a character by success, are not fit to sit in judgment on a man like John Brown, or the nature of his enterprise. A martyr's death must always, at the time, be ignominious. When Stephen was stoned, it was not amid plaudits of his cause and character. When Latimer was burned, it was not on a theatre of popular applause, so that his departing spirit could be wafted away upon the very hallelujahs of his persecutors. A martyr is always put to death by the hatred and cruelty of men under a cloud of obloquy and odium, under authority of wicked law ; what men suppose to be the highest triumph of their cause being, in fact, but the climax and highest demonstration of their wickedness— the filling up of the measure of their iniquity.

We thank God that the first public victim of the cruelty of slave law and of the slave despotism in our land should have been found a faithful servant of Christ, so unblemished, so entire, so pure, for such an offering. We thank God that this immolation, so awful, so solemn, on the altar of this Moloch, with ostentatious military ministration of Federal and State powers, as the willing priests of its worship, has been the sacrifice of a man in whom, as in Daniel of old, no fault could be found, except concerning the law of his God, applied and obeyed by him against the reigning iniquity of the nation. It is matter for profoundest thoughtful praise, that after the moral assassination of the race by Federal justice, declaring that black men have no rights that white men are bound to respect, this culminating State crime of the murder of the first man who openly struck for their deliverance, has been signalized by finding in its victim a being with God's seal, God's baptism, God's commission, God's truth manifestly upon him and within him.

That such a man should have been hanged by a professedly civilized and Christian State, for the benevolent attempt to rescue a few of his oppressed and enslaved fellow-beings from the bondage and cruelties of Slavery ; and hanged on the pretence that he had committed treason against the State and the government ; and hanged on the principle of expediency announced by Caiaphas of old, that if he were permitted to live, the State was in danger; all this brings both the State and the crime of hanging such a victim into a dreadful resemblance with the Jewish murderers of Christ, on the plea that it was expedient that one man should die rather than the whole nation stand in danger of perishing. Doubtless the death of John Brown is the beginning of the end. God in his infinite mercy grant that through the faithfulness of his servants with his Word, attended by his Spirit, the end may come in a peaceful emancipation of the slaves, and not in a whirlwind of the Divine vengeance.

MR. RALPH WALDO EMERSON.

From a speech delivered at the Tremont Temple, Boston, at a meeting held Dec. 18th, 1860, to adopt measures of relief for the family of John Brown.

THIS commanding event, the sequel to which has brought us together to-night, eclipses all others which have occurred for a long time in our history. *   *   *   *   As for Captain Brown himself, he is so transparent that all men can see through him. He is a man to make himself felt wherever in the world courage and integrity are esteemed—the rarest of heroes, and yet a pure idealist.   Every one who has heard him speak has been impressed alike by his simple and artless goodness and his sublime courage. He joins the high faith of the good man with the revolutionary spirit of his grandfather.   He believes in two instruments—the golden rule and the Declaration of Independence.   When he was here, he used in conversation these words :—" Better that a whole generation of men, women, and children should pass away by violent death, than that one word of these two should be broken in this country."   There is a unionist and a strict constructionist for you.   He believes in the union of American states, and he conceives that the only enemy of the Union is slavery, and for this reason, as a patriot, he seeks its abolition.   Governor Wise has pronounced his eulogy in a manner that does discredit to the moderation of our own timid partisans.   Captain Brown's speeches to the court have interested a nation in him.   What artlessness and plainness !   If he had interfered in behalf of the great, or the wealthy, or the wise, he said, no one would have blamed him ; but he believed that, when he interfered in behalf of a poor and despised people, he was doing right.   What a favourite will he be in history, which plays such pranks with mere temporary reputations.   Nothing can resist it.   If he suffers death, it is plain that he will drag certain official gentlemen into an immortality most undesirable, and of which they have already some disagreeable forebodings.   Indeed, it is the resolution of the governor of Virginia to hang the man who, he says, possesses the greatest integrity, truthfulness, and courage that he ever met.   Is that the kind of men for whom the gallows is built ?   No man dare believe that there exists in Virginia another man as worthy to live, as deserving of public and private honours, as this poor prisoner.   I said, just now, that John Brown is an idealist, but he believes in his ideas to such an extent that he laboured to put them all into action.   He did not believe in moral suasion, but in putting things through."

REV. THEODORE PARKER.

Extract of a letter written from Rome on the 24th of November, 1859, to Francis Jackson, Esq. Boston.

OF course I was not astonished to hear that an attempt had been made to free the slaves in a certain part of Virginia. Such things are to be expected : for they do not depend merely on the private will of men like Captain Brown and his associates, but on the great general causes which move all human kind to hate wrong and love right. Such "insurrections" will continue as long as slavery lasts, and will increase, both in frequency and in power, just as the people become intelligent and moral. Virginia may hang John Brown and all that family, but she cannot hang the human race ; and until that is done, noble men will rejoice in the motto of that once magnanimous state, " *Sic semper tyrannis !*"—" Let such be the end of every oppressor."

It is a good anti-slavery picture on the Virginian shield—a man standing on a tyrant and chopping his head off with a sword ; only I would paint the swordholder *black*, and the tyrant *white*, to show the *immediate application* of the principle. The American people will have to march to rather severe music, I think, and it is better for them to face it in season.

Look at a few notorious facts : There are four millions of slaves in the United States, violently withheld from their natural right to life, liberty, and the pursuit of happiness. Now, they are our fellow-countrymen—yours and mine, just as much as any four millions of white men. Of course you and I owe them the duty which one man owes another of his own nation—the duty of instruction, advice, and protection of natural rights. If they are starving, we ought to help to feed them. The colour of their skins, their degraded social condition, their ignorance, abates nothing from their natural claim on us, or from our natural duty toward them.

There are men in all the northern states who feel the obligation which citizenship imposes on them—the duty to help those slaves.   Hence arose the [American] Anti-Slavery Society, which seeks simply to excite the white people to perform their natural duty to their dark fellow-countrymen.   Hence comes Captain Brown's expedition—an attempt to help his countrymen to enjoy their natural right to life, liberty, and the pursuit of happiness. He sought by violence what the Anti-Slavery Society works for with other weapons.   The two agree in the end, and differ only in the means.   Men like Captain Brown will be continually rising up among the white people of the free states, attempting to do their natural duty to their black countrymen—that is, help them to freedom.   Some of these efforts will be successful.   Thus, last winter, Captain Brown himself escorted eleven of his countrymen from bondage in Missouri to freedom in Canada.   He did not snap a gun, I think ; although then, as more recently, he had his fighting tools at hand, and would have used them, if necessary. Even now, the underground railroad is in constant and beneficent operation.   By and by it will be an overground railroad from Mason and Dixon's line clear to Canada ; the only *tunnelling* will be in the slave states.   Northern men applaud the brave con-ductors of that locomotive of liberty.

When Thomas Garrett was introduced to a meeting of political free-soilers in Boston, as " the man who helped 1,800 slaves to their natural liberty," even that meeting gave the righteous Quaker *three times three.*   All honest northern hearts beat with admiration of such men ; nay, with love for them.   Young lads say, "I wish that Heaven would make me such a man."   The wish will now and then be father to the fact.   You and I have had opportunity enough, in twenty years, to see that this philan-thropic patriotism is on the increase at the north, and the special direction it takes is toward the liberation of their countrymen in bondage.

Captain Brown's expedition was a failure, I hear it said.   I am not quite sure of that.   True, it kills fifteen men by sword and shot, and four or five men by the gallows.   But it shows the weakness of the greatest slave state in America, the worthlessness of her soldiery, and the utter fear which slavery genders in the bosoms of the masters.

Brown will die, I think, like a martyr, and also like a saint. His noble demeanour, his unflinching bravery, his gentleness, his calm, religious trust in God, and his words of truth and soberness, cannot fail to make a profound impression on the hearts of northern men ; yes, and on southern men. " For every human heart is human," &c. I do not think the money wasted, nor the lives thrown away. Many acorns must be sown to have one come up ; even then, the plant grows slow ; but it is an oak at last. None of the Christian martyrs died in vain ; and from Stephen, who was stoned at Jerusalem, to Mary Dyer, whom our fathers hanged on a bough of " the great tree" on Boston Common, I think there have been few spirits more pure and devoted than John Brown's, and none that gave up their breath in a nobler cause. The blessing of such as are ready to perish will fall on him, and God will take him welcome home. The road to heaven is as short from the gallows as from a throne ; perhaps, also, as easy.

MR. WILLIAM LLOYD GARRISON.
From the *Liberator*.

As to Captain Brown, all who know him personally are united in the conviction that a more honest, conscientious, truthful, brave, disinterested man (however misguided or unfortunate) does not exist; that he possesses a deeply religious nature, powerfully wrought upon by the trials through which he has passed ; that he as sincerely believes himself to have been raised up by God to deliver the oppressed in this country, in the way he has chosen, as did Moses in relation to the deliverance of the captive Israelities ; that when he says he aims to be guided by the golden rule, it is no cant from his lips, but a vital application of it to his own soul, "remembering them that are in bonds as bound with them;" that when he affirms that he had no other motive for his conduct at Harper's Ferry except to break the chains of the oppressed, by the shedding of the least possible amount of human blood, he speaks " the truth, the whole truth, and nothing but the truth;" and that if he shall be (as he will speedily, beyond a peradventure) put to death, he will not die ignobly, but as a martyr to his sympathy for a suffering race, and in defence of the sacred and inalienable rights of man, and will therefore deserve to be held in grateful and honourable remembrance to the latest posterity, by all those who glory in the deeds of a Wallace or Tell, a Washington or Warren. Read his replies to the interrogatories propounded to him by Senator Mason and others! Is there another man, of all the thirty millions of people inhabiting this country, who could have answered more wisely, more impressively, more courageously, or with greater moral dignity, under such a trying ordeal? How many hearts will be thrilled and inspired by his utterances! Read, too, his replies in court with reference to his counsel! Where shall a more undaunted spirit be found? In vain will the sanguinary tyrants of the south, and their northern minions, seek to cover him with infamy :—

> Courts, judges can inflict no brand of shame,
> Or shape of death, to shroud him from applause;

for, by the logic of Concord, Lexington, and Bunker Hill, and by the principles enforced by this nation in its Declaration of Independence, Captain Brown was a hero—struggling against fearful odds, not for his own advantage, but to redeem others from a horrible bondage—to be justified in all that he aimed to achieve, however lacking in sound discretion. And by the same logic and the same principles, every slaveholder has forfeited his right to live, if his destruction be necessary to enable his victims to break the yoke of bondage; and they, and all who are disposed to aid them by force and arms, are fully warranted in carrying rebellion to any extent, and securing freedom at whatever cost.

It will be a terrible losing day for all slavedom when John

Brown and his associates are brought to the gallows. It will be sowing seed broadcast for a harvest of retribution. Their blood will cry trumpet-tongued from the ground, and that cry will be responded to by tens of thousands in a manner that shall cause the knees of the southern slave-mongers to smite together, as did those of Belshazzar of old ! O that they might avoid all this by a timely repentance !

MR. OLIVER JOHNSON.

From the *National Anti-Slavery Standard.*

To look at the disastrous issue of this affair, one would think that there could be but one opinion on the subject. No insurrection was created ; no men, white or black, came to their aid. Of the men engaged in the movement all but a few are either already dead or in the hands of their executioners. On the other side, a handful of slaves were carried off and three harmless railway employès and one marine killed. The balance certainly does not seem to incline in favor of the wisdom of the invading party. To look at this state of things, it is no wonder that it is characterized as an insane attempt, and John Brown as a madman. But we must remember that we do not know, and perhaps never shall know, all the facts of the case. Captain Brown certainly showed himself anything but a madman in Kansas. And his whole demeanor since his captivity, as well as his coolness and courage during the conflict, which have won the admiration of the men he had so greatly alarmed and incensed, prove that, if mad, there is extraordinary method in his madness. We believe him to be an enthusiast, a fanatic if you will, but in no proper sense of the word a madman. He intimates in his conversations in prison that he had reason to expect help that did not come, and the preparations he had made of arms and munitions of war make this supposition the more probable. He probably, like most men of his tempera-

ment, believed other men made like himself, and trusted to the
existence of a degree of spirit among the slaves he had come to
deliver, which many generations of hereditary servitude had
ground out of them. What he strongly wished, he believed.
Hence his attempt. Those on whom he relied for help failed him.
Hence his discomfiture.

For ourselves, differing as we do from these brave men as to
the wisdom of their enterprise, and regretting deeply its bloody
termination, we cannot withhold our admiration from the self-
devotion and constancy with which they faced and met their
death in a great and unselfish, however mistaken, attempt for
the liberty of the oppressed race. As a display of personal courage
and resolute opposition to deadly odds, we know of nothing
in the annals of heroism that excels it. In this age of compromise
and cowardice, of calculators and economists, it is an encouragement to know that there could be found twenty men ready to
dash themselves against the wall of our Bastile as the forlorn-hope
of what they believed to be the army of liberation. We think
better of the country and the race because of them.

The point of view in which John Brown's movement may most
appropriately be called a success, is the absolute compulsion it has
laid upon all sections of the country to think, speak, and act in
relation to slavery. We, the abolitionists, have for twenty-eight
years been seeking the peaceful abolition of this system of unspeak-
able wickedness. Believing that if the people of this country
would look fairly at the enormities which are inseparable from its
character, they would see that duty and interest combine to require its immediate and unconditional abolition, we have sought
to call their attention to the facts in question. But they would
not hear. As far as strenuous and vigilant efforts would avail,
the clergy shut the subject out of their pulpits—the clerical editors
out of their newspapers—the deacons out of their prayer-meetings
—the political editors out of their party "organs"—the church
committees out of their meeting-houses—and the people at large
out of their mouths and minds. They found the subject of sla-

very a bore.   Like the members of the American Board of Com-
missioners for Foreign Missions, on the presentation of Dr.
Cheever's Memorial against the slave trade, they asked, both in
speech and equally unequivocal action—"Why are we to be teazed
with this everlasting fuss about niggers?"   Our constant effort
to make all these classes attend to the subject of slavery, discuss
it and act upon it—however successful, considering the obstacles—
advanced but by slow degrees towards absolute success.   John
Brown, in two days, by his different method, has irresistibly compelled all these people to do what we have been trying, all these
years, to persuade them to do.   Is not this success?

* * * None of the tests which have been applied to the
national heart and conscience from time to time, since the conflict with slavery began—and God has never left himself without
this witness of his concern in the matter—has been so electrical
and so decisive as this.   That desperate night and day at Harper's
Ferry, and the chain of events which has depended therefrom, has
put forward the hands on the dial-plate of our national destiny
many years, which are moments of History.   It has done more
to develop the state of feeling in regard to slavery and its issues,
both at the North and the South, than anything that has gone
before it.   At the North, the all but unanimous sympathy which
has been felt and uttered for the fate, if not for the deed, of John
Brown shows how much the old pro-slavery glamour has been dis-
pelled that formerly darkened men's eyes.   An assault on the
legalized property of a Southern State, in which lives were lost
was not a thing likely at first sight to awaken the sympathy and
admiration of the hard working and calm thinking North.   It
was because the true nature of that pretended property, and the
mischiefs flowing from its permissive existence were understood
and appreciated, as never before, that John Brown stood up before
the masses of the North as a Hero instead of a Felon, and his act
looked to them like a virtue instead of a crime.

All the history of the country for the last thirty years had been
conducting the general mind up to this plane of opinion and feel-

29

ing. Five and twenty years ago such an act as Brown's had been impossible, and such a state of sentiment concerning it an absurd supposition. Texas and Mexico, the war of the Right of Petition, the Compromise Measures, the Repeal of the Missouri Compromise, the Kansas War, the attempted assassination of Sumner, the proposed reopening of the slave trade, had all been teaching great lessons to the people of the North. Slavery would not suffer the North to forget her existence or to shut its heavy eyes to her forward footsteps. The Northern people were forced to see, whether they liked it or not, that their liberties were inextricably entangled with the fetters of the slave, and that the one could not be secure until the other had been broken. And so when an earnest hand struck a blow for the deliverance of the slaves, that blow, though baffled, awakened a thrill and an echo in thousands of Northern hearts.

And while these passions have been developed at the North, antagonist passions have blazed up in the South with a fury never yet seen in action. Never before was the South—meaning thereby the controlling slaveholding element of the slaveholders which holds all else in check—in so frantic a state of excitement as at present. It is an excitement of mingled terror and hatred—fear of the blacks at the South, and hatred of the whites at the North. Their whole course is one tending yet more to alienate the North, and to make its inhabitants feel that there is not much Union left to save or to dissolve.

This success of John Brown in forwarding our ends by his means—in compelling the whole nation to give immediate and earnest attention to the subject of slavery, by personally undertaking the rescue of a limited number of slaves—does not alter our opinion respecting the *best* method ; we still adhere to *our* method, a method from which we have never varied, the advocacy of the peaceful abolition of slavery. We do not pretend to dictate in regard to the faith or the actions of others, and we welcome opposition to slavery from all sorts of persons and in every manner. Thus, though our counsel is to adopt the *Christian* manner of overthrowing slavery, overcoming evil with good, we willingly accept aid from the infidel, if he feels disposed to give it ; and, though we seek the *peaceful* deliverance of the slave, if all the fighting men in the nation would turn their arms against slavery, we should heartily rejoice at it. We want men to use against slavery whatever arms they are accustomed to use against other vices and evils.

We honour John Brown for his hearty, disinterested, self-sacrificing devotion of himself, all that he has, and all that he is, on the altar of liberty. He made it his business in this world " to seek and to save them that were lost." For the sake of what we deem an error in his method, shall we undervalue and set at nought his noble, truthful and magnanimous character ? Nay, verily ! We do not represent him as a perfect man. Nay, we put our finger on the spot where we judge him to have been' in error. But, as the Lord liveth, in comparison with the pro-slavery clergyman who edits the *Observer*, putting into its " Secular Department" his plea for the judicial murder of John Brown, and into its " Religious Department" his welcome to the communion-table of every common stabber by land or sea, who can get the certificate of the American Church—and again, in comparison with that other pro-slavery clergyman* who volunteered to buckle on his knapsack and march with his musket to fight for slavery, and then volunteered to aid in raising a monument to one who fought for liberty—in comparison with these, the stern, gray, sabre-hacked man who now lies fettered, and awaiting death in that den of Virginia robbers whose victims he went to save, swells into proportions of colossal nobleness and excellence.

* The Hon. Edward Everett, a distinguished American statesman and scholar, is here referred to. He was, in the early part of his career, a Unitarian minister. As a member of Congress, he declared his readiness to buckle on his knapsack, and march with his musket to suppress a servile insurrection. Latterly he has been much engaged in delivering a lecture in praise of Washington, with a view to collect funds for erecting at Mount Vernon an appropriate mausoleum for the Father of his country.

MR. WENDELL PHILLIPS.

From a Lecture entitled, "The Lesson of the Hour," delivered at Brooklyn,
New York, November 1st, 1859.

I APPEAL from Philip drunk to Philip sober; I appeal from the
American people, drunk with cotton, to the American people
fifty years hence, when the light of civilization has had more time
to penetrate, when self-interest has been rebuked by the world
rising and giving its verdict on these great questions, when it is
not a small band of abolitionists, but the civilization of the twen-
tieth century, in all its varied forms, interests, and elements, that
undertakes to enter the arena, and discuss this last great reform.
When that day comes, what will be thought of these first martyrs,
who teach us how to live and how to die?

Has the slave a right to resist his master? I will not argue
that question to a people hoarse with shouting ever since July 4,
1776, that all men are created equal, that the right to liberty is
inalienable, and that "resistance to tyrants is obedience to God."
But may he resist to blood—with rifles? What need of proving
that to a people who load down Bunker Hill with granite, and
crowd their public squares with images of Washington. But may
one help the slave to resist, as Brown did? Ask Byron on his
death-bed in the marshes of Missolonghi.

But John Brown violated the law. Yes. On yonder desk lie
the inspired words of men who died violent deaths for breaking
the laws of Rome. Why do you listen to them so reverently?
Huss and Wickliffe violated laws, why honour them? George
Washington, had he been caught before 1783, would have died
on the gibbet for breaking the laws of his sovereign. Yes, you
say, but these men broke *bad* laws. Just so. It is honourable,
then, to break *bad* laws, and such law-breaking History loves
and God blesses! Who says, then, that slave laws are not ten
thousand times worse than any those men resisted? Whatever
argument *excuses* them, makes John Brown a saint.

" The most resolute man I ever saw," says Governor Wise, "the most daring, the coolest. I would trust his truth about any question. The sincerest !" Sincerity, courage, resolute daring, beating in a heart that feared God, and dared all to help his brother to liberty : Virginia has nothing, nothing for those qualities but a scaffold ! (Applause.) In her broad dominion she can only afford him six feet for a grave ! God help the commonwealth that bids such welcome to the noblest qualities that can grace poor human nature ! Yet that is the acknowledgment of Governor Wise himself ! I will not dignify such a horde with the name of a *despotism ;* since despotism is sometimes magnanimous. Witness Russia covering Schamyl with generous protection. Compare that with mad Virginia, hurrying forward that ghastly trial.

> "Right forever on the scaffold, Wrong forever on the throne;
> But that scaffold sways the future, and behind the dim unknown
> Standeth God within the shadow, keeping watch above his own."

PRINTED BY ALFRED WEBB, GREAT BRUNSWICK-STREET, DUBLIN.